FABLE COMICS

:01

First Second

New York

First Second
New York

Compilation copyright © 2015 First Second
Editor's note © 2015 Chris Duffy

Published by First Second
First Second is an imprint of Roaring Book Press,
a division of Holtzbrinck Publishing Holdings Limited Partnership
175 Fifth Avenue, New York, New York, 10010
All rights reserved

Cataloging-in-Publication Data is on file at the Library of Congress.
ISBN: 978-1-62672-107-4

First Second books may be purchased for business or promotional use.
For information on bulk purchases please contact Macmillan Corporate and Premium Sales Department at (800) 221-7945 x5442 or by email at specialmarkets@macmillanbooks.com.

Edited by Chris Duffy
Book design by Gordon Whiteside

FIRST

EDITION

First edition 2015
Printed in China by RR Donnelley Asia Printing Solutions Ltd.,
Dongguan City, Guangdong Province

3 5 7 9 10 8 6 4 2

BY ART WE LIVE

CONTENTS

THE FOX AND THE GRAPES James Kochalka 1

THE TOWN MOUSE AND THE COUNTRY MOUSE Tom Gauld 6

HERMES AND THE MAN WHO WAS BITTEN BY AN ANT George O'Connor 9

LEOPARD DRUMS UP DINNER Sophie Goldstein 10

THE BELLY AND THE BODY MEMBERS Charise Harper 16

LION + MOUSE R. Sikoryak 20

FOX AND CROW Jennifer L. Meyer 26

THE OLD MAN AND DEATH Eleanor Davis 31

THE BOY WHO CRIED WOLF Jaime Hernandez 34

THE CROW AND THE PITCHER Simone Lia 40

HERMES AND THE WOODSMAN George O'Connor 45

THE DOG AND HIS REFLECTION Graham Chaffee 48

THE DOLPHINS, THE WHALES, AND THE SPRAT Maris Wicks 53

THE FROGS WHO DESIRED A KING George O'Connor 59

THE HARE AND THE PIG Vera Brosgol 64

THE DEMON, THE THIEF, AND THE HERMIT Keny Widjaja 66

THE ELEPHANT IN FAVOR Corinne Mucha 71

THE MOUSE COUNCIL Liniers 76

MAN AND WART Mark Newgarden 79

THE MILKMAID AND HER PAIL Israel Sanchez 83

THE GREAT WEASEL WAR Ulises Farinas 87

THE SUN AND THE WIND R. O. Blechman 93

THE HARE AND THE TORTOISE Graham Annable 97

THE GRASSHOPPER AND THE ANTS John Kerschbaum 103

THE THIEF AND THE WATCHDOG Braden Lamb and Shelli Paroline 109

HERMES AND THE SCULPTOR George O'Connor 113

THE HEN AND THE MOUNTAIN TURTLE Gregory Benton 114

DEMADES AND HIS FABLE Roger Langridge 120

EDITOR'S NOTE 122

CONTRIBUTORS 122

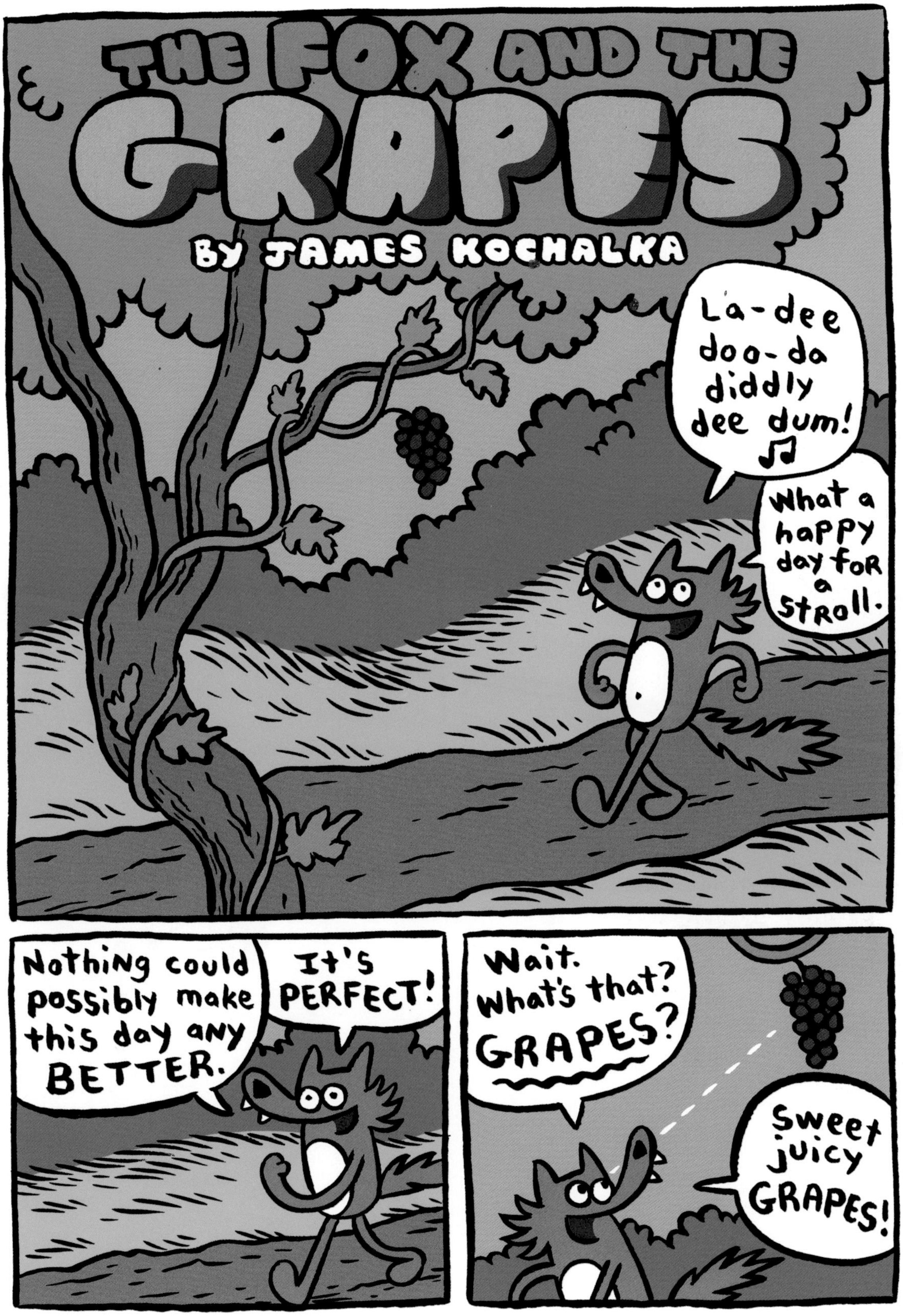
THE FOX AND THE GRAPES
BY JAMES KOCHALKA
La-dee doo-da diddly dee dum!
What a happy day for a stroll.
Nothing could possibly make this day any BETTER.
It's PERFECT!
Wait. What's that? GRAPES?
Sweet juicy GRAPES!

From Aesop

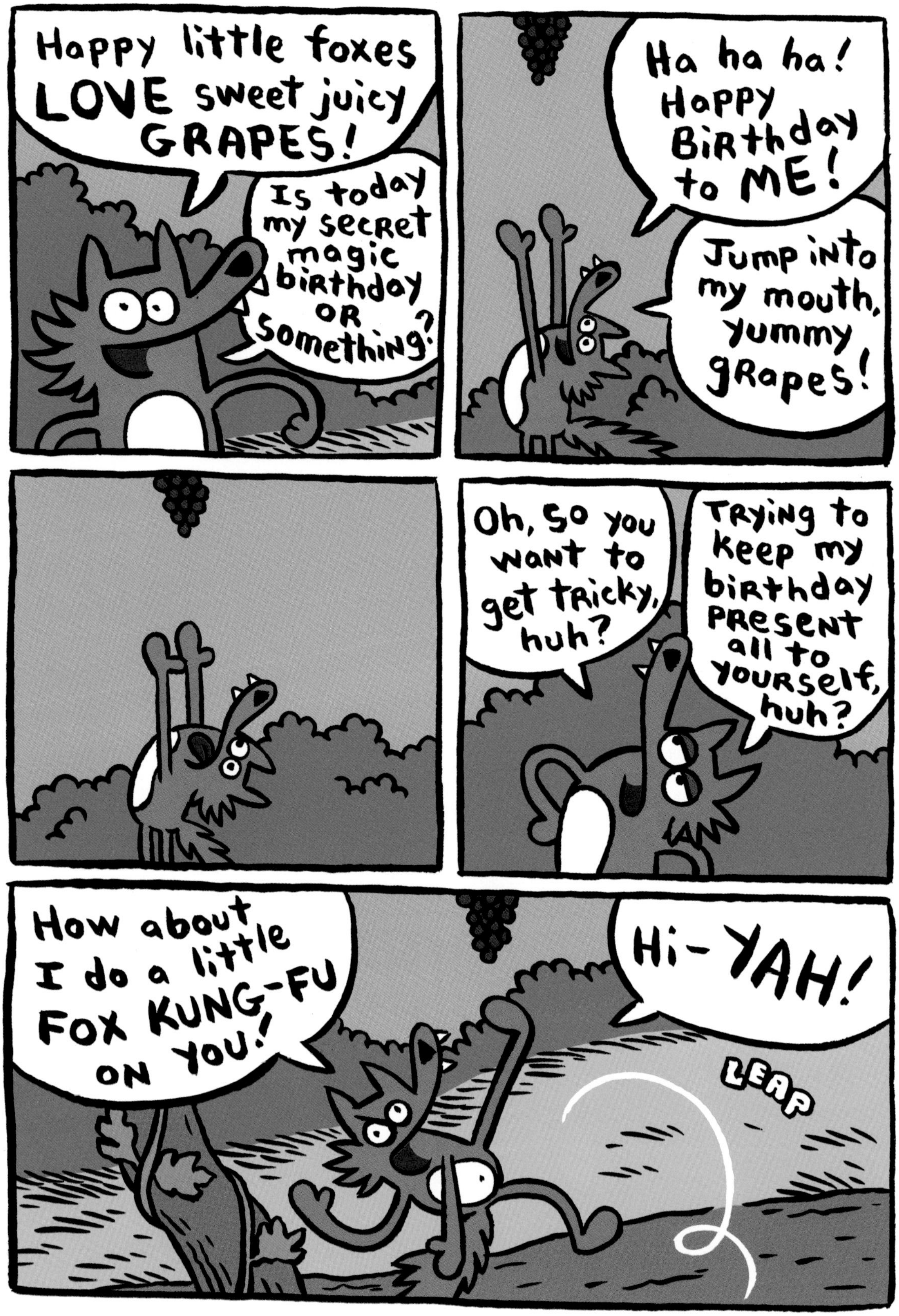
Happy little foxes LOVE sweet juicy GRAPES!
Is today my secret magic birthday OR something?
Ha ha ha! Happy BiRthday to ME!
Jump into my mouth, yummy grapes!
Oh, so you want to get tricky, huh?
TRying to keep my birthday PResent all to yourself, huh?
How about I do a little FOX KUNG-FU ON YOU!
Hi-YAH!
LEAP

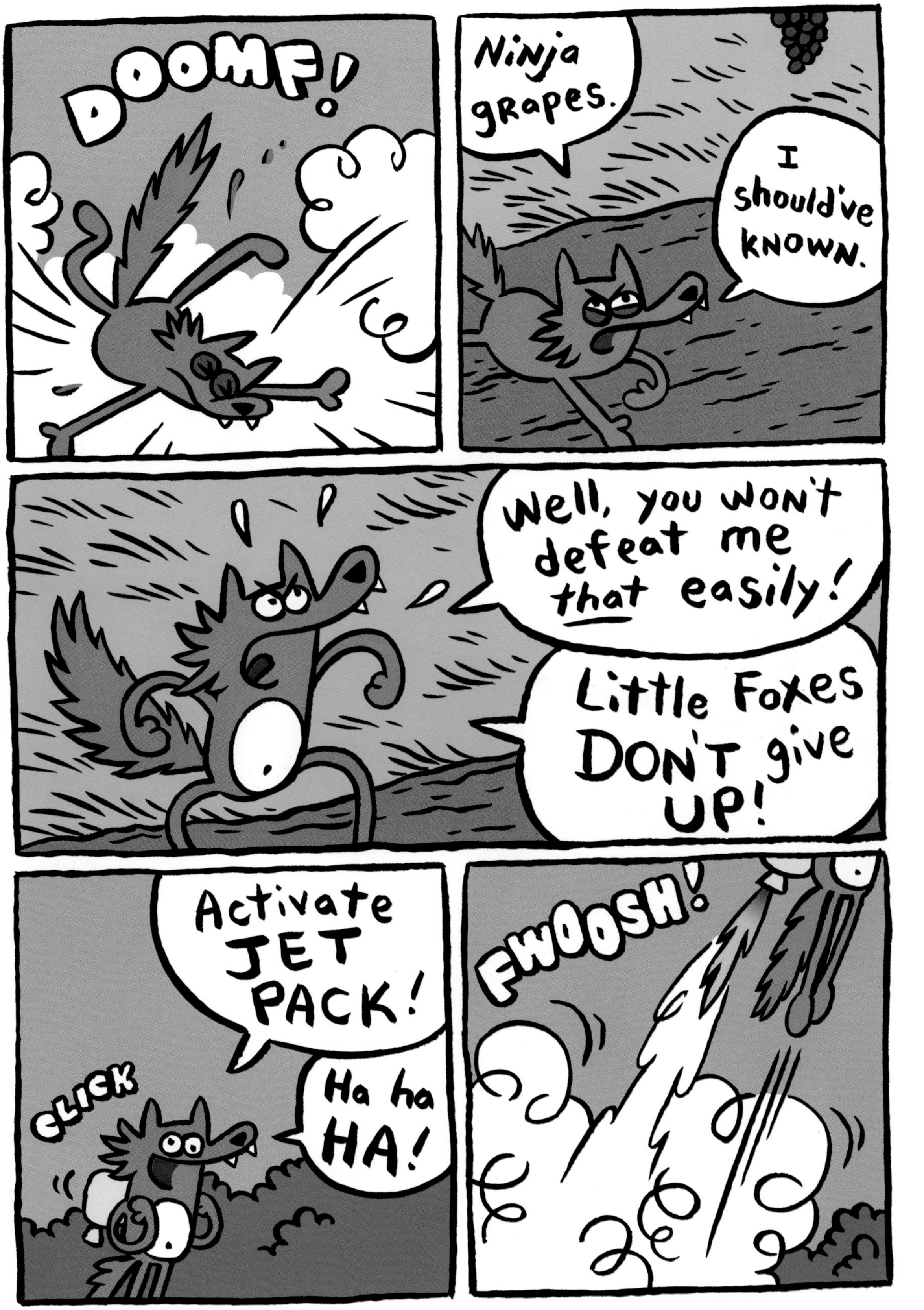
DOOMF!
Ninja grapes.
I should've KNOWN.
Well, you won't defeat me that easily!
Little Foxes DON'T give UP!
Activate JET PACK!
CLICK
Ha ha HA!
FWOOSH!

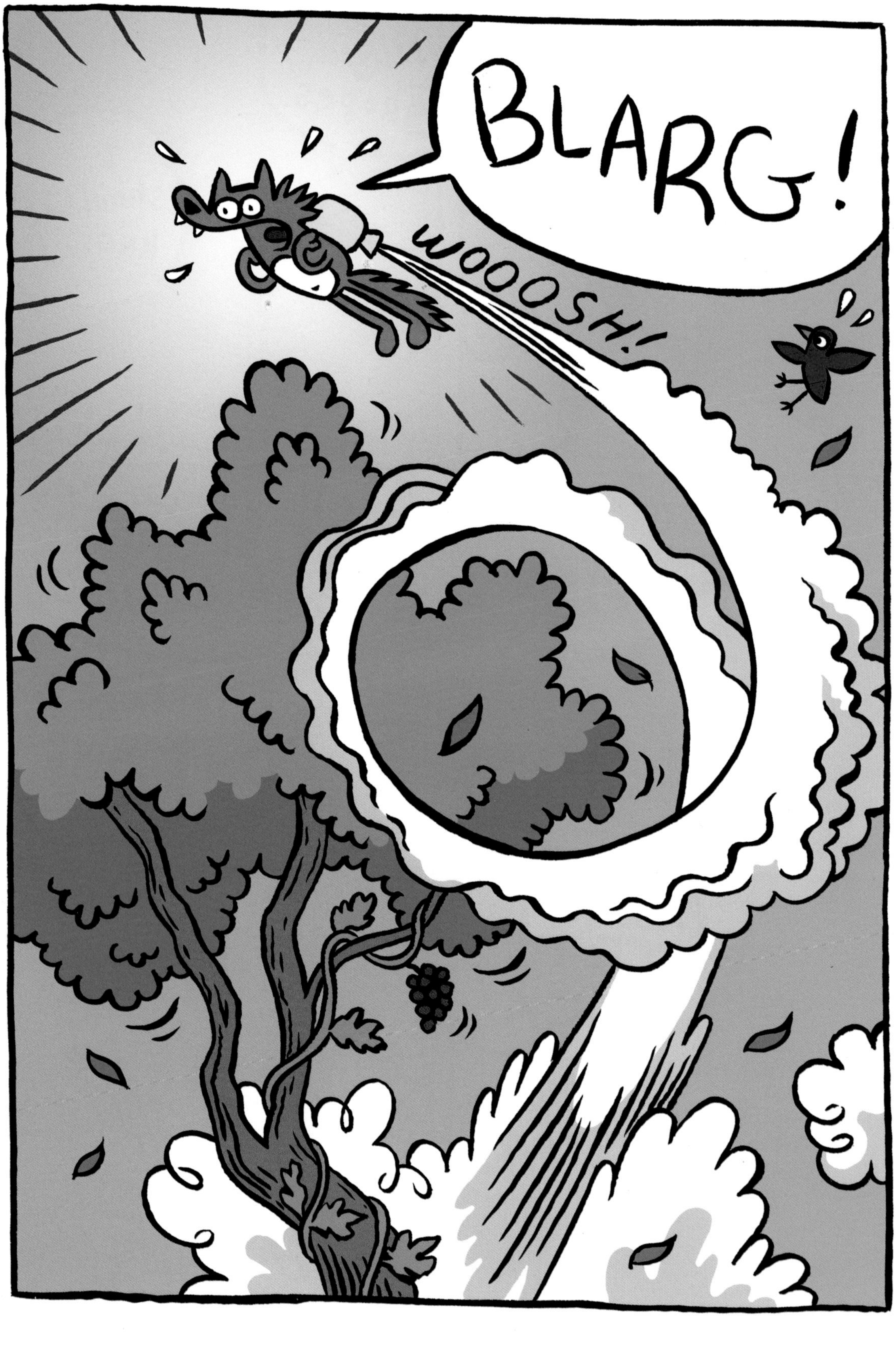
BLARG!
WOOOSH!

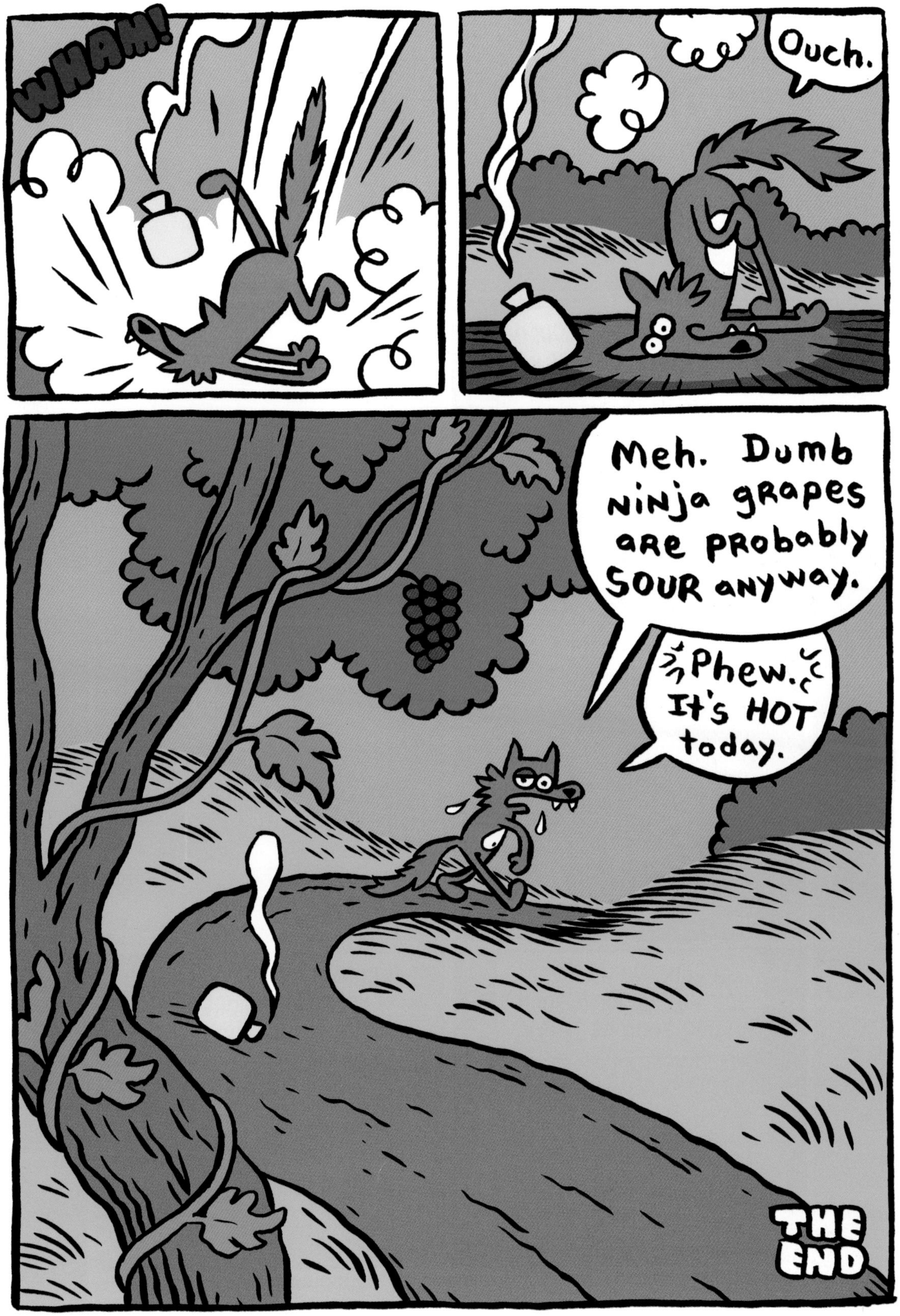
WHAM!
Ouch.
Meh. Dumb ninja grapes are probably SOUR anyway.
Phew. It's HOT today.
THE END

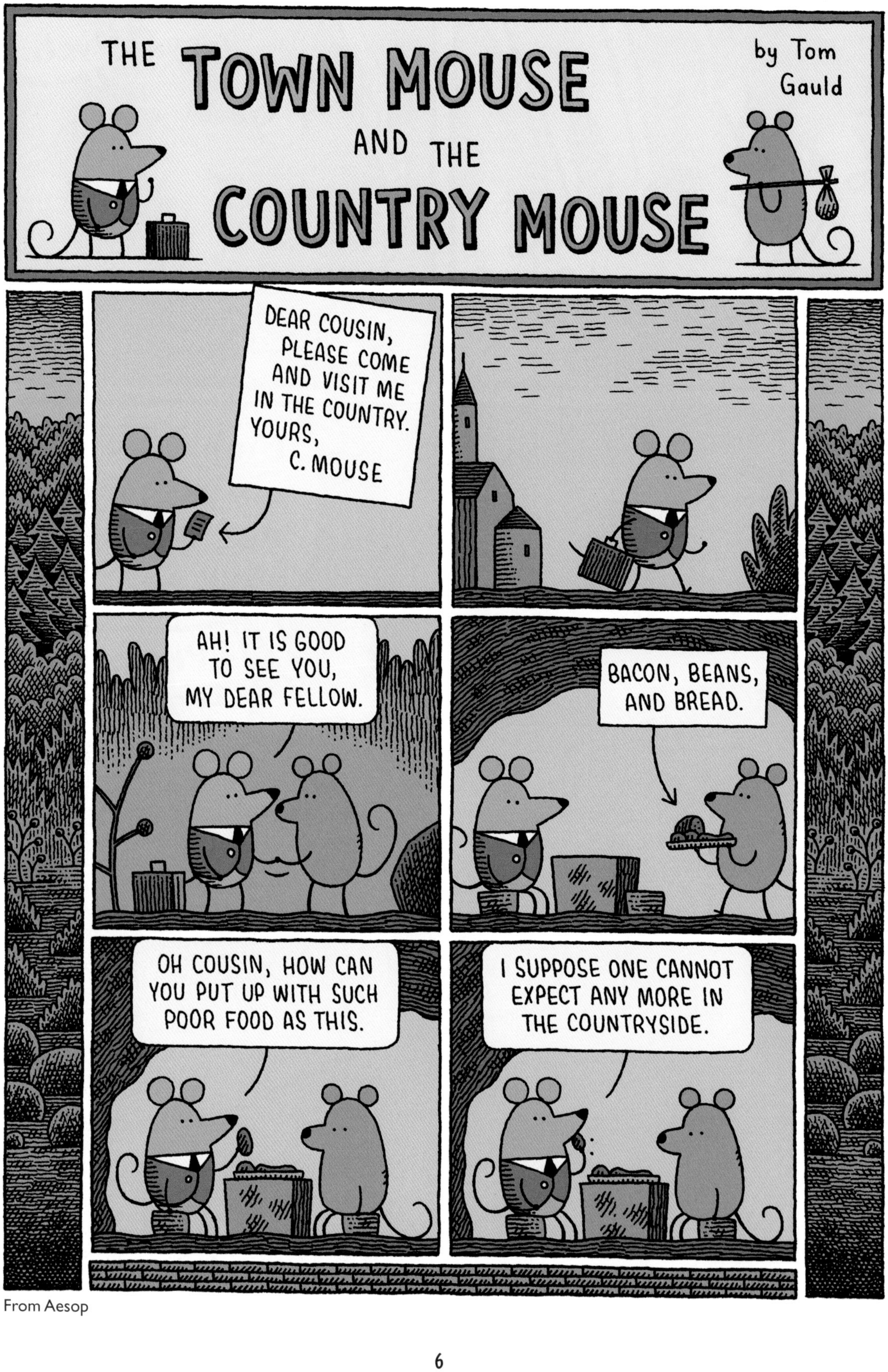
THE TOWN MOUSE AND THE COUNTRY MOUSE
by Tom Gauld
DEAR COUSIN, PLEASE COME AND VISIT ME IN THE COUNTRY. YOURS, C. MOUSE
AH! IT IS GOOD TO SEE YOU, MY DEAR FELLOW.
BACON, BEANS, AND BREAD.
OH COUSIN, HOW CAN YOU PUT UP WITH SUCH POOR FOOD AS THIS.
I SUPPOSE ONE CANNOT EXPECT ANY MORE IN THE COUNTRYSIDE.

From Aesop

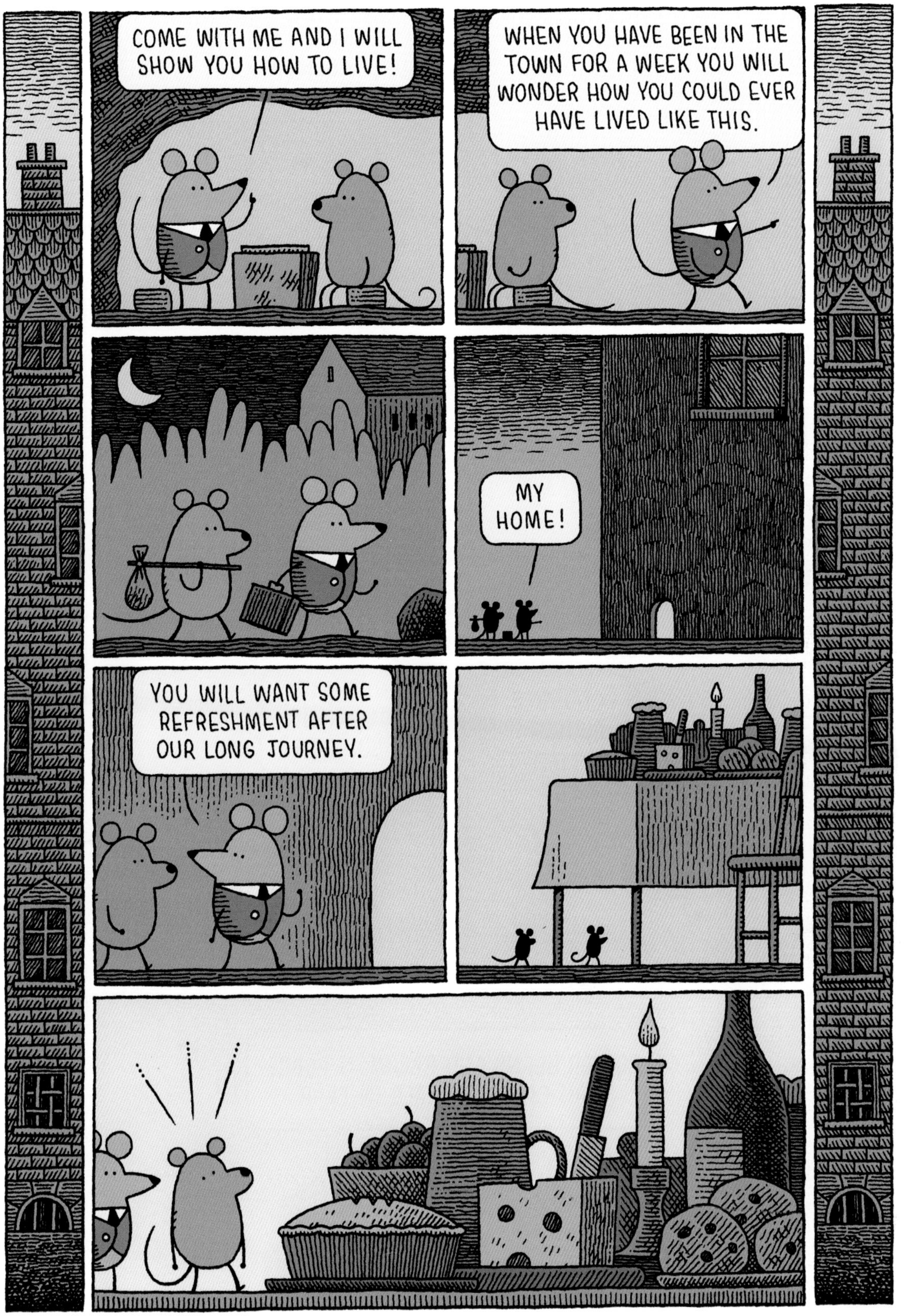
COME WITH ME AND I WILL SHOW YOU HOW TO LIVE!
WHEN YOU HAVE BEEN IN THE TOWN FOR A WEEK YOU WILL WONDER HOW YOU COULD EVER HAVE LIVED LIKE THIS.
MY HOME!
YOU WILL WANT SOME REFRESHMENT AFTER OUR LONG JOURNEY.

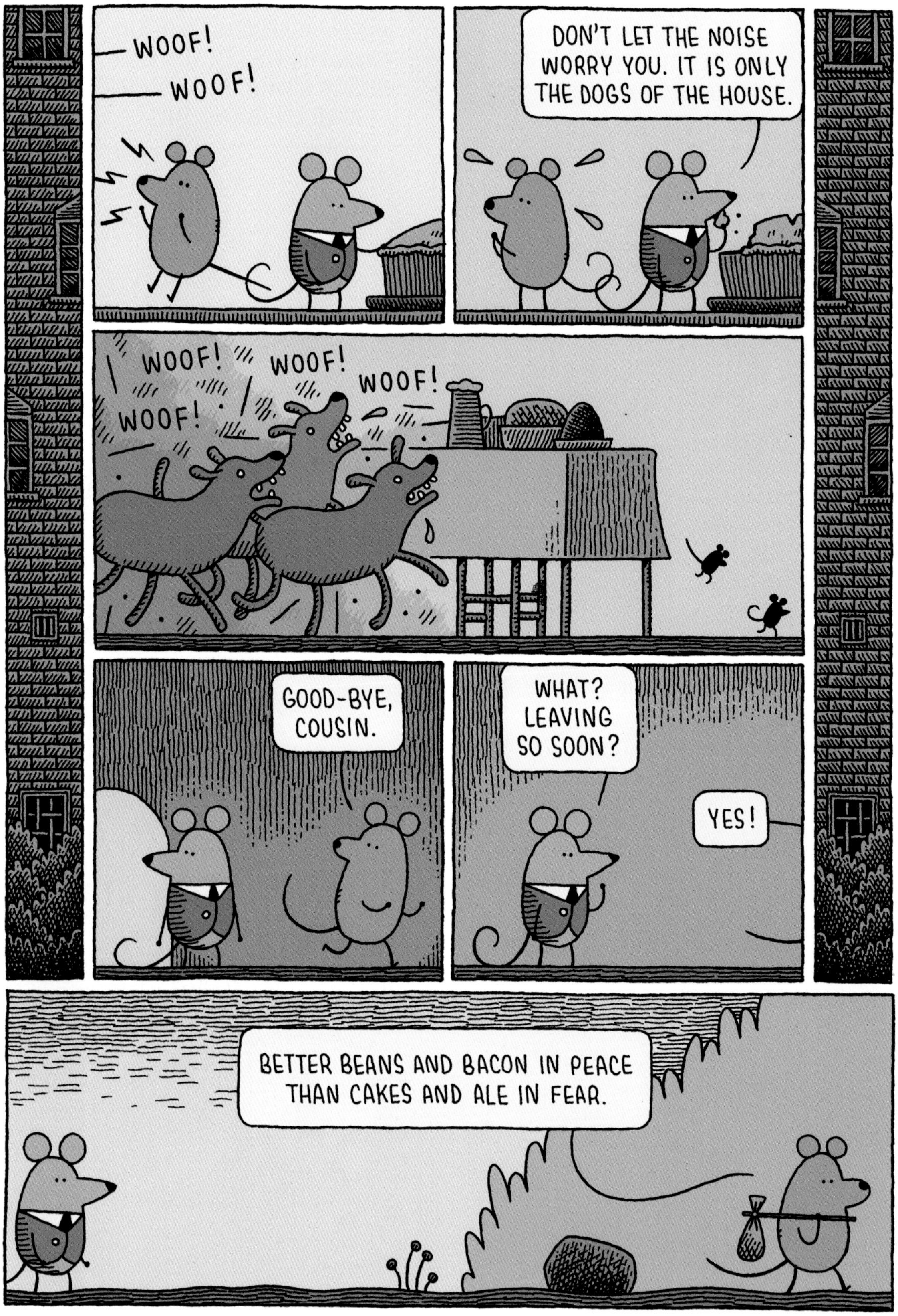
WOOF!
WOOF!
DON'T LET THE NOISE WORRY YOU. IT IS ONLY THE DOGS OF THE HOUSE.
WOOF!
WOOF!
WOOF!
WOOF!
GOOD-BYE, COUSIN.
WHAT? LEAVING SO SOON?
YES!
BETTER BEANS AND BACON IN PEACE THAN CAKES AND ALE IN FEAR.

HERMES AND THE MAN WHO WAS BITTEN BY AN ANT

retold by George O'Connor

BEHOLD! MOUNT OLYMPUS, HOME OF THE GODS! THE ALOOF, UNCARING GODS!

ONCE I SAW A SHIP SINK WITH EVERYONE ON BOARD! THE GODS DID NOTHING TO SAVE THEM!

THEY CARE NOTHING FOR A PERSON'S CHARACTER, BUT LET THE GOOD AND BAD GO TO THEIR DEATHS TOGETHER!

WHY, THEY-- OW!!

A STUPID ANT BIT ME!!

YOU GO SMASH NOW, STUPID ANTS!!

WAP! WAP! WAP!

---UH---

THE MORAL IS: WATCH WHERE YOU STEP OR IRONY IS LOST ON THE STUPID

From Aesop

LEOPARD DRUMS UP DINNER

BY SOPHIE GOLDSTEIN

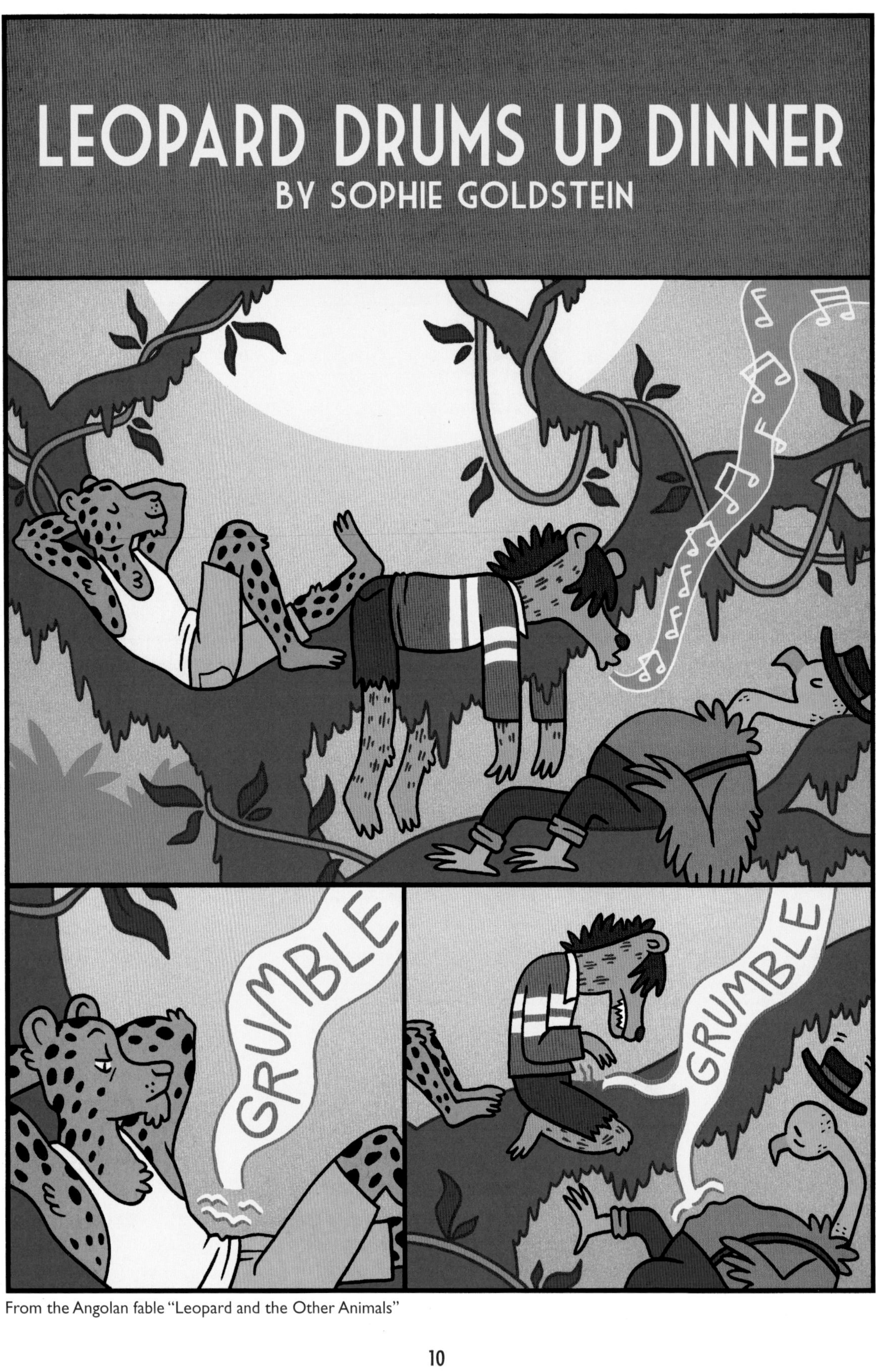
GRUMBLE
GRUMBLE

From the Angolan fable "Leopard and the Other Animals"

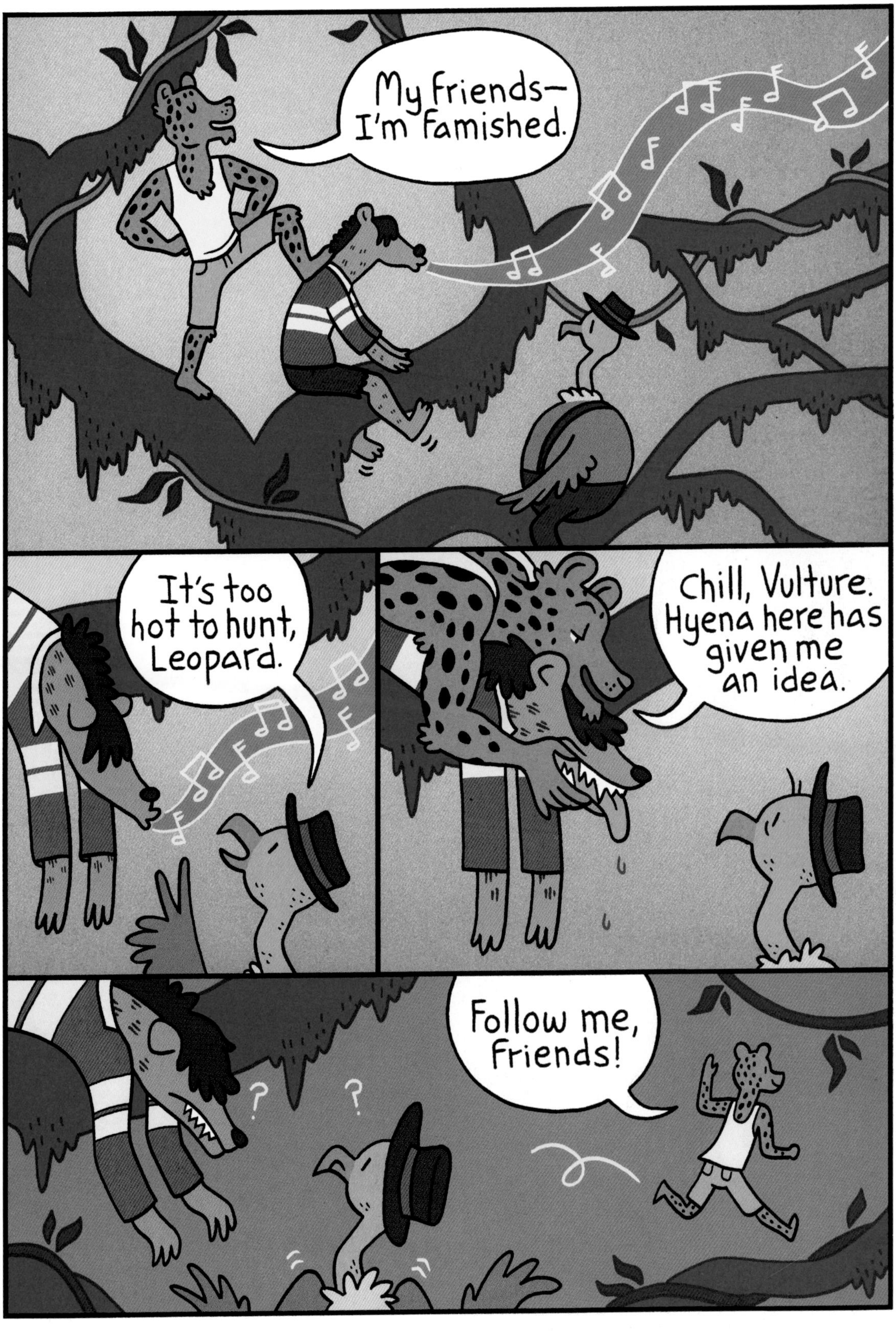

My friends—
I'm famished.
It's too hot to hunt, Leopard.
Chill, Vulture. Hyena here has given me an idea.
?
?
Follow me, Friends!

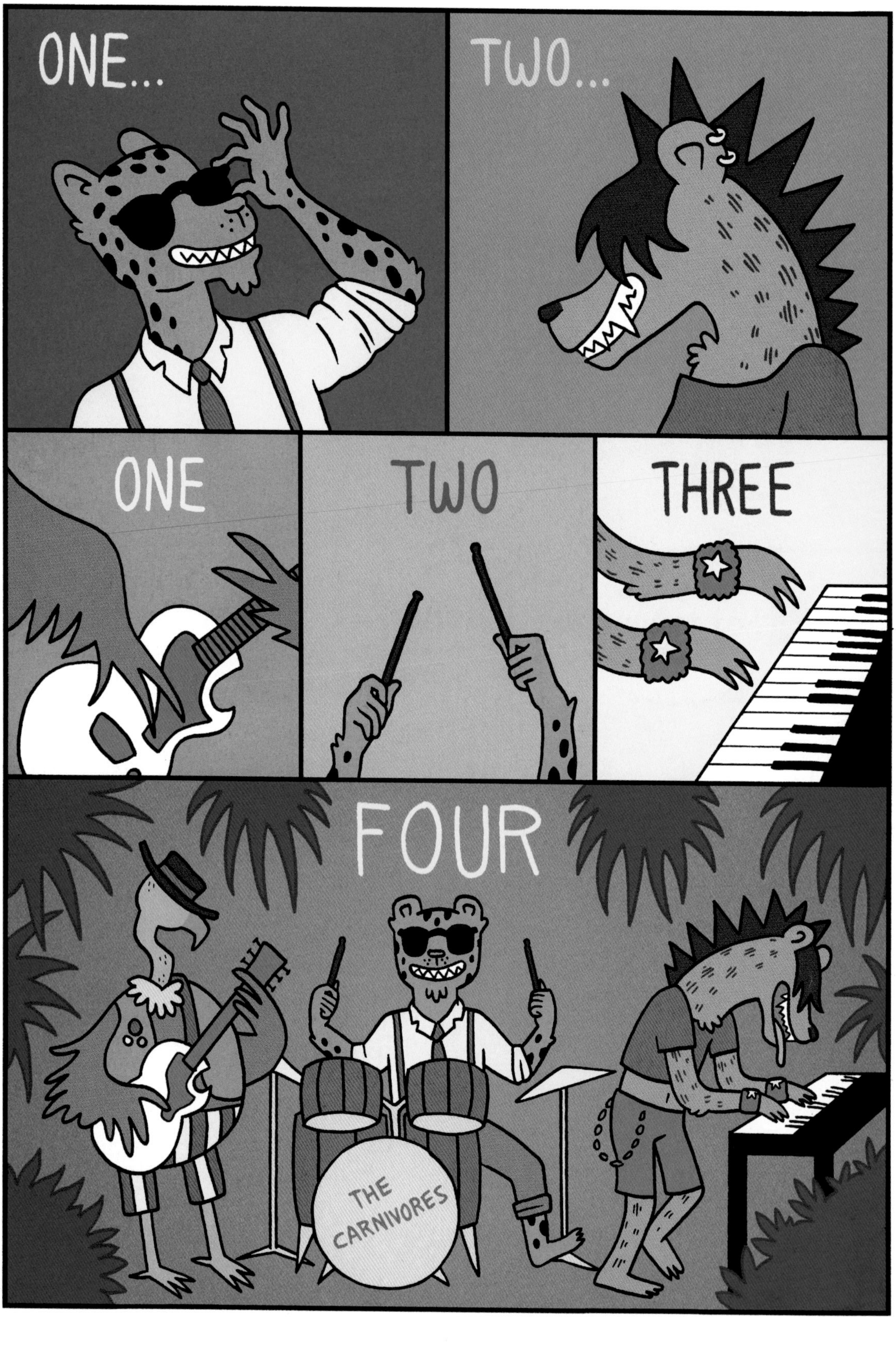
ONE...
TWO...
ONE
TWO
THREE
FOUR
THE CARNIVORES

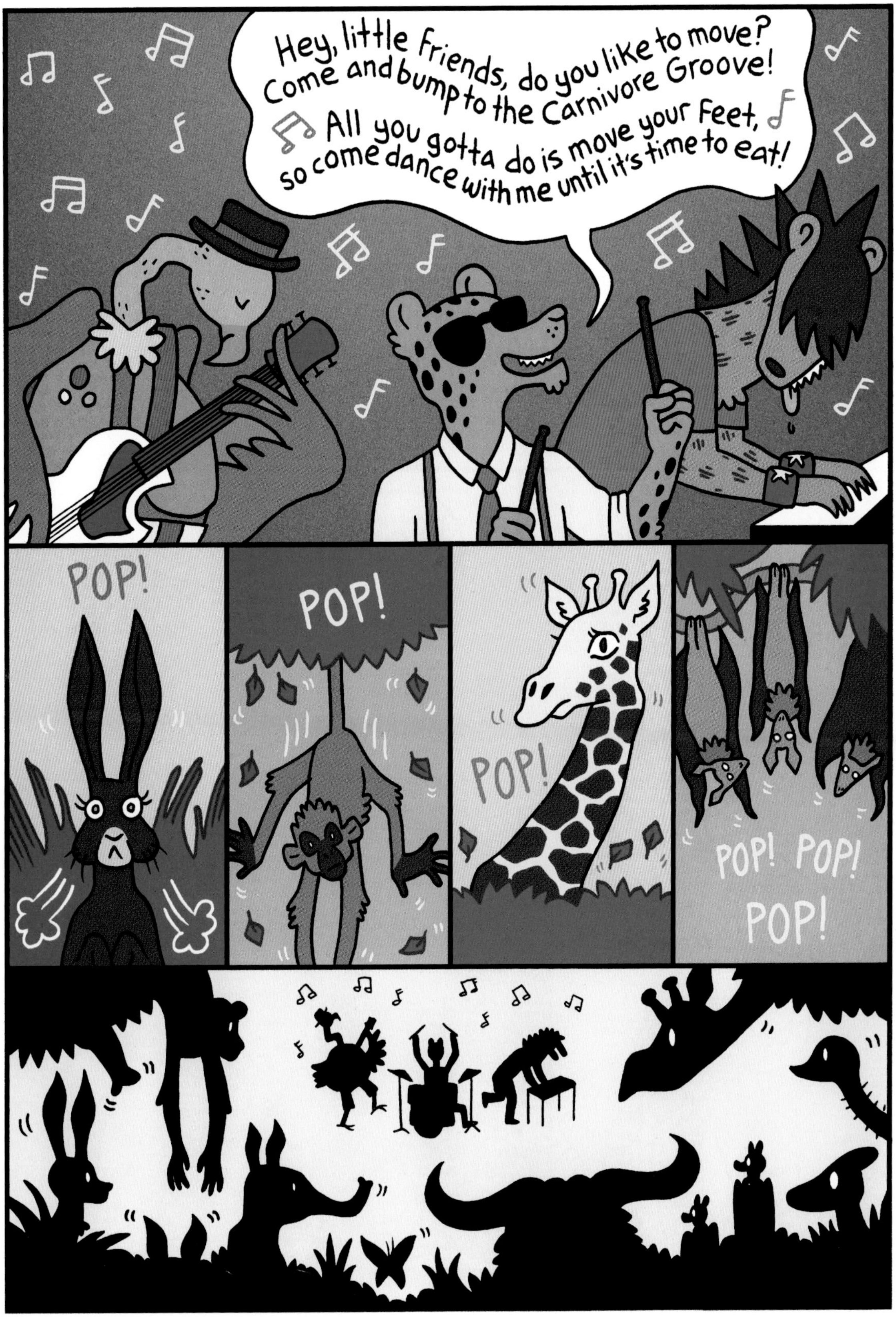
Hey, little friends, do you like to move?
Come and bump to the Carnivore Groove!
All you gotta do is move your feet, so come dance with me until it's time to eat!
POP!
POP!
POP!
POP! POP!
POP!

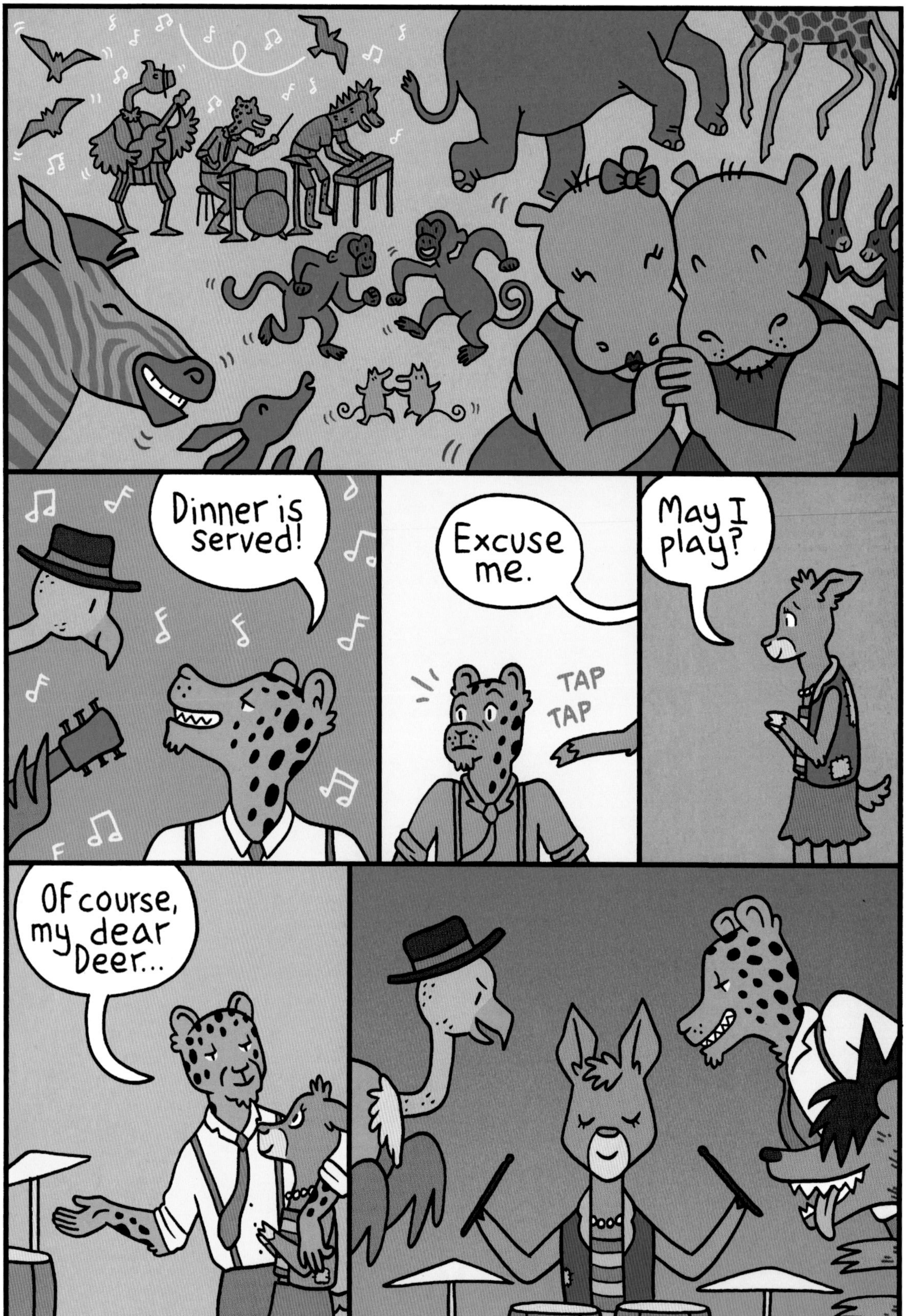

Dinner is served!
Excuse me.
TAP TAP
May I play?
Of course, my dear Deer...

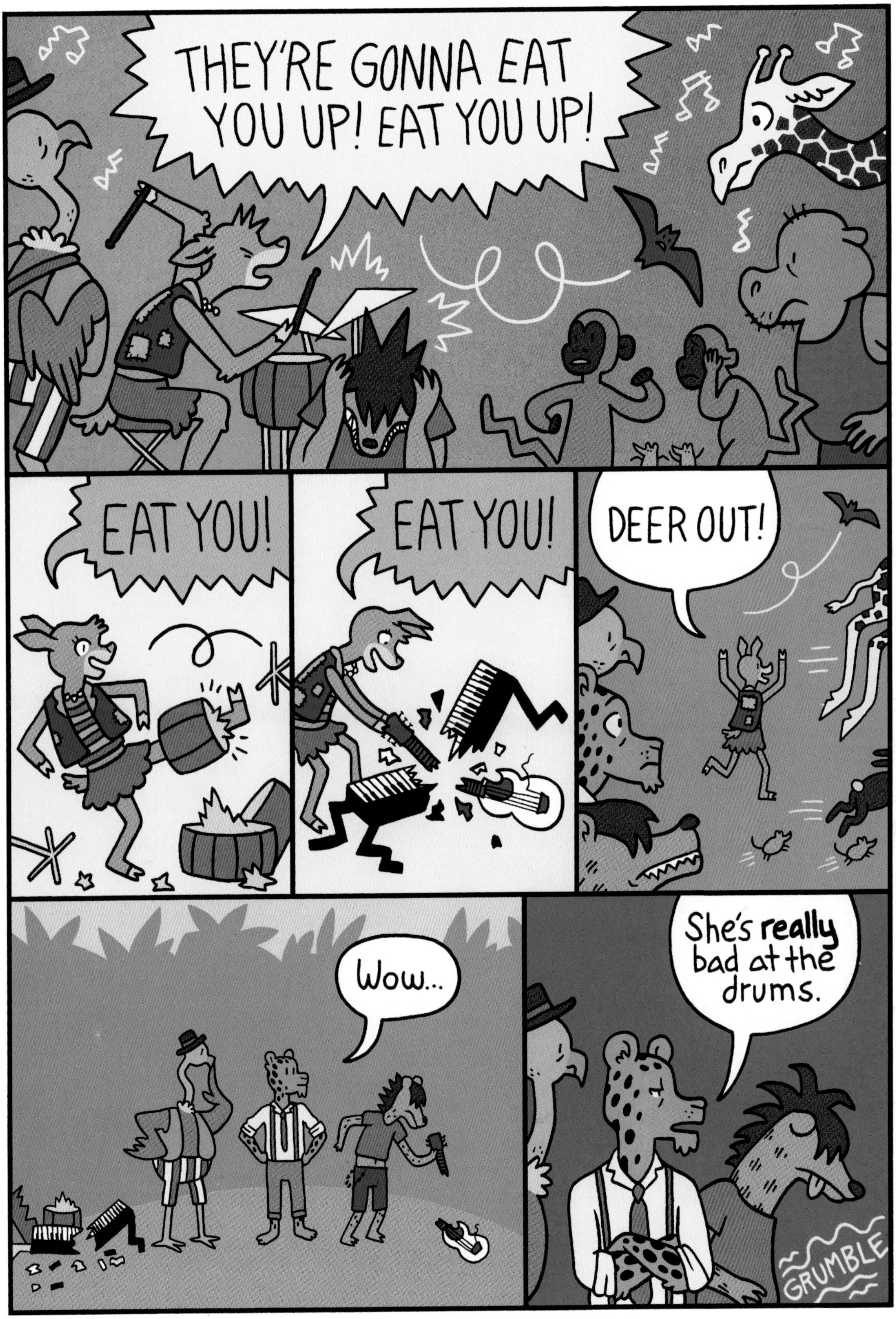
THEY'RE GONNA EAT YOU UP! EAT YOU UP!
EAT YOU!
EAT YOU!
DEER OUT!
Wow...
She's **really** bad at the drums.
GRUMBLE

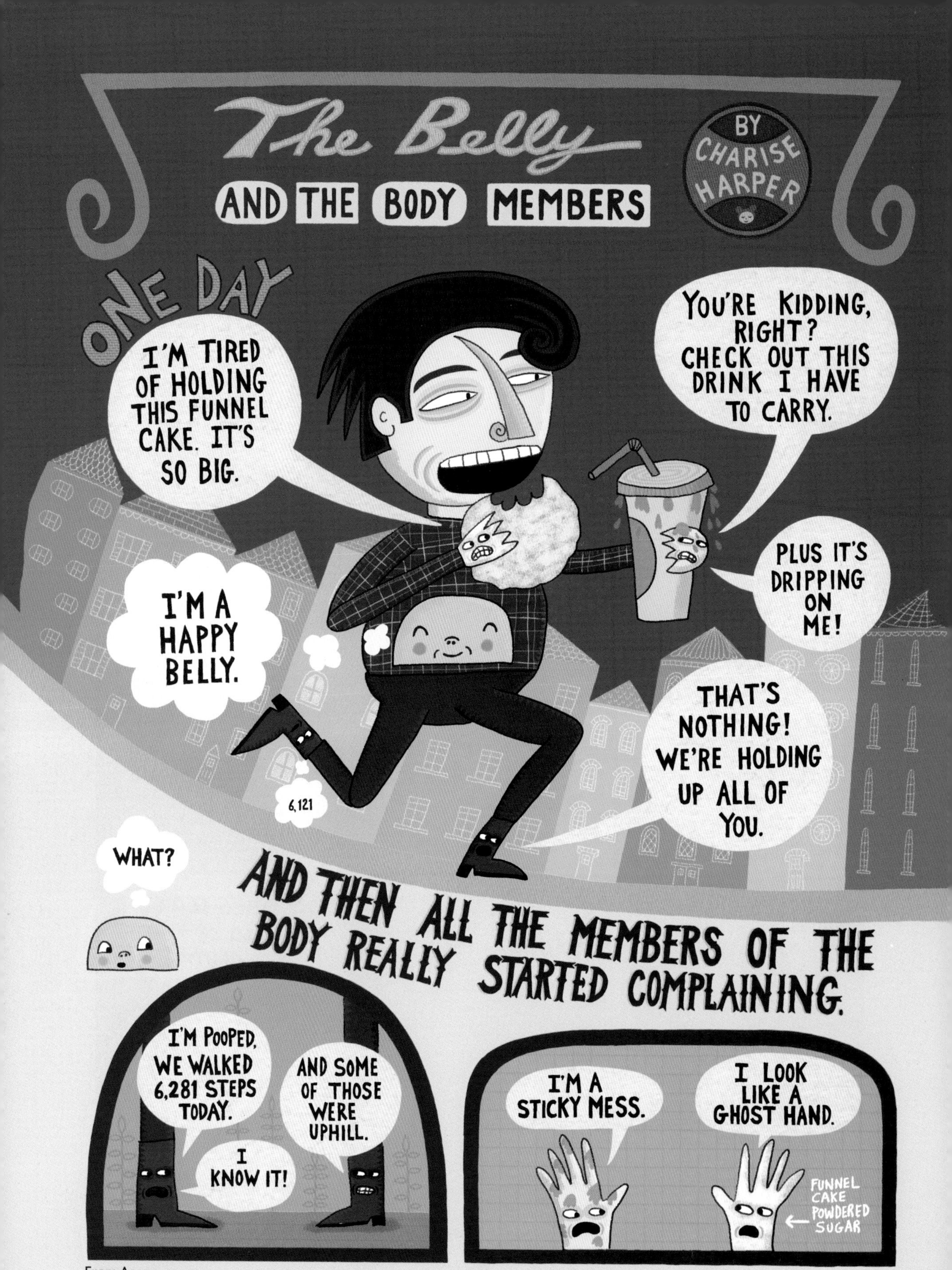
The Belly
AND THE BODY MEMBERS
BY CHARISE HARPER
ONE DAY
I'M TIRED OF HOLDING THIS FUNNEL CAKE. IT'S SO BIG.
YOU'RE KIDDING, RIGHT? CHECK OUT THIS DRINK I HAVE TO CARRY.
PLUS IT'S DRIPPING ON ME!
I'M A HAPPY BELLY.
THAT'S NOTHING! WE'RE HOLDING UP ALL OF YOU.
6,121
WHAT?
AND THEN ALL THE MEMBERS OF THE BODY REALLY STARTED COMPLAINING.
I'M POOPED. WE WALKED 6,281 STEPS TODAY.
AND SOME OF THOSE WERE UPHILL.
I KNOW IT!
I'M A STICKY MESS.
I LOOK LIKE A GHOST HAND.
FUNNEL CAKE POWDERED SUGAR

From Aesop

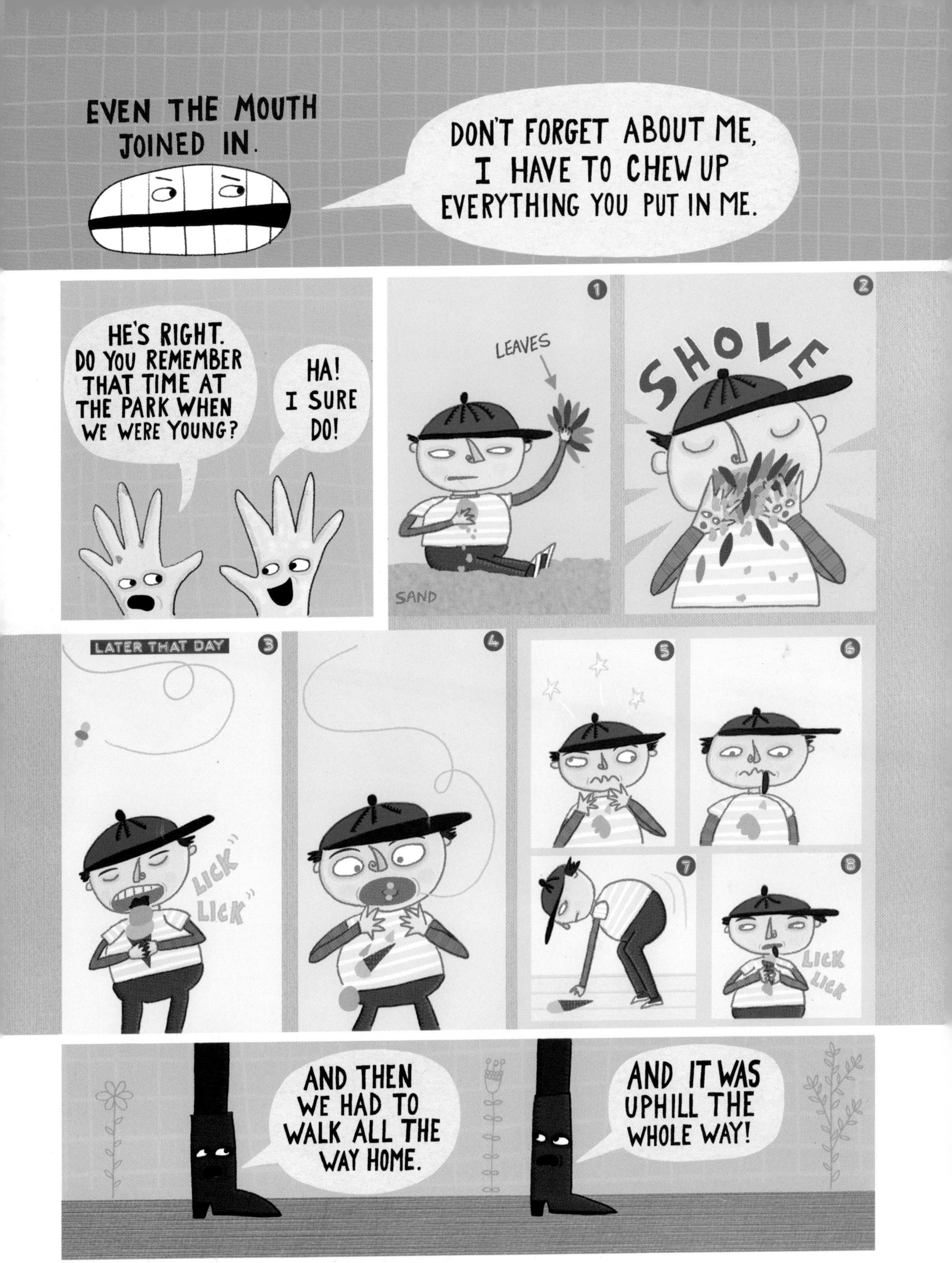

EVEN THE MOUTH JOINED IN.
DON'T FORGET ABOUT ME, I HAVE TO CHEW UP EVERYTHING YOU PUT IN ME.
HE'S RIGHT. DO YOU REMEMBER THAT TIME AT THE PARK WHEN WE WERE YOUNG?
HA! I SURE DO!
1
LEAVES
SAND
2
SHOVE
LATER THAT DAY
3
LICK LICK
4
5
6
7
8
LICK LICK
AND THEN WE HAD TO WALK ALL THE WAY HOME.
AND IT WAS UPHILL THE WHOLE WAY!

WORK "O" METER

1	2	3	4	5	6
LIVING THE DREAM	HARDLY WORKING	SORT OF WORKING	WORKING	WORKING HARD	WORKING TO THE BONE

I'M A 6!

I'M A 6 PLUS!

WAIT, THERE'S NO 6 PLUS.

WELL THERE SHOULD BE. THIS GUY IS RIGHT-HANDED.

WE'RE 6 ALONE AND 12 TOGETHER!

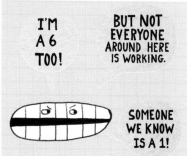

I'M A 6 TOO!

BUT NOT EVERYONE AROUND HERE IS WORKING.

SOMEONE WE KNOW IS A 1!

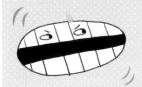

DO YOU KNOW WHO IT IS?

IT'S THE BELLY!

HAVE YOU NOTICED THAT WE DO ALL THE WORK AND HE DOES NOTHING?

YOU'RE RIGHT! THAT'S NOT FAIR!

I'VE NEVER SEEN THE BELLY DO A SINGLE THING!

WAIT! THAT'S NOT TRUE!

I WORK ALL THE TIME!

YOU JUST CAN'T SEE IT!

WELL, IF I DON'T SEE IT, I DON'T BELIEVE IT!

NICE STORY! WHY SHOULD I WORK, IF YOU DO NOTHING?

FROM NOW ON, I'M NOT GOING TO LIFT A FINGER!

18

THE OTHER BODY MEMBERS QUICKLY AGREED WITH THE HANDS.

NO MORE CHEWING FOR ME.

MY TEETH ARE ON STRIKE.

I WON'T TOUCH FOOD, NOT EVEN A CRUMB.

THE FIST PICKS UP NOTHING!

AND WE WON'T MOVE AN INCH!

AGREED!

THE BELLY BEGGED THE BODY MEMBERS TO CHANGE THEIR MINDS, BUT THEY REFUSED.

PLEASE!

DON'T DO THIS!

WE NEED TO WORK TOGETHER.

THE FIST HEARS NOTHING!

AND THEN THINGS WENT FROM BAD TO WORSE.

THE FEET DID NOT WALK TOWARD FOOD.

❶ NOT MOVING.

THE HANDS DID NOT PICK UP FOOD.

❷ THIS IS BORING.

SO THE MOUTH HAD NOTHING TO CHEW.

❸ YAWN.

TWO DAYS LATER EVERYONE WAS OUT OF

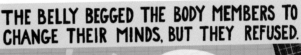

I FEEL WEAK.

AND TIRED.

I'M SO HUNGRY.

I COULD EAT...

...LEAVES.

UH OH.

ENERGY

IT WAS A SAD BIRTHDAY.

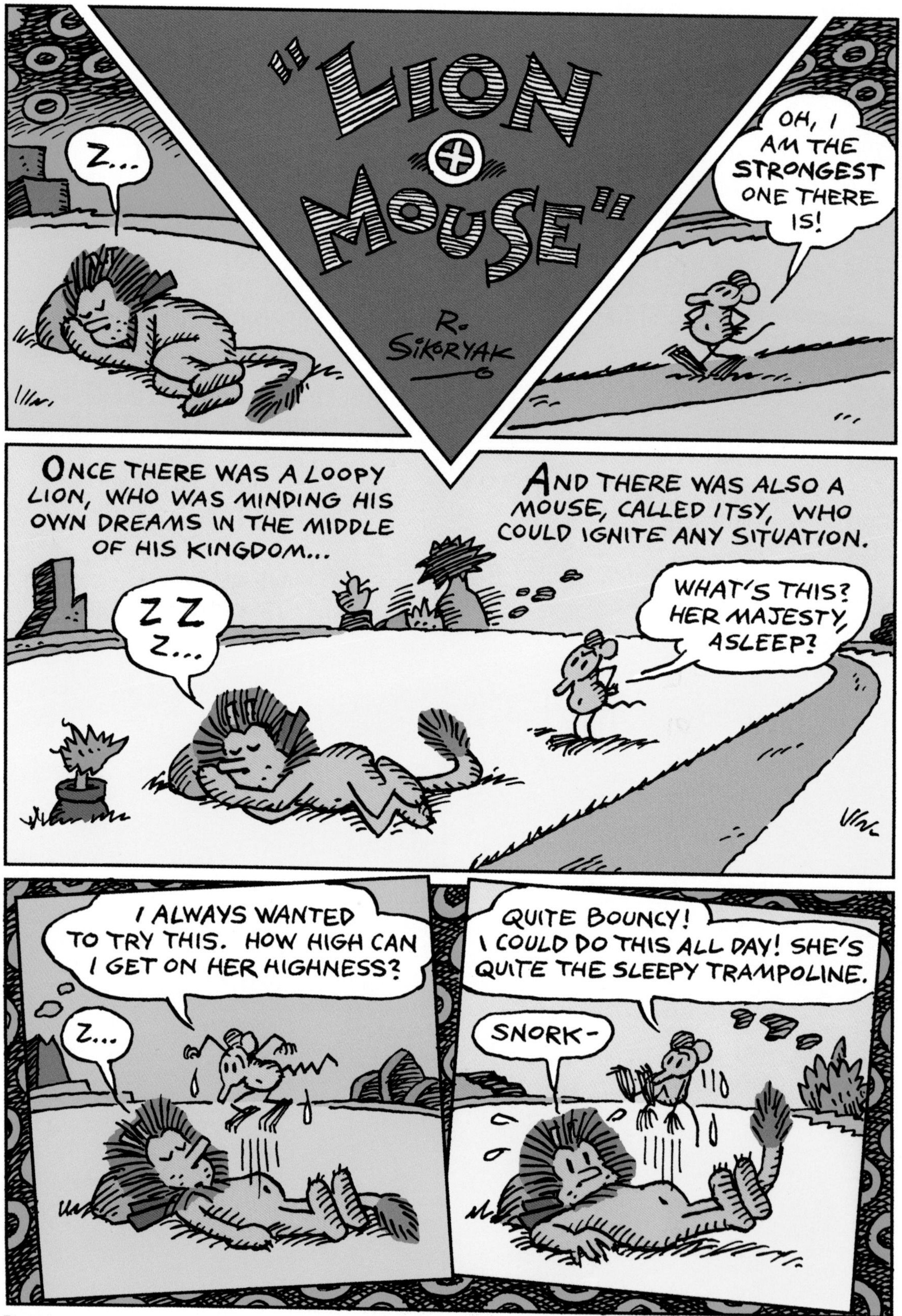
Z...
"LION + MOUSE"
R. SIKORYAK
OH, I AM THE STRONGEST ONE THERE IS!
ONCE THERE WAS A LOOPY LION, WHO WAS MINDING HIS OWN DREAMS IN THE MIDDLE OF HIS KINGDOM...
AND THERE WAS ALSO A MOUSE, CALLED ITSY, WHO COULD IGNITE ANY SITUATION.
Z Z Z...
WHAT'S THIS? HER MAJESTY, ASLEEP?
I ALWAYS WANTED TO TRY THIS. HOW HIGH CAN I GET ON HER HIGHNESS?
Z...
QUITE BOUNCY! I COULD DO THIS ALL DAY! SHE'S QUITE THE SLEEPY TRAMPOLINE.
SNORK-

From Aesop

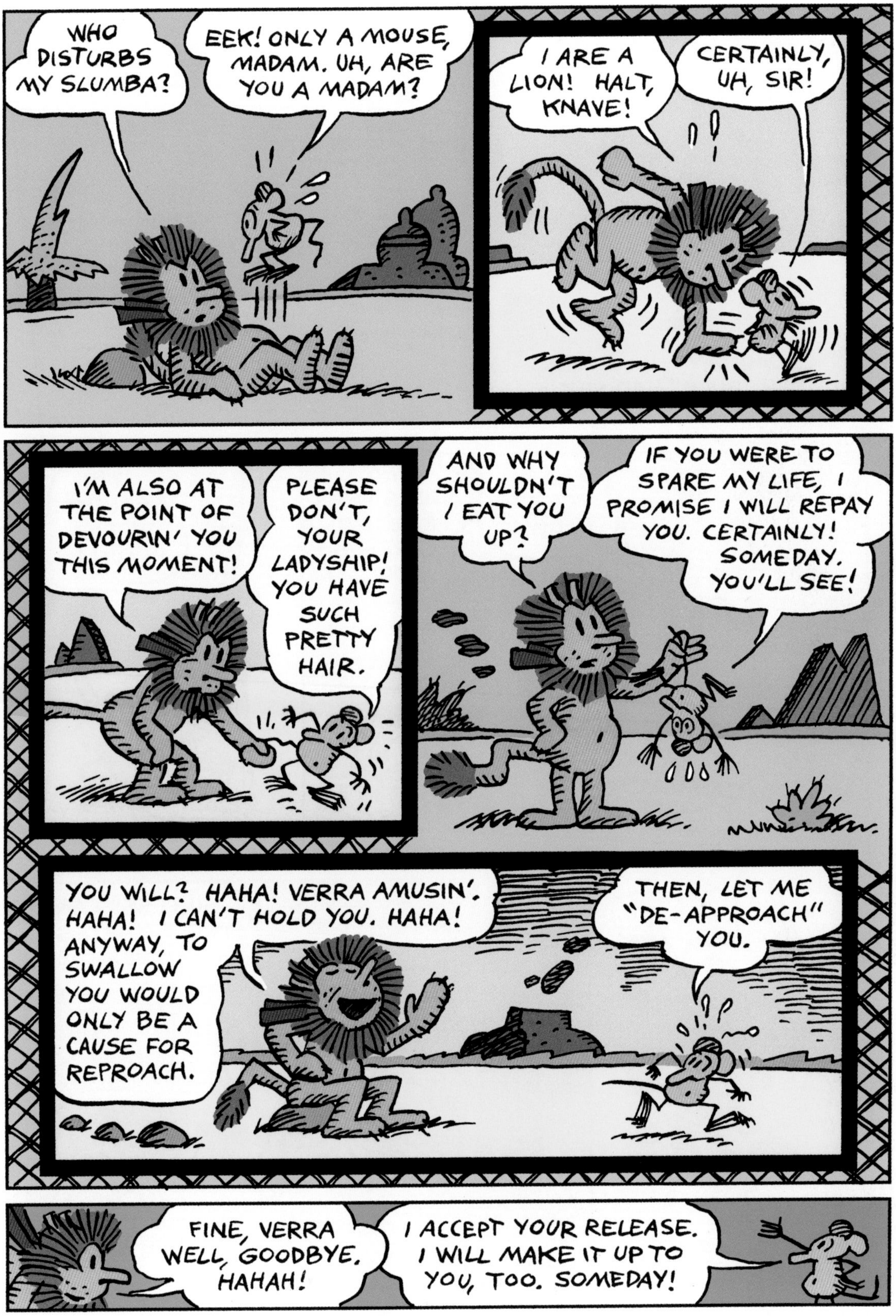
WHO DISTURBS MY SLUMBA?
EEK! ONLY A MOUSE, MADAM. UH, ARE YOU A MADAM?
I ARE A LION! HALT, KNAVE!
CERTAINLY, UH, SIR!
I'M ALSO AT THE POINT OF DEVOURIN' YOU THIS MOMENT!
PLEASE DON'T, YOUR LADYSHIP! YOU HAVE SUCH PRETTY HAIR.
AND WHY SHOULDN'T I EAT YOU UP?
IF YOU WERE TO SPARE MY LIFE, I PROMISE I WILL REPAY YOU. CERTAINLY! SOMEDAY. YOU'LL SEE!
YOU WILL? HAHA! VERRA AMUSIN'. HAHA! I CAN'T HOLD YOU. HAHA! ANYWAY, TO SWALLOW YOU WOULD ONLY BE A CAUSE FOR REPROACH.
THEN, LET ME "DE-APPROACH" YOU.
FINE, VERRA WELL, GOODBYE. HAHAH!
I ACCEPT YOUR RELEASE. I WILL MAKE IT UP TO YOU, TOO. SOMEDAY!

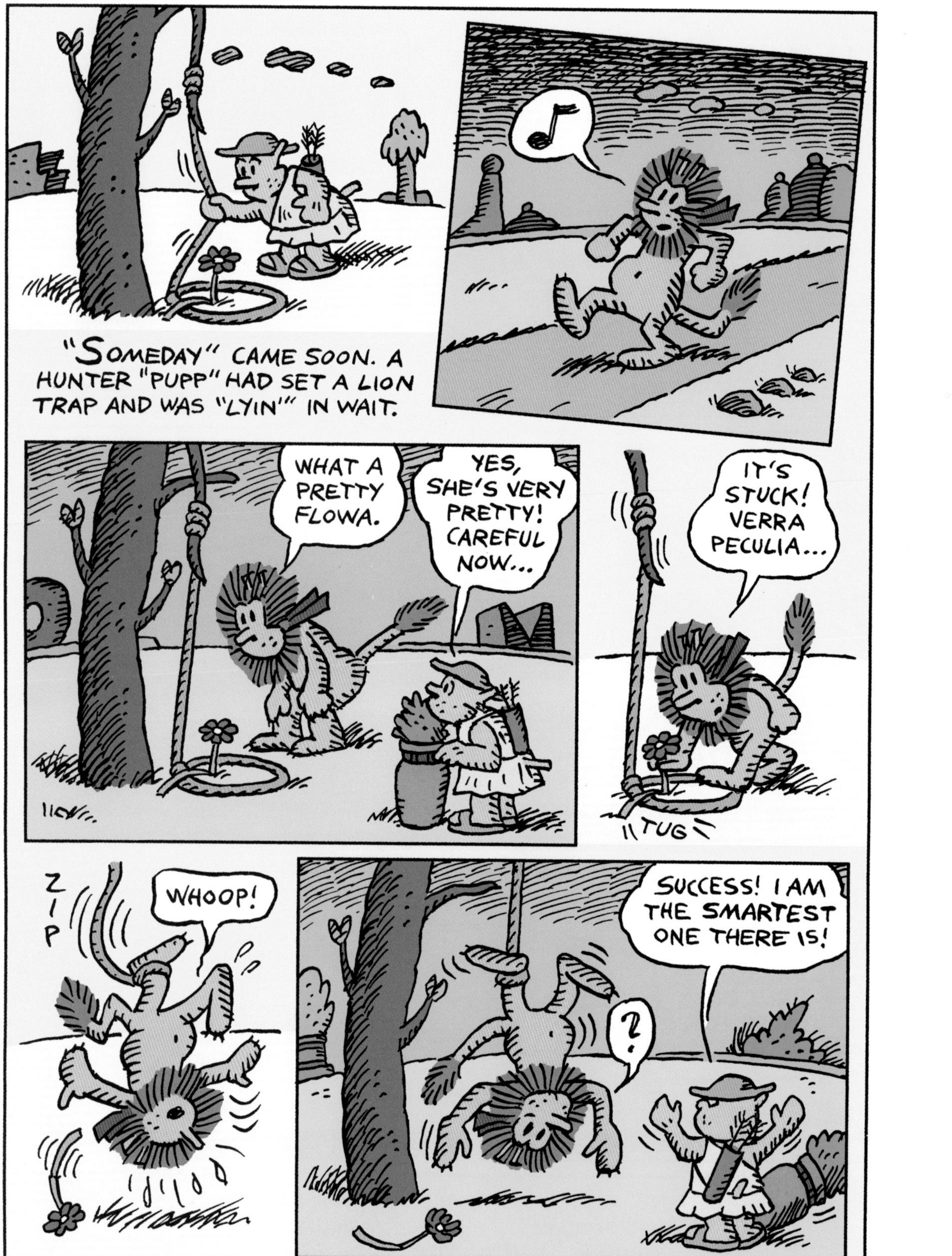
"SOMEDAY" CAME SOON. A HUNTER "PUPP" HAD SET A LION TRAP AND WAS "LYIN'" IN WAIT.
WHAT A PRETTY FLOWA.
YES, SHE'S VERY PRETTY! CAREFUL NOW...
IT'S STUCK! VERRA PECULIA...
TUG
ZIP
WHOOP!
SUCCESS! I AM THE SMARTEST ONE THERE IS!
?

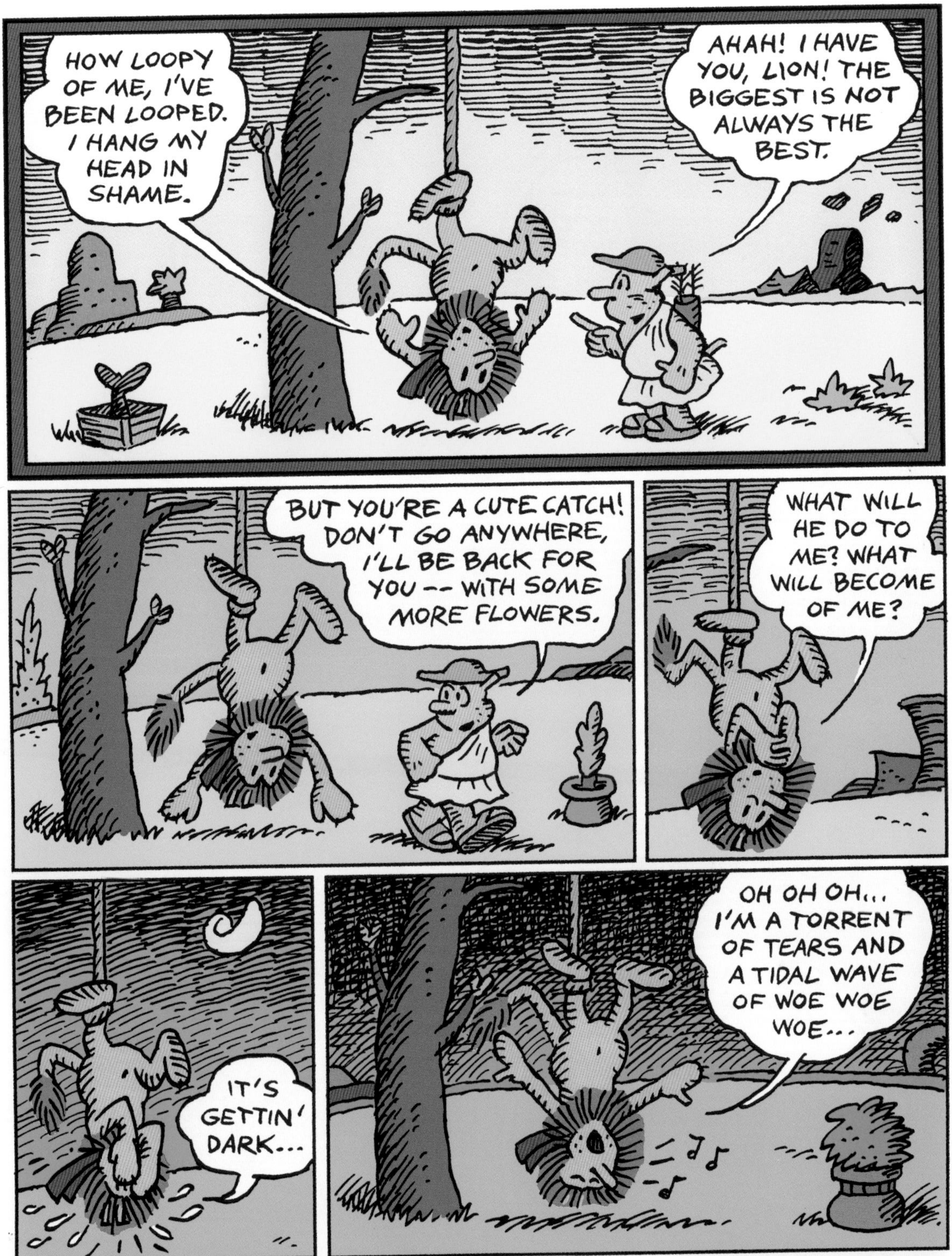
HOW LOOPY OF ME, I'VE BEEN LOOPED. I HANG MY HEAD IN SHAME.
AHAH! I HAVE YOU, LION! THE BIGGEST IS NOT ALWAYS THE BEST.
BUT YOU'RE A CUTE CATCH! DON'T GO ANYWHERE, I'LL BE BACK FOR YOU -- WITH SOME MORE FLOWERS.
WHAT WILL HE DO TO ME? WHAT WILL BECOME OF ME?
IT'S GETTIN' DARK...
OH OH OH... I'M A TORRENT OF TEARS AND A TIDAL WAVE OF WOE WOE WOE...
WOE OH WOE...

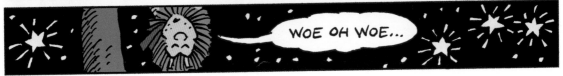

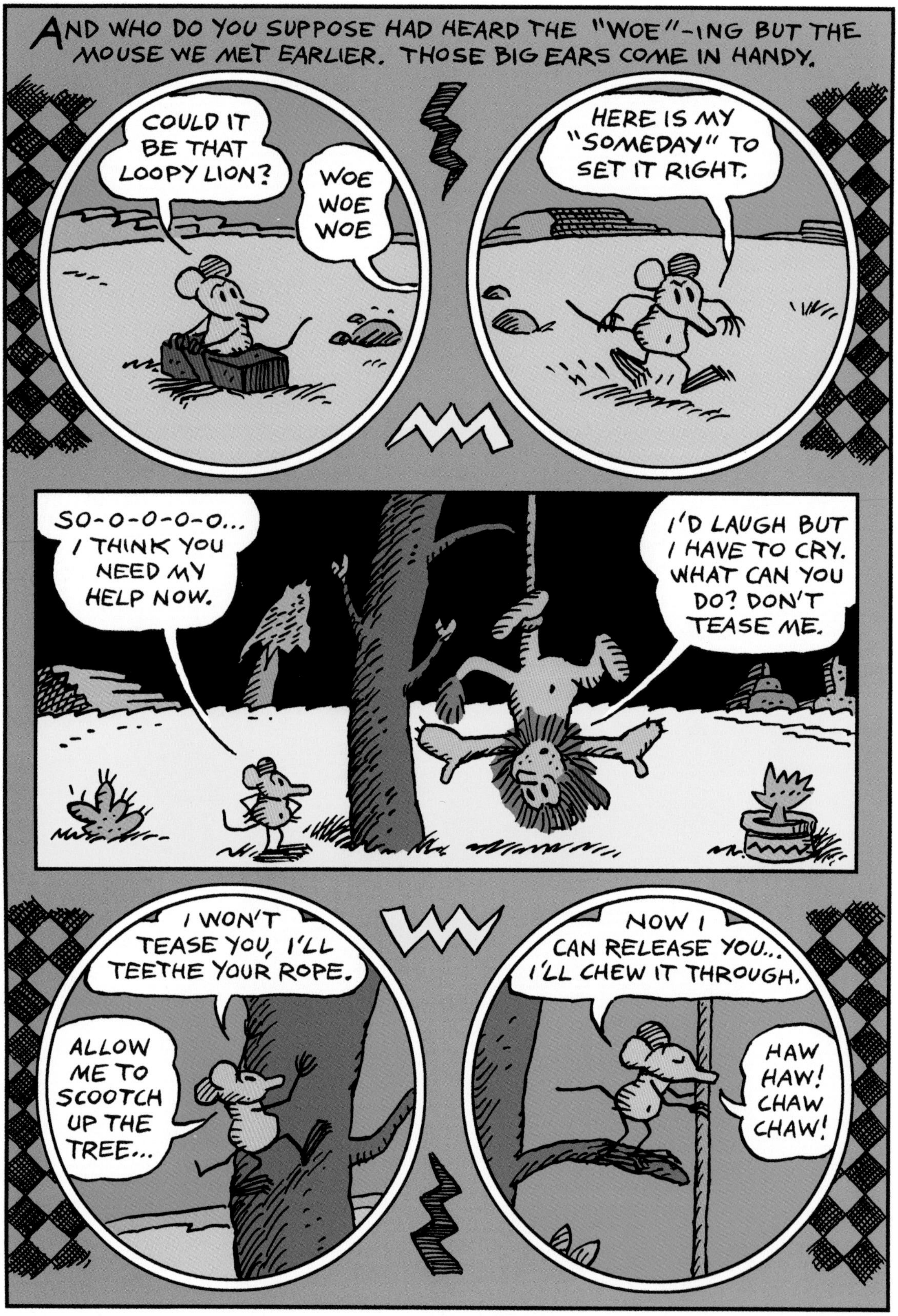
AND WHO DO YOU SUPPOSE HAD HEARD THE "WOE"-ING BUT THE MOUSE WE MET EARLIER. THOSE BIG EARS COME IN HANDY.
COULD IT BE THAT LOOPY LION?
WOE WOE WOE
HERE IS MY "SOMEDAY" TO SET IT RIGHT.
SO-O-O-O-O... I THINK YOU NEED MY HELP NOW.
I'D LAUGH BUT I HAVE TO CRY. WHAT CAN YOU DO? DON'T TEASE ME.
I WON'T TEASE YOU, I'LL TEETHE YOUR ROPE.
ALLOW ME TO SCOOTCH UP THE TREE...
NOW I CAN RELEASE YOU... I'LL CHEW IT THROUGH.
HAW HAW! CHAW CHAW!

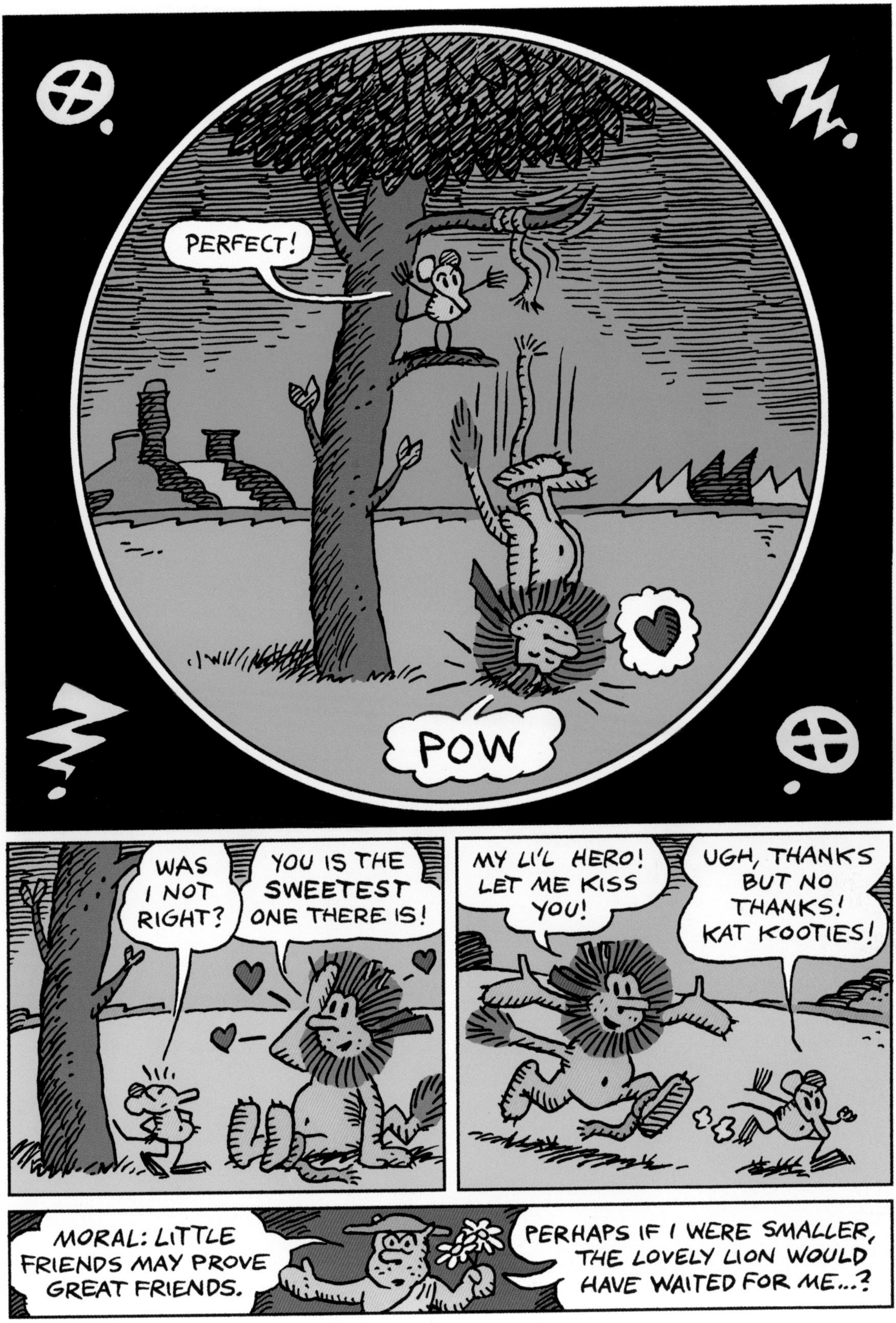
PERFECT!
POW
WAS I NOT RIGHT?
YOU IS THE SWEETEST ONE THERE IS!
MY LI'L HERO! LET ME KISS YOU!
UGH, THANKS BUT NO THANKS! KAT KOOTIES!
MORAL: LITTLE FRIENDS MAY PROVE GREAT FRIENDS.
PERHAPS IF I WERE SMALLER, THE LOVELY LION WOULD HAVE WAITED FOR ME...?

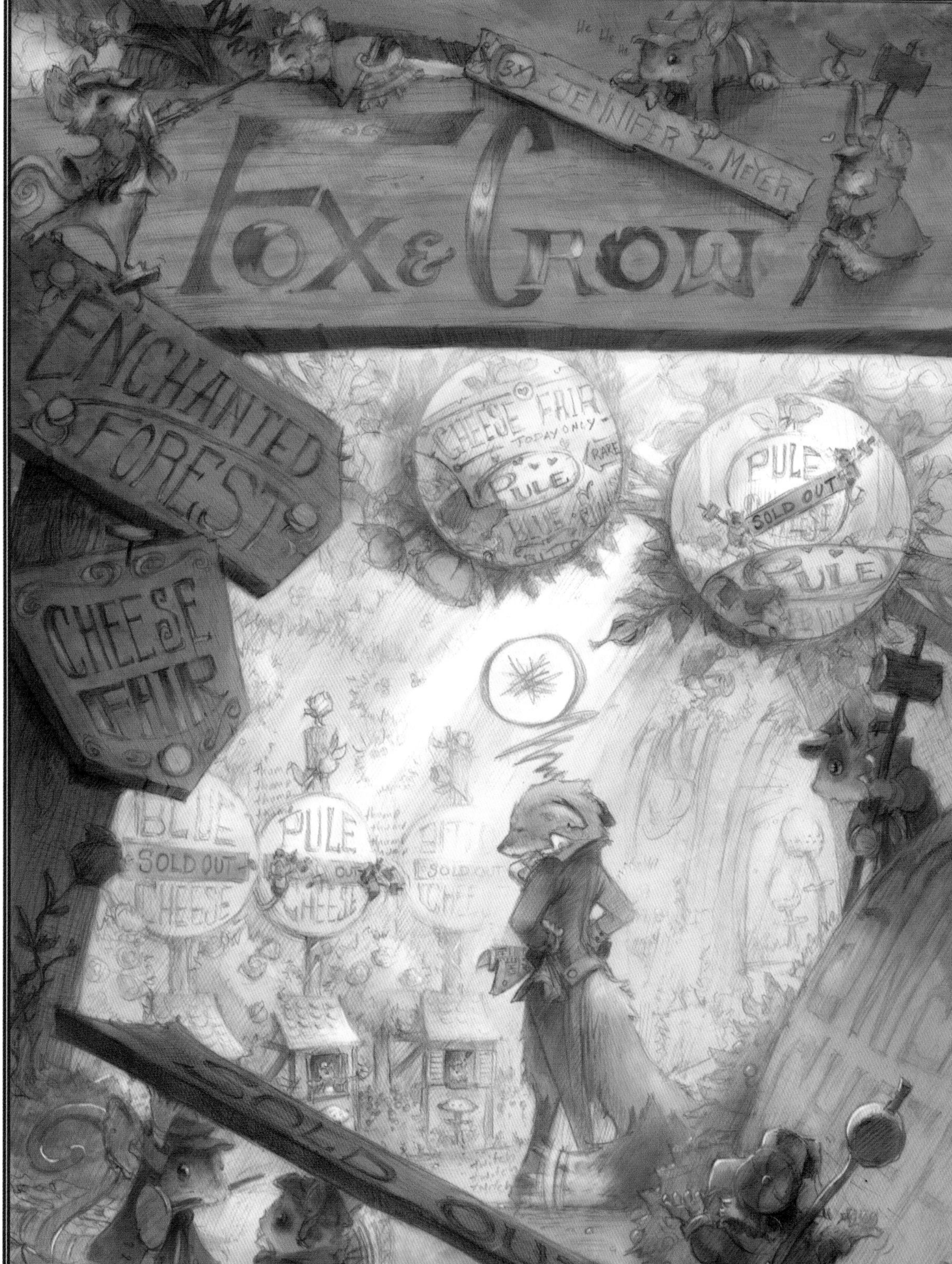
BY JENNIFER L. MEYER
FOX & CROW
ENCHANTED FOREST
CHEESE FAIR
CHEESE FAIR
TODAY ONLY
PULE
SOLD OUT
BLUE
SOLD OUT
CHEESE
PULE
CHEESE
SOLD OUT

From Aesop

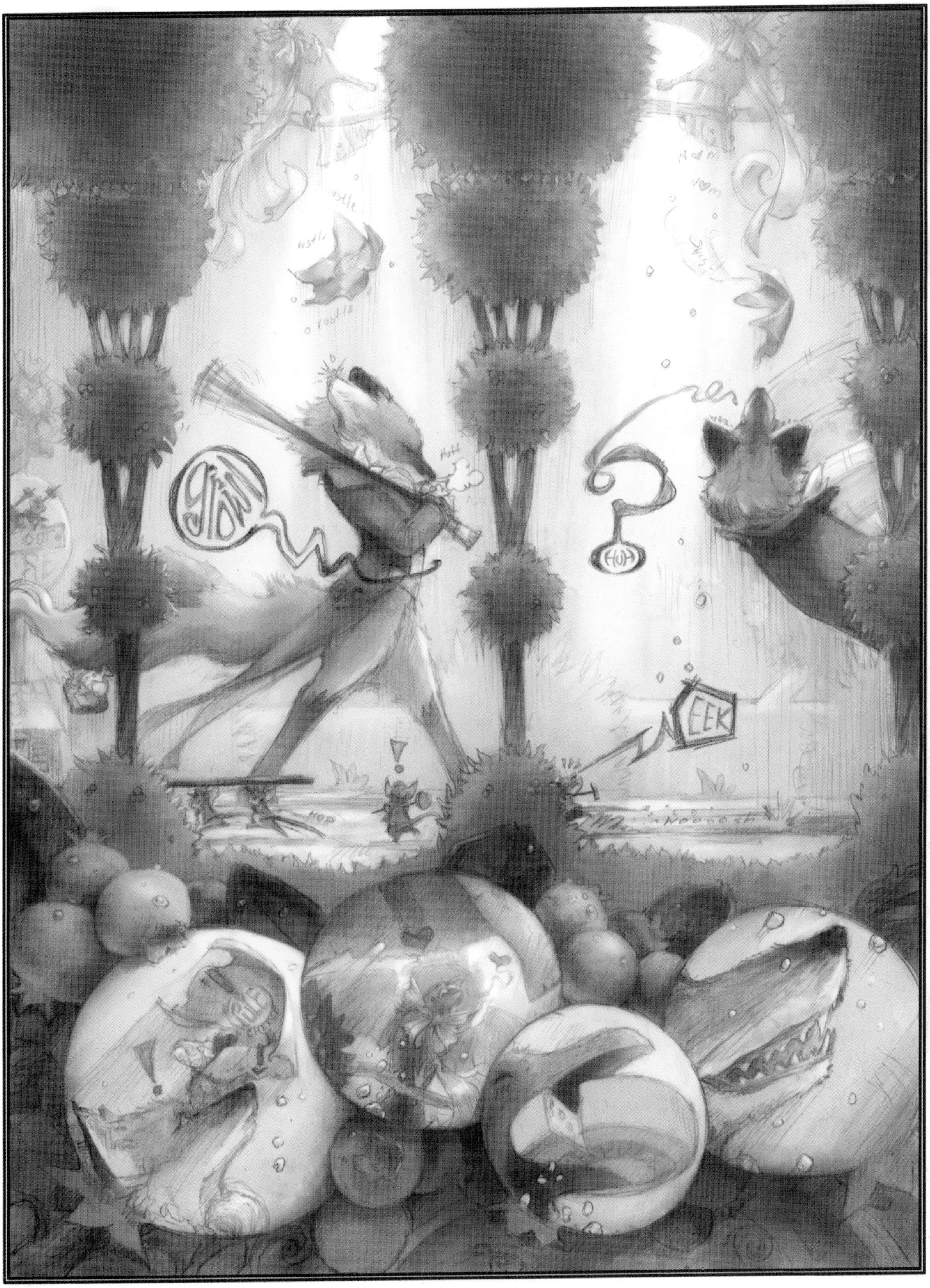
HUH
EEK

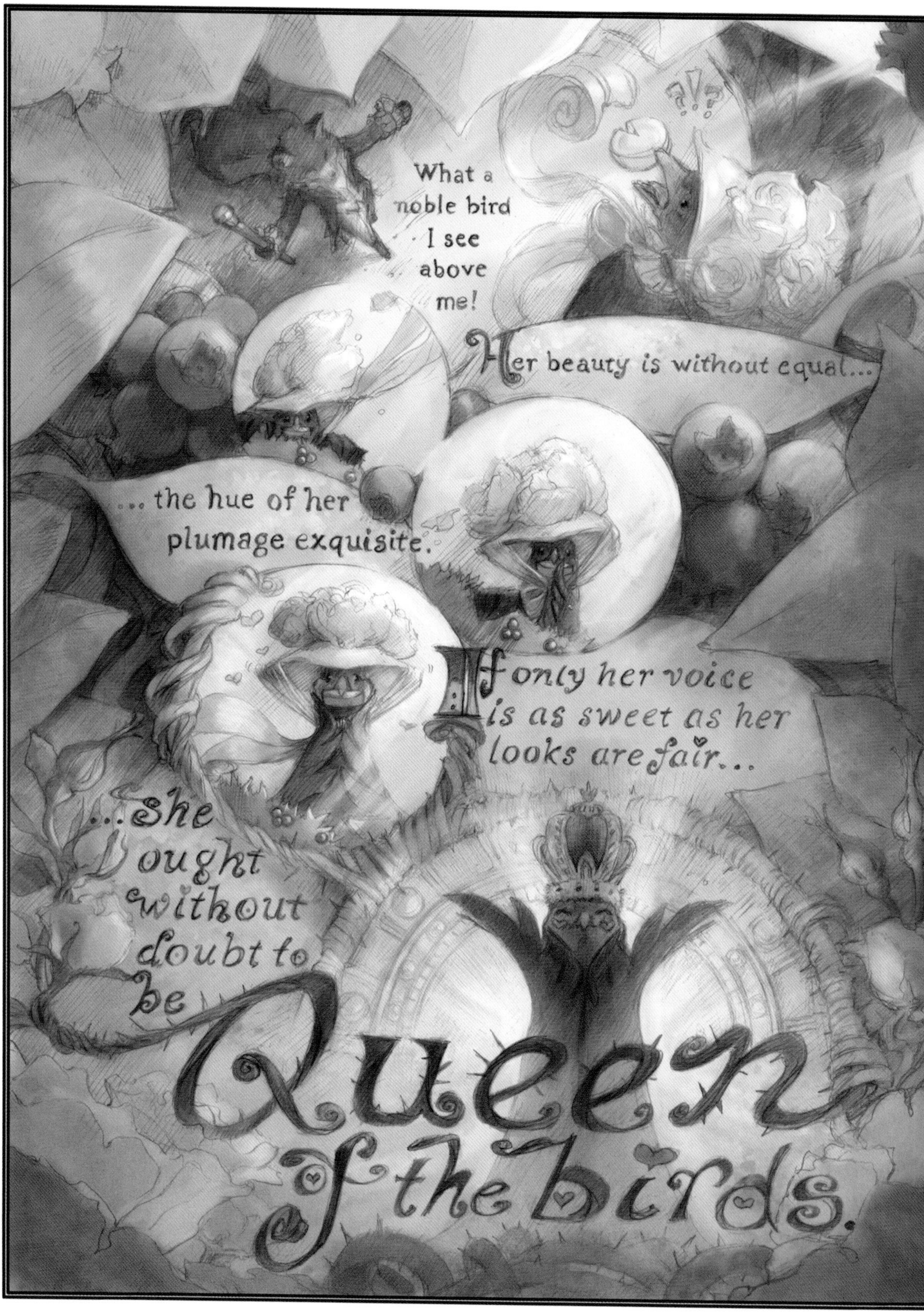
?!?
What a noble bird I see above me!
Her beauty is without equal...
... the hue of her plumage exquisite.
If only her voice is as sweet as her looks are fair...
...she ought without doubt to be
Queen of the birds.

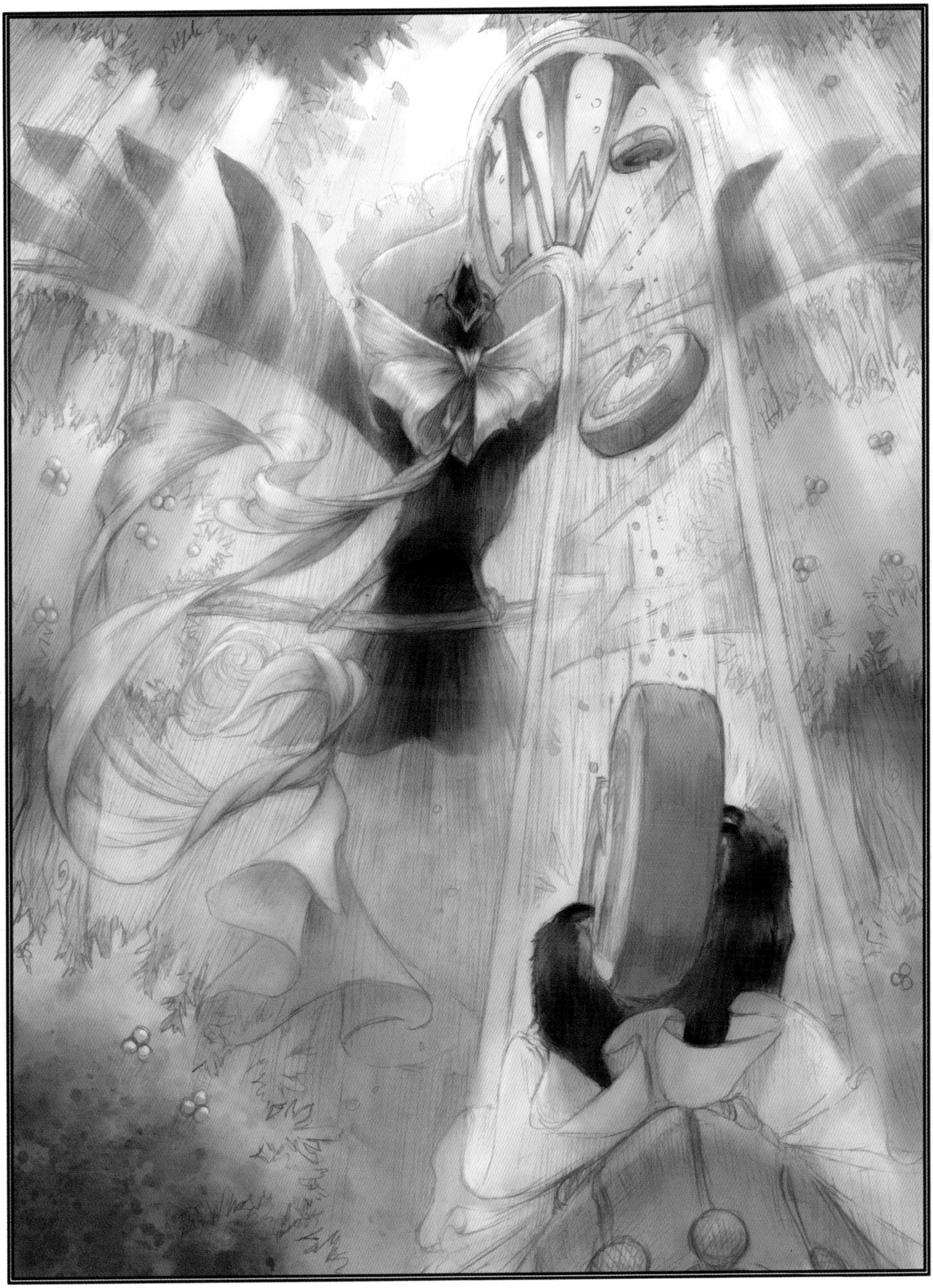

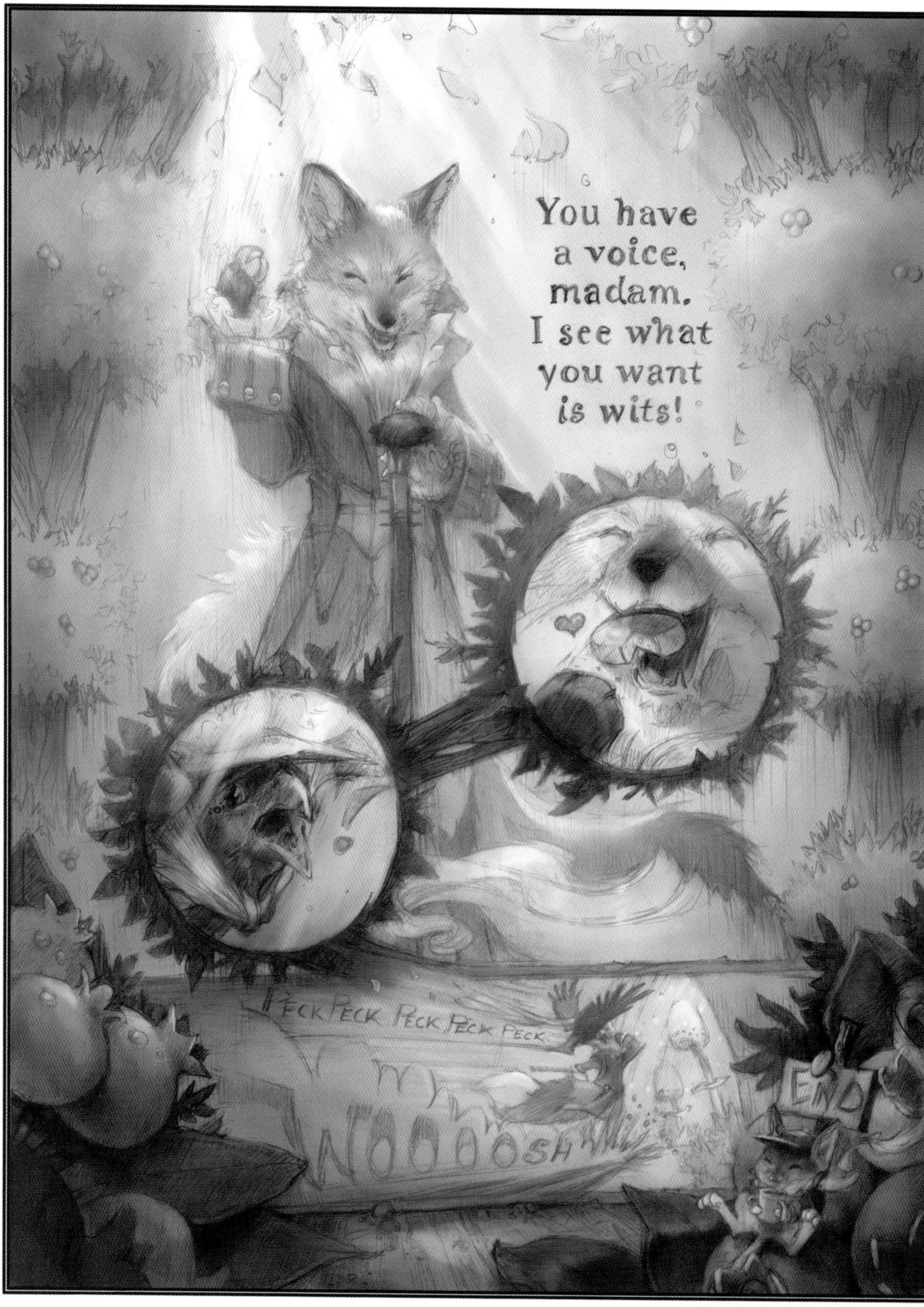
You have
a voice,
madam.
I see what
you want
is wits!
PECK PECK PECK PECK PECK
WOOOOOSH
END

THE OLD MAN AND DEATH

ADAPTED BY ELEANOR DAVIS

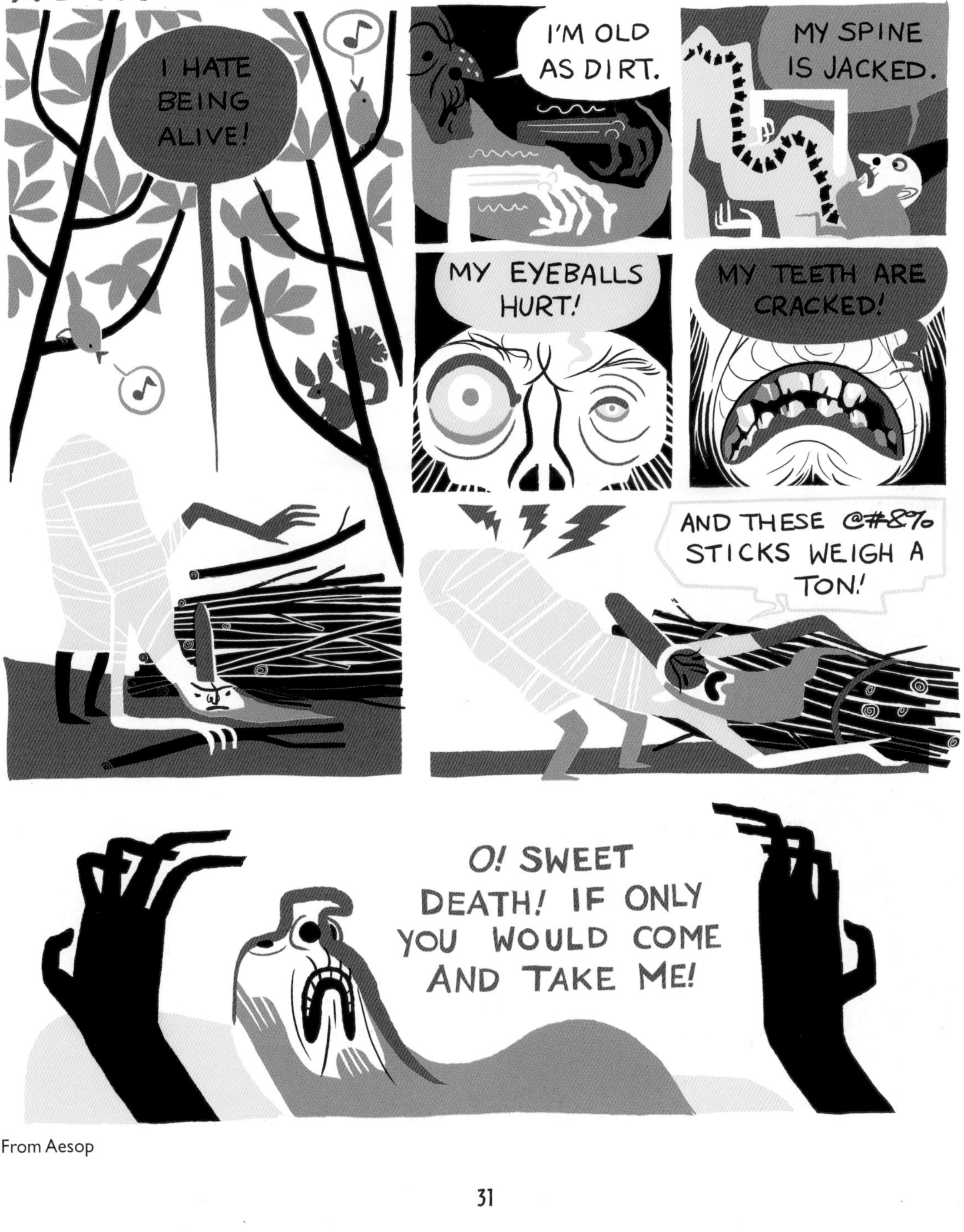
I HATE BEING ALIVE!
I'M OLD AS DIRT.
MY SPINE IS JACKED.
MY EYEBALLS HURT!
MY TEETH ARE CRACKED!
AND THESE @#&% STICKS WEIGH A TON!
O! SWEET DEATH! IF ONLY YOU WOULD COME AND TAKE ME!

From Aesop

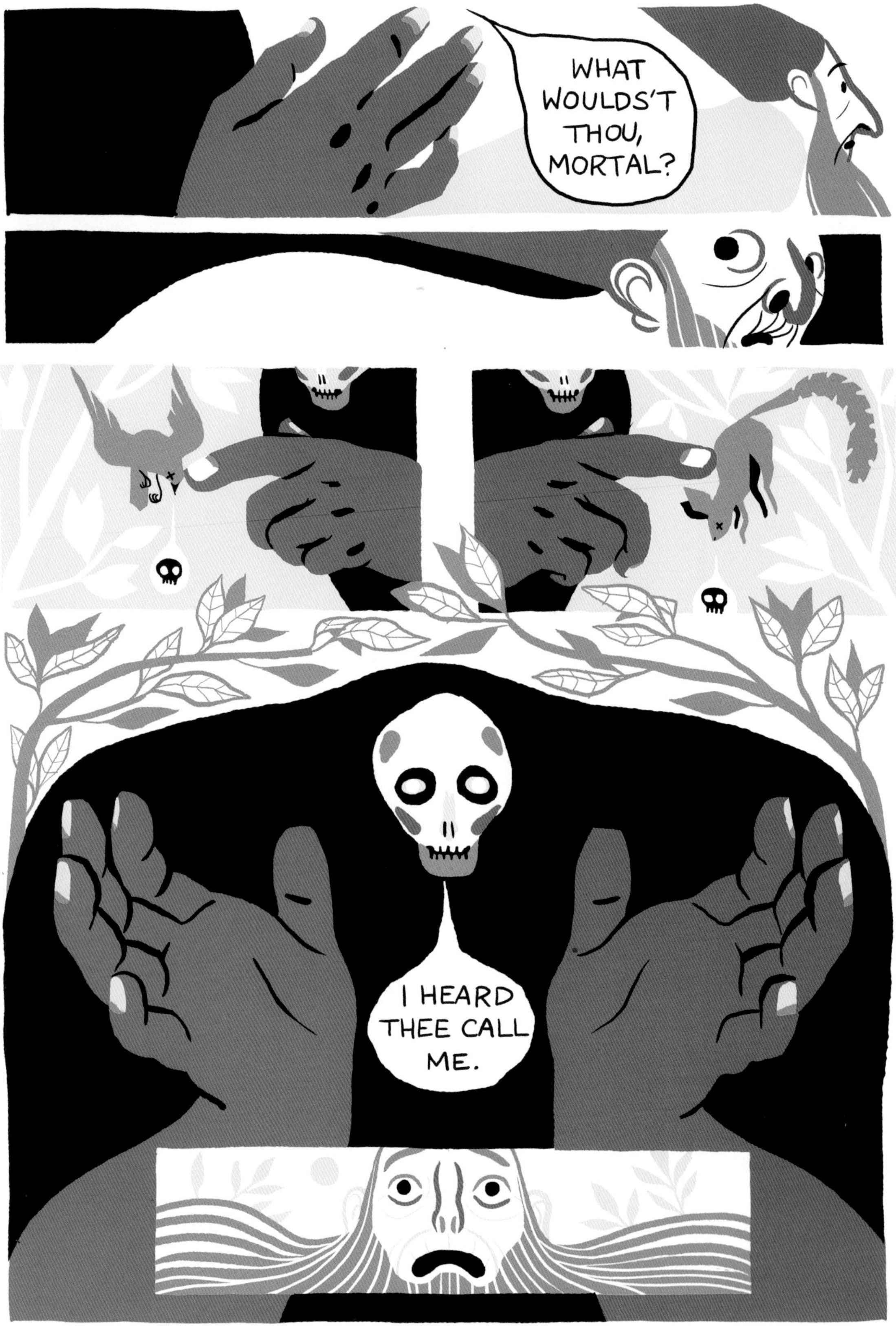
WHAT WOULDS'T THOU, MORTAL?
I HEARD THEE CALL ME.

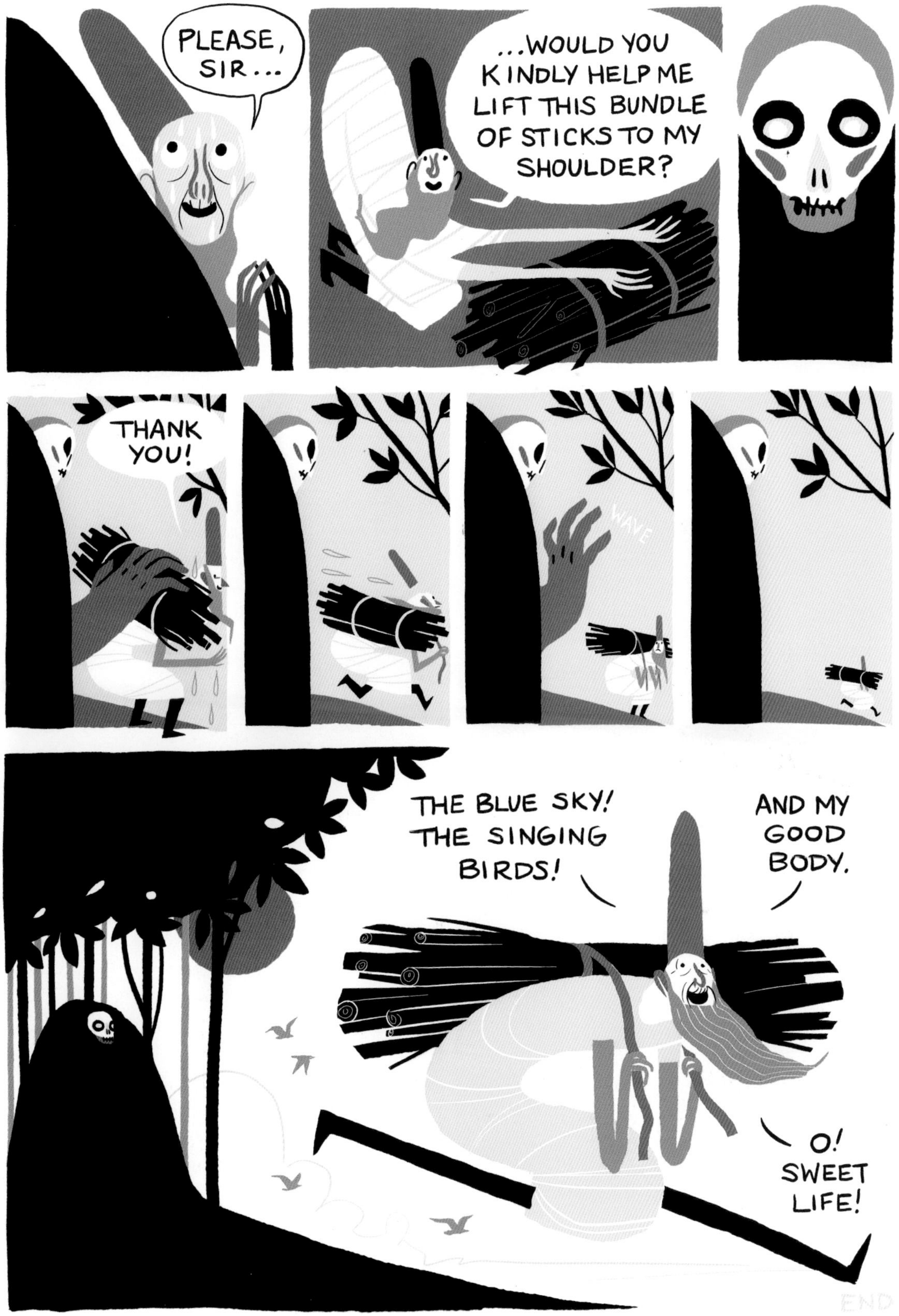
PLEASE, SIR...
...WOULD YOU KINDLY HELP ME LIFT THIS BUNDLE OF STICKS TO MY SHOULDER?
THANK YOU!
WAVE
THE BLUE SKY! THE SINGING BIRDS!
AND MY GOOD BODY.
O! SWEET LIFE!
END

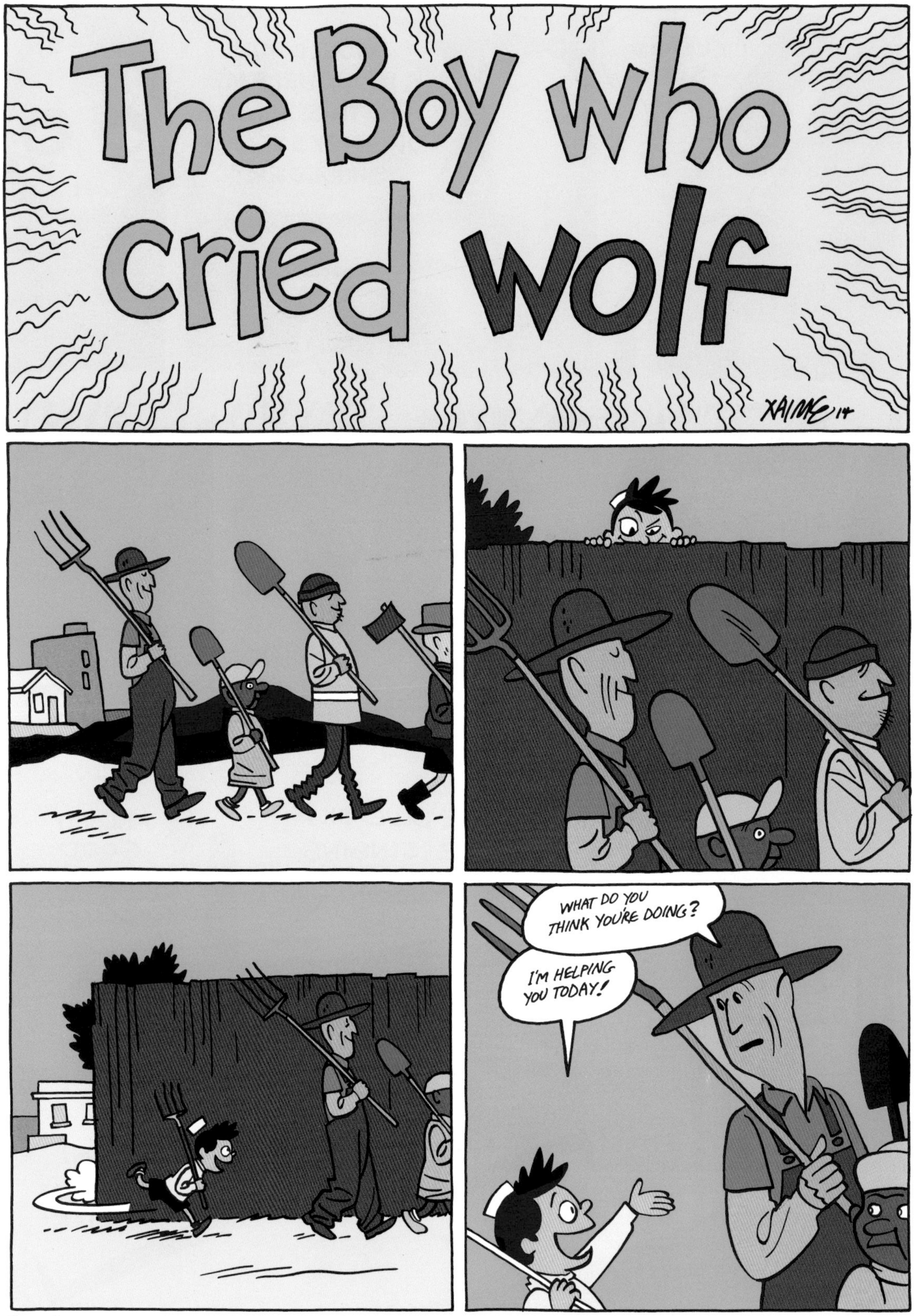
The Boy who cried wolf
XAIME '14
WHAT DO YOU THINK YOU'RE DOING?
I'M HELPING YOU TODAY!

From Aesop

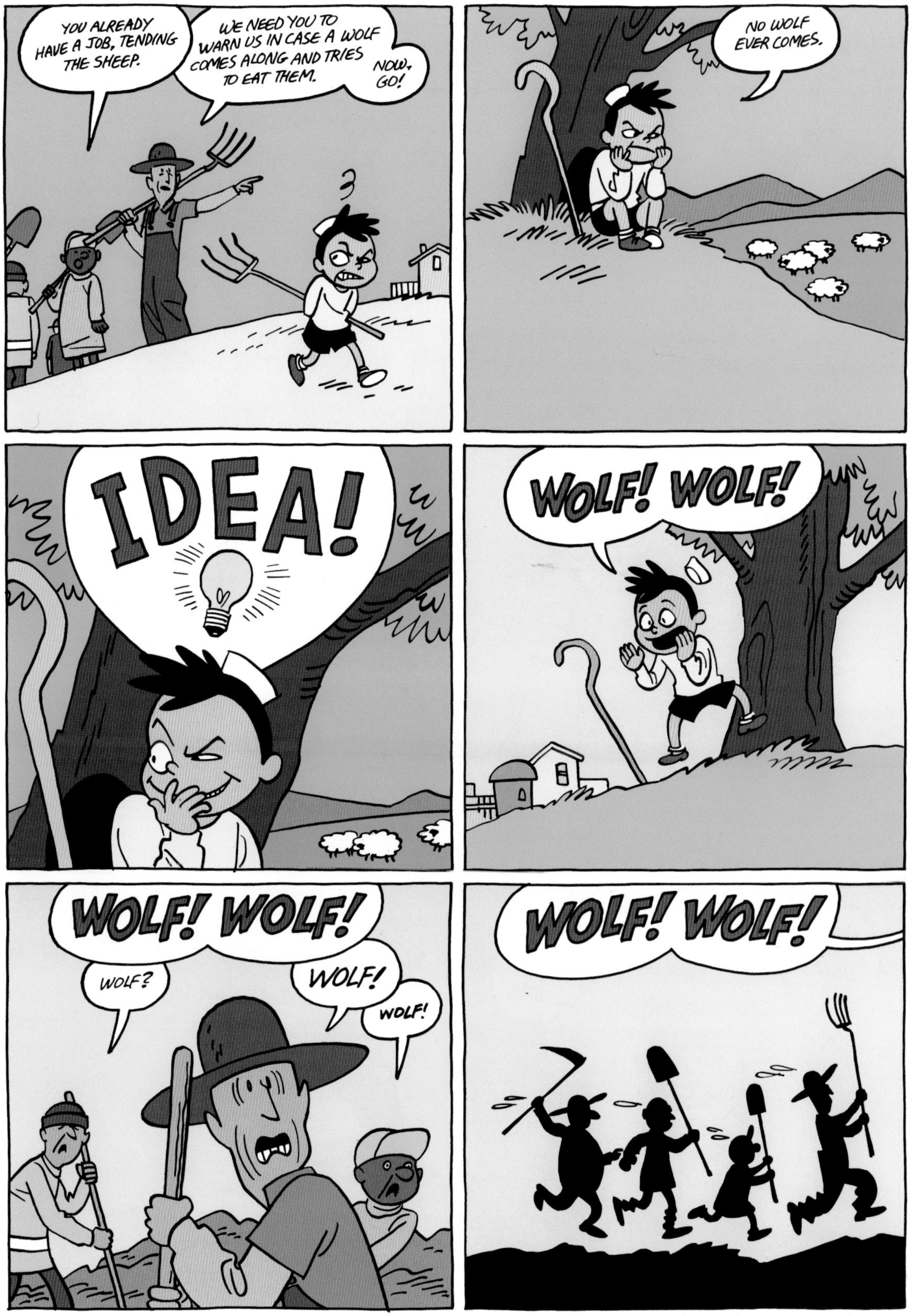
YOU ALREADY HAVE A JOB, TENDING THE SHEEP.
WE NEED YOU TO WARN US IN CASE A WOLF COMES ALONG AND TRIES TO EAT THEM.
NOW, GO!
NO WOLF EVER COMES.
IDEA!
WOLF! WOLF!
WOLF! WOLF!
WOLF?
WOLF!
WOLF!
WOLF! WOLF!

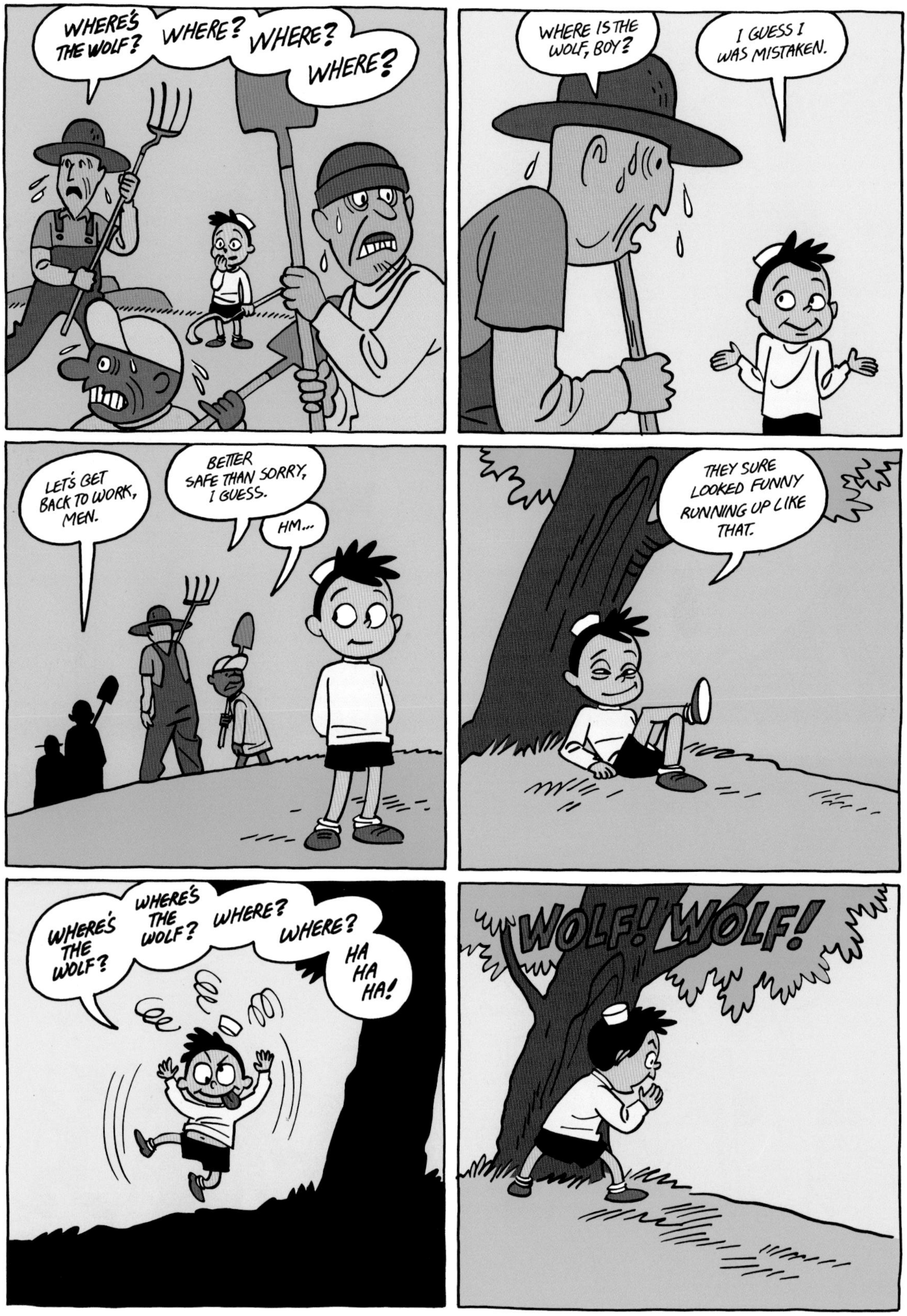
WHERE'S THE WOLF?
WHERE?
WHERE?
WHERE?
WHERE IS THE WOLF, BOY?
I GUESS I WAS MISTAKEN.
LET'S GET BACK TO WORK, MEN.
BETTER SAFE THAN SORRY, I GUESS.
HM...
THEY SURE LOOKED FUNNY RUNNING UP LIKE THAT.
WHERE'S THE WOLF?
WHERE'S THE WOLF?
WHERE?
WHERE?
HA HA HA!
WOLF! WOLF!

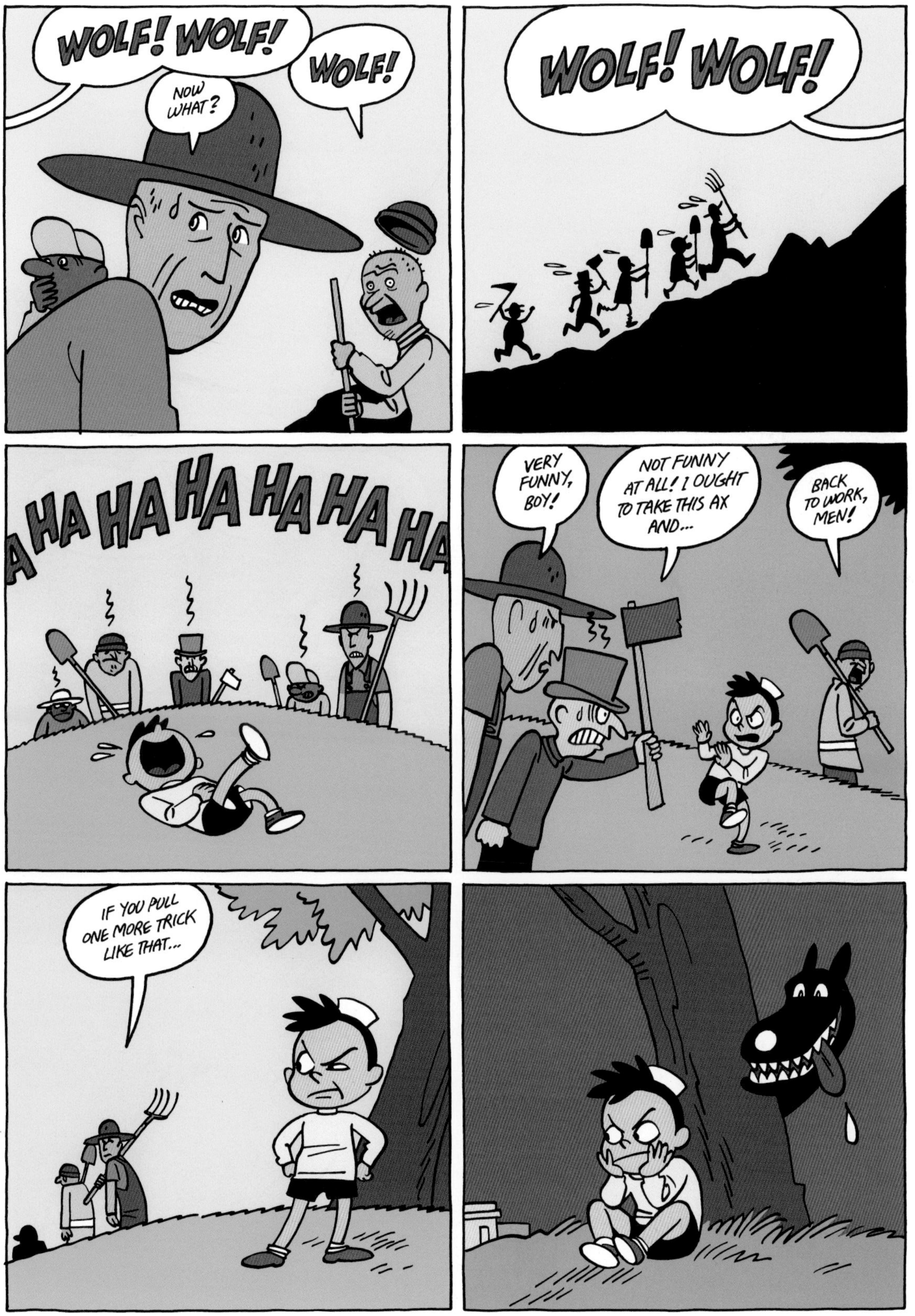
WOLF! WOLF!
NOW WHAT?
WOLF!
WOLF! WOLF!
HAHAHAHAHAHAHAHAHA
VERY FUNNY, BOY!
NOT FUNNY AT ALL! I OUGHT TO TAKE THIS AX AND...
BACK TO WORK, MEN!
IF YOU PULL ONE MORE TRICK LIKE THAT...

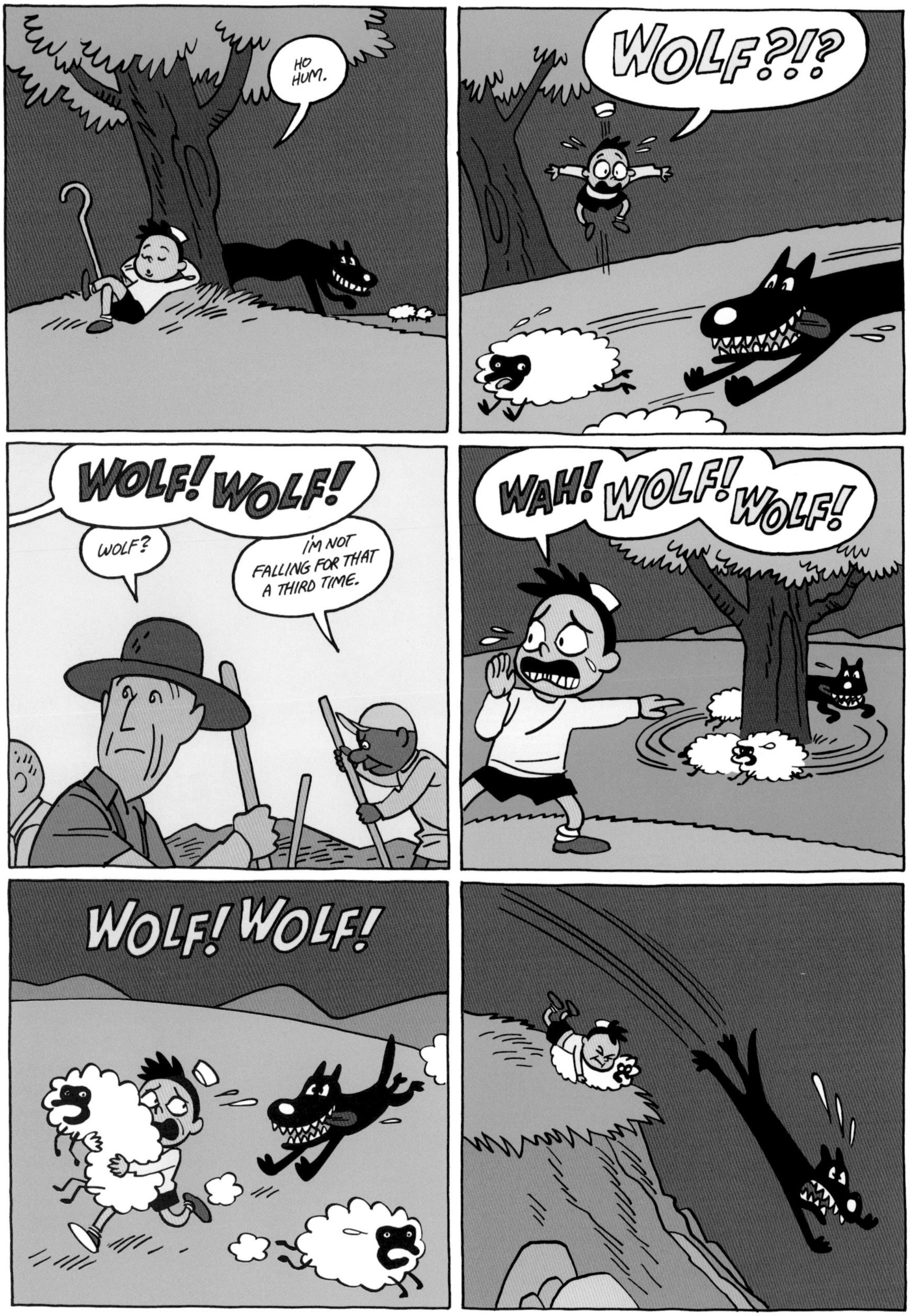
HO HUM.
WOLF?!?
WOLF! WOLF!
WOLF?
I'M NOT FALLING FOR THAT A THIRD TIME.
WAH! WOLF! WOLF!
WOLF! WOLF!

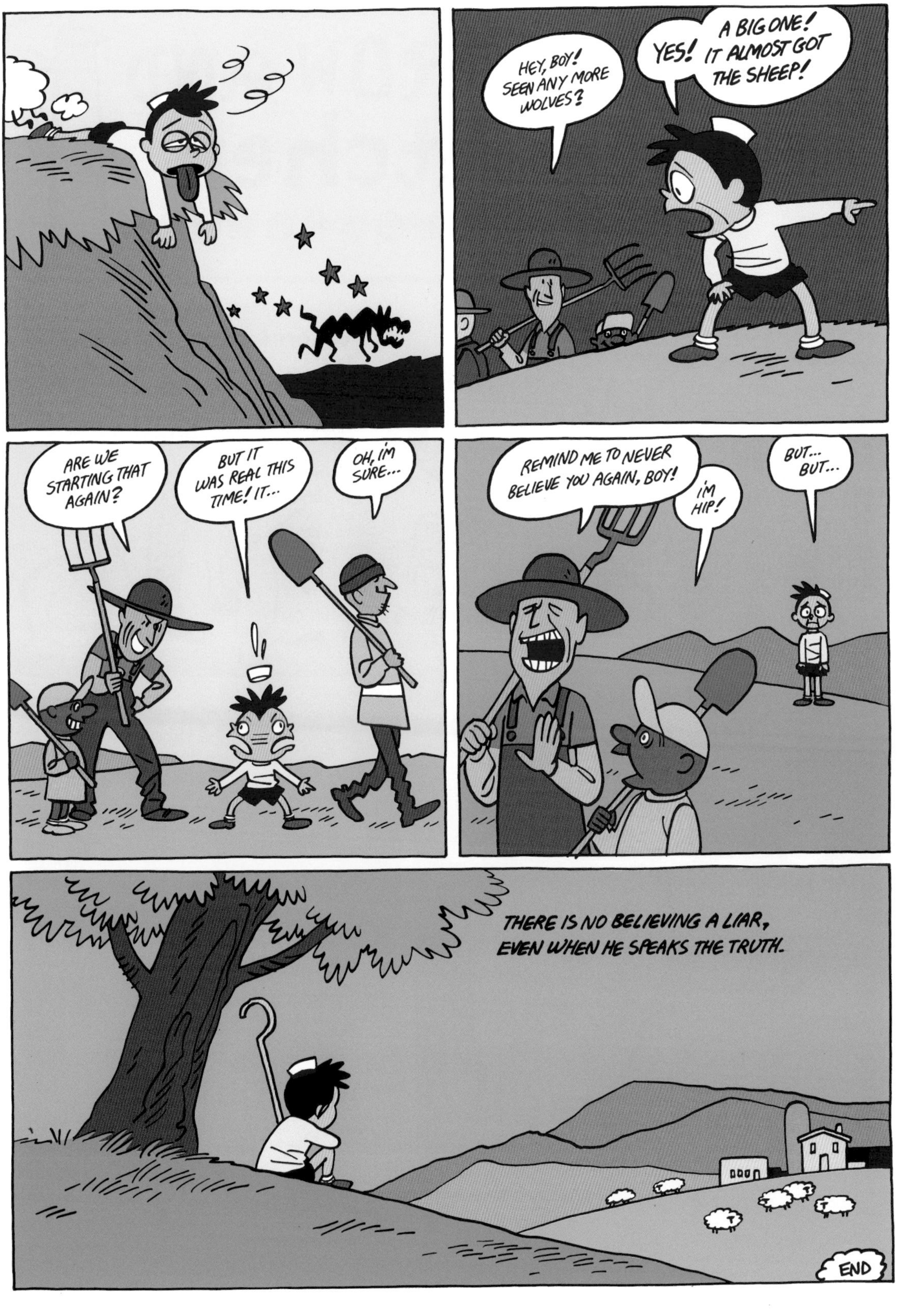
HEY, BOY! SEEN ANY MORE WOLVES?
YES!
A BIG ONE! IT ALMOST GOT THE SHEEP!
ARE WE STARTING THAT AGAIN?
BUT IT WAS REAL THIS TIME! IT...
OH, I'M SURE...
REMIND ME TO NEVER BELIEVE YOU AGAIN, BOY!
I'M HIP!
BUT... BUT...
THERE IS NO BELIEVING A LIAR, EVEN WHEN HE SPEAKS THE TRUTH.
END

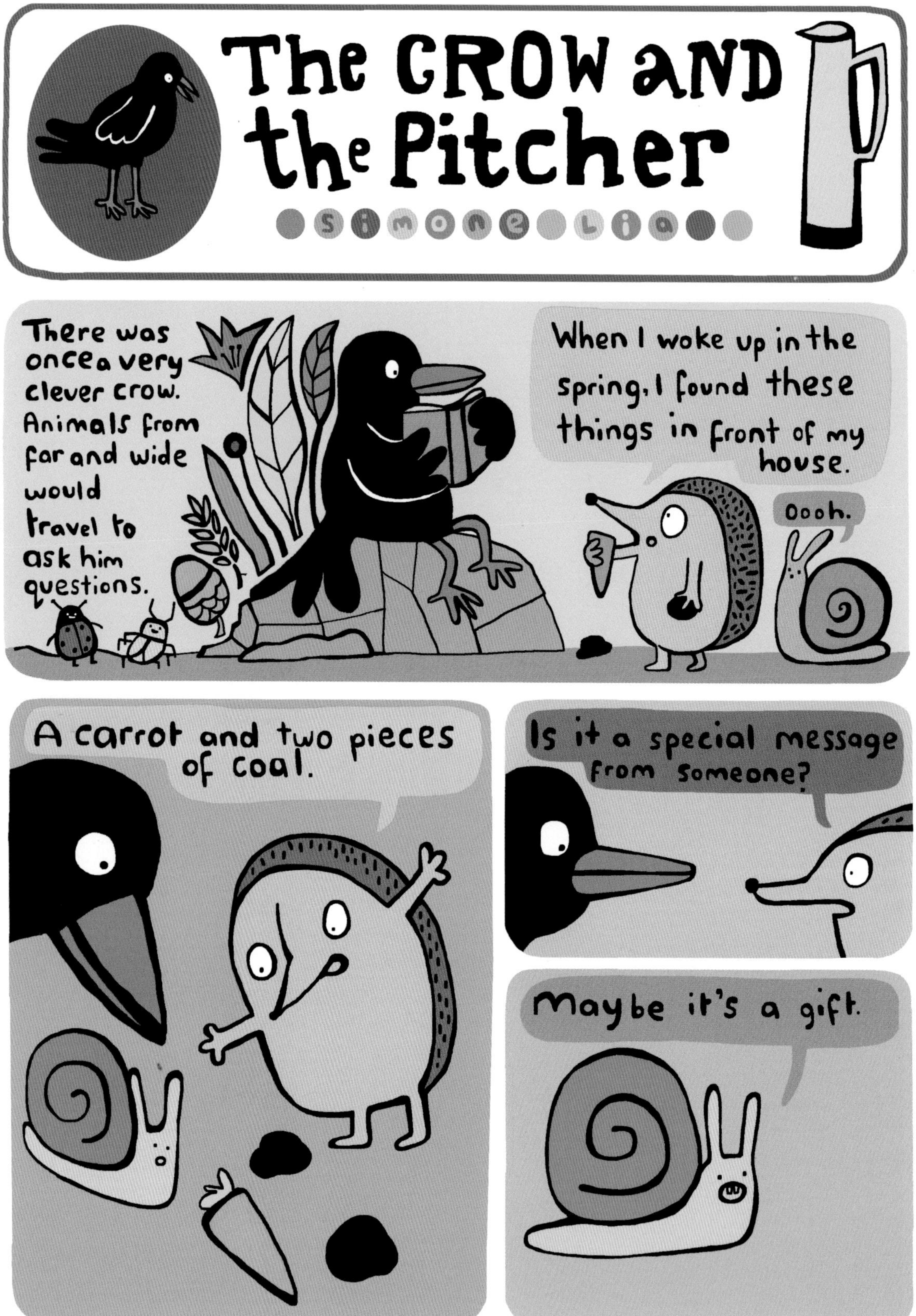
The CROW AND the Pitcher
Simone Lia
There was once a very clever crow. Animals from far and wide would travel to ask him questions.
When I woke up in the spring, I found these things in front of my house.
Oooh.
A carrot and two pieces of coal.
Is it a special message from someone?
Maybe it's a gift.

From Aesop

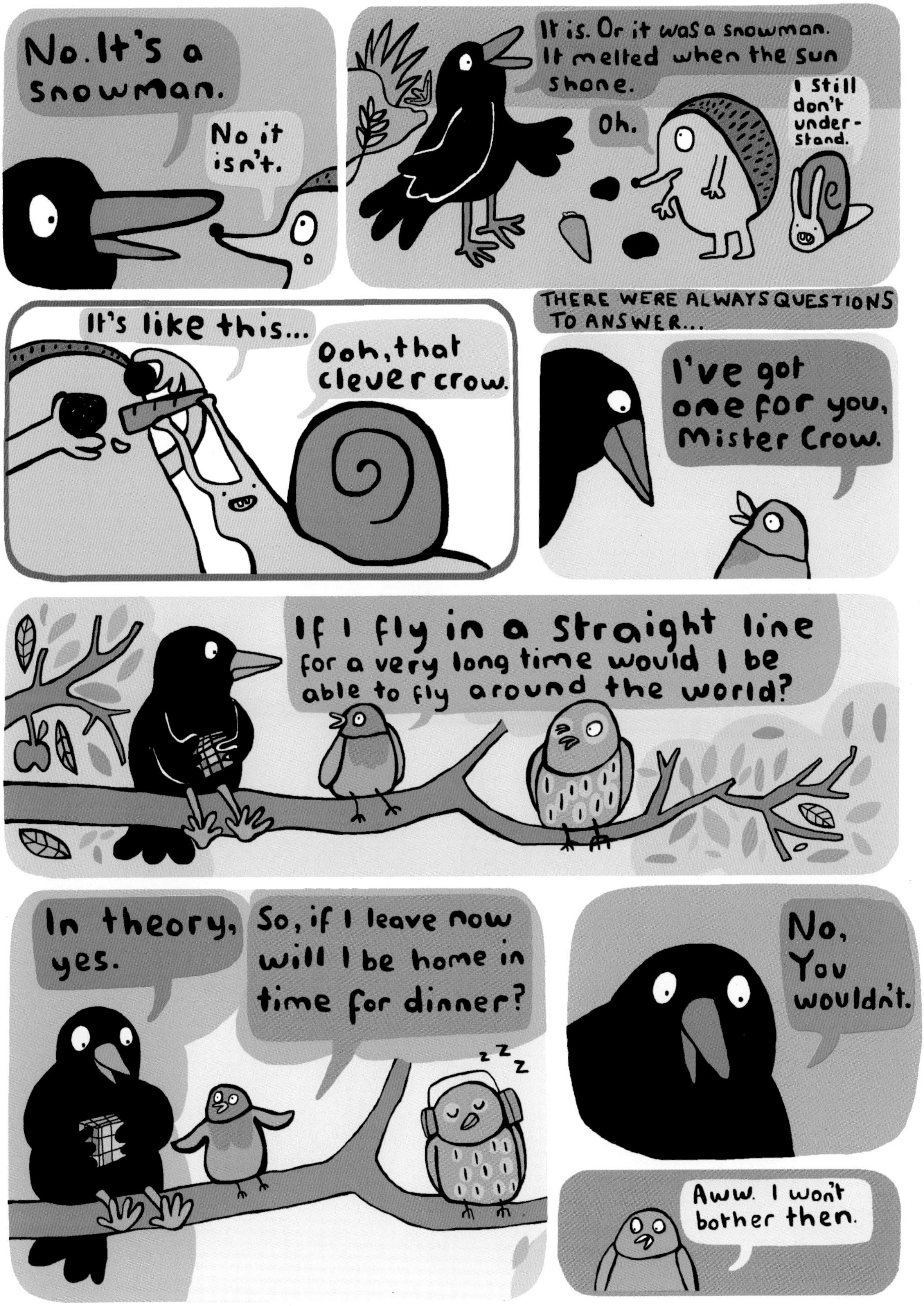

No. It's a snowman.
No it isn't.
It is. Or it was a snowman. It melted when the sun shone.
Oh.
I still don't under-stand.
It's like this...
Ooh, that clever crow.
THERE WERE ALWAYS QUESTIONS TO ANSWER...
I've got one for you, Mister Crow.
If I fly in a straight line for a very long time would I be able to fly around the world?
In theory, yes.
So, if I leave now will I be home in time for dinner?
z z z
No, You wouldn't.
Aww. I won't bother then.

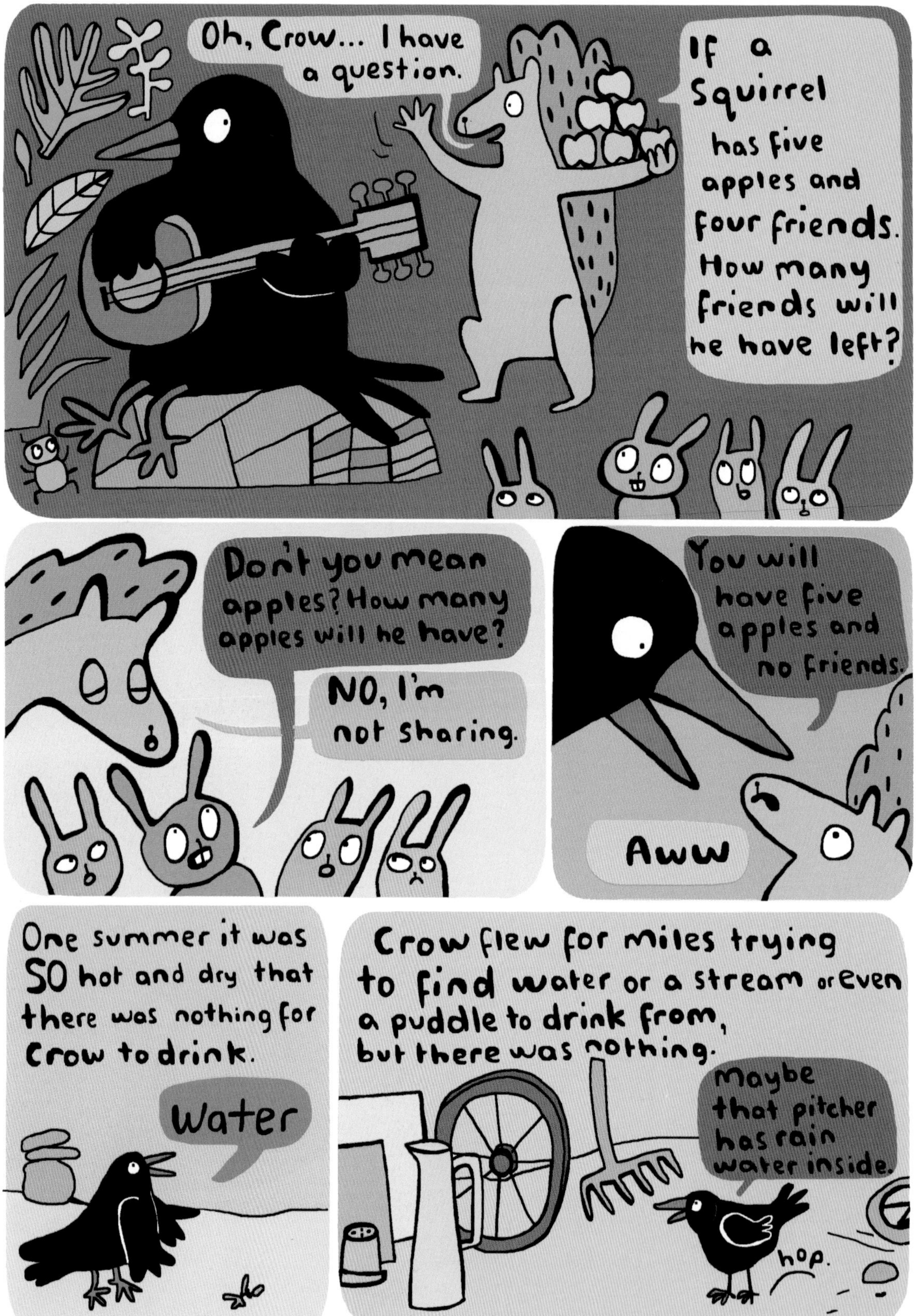
Oh, Crow... I have a question.
If a Squirrel has five apples and four friends. How many friends will he have left?
Don't you mean apples? How many apples will he have?
NO, I'm not sharing.
You will have five apples and no friends.
Aww
One summer it was SO hot and dry that there was nothing for Crow to drink.
Water
Crow flew for miles trying to find water or a stream or even a puddle to drink from, but there was nothing.
Maybe that pitcher has rain water inside.
hop.

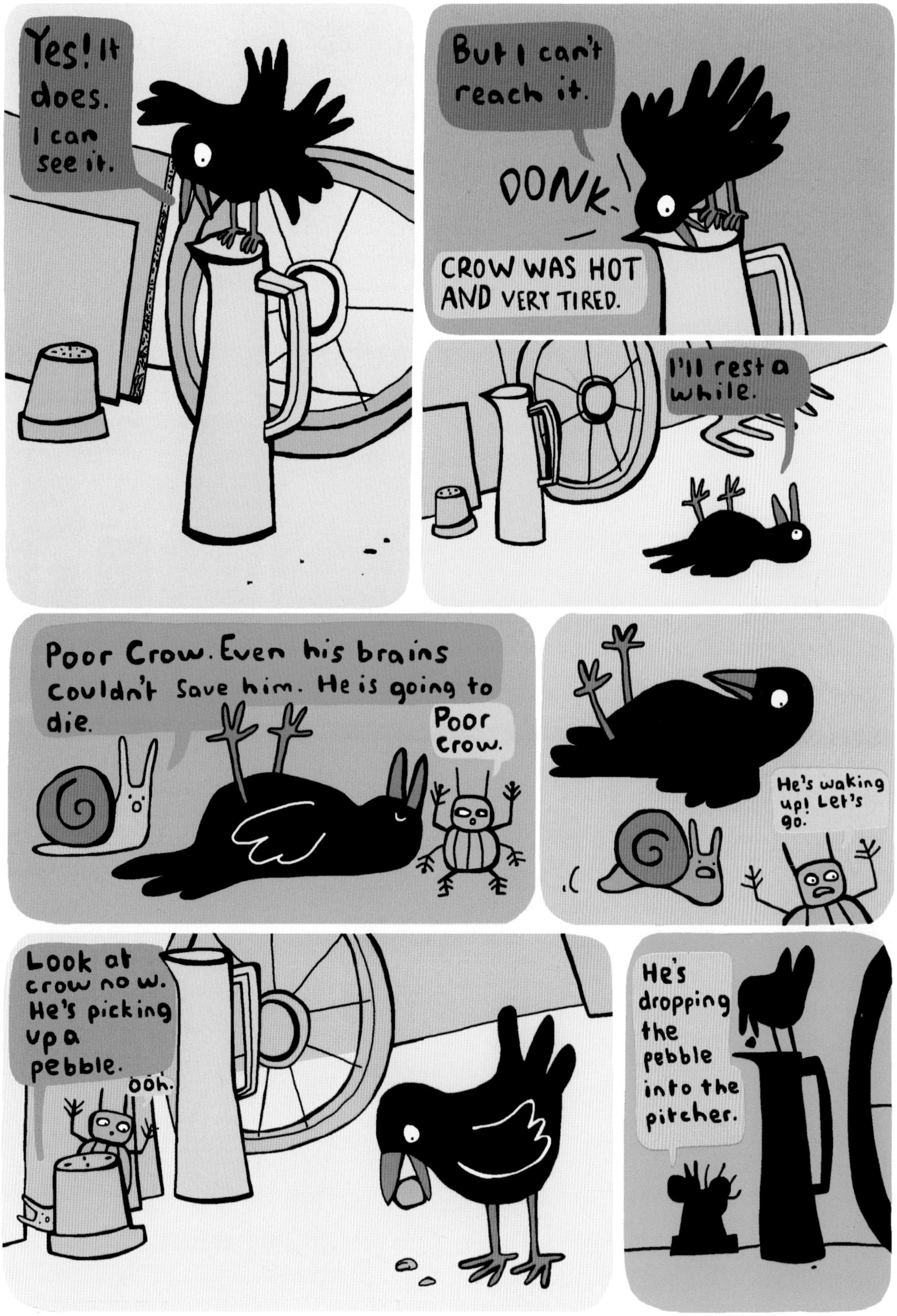
Yes! It does. I can see it.
But I can't reach it.
DONK
CROW WAS HOT AND VERY TIRED.
I'll rest a while.
Poor Crow. Even his brains couldn't save him. He is going to die.
Poor crow.
He's waking up! Let's go.
Look at crow now. He's picking up a pebble.
ooh.
He's dropping the pebble into the pitcher.

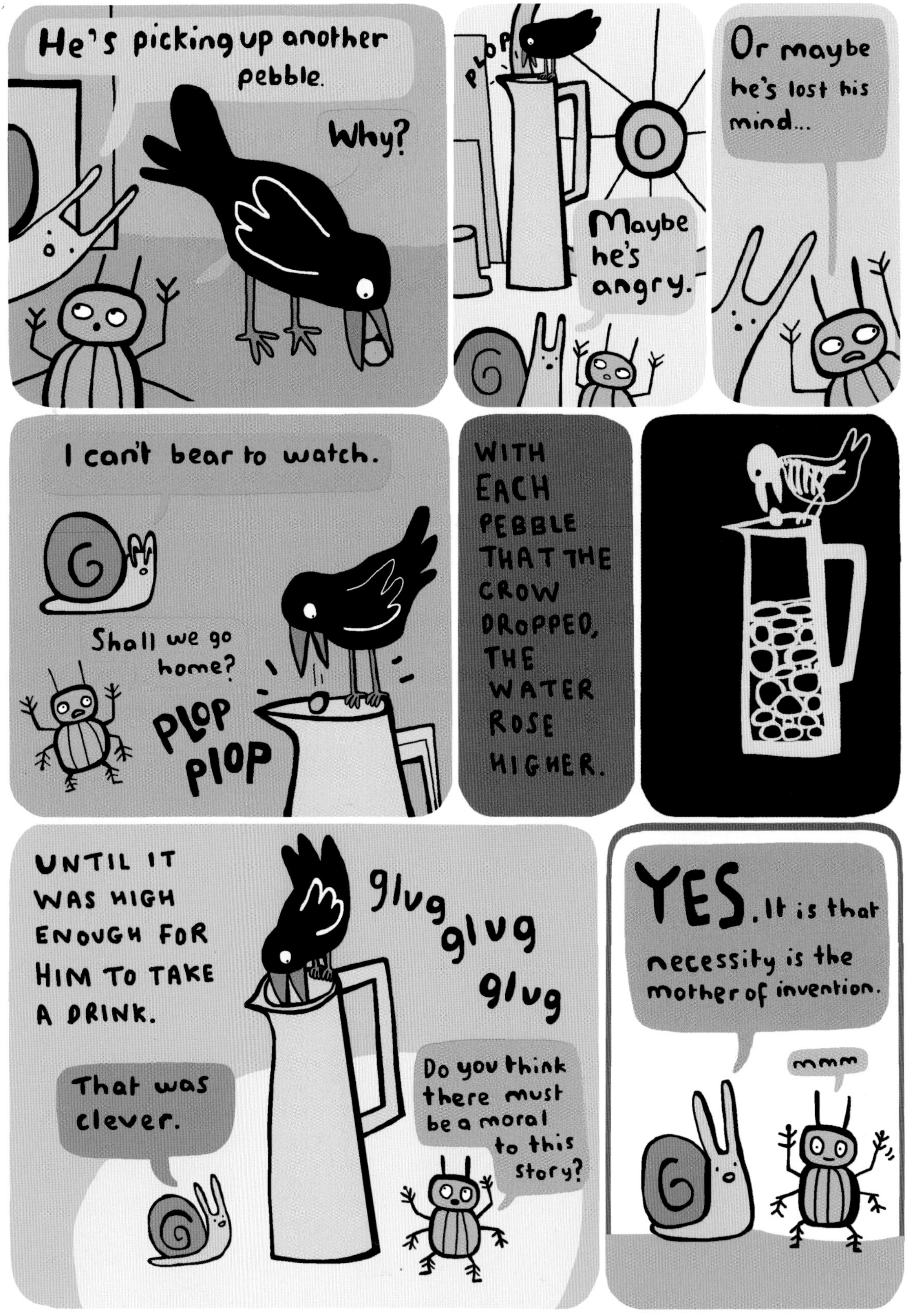
He's picking up another pebble.
Why?
PLOP
Maybe he's angry.
Or maybe he's lost his mind...
I can't bear to watch.
Shall we go home?
PLOP PLOP
WITH EACH PEBBLE THAT THE CROW DROPPED, THE WATER ROSE HIGHER.
UNTIL IT WAS HIGH ENOUGH FOR HIM TO TAKE A DRINK.
glug glug glug
That was clever.
Do you think there must be a moral to this story?
YES. It is that necessity is the mother of invention.
mmm

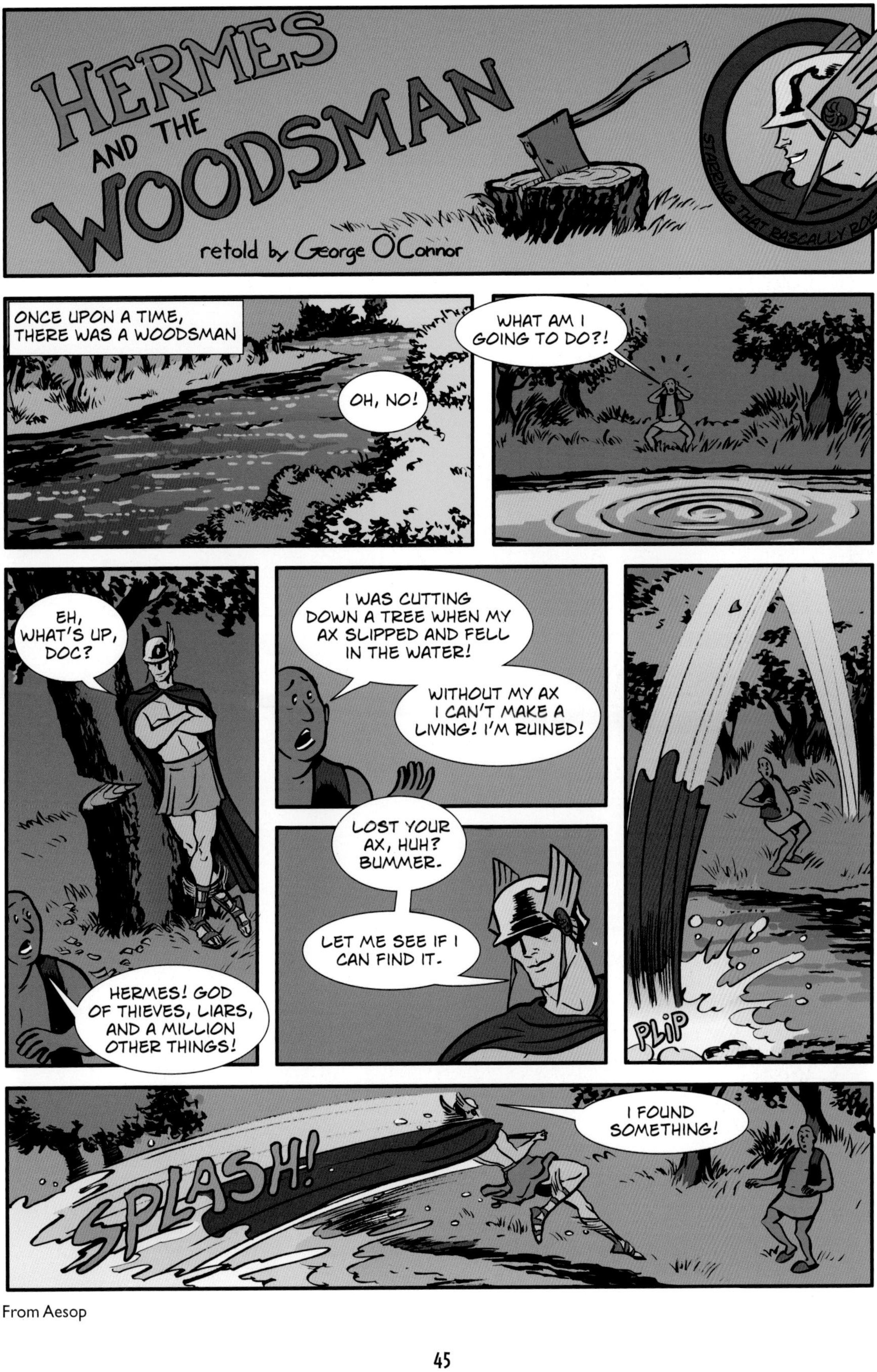
HERMES AND THE WOODSMAN
retold by George O'Connor
STARRING THAT RASCALLY ROGUE, HERMES
ONCE UPON A TIME, THERE WAS A WOODSMAN
OH, NO!
WHAT AM I GOING TO DO?!
EH, WHAT'S UP, DOC?
HERMES! GOD OF THIEVES, LIARS, AND A MILLION OTHER THINGS!
I WAS CUTTING DOWN A TREE WHEN MY AX SLIPPED AND FELL IN THE WATER!
WITHOUT MY AX I CAN'T MAKE A LIVING! I'M RUINED!
LOST YOUR AX, HUH? BUMMER.
LET ME SEE IF I CAN FIND IT.
PLIP
SPLASH!
I FOUND SOMETHING!

From Aesop

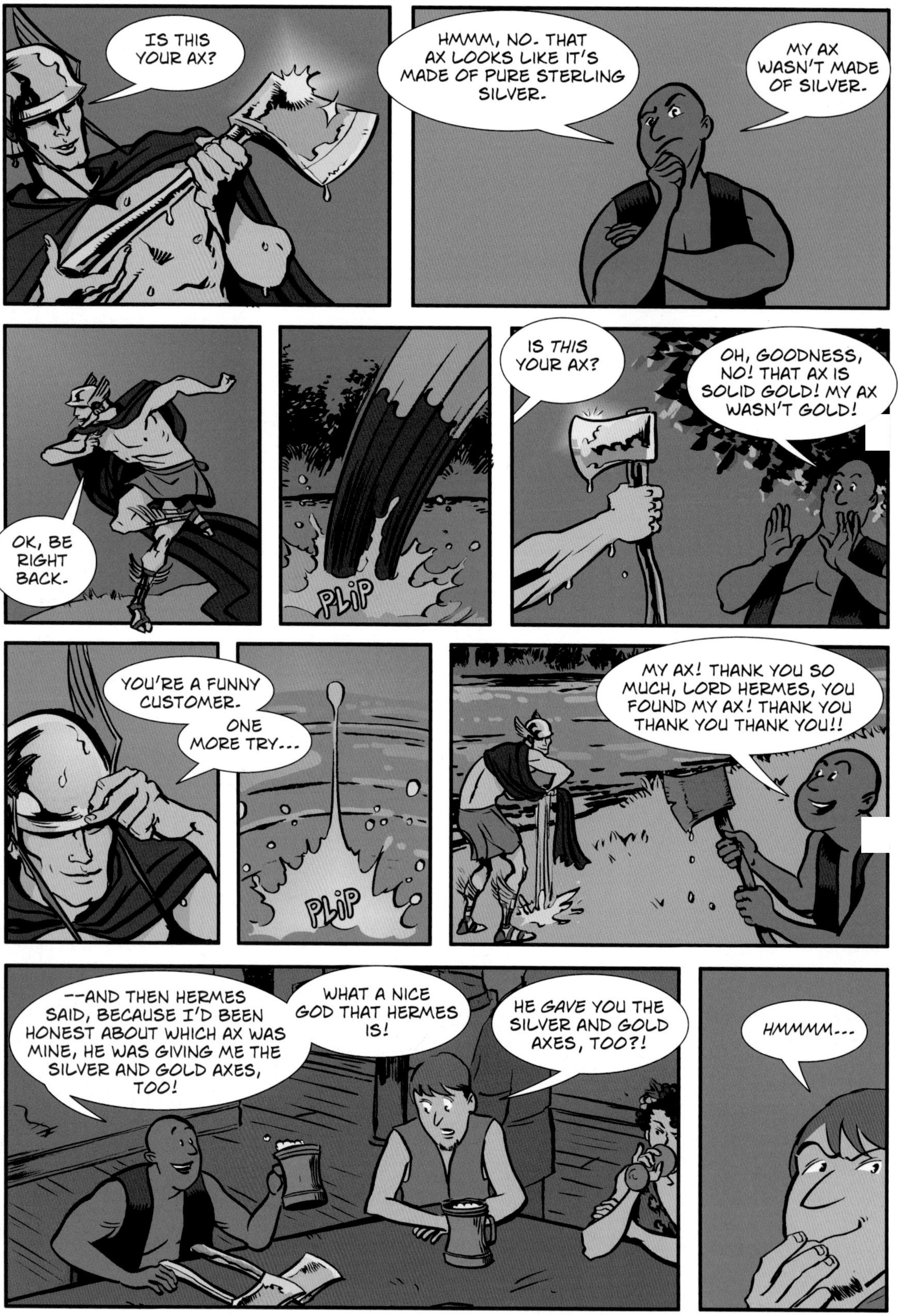
IS THIS YOUR AX?
HMMM, NO. THAT AX LOOKS LIKE IT'S MADE OF PURE STERLING SILVER.
MY AX WASN'T MADE OF SILVER.
OK, BE RIGHT BACK.
PLIP
IS *THIS* YOUR AX?
OH, GOODNESS, NO! THAT AX IS SOLID GOLD! MY AX WASN'T GOLD!
YOU'RE A FUNNY CUSTOMER.
ONE MORE TRY...
PLIP
MY AX! THANK YOU SO MUCH, LORD HERMES, YOU FOUND MY AX! THANK YOU THANK YOU THANK YOU!!
--AND THEN HERMES SAID, BECAUSE I'D BEEN HONEST ABOUT WHICH AX WAS MINE, HE WAS GIVING ME THE SILVER AND GOLD AXES, TOO!
WHAT A NICE GOD THAT HERMES IS!
HE *GAVE* YOU THE SILVER AND GOLD AXES, TOO?!
HMMMM...

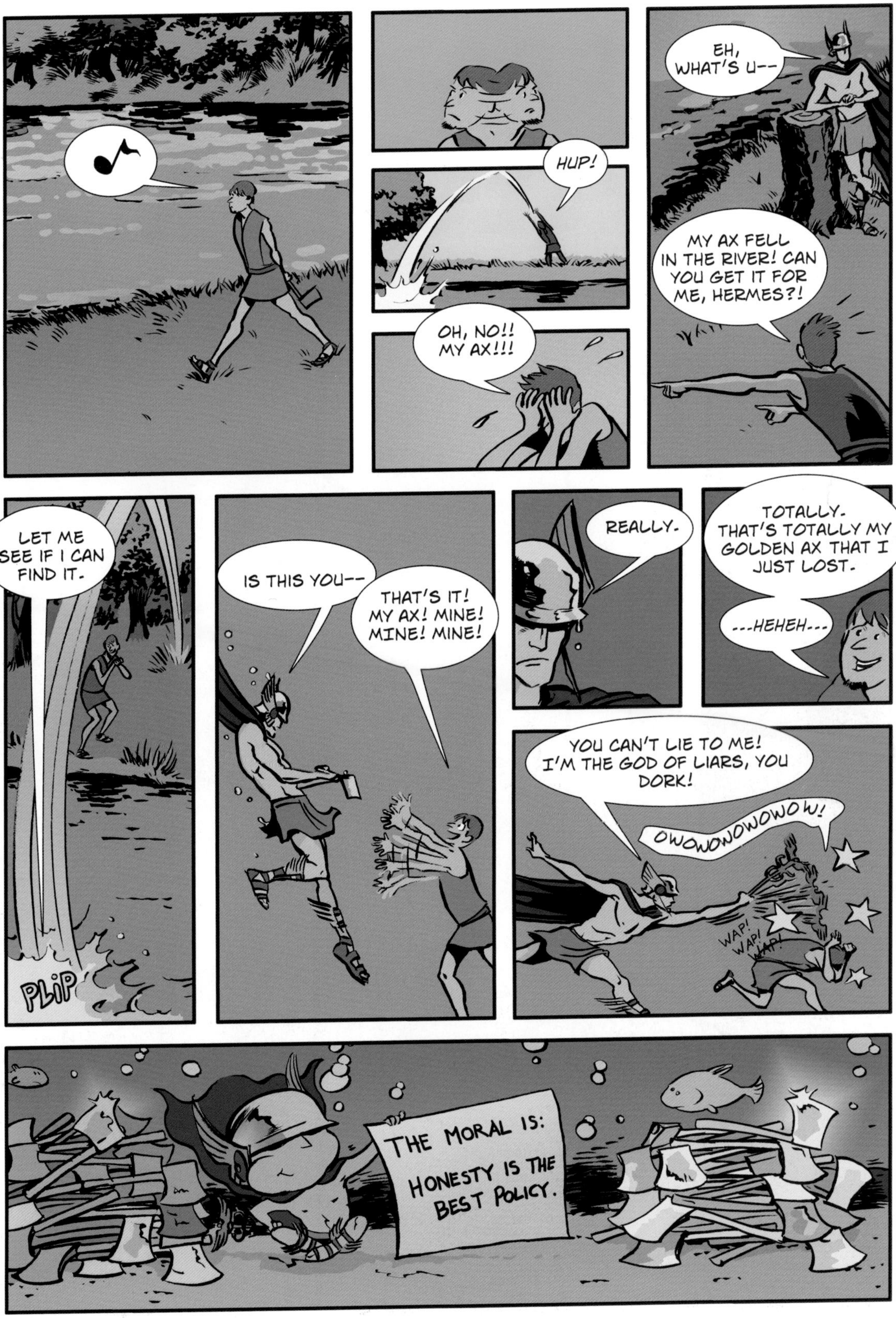
♪
HUP!
OH, NO!! MY AX!!!
EH, WHAT'S U--
MY AX FELL IN THE RIVER! CAN YOU GET IT FOR ME, HERMES?!
LET ME SEE IF I CAN FIND IT.
PLIP
IS THIS YOU--
THAT'S IT! MY AX! MINE! MINE! MINE!
REALLY.
TOTALLY. THAT'S TOTALLY MY GOLDEN AX THAT I JUST LOST.
---HEHEH---
YOU CAN'T LIE TO ME! I'M THE GOD OF LIARS, YOU DORK!
OWOWOWOWOWOW!
WAP! WAP! WAP!
THE MORAL IS:
HONESTY IS THE BEST POLICY.

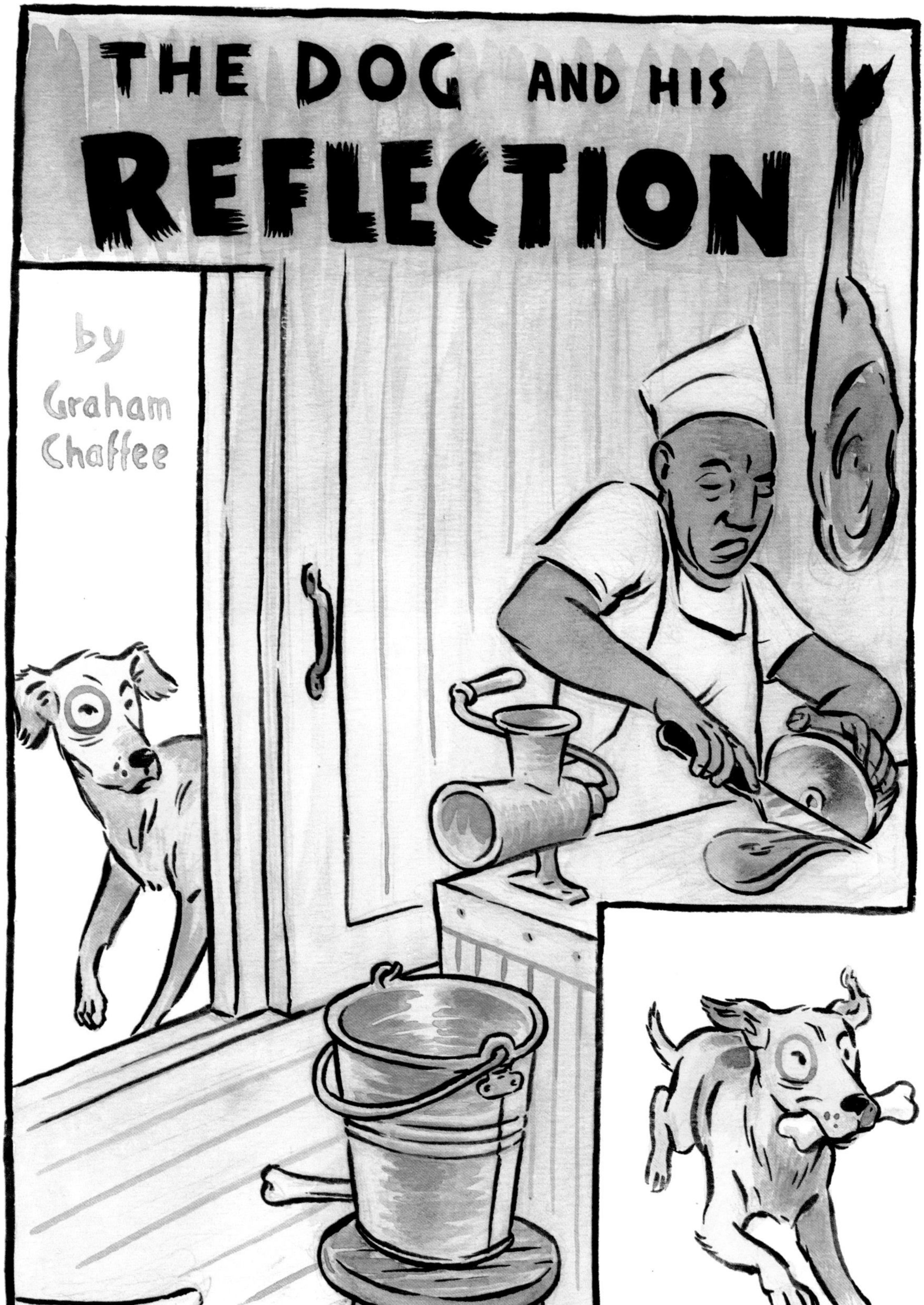
THE DOG AND HIS REFLECTION
by Graham Chaffee

From Aesop

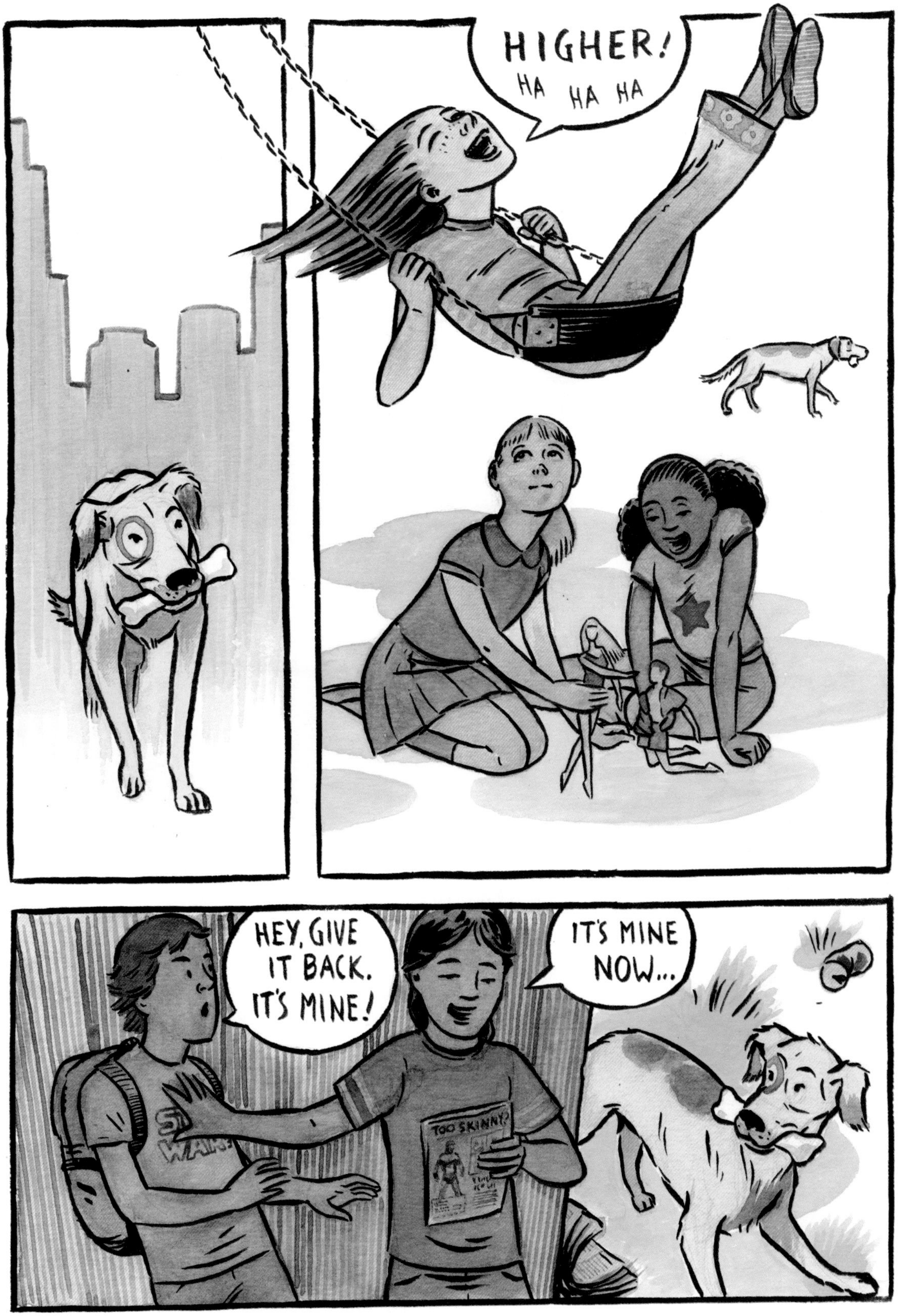
HIGHER!
HA HA HA
HEY, GIVE IT BACK. IT'S MINE!
IT'S MINE NOW...
TOO SKINNY?

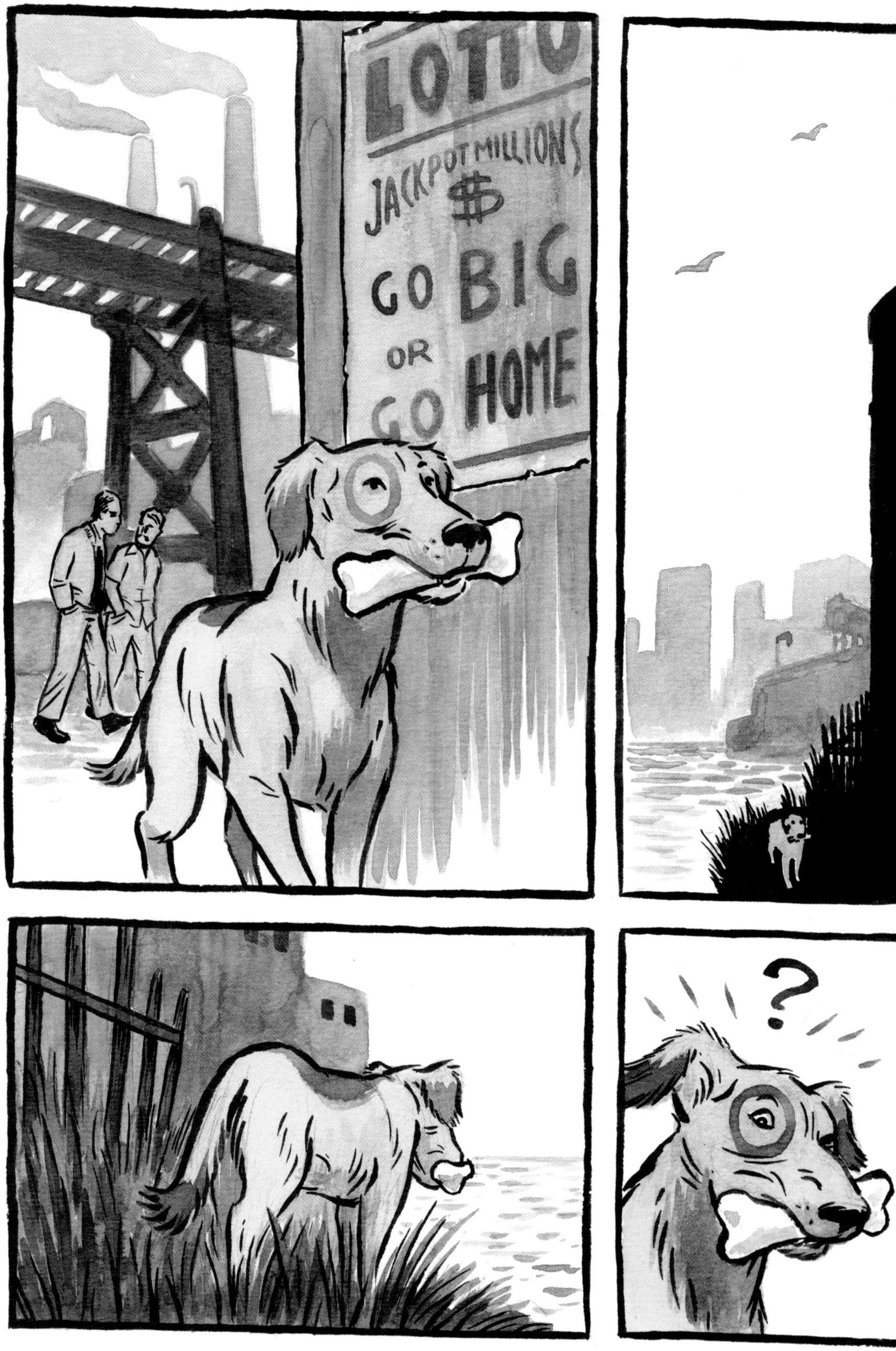
LOTTO
JACKPOT MILLIONS
$
GO BIG
OR
GO HOME
?

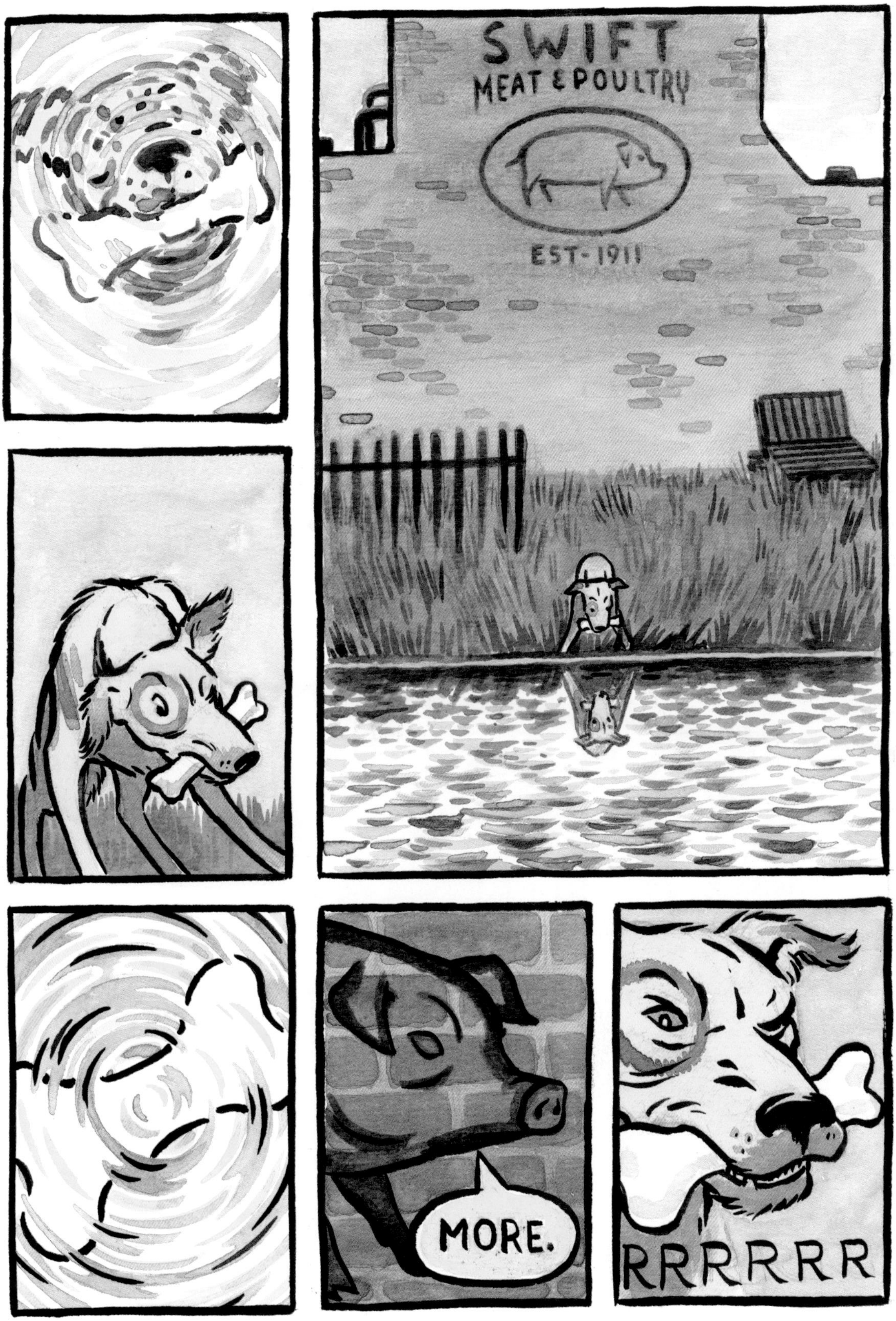
SWIFT
MEAT & POULTRY
EST-1911
MORE.
RRRRRRR

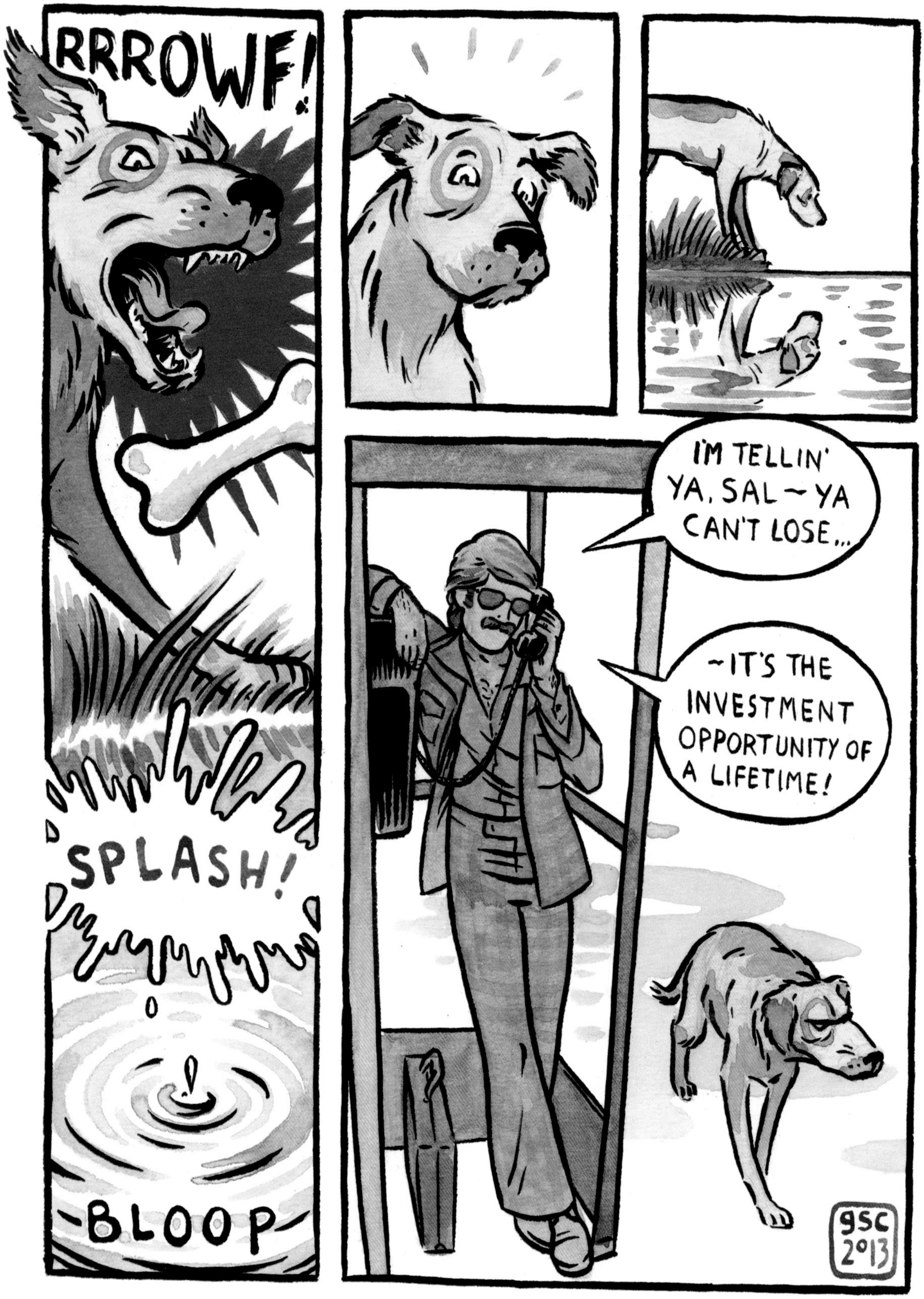
RRROWF!
SPLASH!
BLOOP
I'M TELLIN' YA, SAL ~ YA CAN'T LOSE...
~IT'S THE INVESTMENT OPPORTUNITY OF A LIFETIME!
GSC 2013

THE DOLPHINS THE WHALES AND THE SPRAT

BY MARIS WICKS

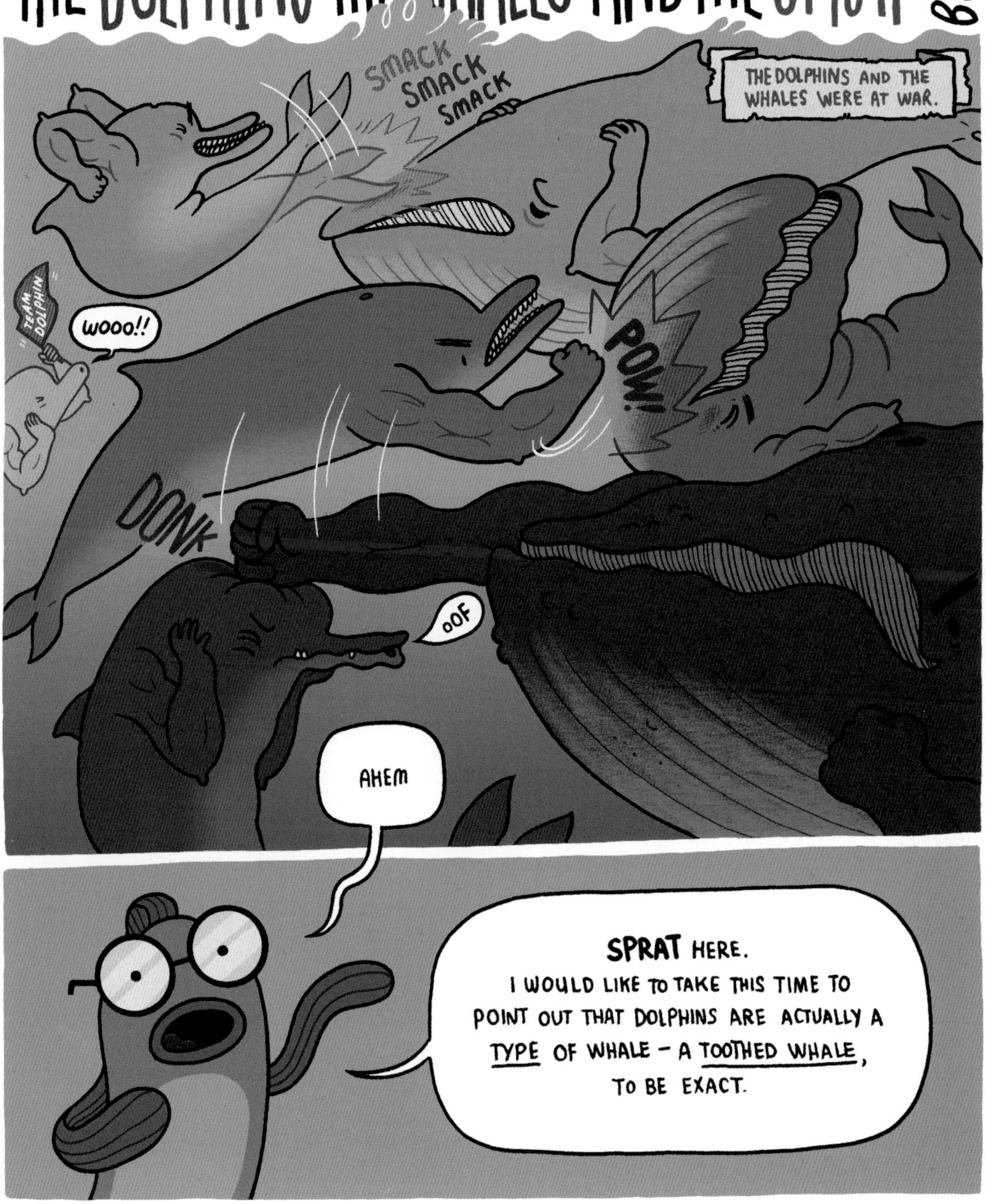

THE DOLPHINS AND THE WHALES WERE AT WAR.
SMACK
SMACK
SMACK
TEAM DOLPHIN
WOOO!!
POW!
DONK
OOF
AHEM
SPRAT HERE.
I WOULD LIKE TO TAKE THIS TIME TO POINT OUT THAT DOLPHINS ARE ACTUALLY A TYPE OF WHALE – A TOOTHED WHALE, TO BE EXACT.

From Aesop

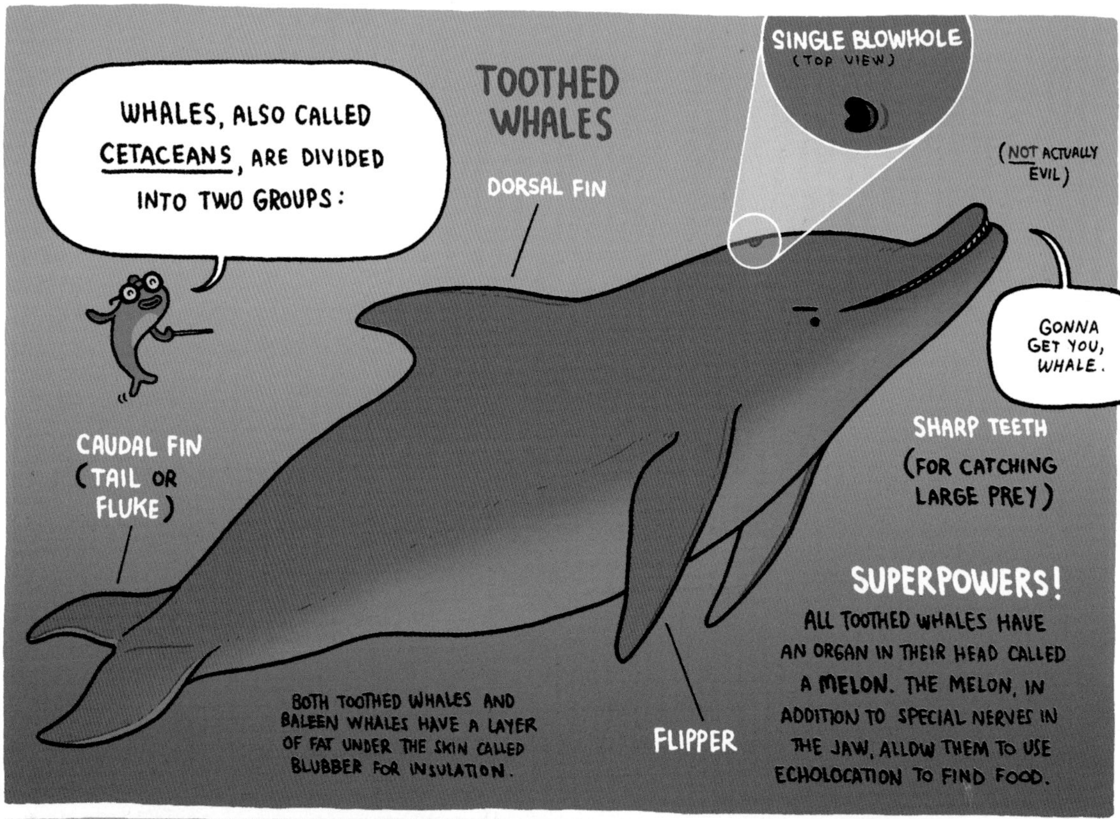
WHALES, ALSO CALLED CETACEANS, ARE DIVIDED INTO TWO GROUPS:
TOOTHED WHALES
SINGLE BLOWHOLE (TOP VIEW)
(NOT ACTUALLY EVIL)
DORSAL FIN
GONNA GET YOU, WHALE.
CAUDAL FIN (TAIL OR FLUKE)
SHARP TEETH (FOR CATCHING LARGE PREY)
SUPERPOWERS!
ALL TOOTHED WHALES HAVE AN ORGAN IN THEIR HEAD CALLED A MELON. THE MELON, IN ADDITION TO SPECIAL NERVES IN THE JAW, ALLOW THEM TO USE ECHOLOCATION TO FIND FOOD.
BOTH TOOTHED WHALES AND BALEEN WHALES HAVE A LAYER OF FAT UNDER THE SKIN CALLED BLUBBER FOR INSULATION.
FLIPPER

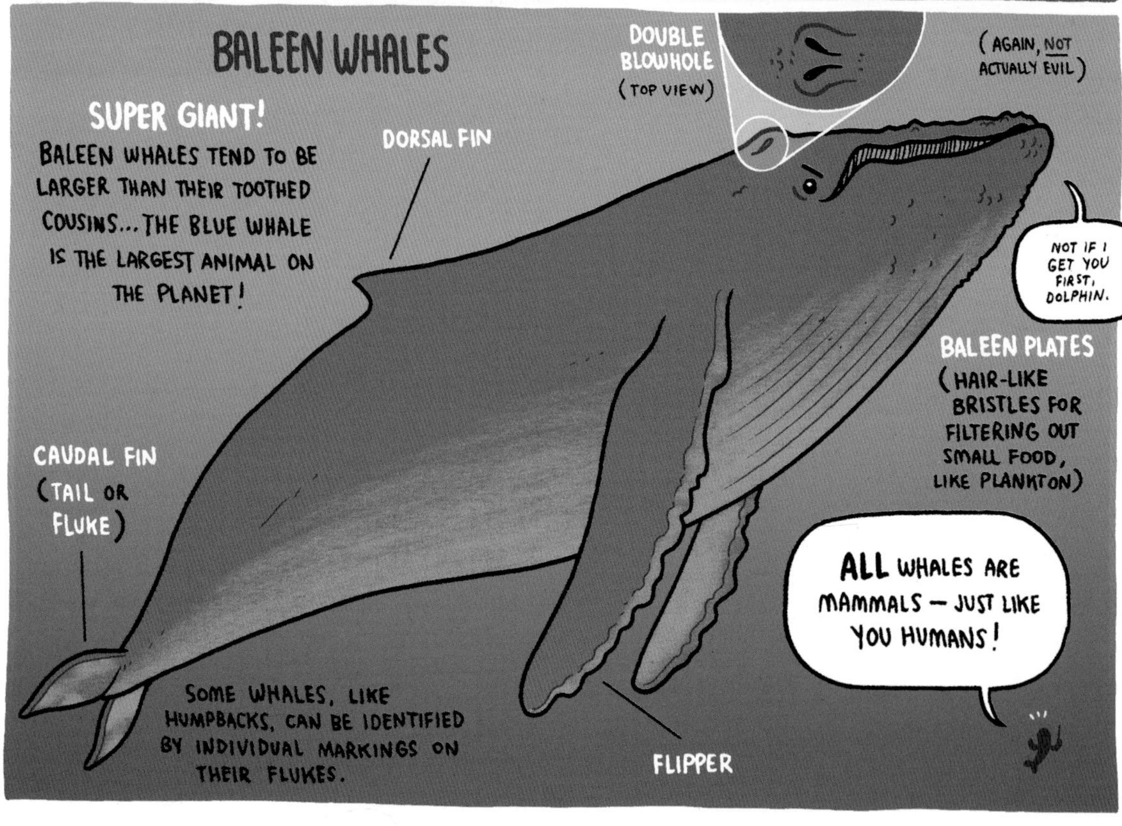
BALEEN WHALES
DOUBLE BLOWHOLE (TOP VIEW)
(AGAIN, NOT ACTUALLY EVIL)
SUPER GIANT!
BALEEN WHALES TEND TO BE LARGER THAN THEIR TOOTHED COUSINS... THE BLUE WHALE IS THE LARGEST ANIMAL ON THE PLANET!
DORSAL FIN
NOT IF I GET YOU FIRST, DOLPHIN.
BALEEN PLATES (HAIR-LIKE BRISTLES FOR FILTERING OUT SMALL FOOD, LIKE PLANKTON)
CAUDAL FIN (TAIL OR FLUKE)
ALL WHALES ARE MAMMALS — JUST LIKE YOU HUMANS!
SOME WHALES, LIKE HUMPBACKS, CAN BE IDENTIFIED BY INDIVIDUAL MARKINGS ON THEIR FLUKES.
FLIPPER

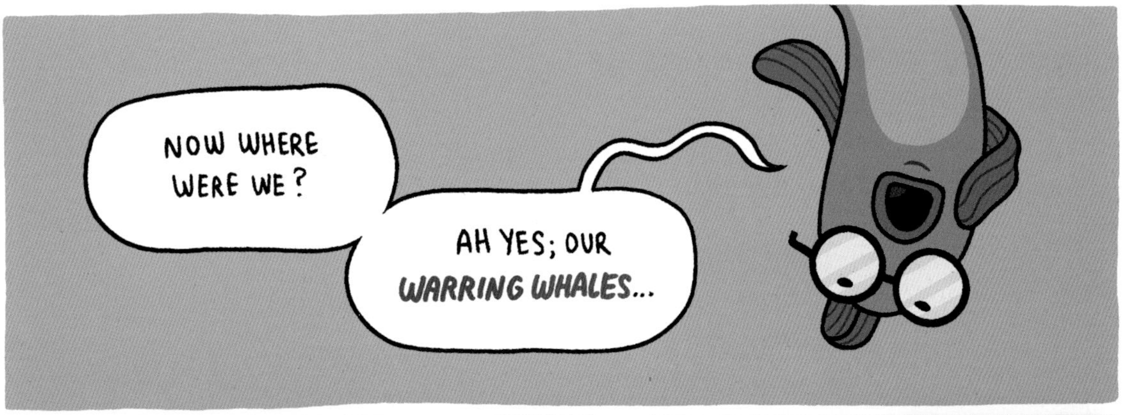
NOW WHERE WERE WE?
AH YES; OUR WARRING WHALES...

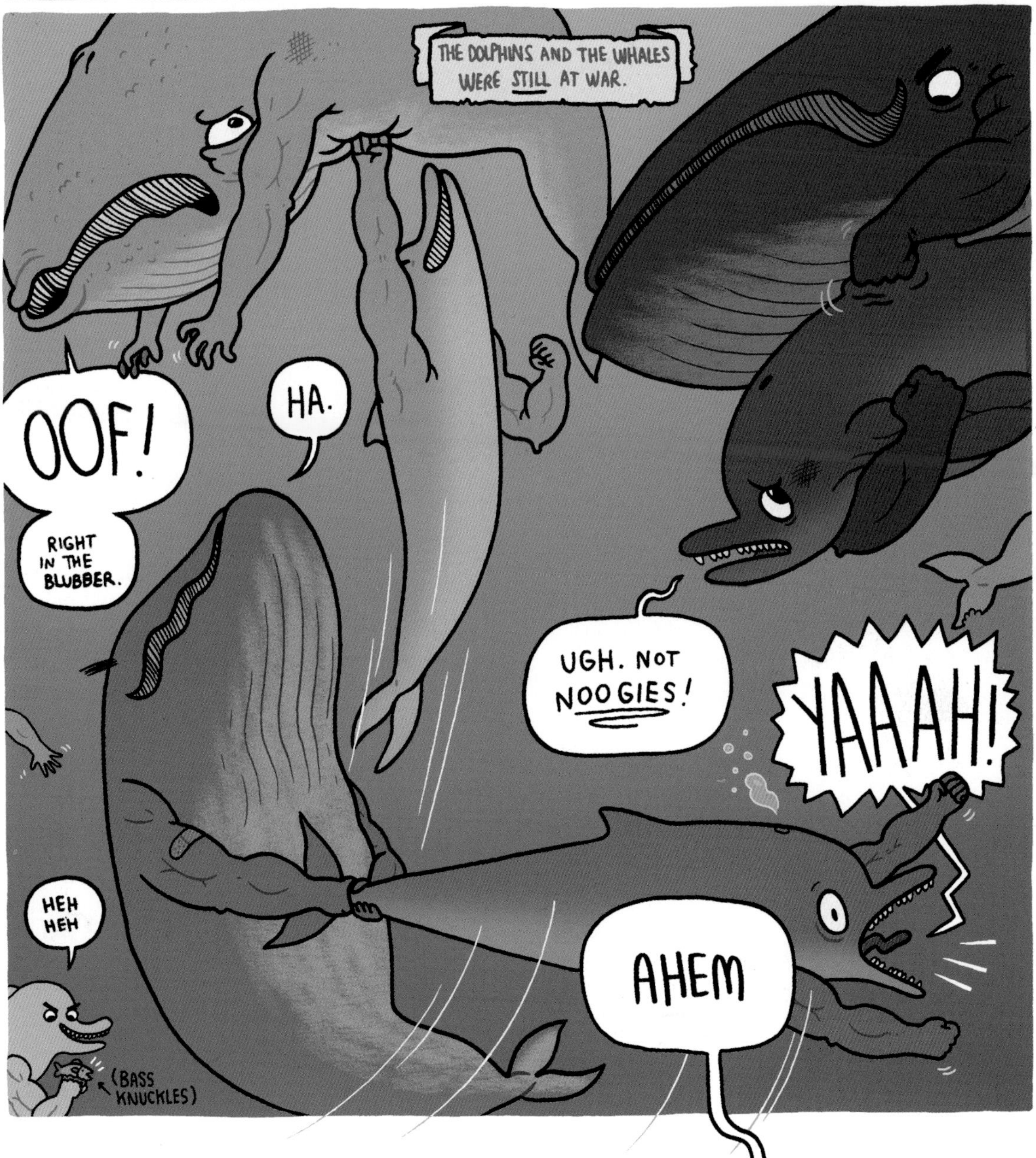
THE DOLPHINS AND THE WHALES WERE STILL AT WAR.
OOF!
RIGHT IN THE BLUBBER.
HA.
UGH. NOT NOOGIES!
YAAAH!
HEH HEH
(BASS KNUCKLES)
AHEM

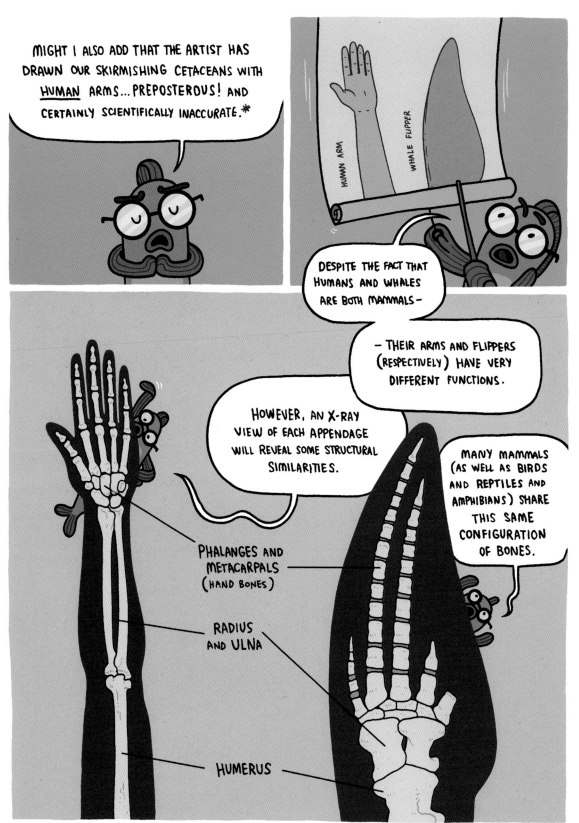

MIGHT I ALSO ADD THAT THE ARTIST HAS DRAWN OUR SKIRMISHING CETACEANS WITH <u>HUMAN</u> ARMS...PREPOSTEROUS! AND CERTAINLY SCIENTIFICALLY INACCURATE.*

HUMAN ARM

WHALE FLIPPER

DESPITE THE FACT THAT HUMANS AND WHALES ARE BOTH MAMMALS—

— THEIR ARMS AND FLIPPERS (RESPECTIVELY) HAVE VERY DIFFERENT FUNCTIONS.

HOWEVER, AN X-RAY VIEW OF EACH APPENDAGE WILL REVEAL SOME STRUCTURAL SIMILARITIES.

MANY MAMMALS (AS WELL AS BIRDS AND REPTILES AND AMPHIBIANS) SHARE THIS SAME CONFIGURATION OF BONES.

PHALANGES AND METACARPALS (HAND BONES)

RADIUS AND ULNA

HUMERUS

* WELL, THE ARTIST WOULD LIKE TO POINT OUT THAT FISH DON'T WEAR GLASSES. OR TALK. SO THERE.

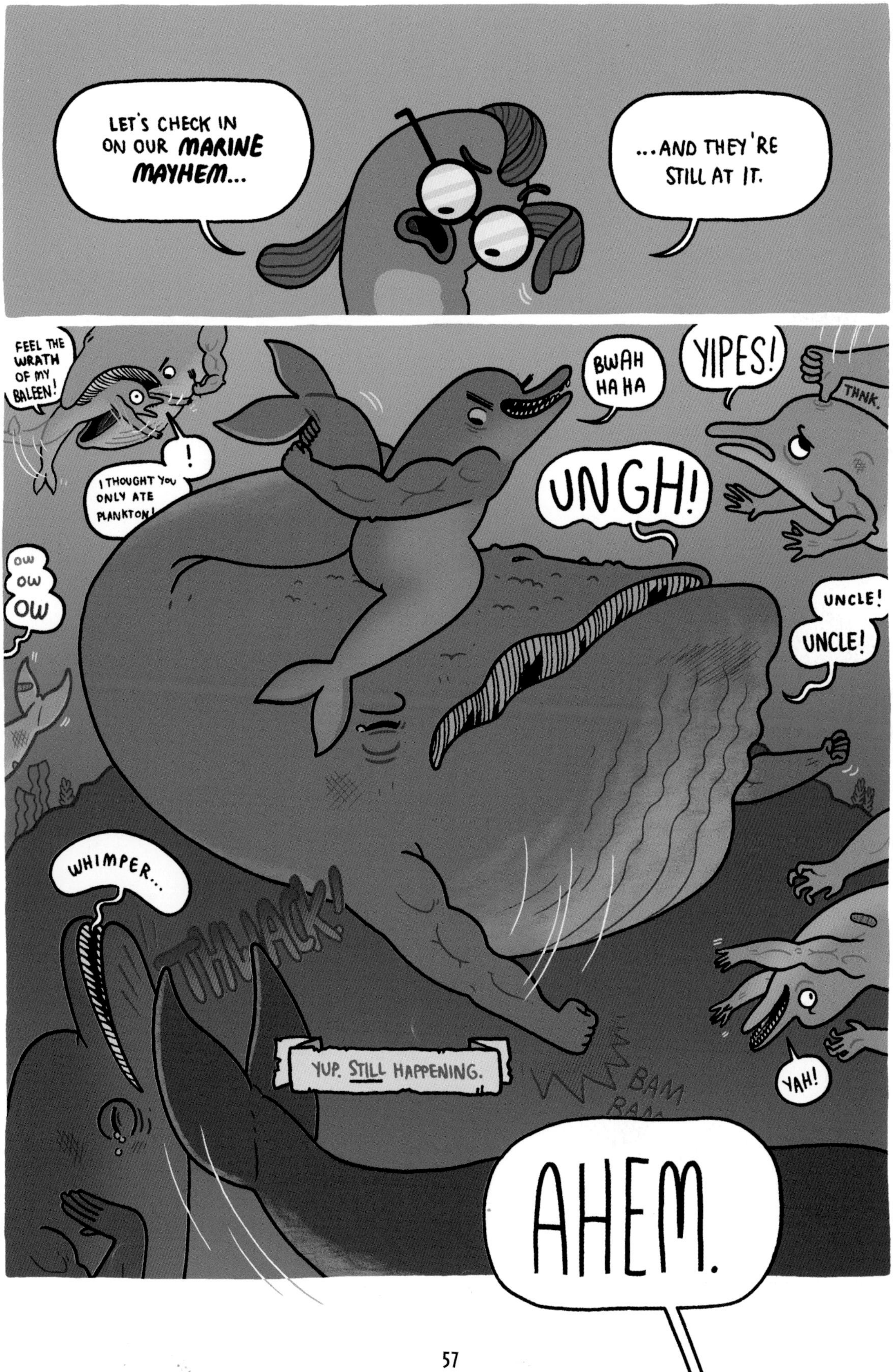
LET'S CHECK IN ON OUR MARINE MAYHEM...
...AND THEY'RE STILL AT IT.
FEEL THE WRATH OF MY BALEEN!
!
I THOUGHT YOU ONLY ATE PLANKTON!
BWAH HA HA
YIPES!
THNK.
UNGH!
OW OW OW
UNCLE!
UNCLE!
WHIMPER...
THWACK!
YUP. STILL HAPPENING.
BAM
YAH!
AHEM.

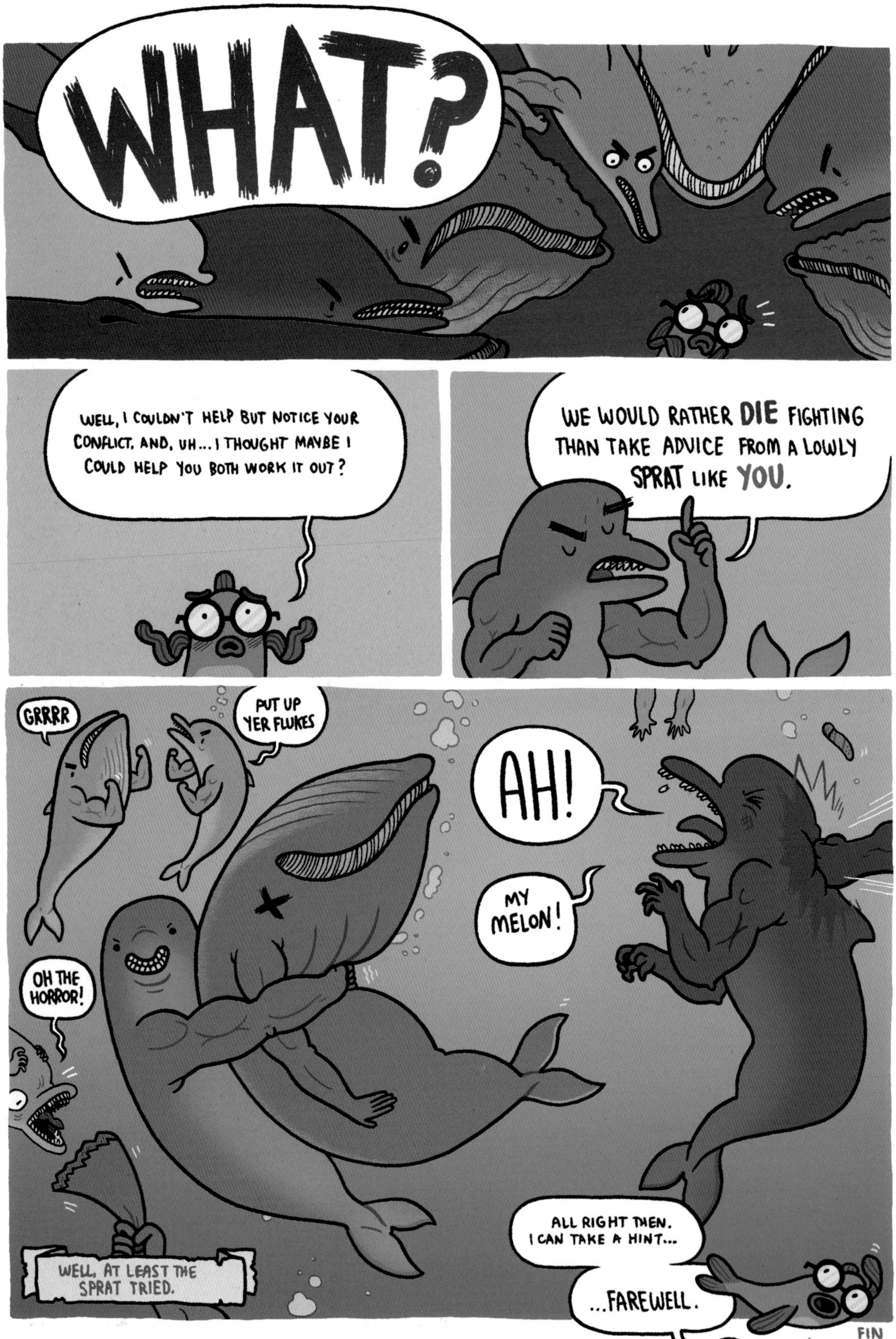
WHAT?
WELL, I COULDN'T HELP BUT NOTICE YOUR CONFLICT. AND, UH... I THOUGHT MAYBE I COULD HELP YOU BOTH WORK IT OUT?
WE WOULD RATHER DIE FIGHTING THAN TAKE ADVICE FROM A LOWLY SPRAT LIKE YOU.
GRRRR
PUT UP YER FLUKES
AH!
MY MELON!
OH THE HORROR!
WELL, AT LEAST THE SPRAT TRIED.
ALL RIGHT THEN. I CAN TAKE A HINT...
...FAREWELL.
FIN

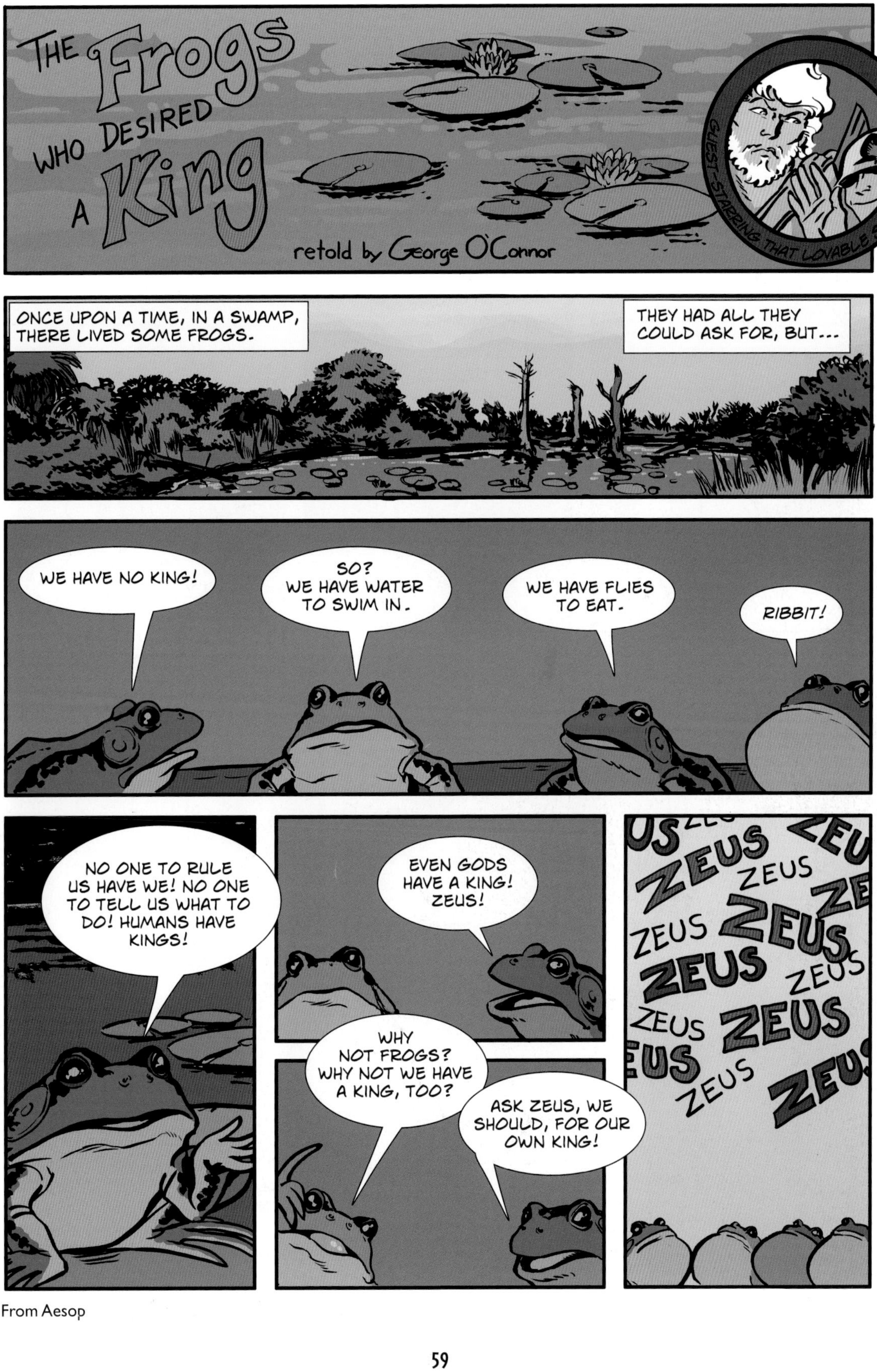
THE Frogs WHO DESIRED A King
retold by George O'Connor
GUEST-STARRING THAT LOVABLE SCAMP, HERMES
ONCE UPON A TIME, IN A SWAMP, THERE LIVED SOME FROGS.
THEY HAD ALL THEY COULD ASK FOR, BUT...
WE HAVE NO KING!
SO? WE HAVE WATER TO SWIM IN.
WE HAVE FLIES TO EAT.
RIBBIT!
NO ONE TO RULE US HAVE WE! NO ONE TO TELL US WHAT TO DO! HUMANS HAVE KINGS!
EVEN GODS HAVE A KING! ZEUS!
WHY NOT FROGS? WHY NOT WE HAVE A KING, TOO?
ASK ZEUS, WE SHOULD, FOR OUR OWN KING!
ZEUS ZEUS ZEUS ZEUS ZEUS ZEUS ZEUS ZEUS ZEUS ZEUS

From Aesop

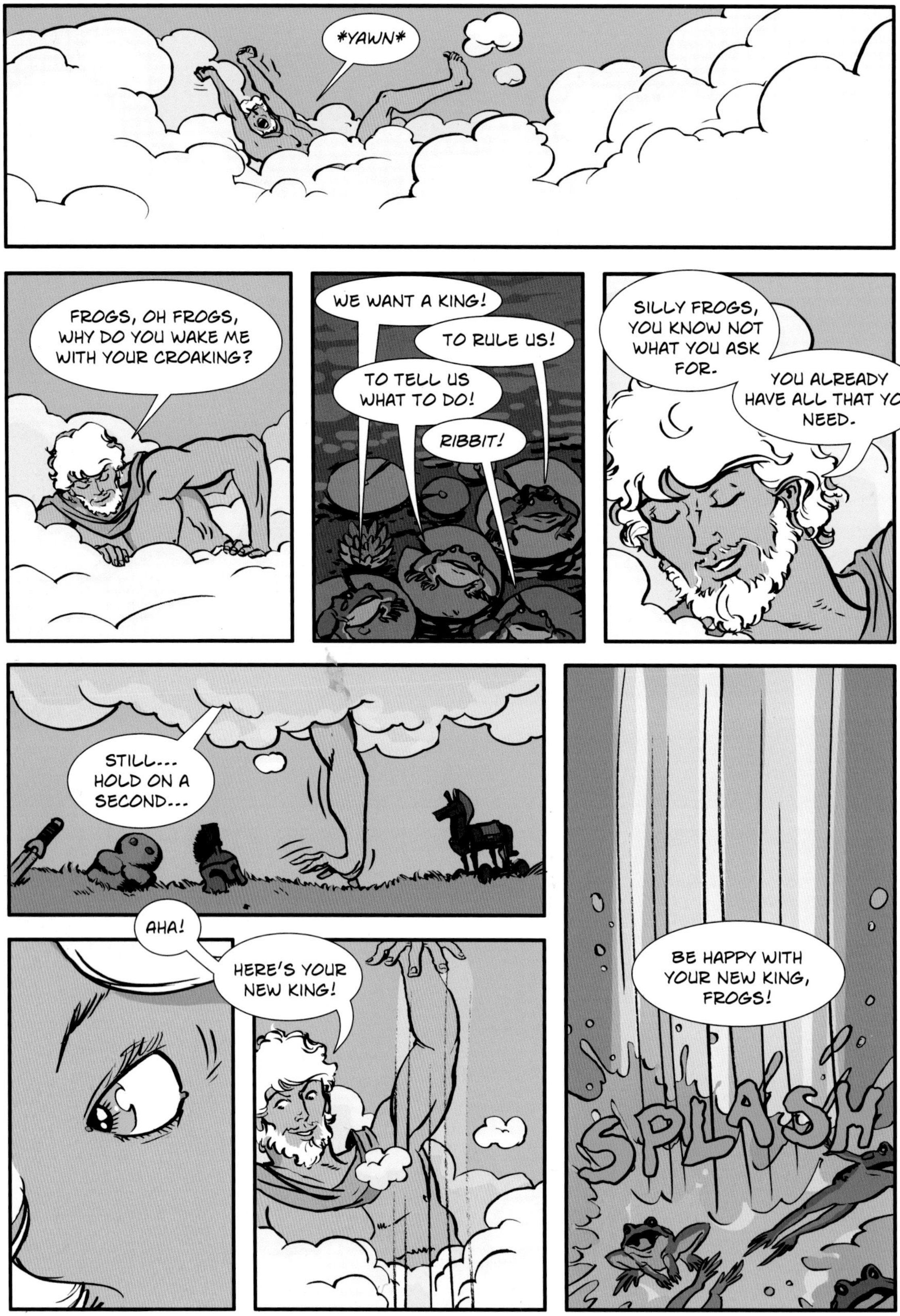
YAWN
FROGS, OH FROGS, WHY DO YOU WAKE ME WITH YOUR CROAKING?
WE WANT A KING!
TO RULE US!
TO TELL US WHAT TO DO!
RIBBIT!
SILLY FROGS, YOU KNOW NOT WHAT YOU ASK FOR.
YOU ALREADY HAVE ALL THAT YOU NEED.
STILL... HOLD ON A SECOND...
AHA!
HERE'S YOUR NEW KING!
BE HAPPY WITH YOUR NEW KING, FROGS!
SPLASH

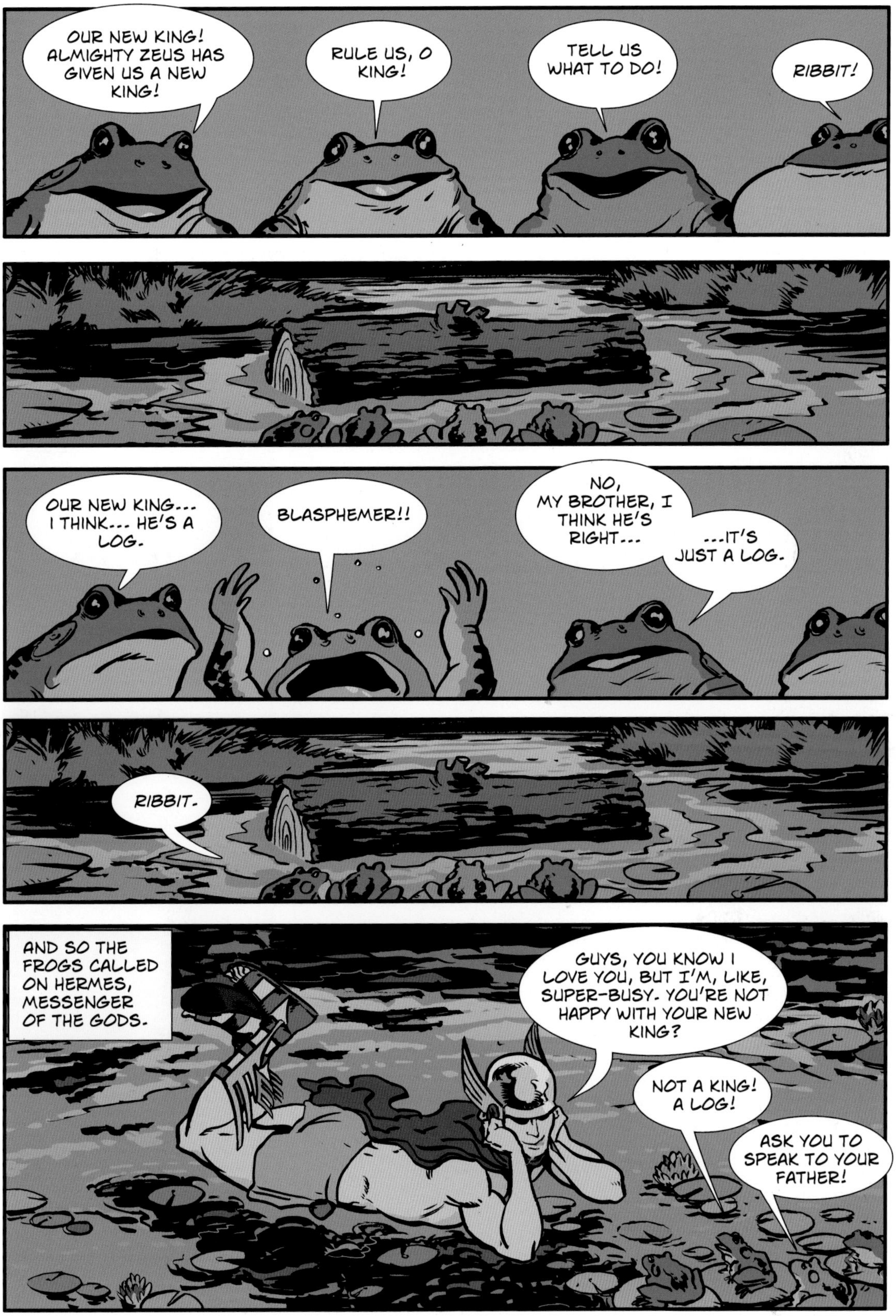
OUR NEW KING! ALMIGHTY ZEUS HAS GIVEN US A NEW KING!
RULE US, O KING!
TELL US WHAT TO DO!
RIBBIT!
OUR NEW KING... I THINK... HE'S A LOG.
BLASPHEMER!!
NO, MY BROTHER, I THINK HE'S RIGHT...
...IT'S JUST A LOG.
RIBBIT.
AND SO THE FROGS CALLED ON HERMES, MESSENGER OF THE GODS.
GUYS, YOU KNOW I LOVE YOU, BUT I'M, LIKE, SUPER-BUSY. YOU'RE NOT HAPPY WITH YOUR NEW KING?
NOT A KING! A LOG!
ASK YOU TO SPEAK TO YOUR FATHER!

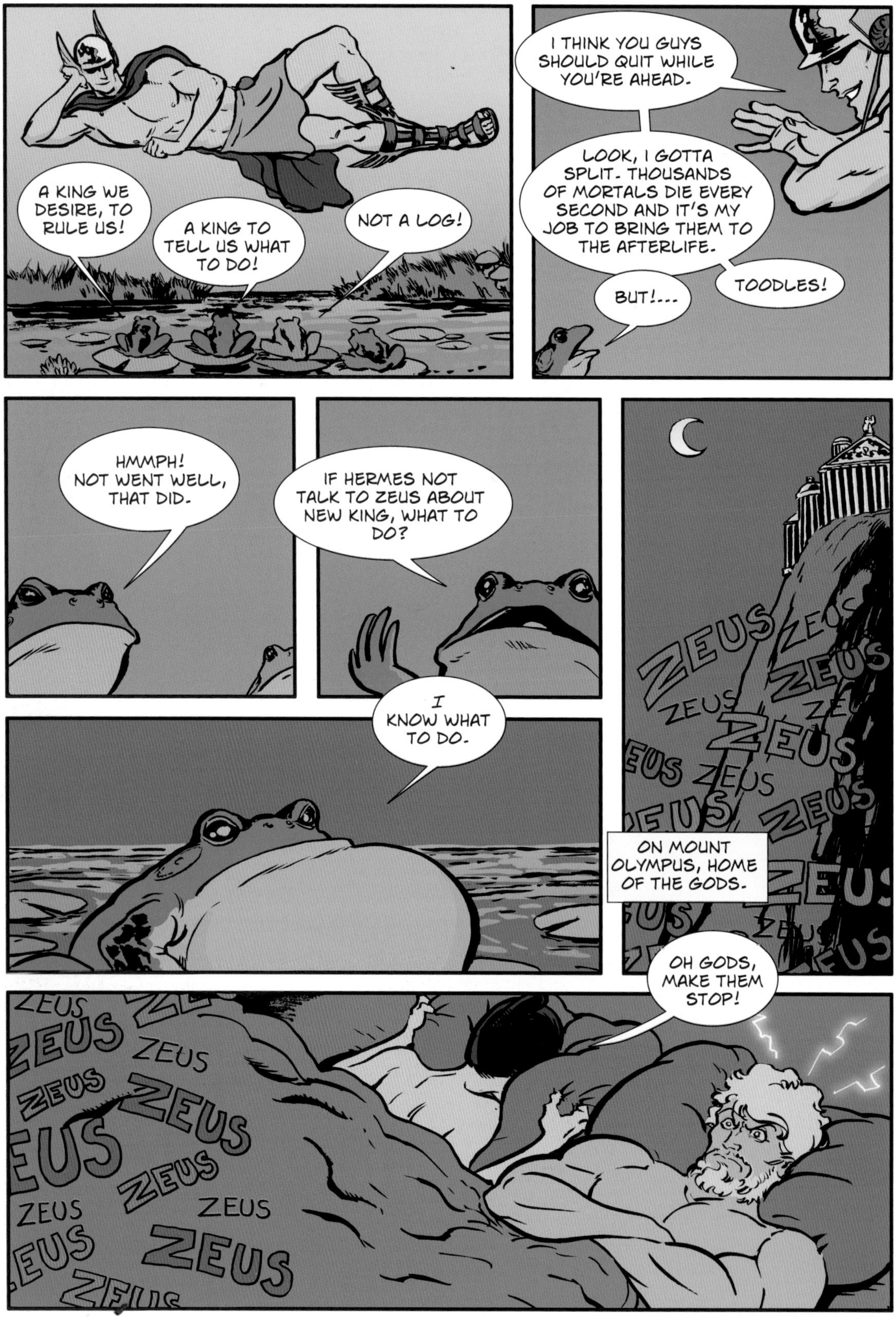
A KING WE DESIRE, TO RULE US!
A KING TO TELL US WHAT TO DO!
NOT A LOG!
I THINK YOU GUYS SHOULD QUIT WHILE YOU'RE AHEAD.
LOOK, I GOTTA SPLIT. THOUSANDS OF MORTALS DIE EVERY SECOND AND IT'S MY JOB TO BRING THEM TO THE AFTERLIFE.
TOODLES!
BUT!...
HMMPH! NOT WENT WELL, THAT DID.
IF HERMES NOT TALK TO ZEUS ABOUT NEW KING, WHAT TO DO?
I KNOW WHAT TO DO.
ON MOUNT OLYMPUS, HOME OF THE GODS.
ZEUS ZEUS ZEUS ZEUS ZEUS ZEUS ZEUS ZEUS ZEUS
OH GODS, MAKE THEM STOP!
ZEUS ZEUS ZEUS ZEUS ZEUS ZEUS ZEUS ZEUS ZEUS ZEUS ZEUS

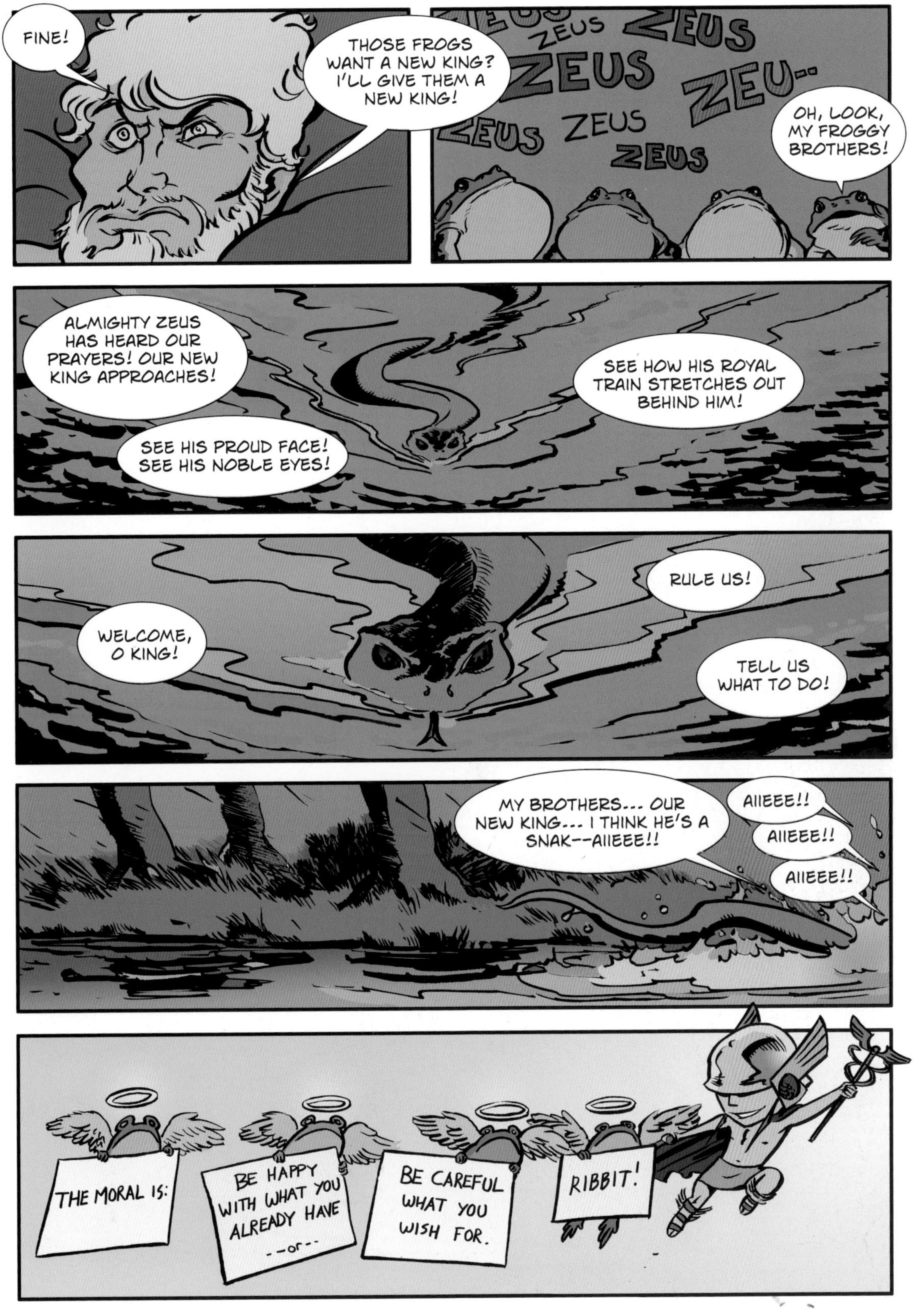
FINE!
THOSE FROGS WANT A NEW KING? I'LL GIVE THEM A NEW KING!
ZEUS ZEUS ZEUS ZEUS ZEU-- ZEUS ZEUS ZEUS
OH, LOOK, MY FROGGY BROTHERS!
ALMIGHTY ZEUS HAS HEARD OUR PRAYERS! OUR NEW KING APPROACHES!
SEE HIS PROUD FACE! SEE HIS NOBLE EYES!
SEE HOW HIS ROYAL TRAIN STRETCHES OUT BEHIND HIM!
WELCOME, O KING!
RULE US!
TELL US WHAT TO DO!
MY BROTHERS... OUR NEW KING... I THINK HE'S A SNAK--AIIEEE!!
AIIEEE!!
AIIEEE!!
AIIEEE!!
THE MORAL IS:
BE HAPPY WITH WHAT YOU ALREADY HAVE
--or--
BE CAREFUL WHAT YOU WISH FOR.
RIBBIT!

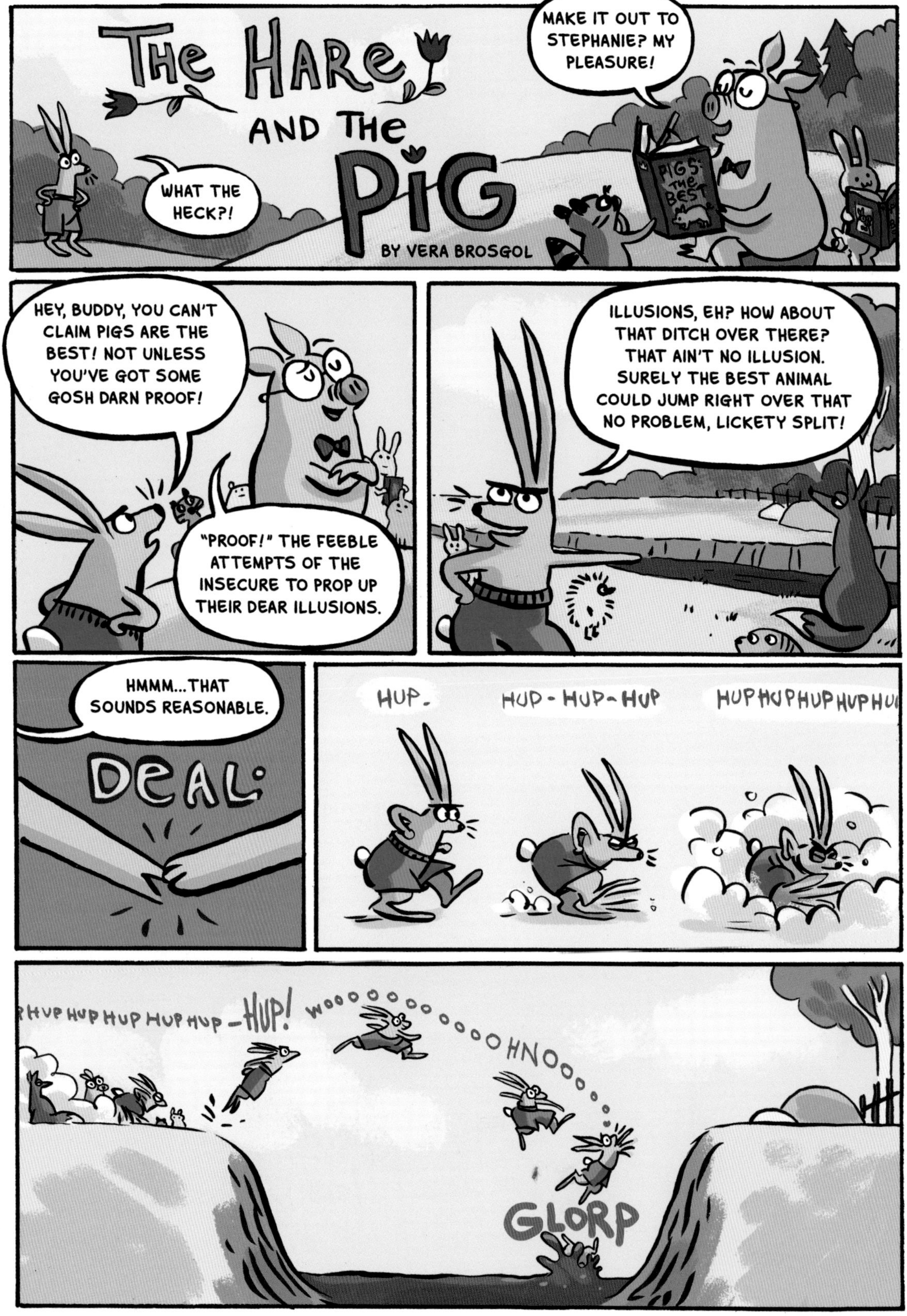
The Hare and the Pig
By Vera Brosgol
What the heck?!
Make it out to Stephanie? My pleasure!
Pigs: the best
Hey, buddy, you can't claim pigs are the best! Not unless you've got some gosh darn proof!
"Proof!" The feeble attempts of the insecure to prop up their dear illusions.
Illusions, eh? How about that ditch over there? That ain't no illusion. Surely the best animal could jump right over that no problem, lickety split!
Hmmm...that sounds reasonable.
Deal:
Hup.
Hup-hup-hup
Huphuphuphuphu
huphuphuphuphup-Hup!
Wooooooooooooohnoooooo
Glorp

From the Indian fable

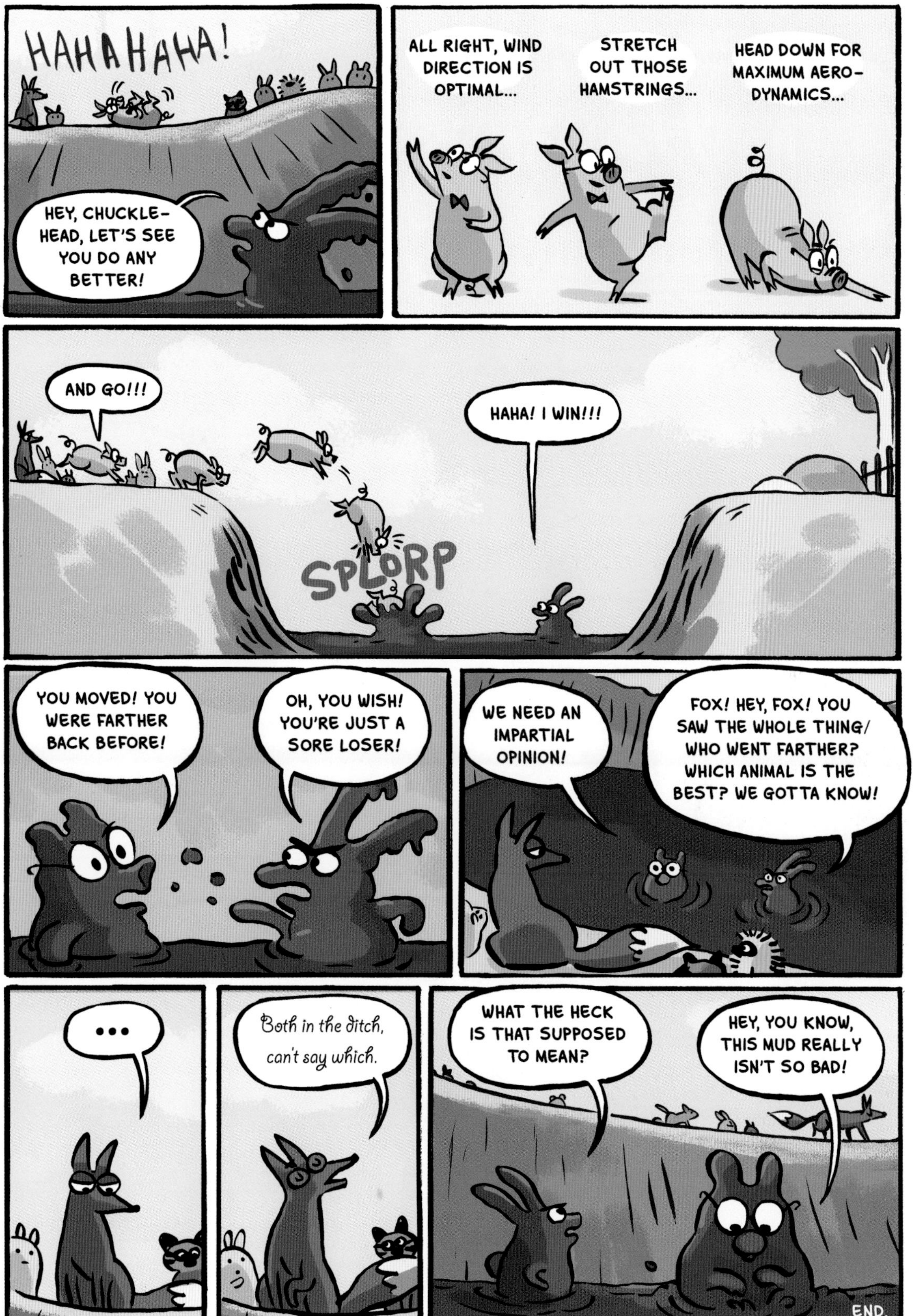
HAHAHAHA!
HEY, CHUCKLE-HEAD, LET'S SEE YOU DO ANY BETTER!
ALL RIGHT, WIND DIRECTION IS OPTIMAL...
STRETCH OUT THOSE HAMSTRINGS...
HEAD DOWN FOR MAXIMUM AERO-DYNAMICS...
AND GO!!!
SPLORP
HAHA! I WIN!!!
YOU MOVED! YOU WERE FARTHER BACK BEFORE!
OH, YOU WISH! YOU'RE JUST A SORE LOSER!
WE NEED AN IMPARTIAL OPINION!
FOX! HEY, FOX! YOU SAW THE WHOLE THING! WHO WENT FARTHER? WHICH ANIMAL IS THE BEST? WE GOTTA KNOW!
...
Both in the ditch, can't say which.
WHAT THE HECK IS THAT SUPPOSED TO MEAN?
HEY, YOU KNOW, THIS MUD REALLY ISN'T SO BAD!
END.

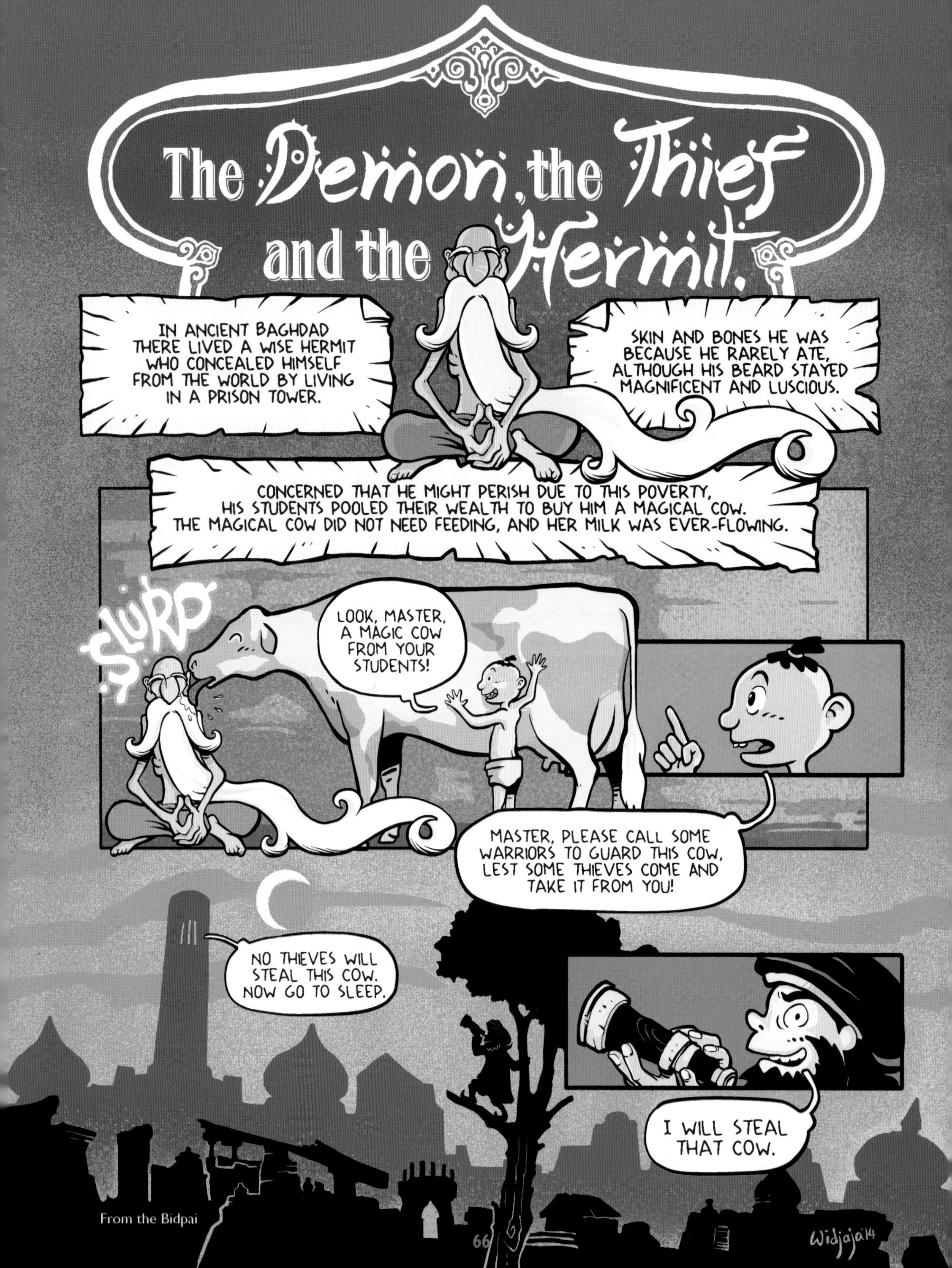

The Demon, the Thief and the Hermit.
IN ANCIENT BAGHDAD THERE LIVED A WISE HERMIT WHO CONCEALED HIMSELF FROM THE WORLD BY LIVING IN A PRISON TOWER.
SKIN AND BONES HE WAS BECAUSE HE RARELY ATE, ALTHOUGH HIS BEARD STAYED MAGNIFICENT AND LUSCIOUS.
CONCERNED THAT HE MIGHT PERISH DUE TO THIS POVERTY, HIS STUDENTS POOLED THEIR WEALTH TO BUY HIM A MAGICAL COW. THE MAGICAL COW DID NOT NEED FEEDING, AND HER MILK WAS EVER-FLOWING.
SLURP
LOOK, MASTER, A MAGIC COW FROM YOUR STUDENTS!
MASTER, PLEASE CALL SOME WARRIORS TO GUARD THIS COW, LEST SOME THIEVES COME AND TAKE IT FROM YOU!
NO THIEVES WILL STEAL THIS COW. NOW GO TO SLEEP.
I WILL STEAL THAT COW.
Widjaja'14

From the Bidpai

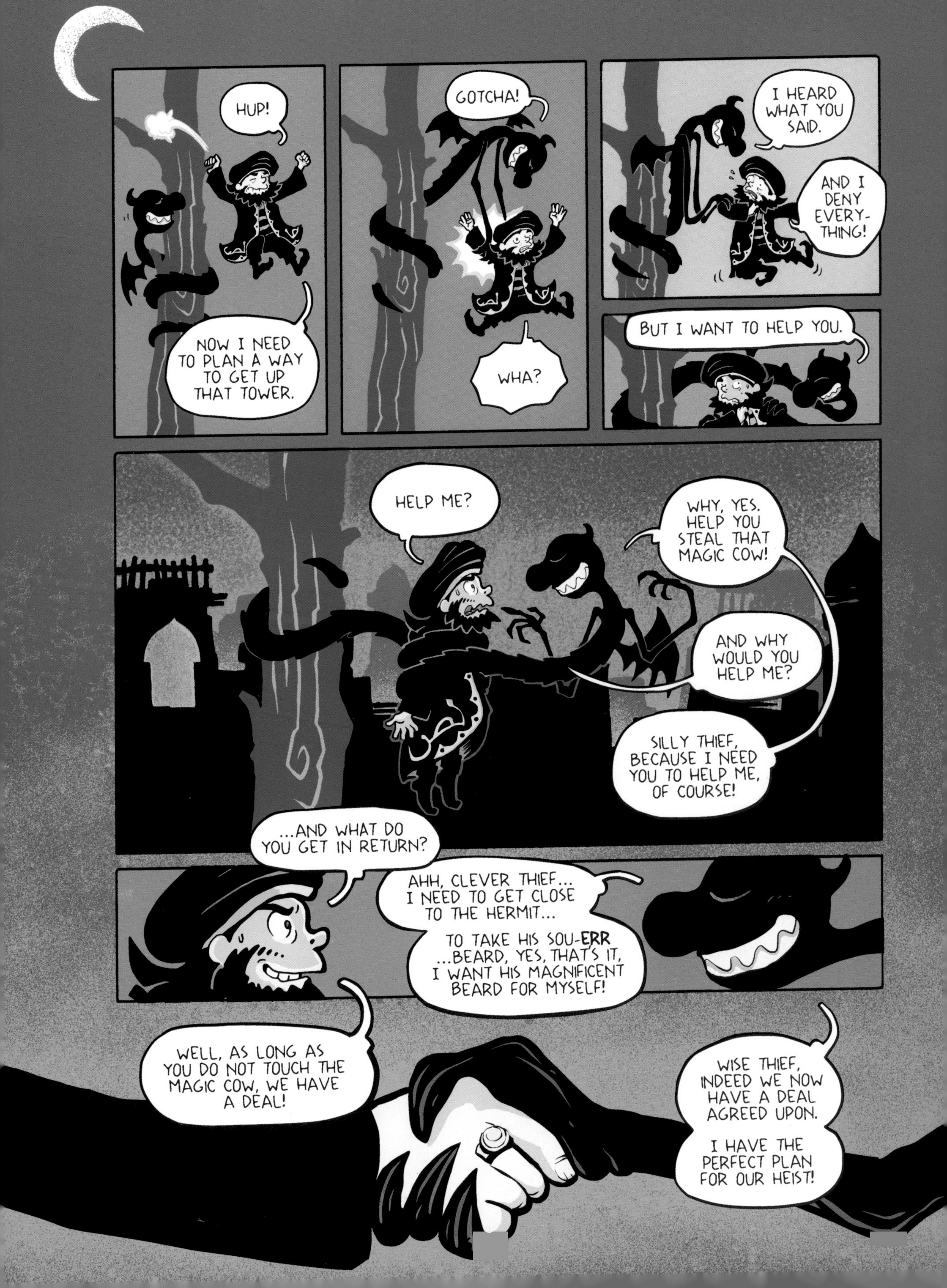
HUP!
NOW I NEED TO PLAN A WAY TO GET UP THAT TOWER.
GOTCHA!
WHA?
I HEARD WHAT YOU SAID.
AND I DENY EVERY-THING!
BUT I WANT TO HELP YOU.
HELP ME?
WHY, YES. HELP YOU STEAL THAT MAGIC COW!
AND WHY WOULD YOU HELP ME?
SILLY THIEF, BECAUSE I NEED YOU TO HELP ME, OF COURSE!
...AND WHAT DO YOU GET IN RETURN?
AHH, CLEVER THIEF... I NEED TO GET CLOSE TO THE HERMIT...
TO TAKE HIS SOU-**ERR** ...BEARD, YES, THAT'S IT, I WANT HIS MAGNIFICENT BEARD FOR MYSELF!
WELL, AS LONG AS YOU DO NOT TOUCH THE MAGIC COW, WE HAVE A DEAL!
WISE THIEF, INDEED WE NOW HAVE A DEAL AGREED UPON.
I HAVE THE PERFECT PLAN FOR OUR HEIST!

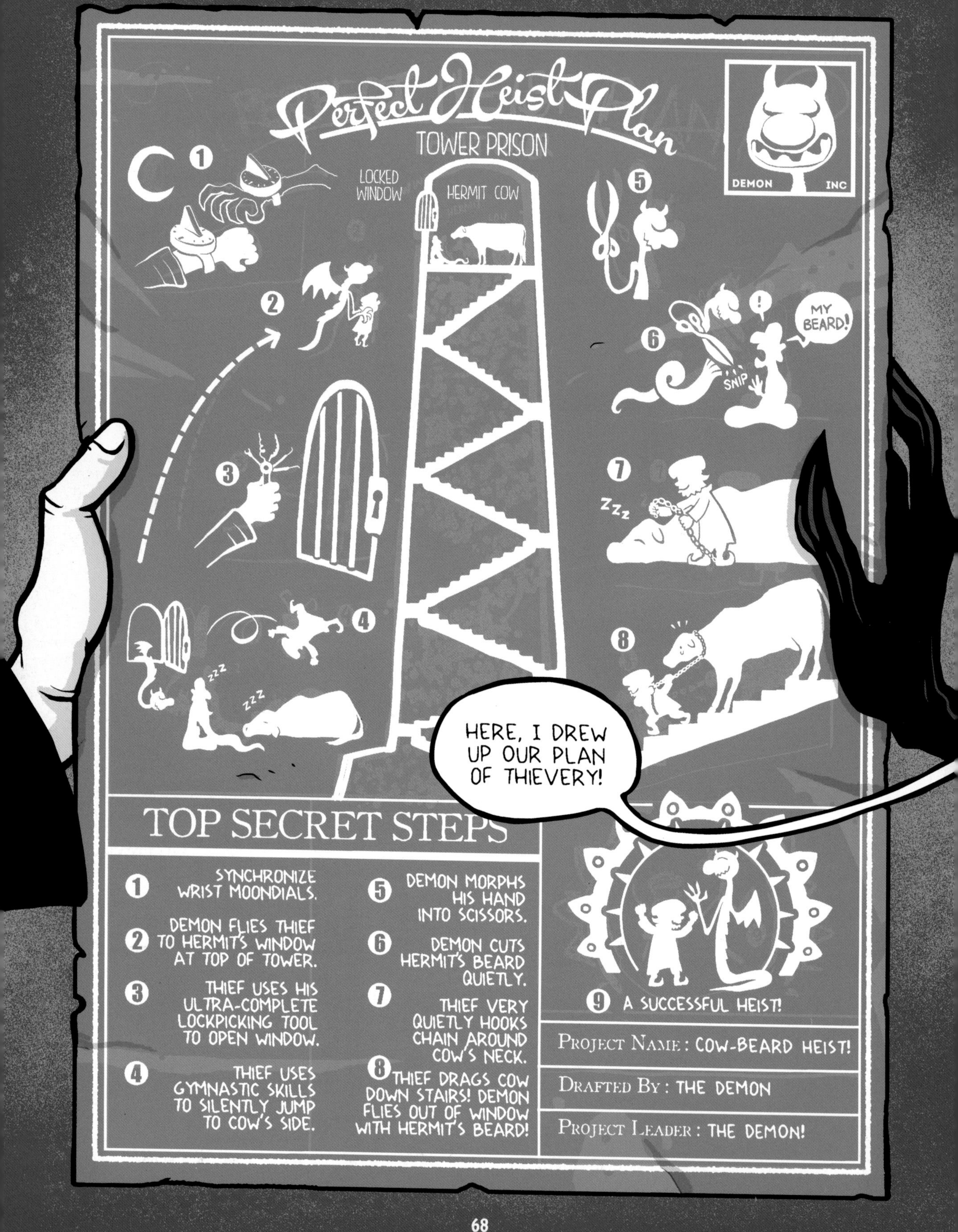
Perfect Heist Plan
TOWER PRISON
DEMON INC
LOCKED WINDOW
HERMIT COW
1
2
3
4
5
6
SNIP
!
MY BEARD!
7
ZZZ
8
HERE, I DREW UP OUR PLAN OF THIEVERY!
TOP SECRET STEPS
1 SYNCHRONIZE WRIST MOONDIALS.
2 DEMON FLIES THIEF TO HERMIT'S WINDOW AT TOP OF TOWER.
3 THIEF USES HIS ULTRA-COMPLETE LOCKPICKING TOOL TO OPEN WINDOW.
4 THIEF USES GYMNASTIC SKILLS TO SILENTLY JUMP TO COW'S SIDE.
5 DEMON MORPHS HIS HAND INTO SCISSORS.
6 DEMON CUTS HERMIT'S BEARD QUIETLY.
7 THIEF VERY QUIETLY HOOKS CHAIN AROUND COW'S NECK.
8 THIEF DRAGS COW DOWN STAIRS! DEMON FLIES OUT OF WINDOW WITH HERMIT'S BEARD!
9 A SUCCESSFUL HEIST!
PROJECT NAME : COW-BEARD HEIST!
DRAFTED BY : THE DEMON
PROJECT LEADER : THE DEMON!

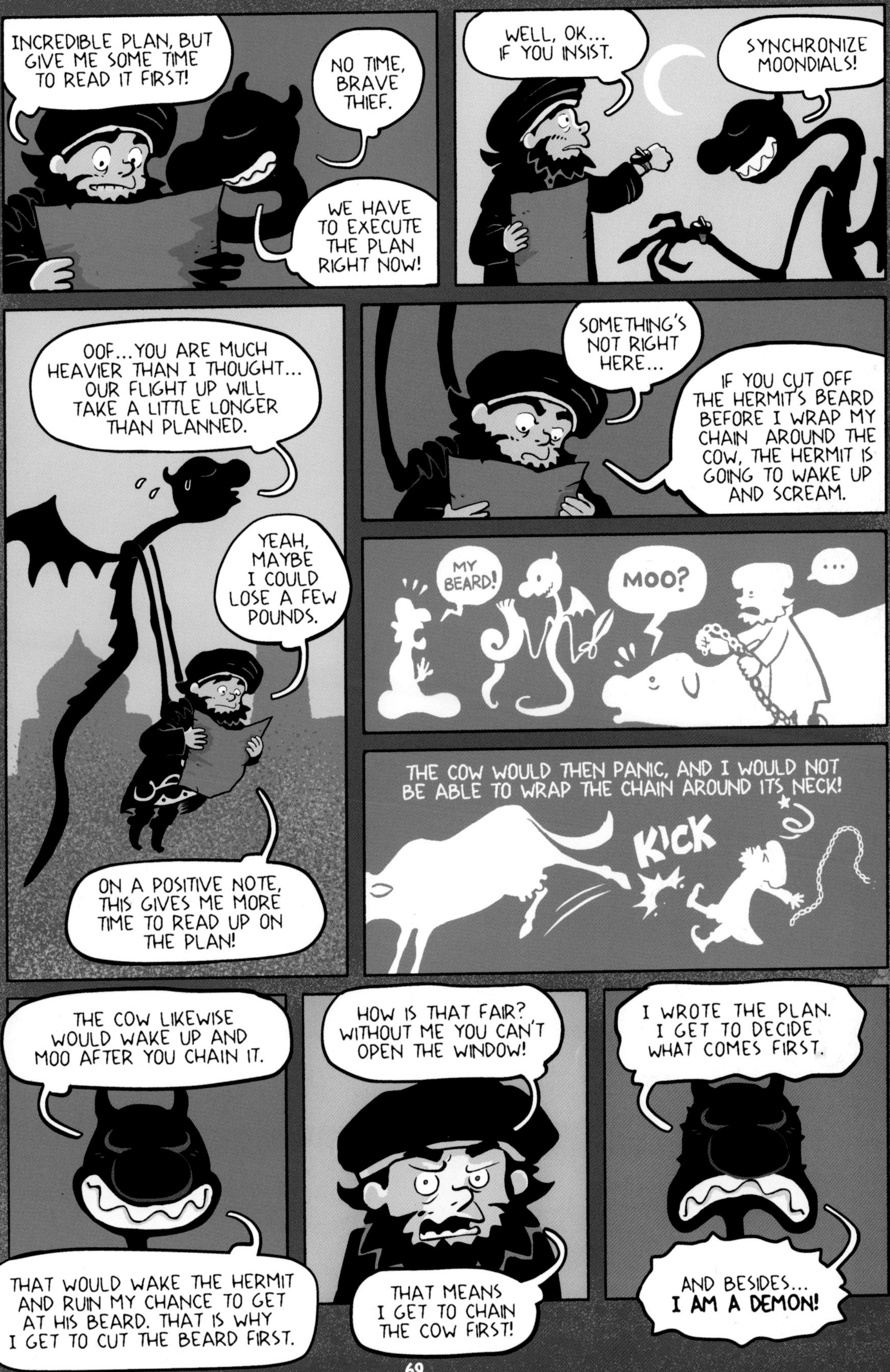
INCREDIBLE PLAN, BUT GIVE ME SOME TIME TO READ IT FIRST!
NO TIME, BRAVE THIEF.
WE HAVE TO EXECUTE THE PLAN RIGHT NOW!
WELL, OK... IF YOU INSIST.
SYNCHRONIZE MOONDIALS!
OOF... YOU ARE MUCH HEAVIER THAN I THOUGHT... OUR FLIGHT UP WILL TAKE A LITTLE LONGER THAN PLANNED.
YEAH, MAYBE I COULD LOSE A FEW POUNDS.
ON A POSITIVE NOTE, THIS GIVES ME MORE TIME TO READ UP ON THE PLAN!
SOMETHING'S NOT RIGHT HERE...
IF YOU CUT OFF THE HERMIT'S BEARD BEFORE I WRAP MY CHAIN AROUND THE COW, THE HERMIT IS GOING TO WAKE UP AND SCREAM.
MY BEARD!
MOO?
...
THE COW WOULD THEN PANIC, AND I WOULD NOT BE ABLE TO WRAP THE CHAIN AROUND ITS NECK!
KICK
THE COW LIKEWISE WOULD WAKE UP AND MOO AFTER YOU CHAIN IT.
THAT WOULD WAKE THE HERMIT AND RUIN MY CHANCE TO GET AT HIS BEARD. THAT IS WHY I GET TO CUT THE BEARD FIRST.
HOW IS THAT FAIR? WITHOUT ME YOU CAN'T OPEN THE WINDOW!
THAT MEANS I GET TO CHAIN THE COW FIRST!
I WROTE THE PLAN. I GET TO DECIDE WHAT COMES FIRST.
AND BESIDES... **I AM A DEMON!**

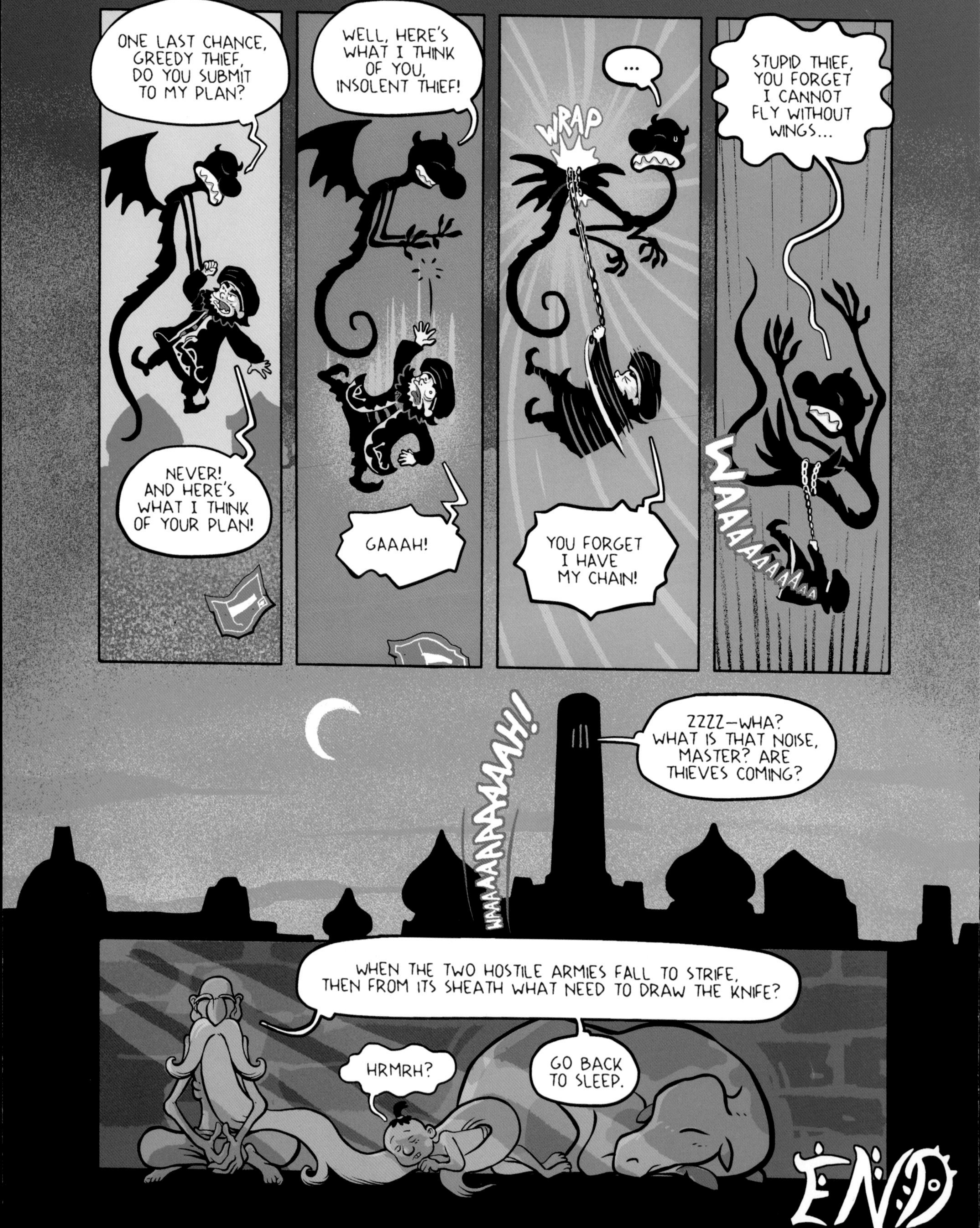
ONE LAST CHANCE, GREEDY THIEF, DO YOU SUBMIT TO MY PLAN?
NEVER! AND HERE'S WHAT I THINK OF YOUR PLAN!
WELL, HERE'S WHAT I THINK OF YOU, INSOLENT THIEF!
GAAAH!
...
WRAP
YOU FORGET I HAVE MY CHAIN!
STUPID THIEF, YOU FORGET I CANNOT FLY WITHOUT WINGS...
WAAAAAAAAAAA
WAAAAAAAAAAAAAH!
ZZZZ—WHA? WHAT IS THAT NOISE, MASTER? ARE THIEVES COMING?
WHEN THE TWO HOSTILE ARMIES FALL TO STRIFE, THEN FROM ITS SHEATH WHAT NEED TO DRAW THE KNIFE?
HRMRH?
GO BACK TO SLEEP.
END

The Elephant in Favor

by Corinne Mucha

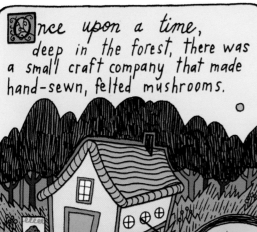

Once upon a time, deep in the forest, there was a small craft company that made hand-sewn, felted mushrooms.

The founder was a cool boss and a decent guy, but guilty of playing favorites.

DUDE!

You are the BEST!

It was rumored that Elephant, a notoriously slow worker, had procured an easy raise.

Great work!

His coffee was always free, his craftsmanship never criticized.

One latté! My treat!

From the fable by Ivan Krilov

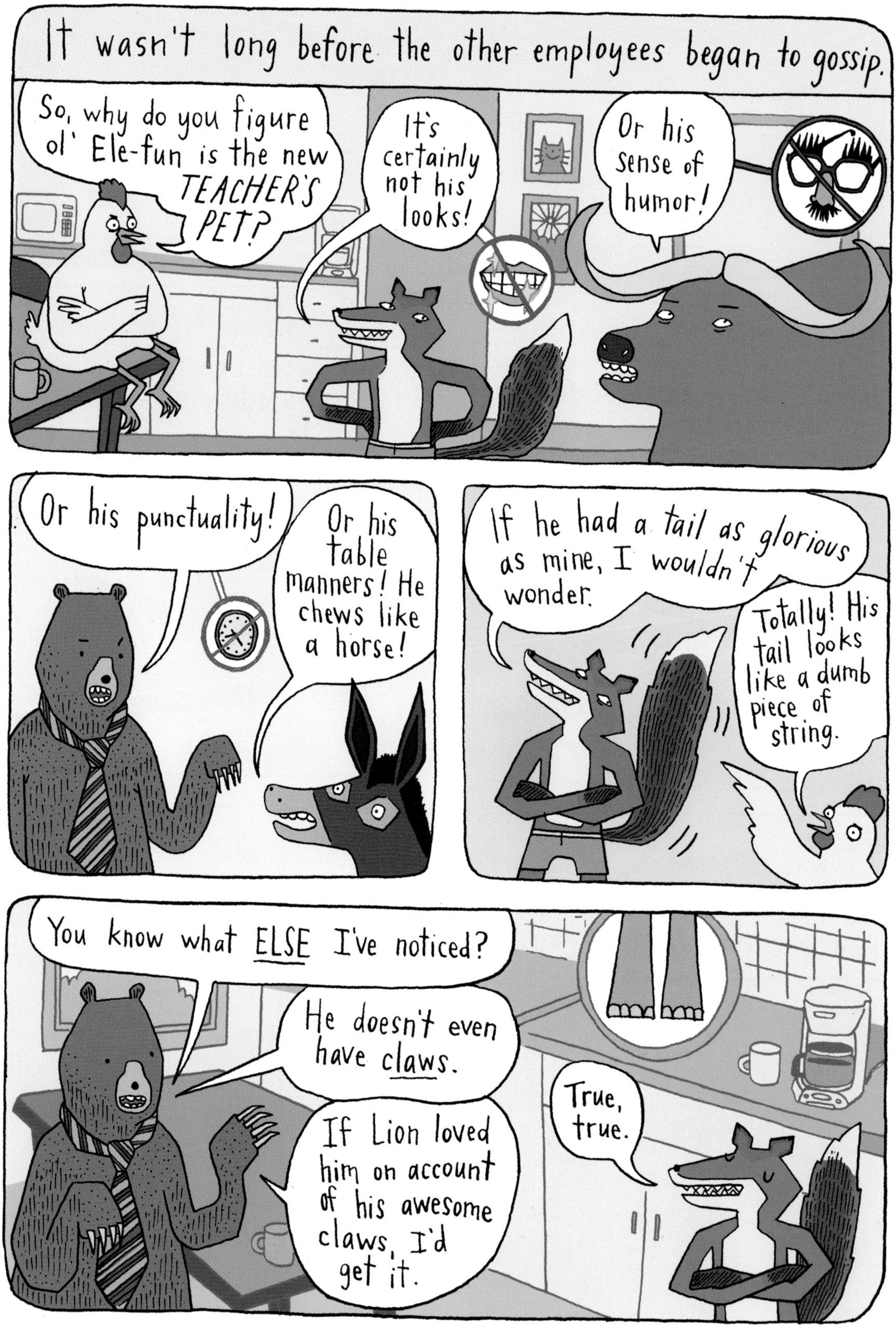
It wasn't long before the other employees began to gossip.
So, why do you figure ol' Ele-fun is the new TEACHER'S PET?
It's certainly not his looks!
Or his sense of humor!
Or his punctuality!
Or his table manners! He chews like a horse!
If he had a tail as glorious as mine, I wouldn't wonder.
Totally! His tail looks like a dumb piece of string.
You know what ELSE I've noticed?
He doesn't even have claws.
If Lion loved him on account of his awesome claws, I'd get it.
True, true.

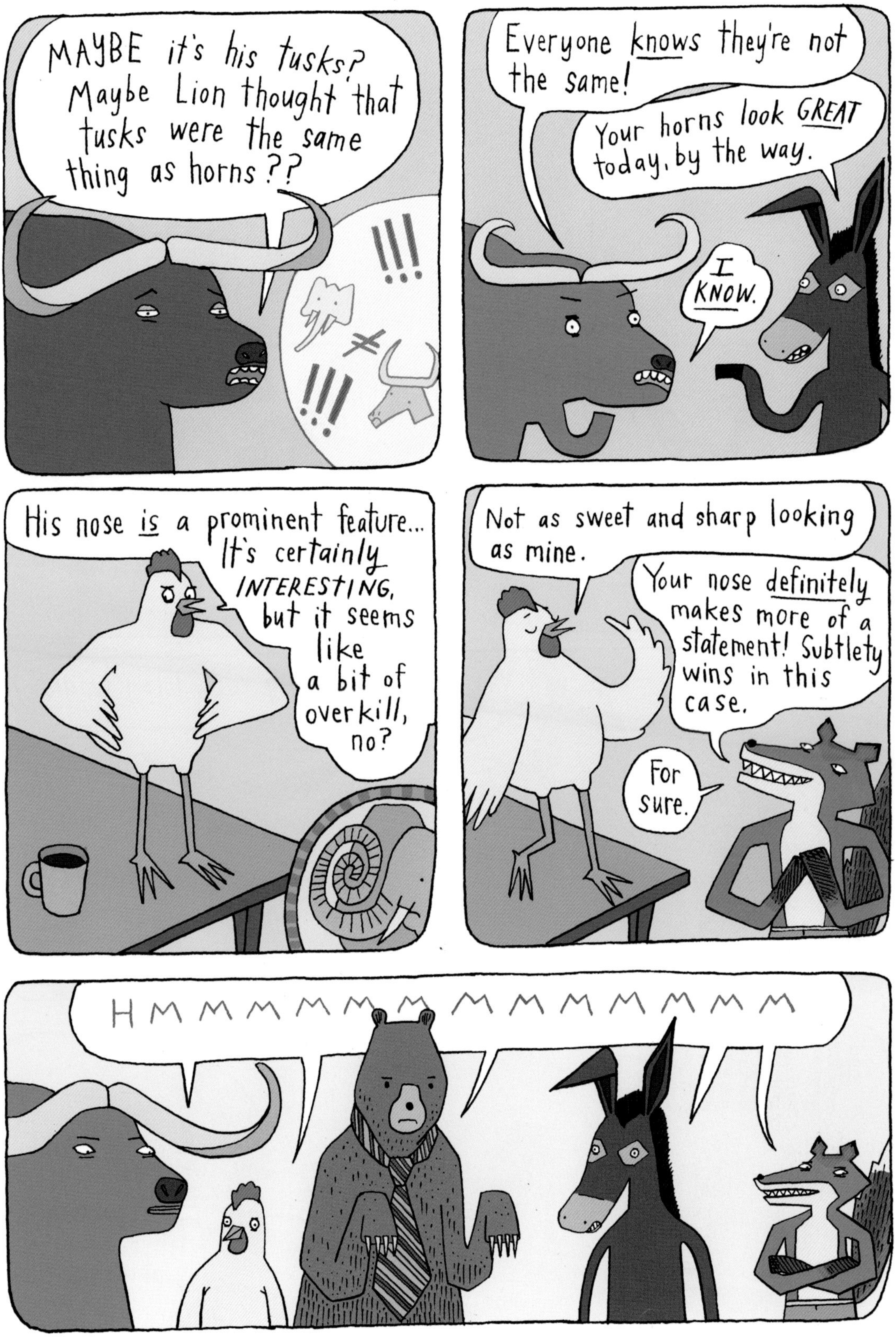
MAYBE it's his tusks? Maybe Lion thought that tusks were the same thing as horns??
!!!
!!!
Everyone knows they're not the same!
Your horns look GREAT today, by the way.
I KNOW.
His nose is a prominent feature... It's certainly INTERESTING, but it seems like a bit of overkill, no?
Not as sweet and sharp looking as mine.
Your nose definitely makes more of a statement! Subtlety wins in this case.
For sure.
HMMMMMMMMMMMMMMM

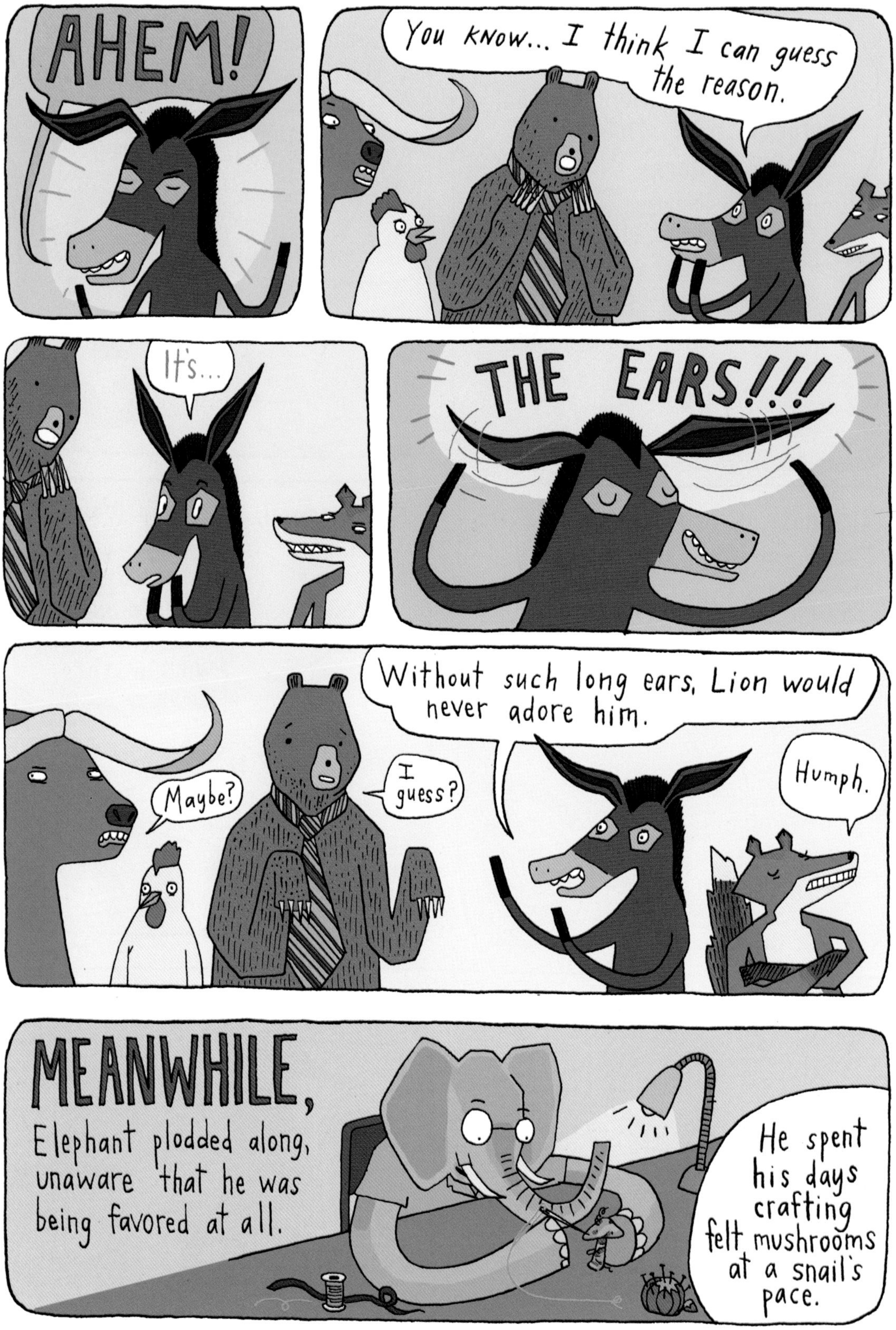
AHEM!
You know... I think I can guess the reason.
It's...
THE EARS!!!
Without such long ears, Lion would never adore him.
Maybe?
I guess?
Humph.
MEANWHILE,
Elephant plodded along, unaware that he was being favored at all.
He spent his days crafting felt mushrooms at a snail's pace.

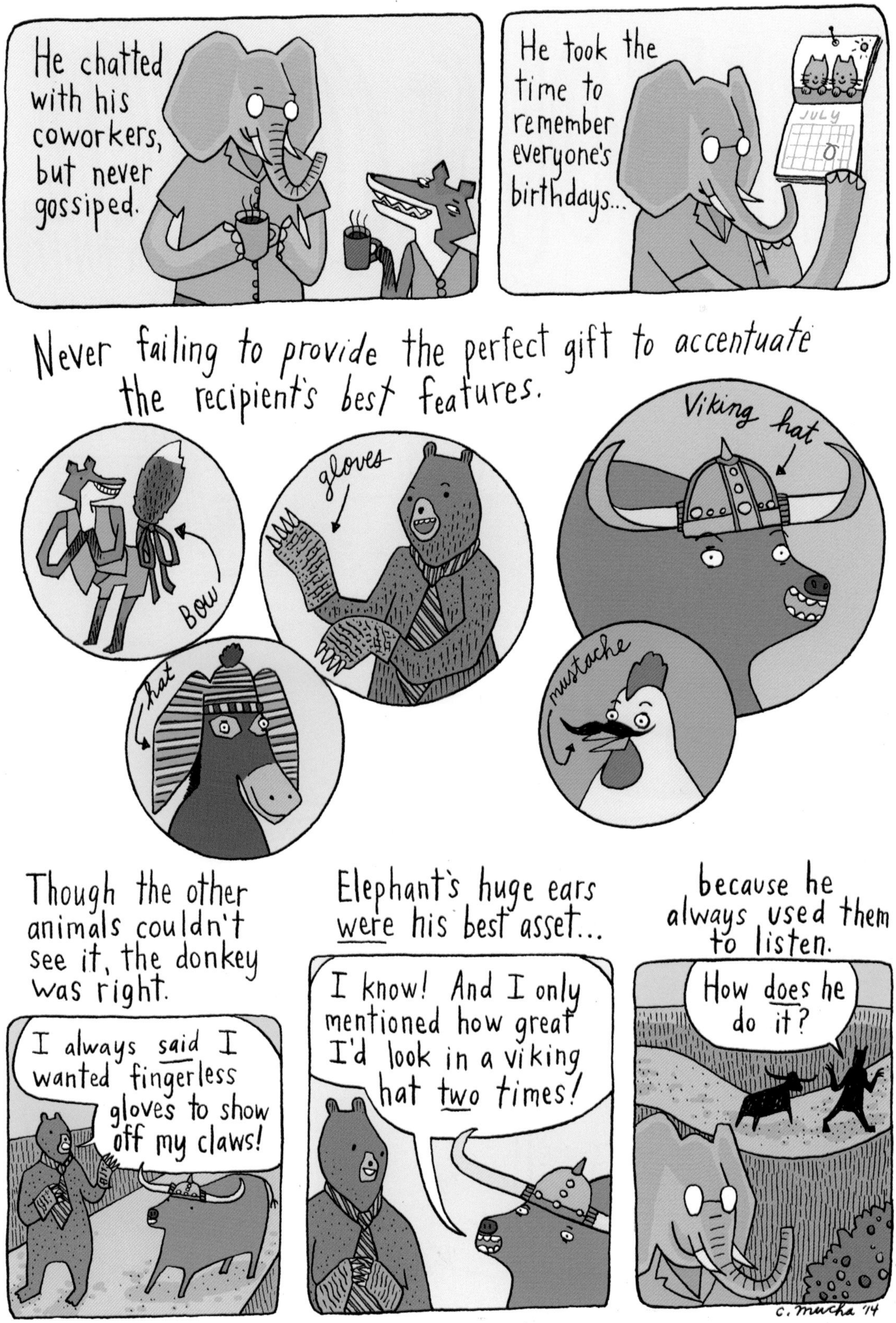
He chatted with his coworkers, but never gossiped.
He took the time to remember everyone's birthdays...
JULY
Never failing to provide the perfect gift to accentuate the recipient's best features.
Bow
gloves
Viking hat
hat
mustache
Though the other animals couldn't see it, the donkey was right.
I always said I wanted fingerless gloves to show off my claws!
Elephant's huge ears were his best asset...
I know! And I only mentioned how great I'd look in a viking hat two times!
because he always used them to listen.
How does he do it?
c. mucha '14

THE MOUSE COUNCIL

BY LINIERS

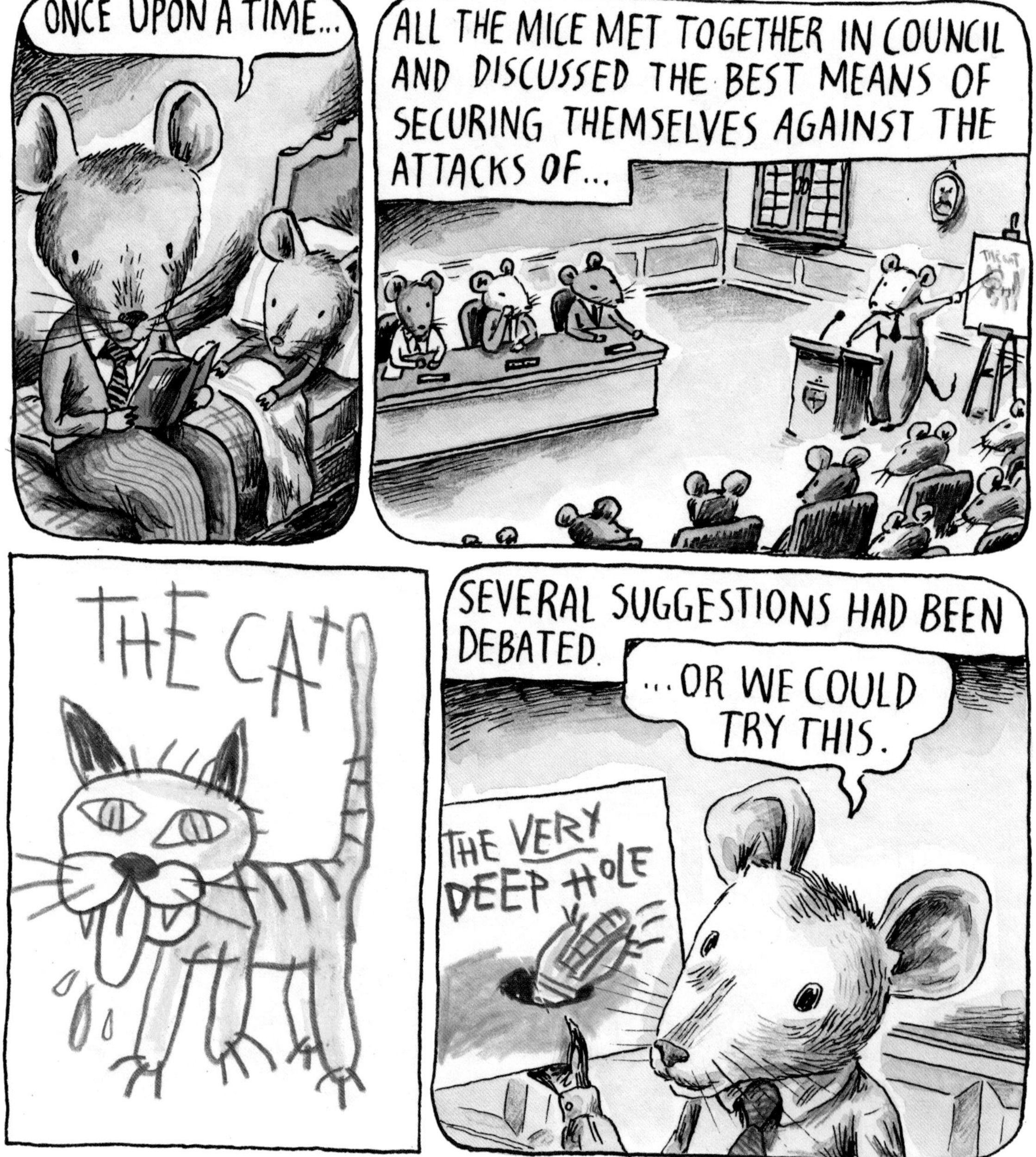
ONCE UPON A TIME...
ALL THE MICE MET TOGETHER IN COUNCIL AND DISCUSSED THE BEST MEANS OF SECURING THEMSELVES AGAINST THE ATTACKS OF...
THE CAT
SEVERAL SUGGESTIONS HAD BEEN DEBATED.
...OR WE COULD TRY THIS.
THE VERY DEEP HOLE

From the medieval European fable

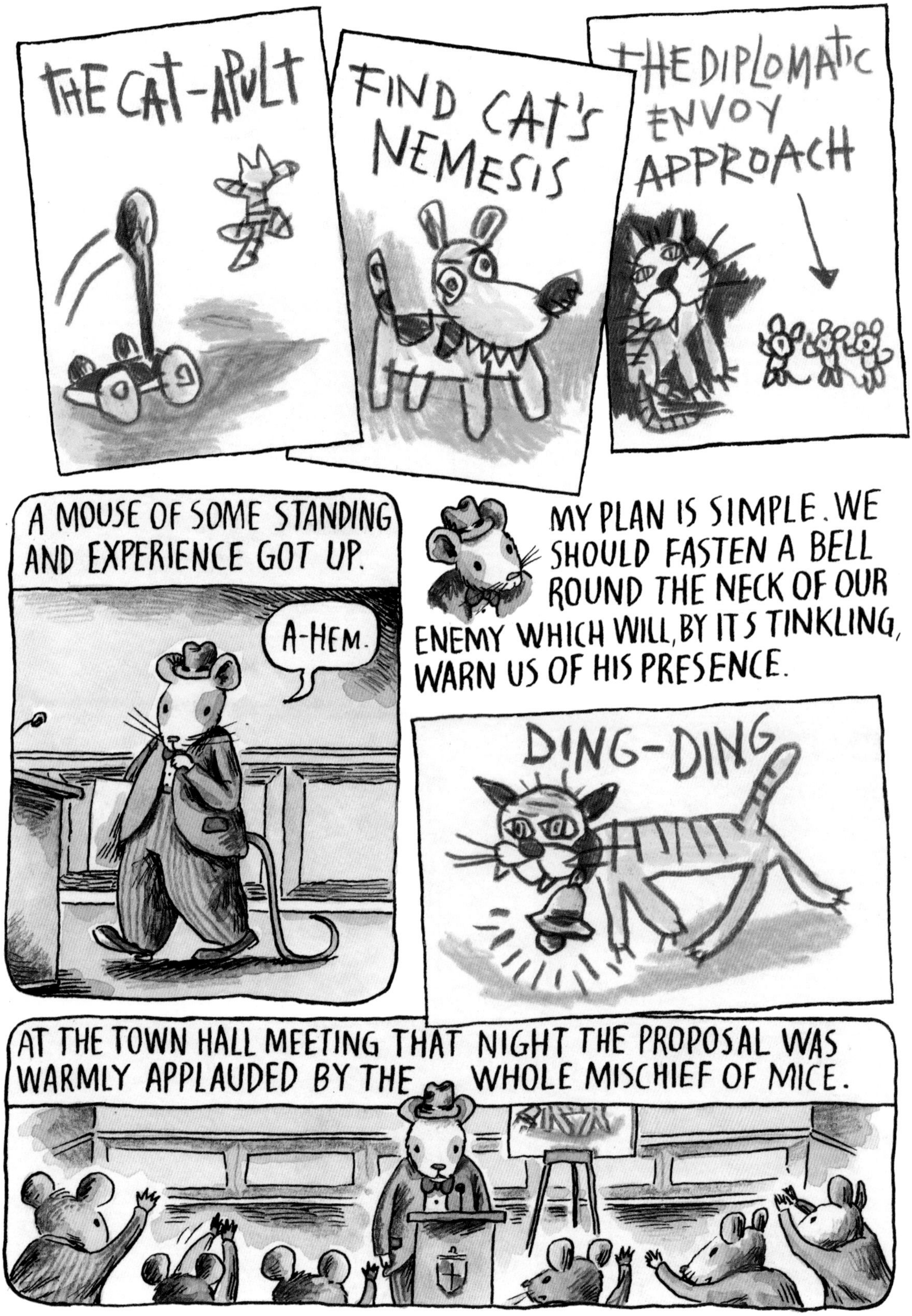
THE CAT-APULT
FIND CAT'S NEMESIS
THE DIPLOMATIC ENVOY APPROACH
A MOUSE OF SOME STANDING AND EXPERIENCE GOT UP.
A-HEM.
MY PLAN IS SIMPLE. WE SHOULD FASTEN A BELL ROUND THE NECK OF OUR ENEMY WHICH WILL, BY ITS TINKLING, WARN US OF HIS PRESENCE.
DING-DING
AT THE TOWN HALL MEETING THAT NIGHT THE PROPOSAL WAS WARMLY APPLAUDED BY THE WHOLE MISCHIEF OF MICE.

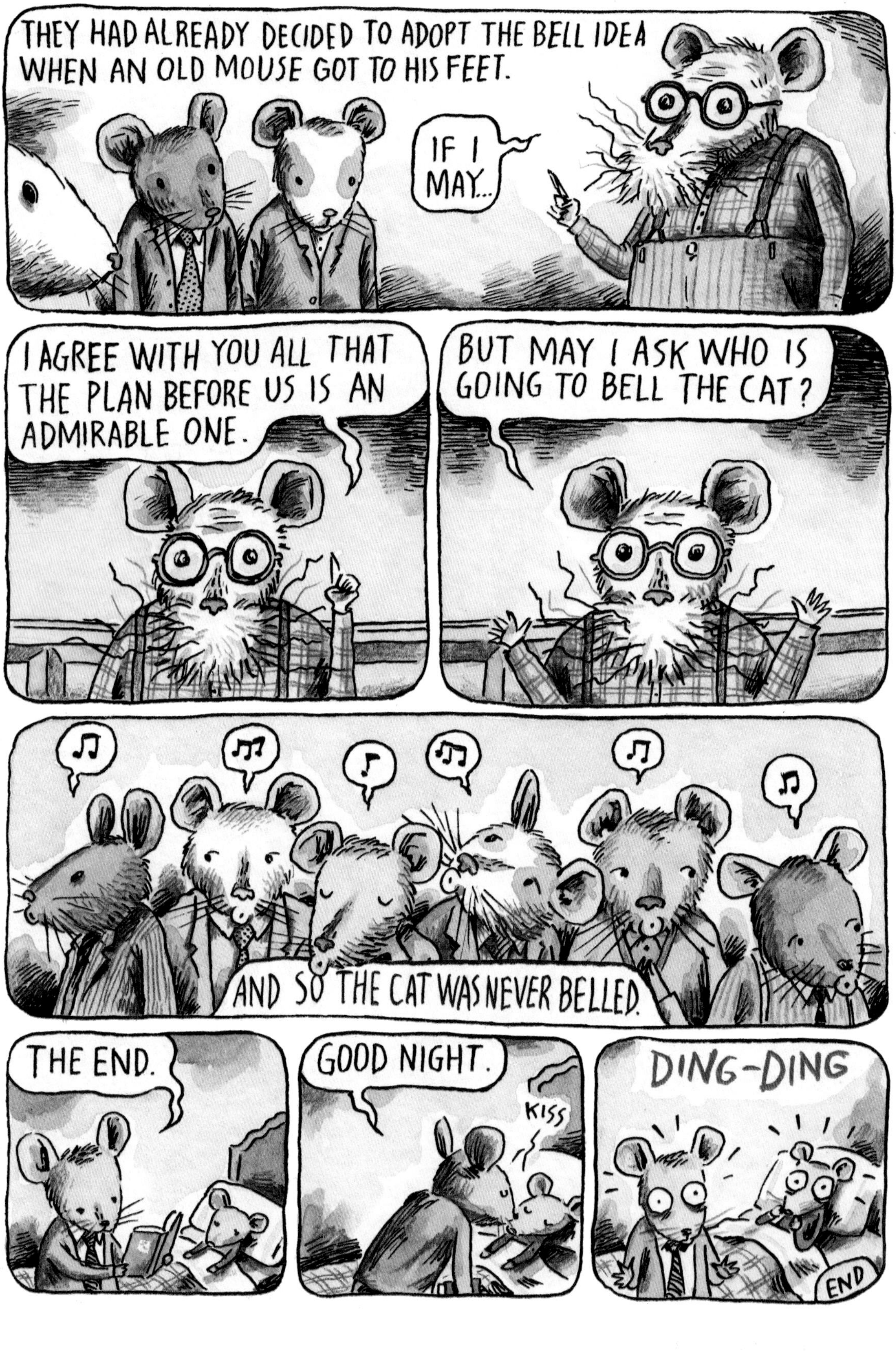
THEY HAD ALREADY DECIDED TO ADOPT THE BELL IDEA WHEN AN OLD MOUSE GOT TO HIS FEET.
IF I MAY...
I AGREE WITH YOU ALL THAT THE PLAN BEFORE US IS AN ADMIRABLE ONE.
BUT MAY I ASK WHO IS GOING TO BELL THE CAT?
AND SO THE CAT WAS NEVER BELLED.
THE END.
GOOD NIGHT.
KISS
DING-DING
END

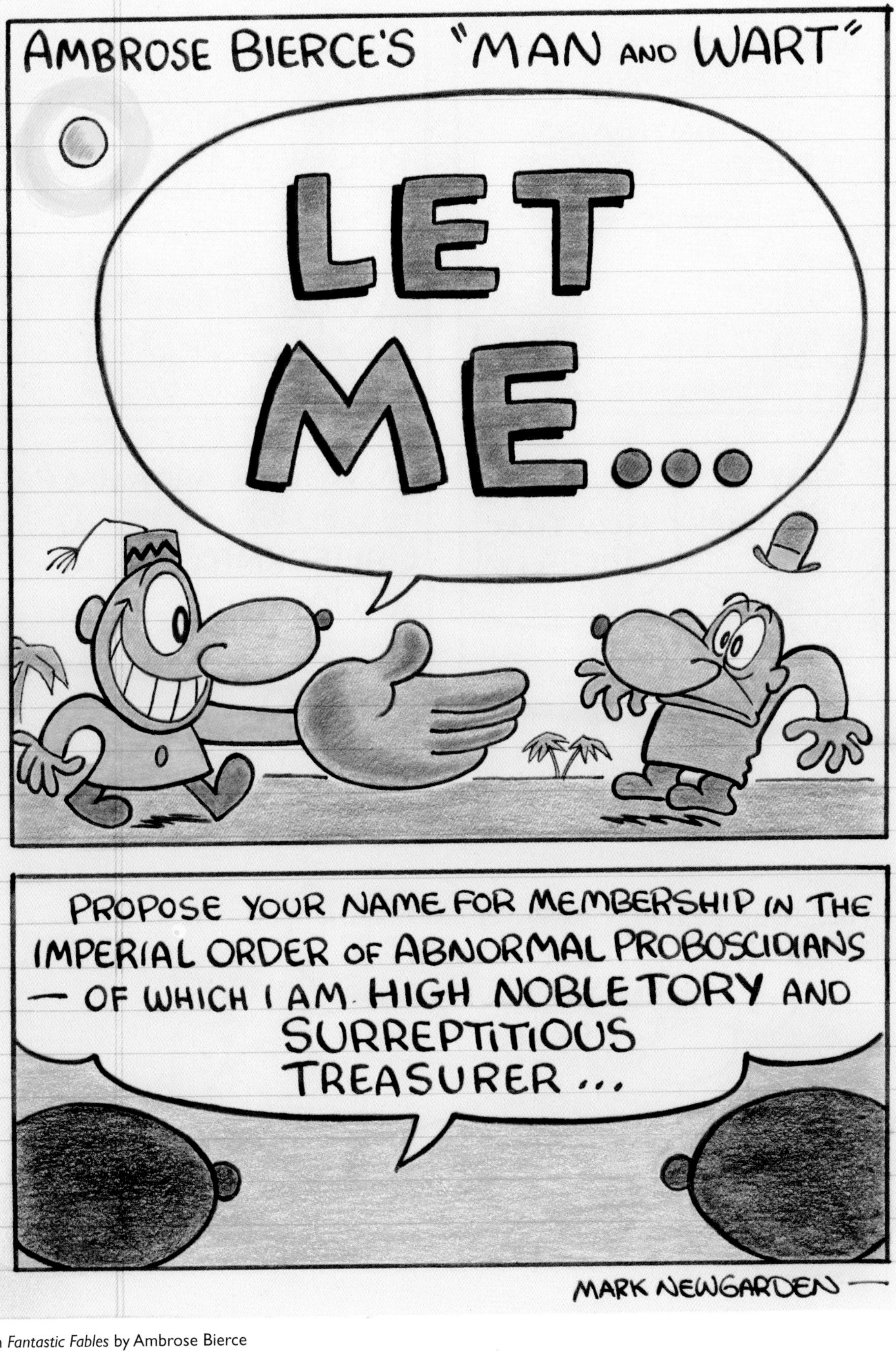
AMBROSE BIERCE'S "MAN AND WART"
LET ME...
PROPOSE YOUR NAME FOR MEMBERSHIP IN THE IMPERIAL ORDER OF ABNORMAL PROBOSCIDIANS — OF WHICH I AM HIGH NOBLETORY AND SURREPTITIOUS TREASURER...
MARK NEWGARDEN

From *Fantastic Fables* by Ambrose Bierce

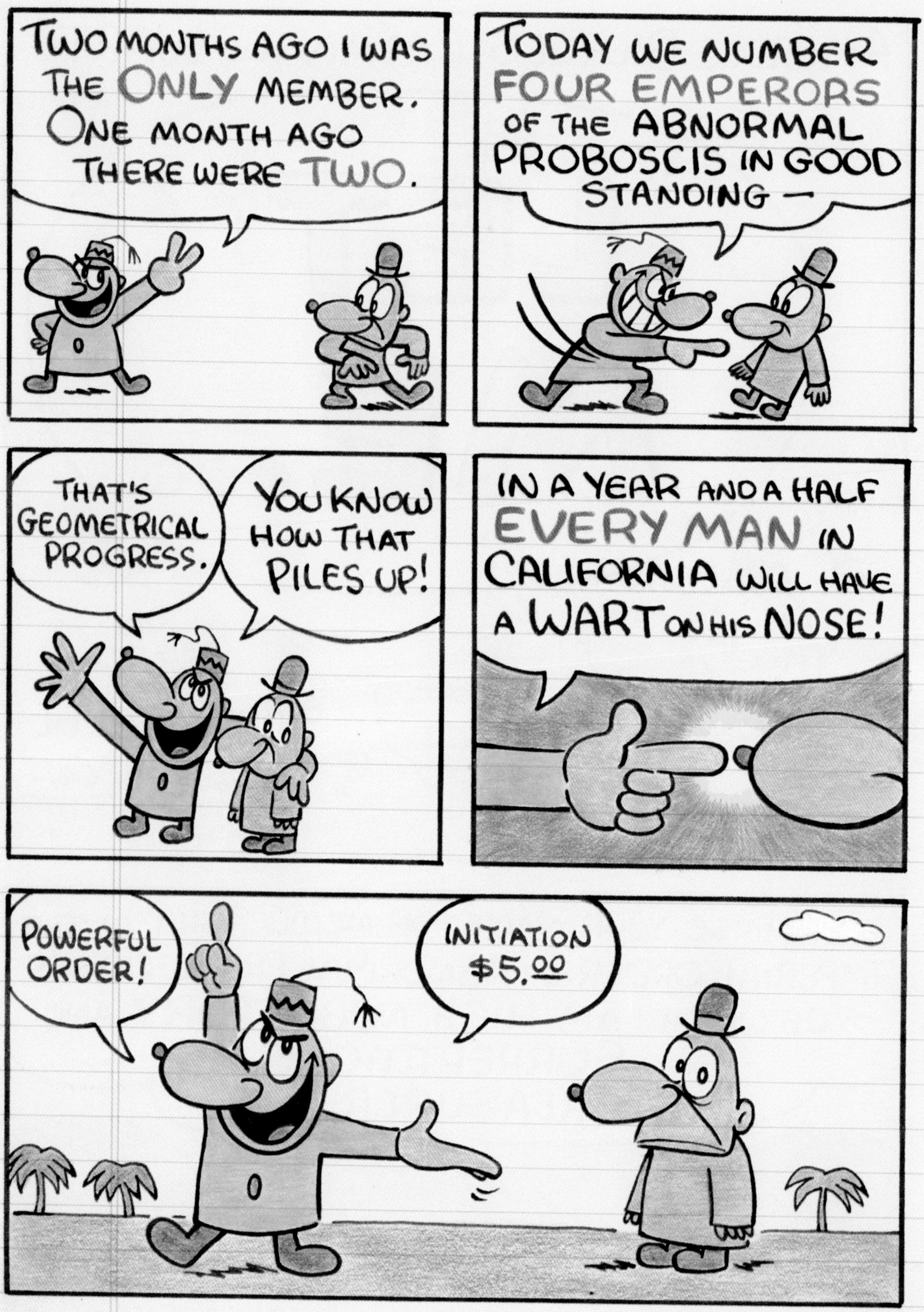
TWO MONTHS AGO I WAS THE ONLY MEMBER. ONE MONTH AGO THERE WERE TWO.
TODAY WE NUMBER FOUR EMPERORS OF THE ABNORMAL PROBOSCIS IN GOOD STANDING —
THAT'S GEOMETRICAL PROGRESS.
YOU KNOW HOW THAT PILES UP!
IN A YEAR AND A HALF EVERY MAN IN CALIFORNIA WILL HAVE A WART ON HIS NOSE!
POWERFUL ORDER!
INITIATION $5.00

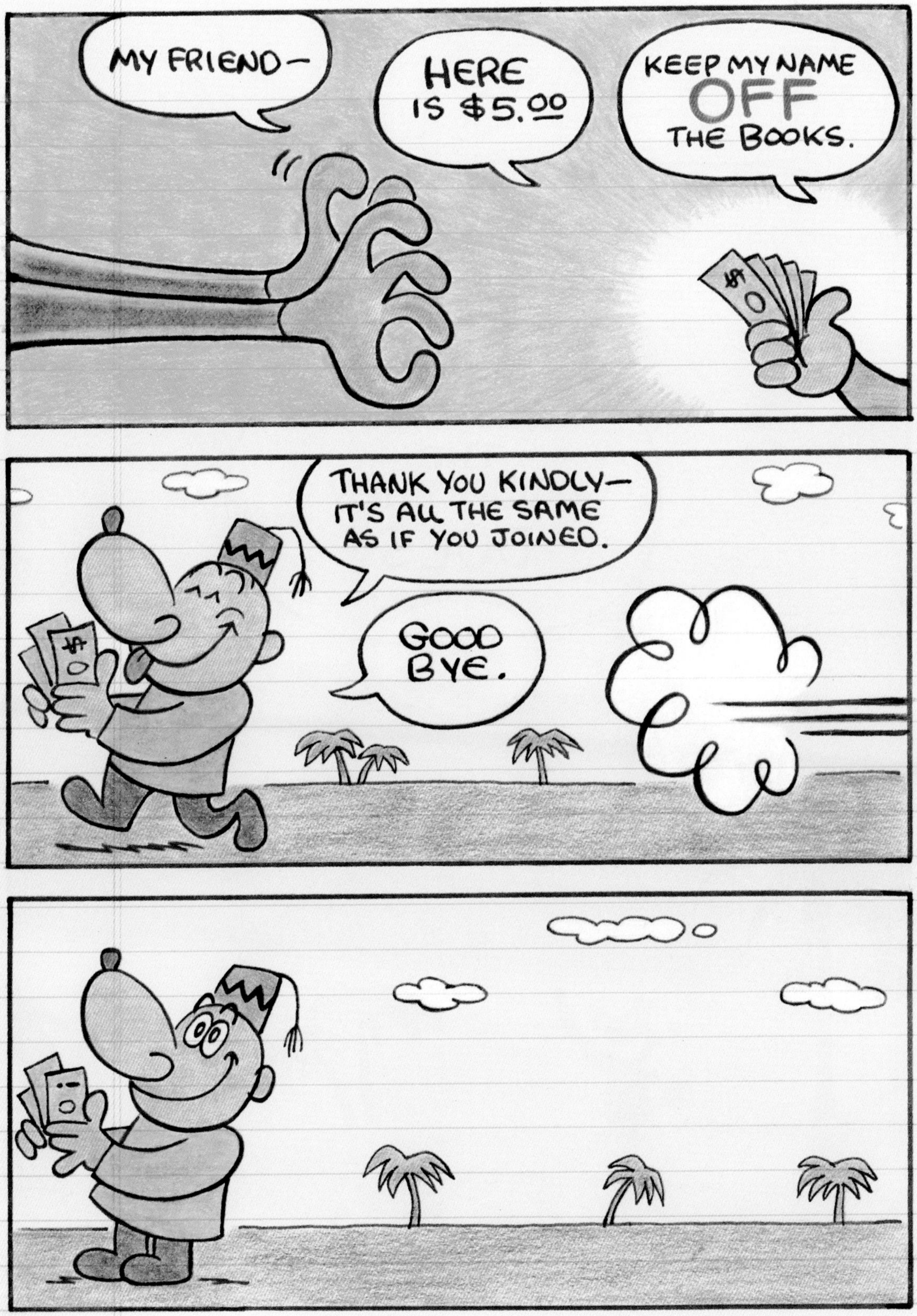
MY FRIEND-
HERE IS $5.00
KEEP MY NAME OFF THE BOOKS.
THANK YOU KINDLY- IT'S ALL THE SAME AS IF YOU JOINED.
GOOD BYE.

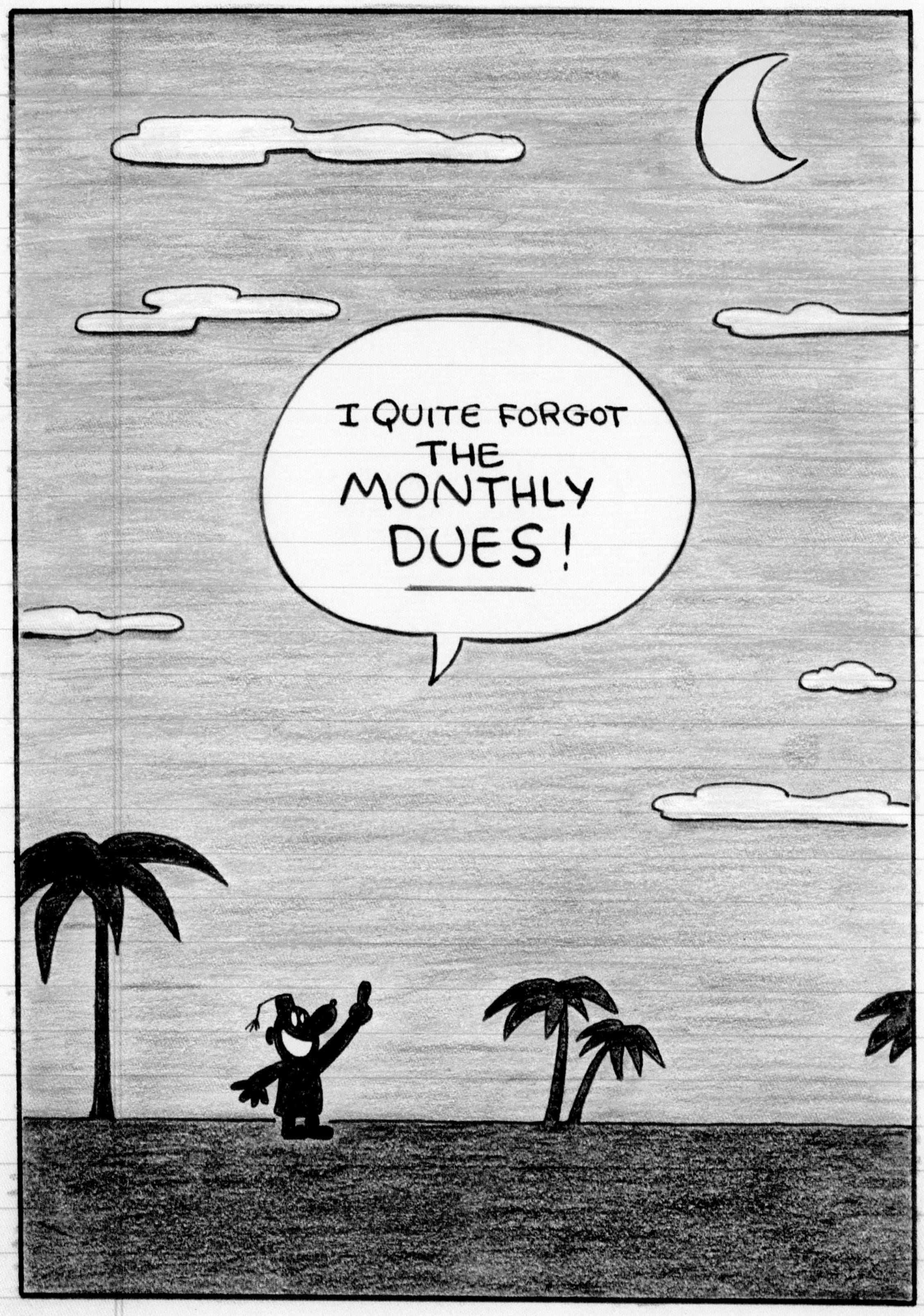
I QUITE FORGOT THE MONTHLY DUES!

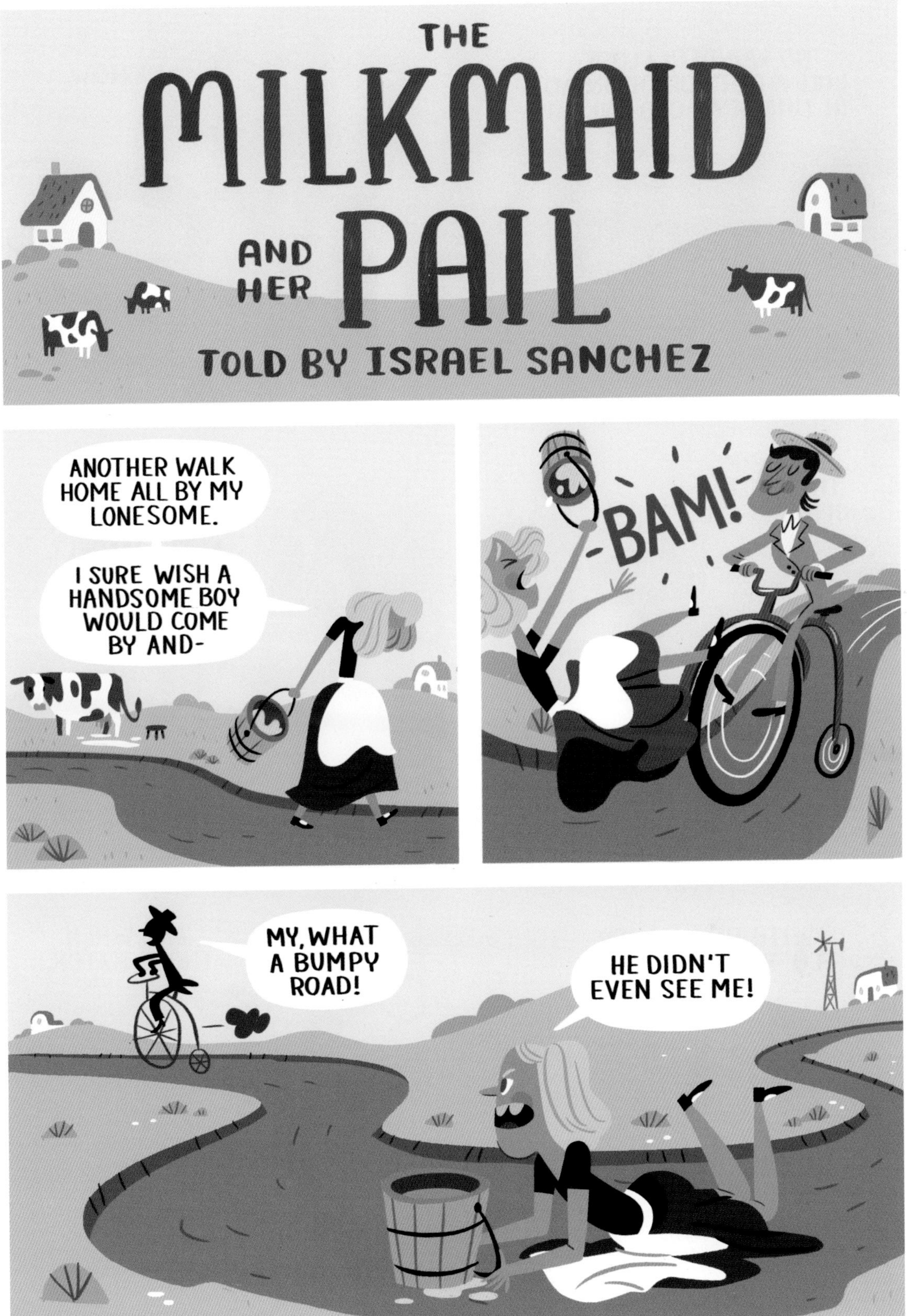
THE MILKMAID AND HER PAIL
TOLD BY ISRAEL SANCHEZ
ANOTHER WALK HOME ALL BY MY LONESOME.
I SURE WISH A HANDSOME BOY WOULD COME BY AND-
BAM!
MY, WHAT A BUMPY ROAD!
HE DIDN'T EVEN SEE ME!

From Aesop

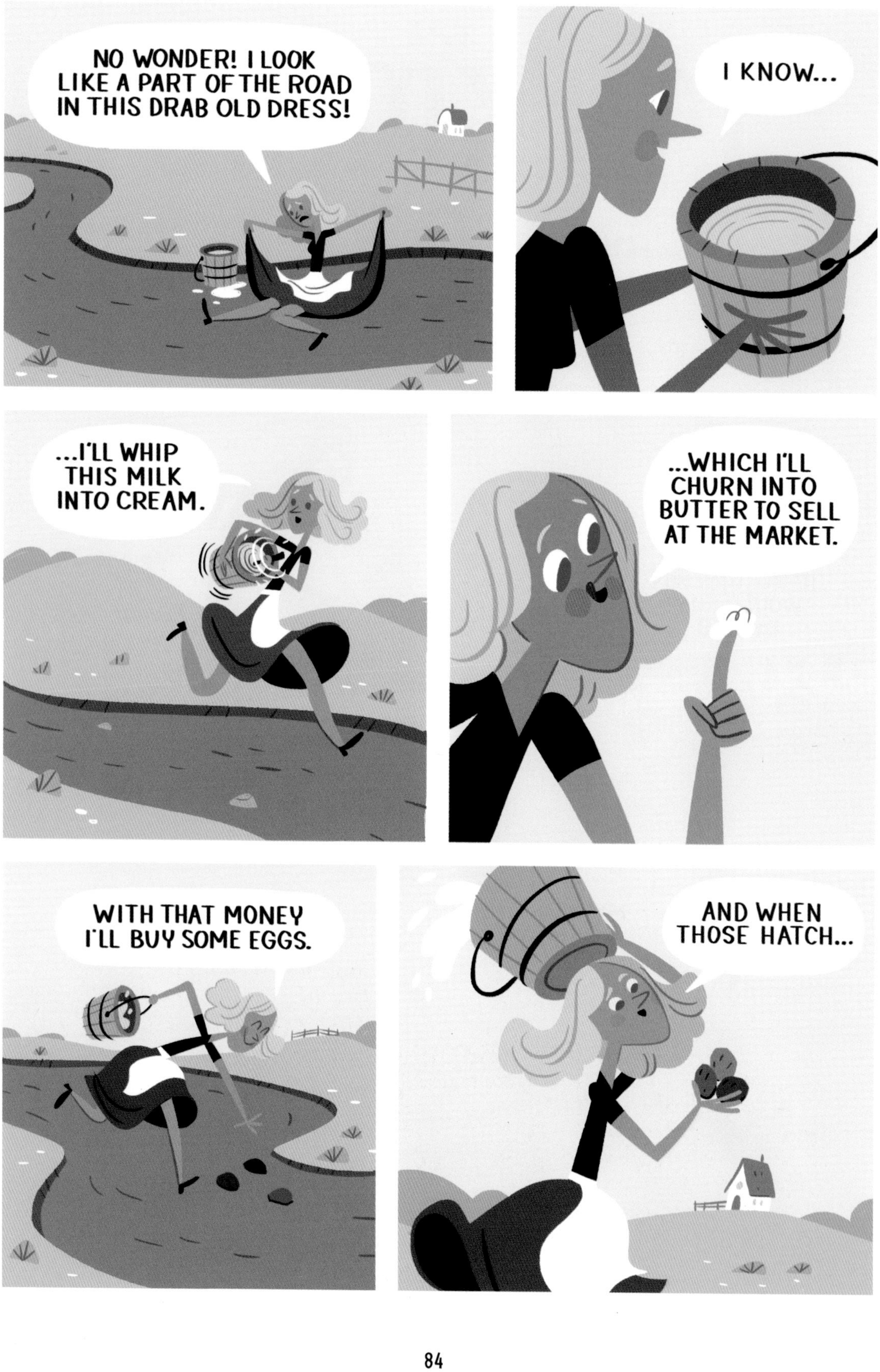
NO WONDER! I LOOK LIKE A PART OF THE ROAD IN THIS DRAB OLD DRESS!
I KNOW...
...I'LL WHIP THIS MILK INTO CREAM.
...WHICH I'LL CHURN INTO BUTTER TO SELL AT THE MARKET.
WITH THAT MONEY I'LL BUY SOME EGGS.
AND WHEN THOSE HATCH...

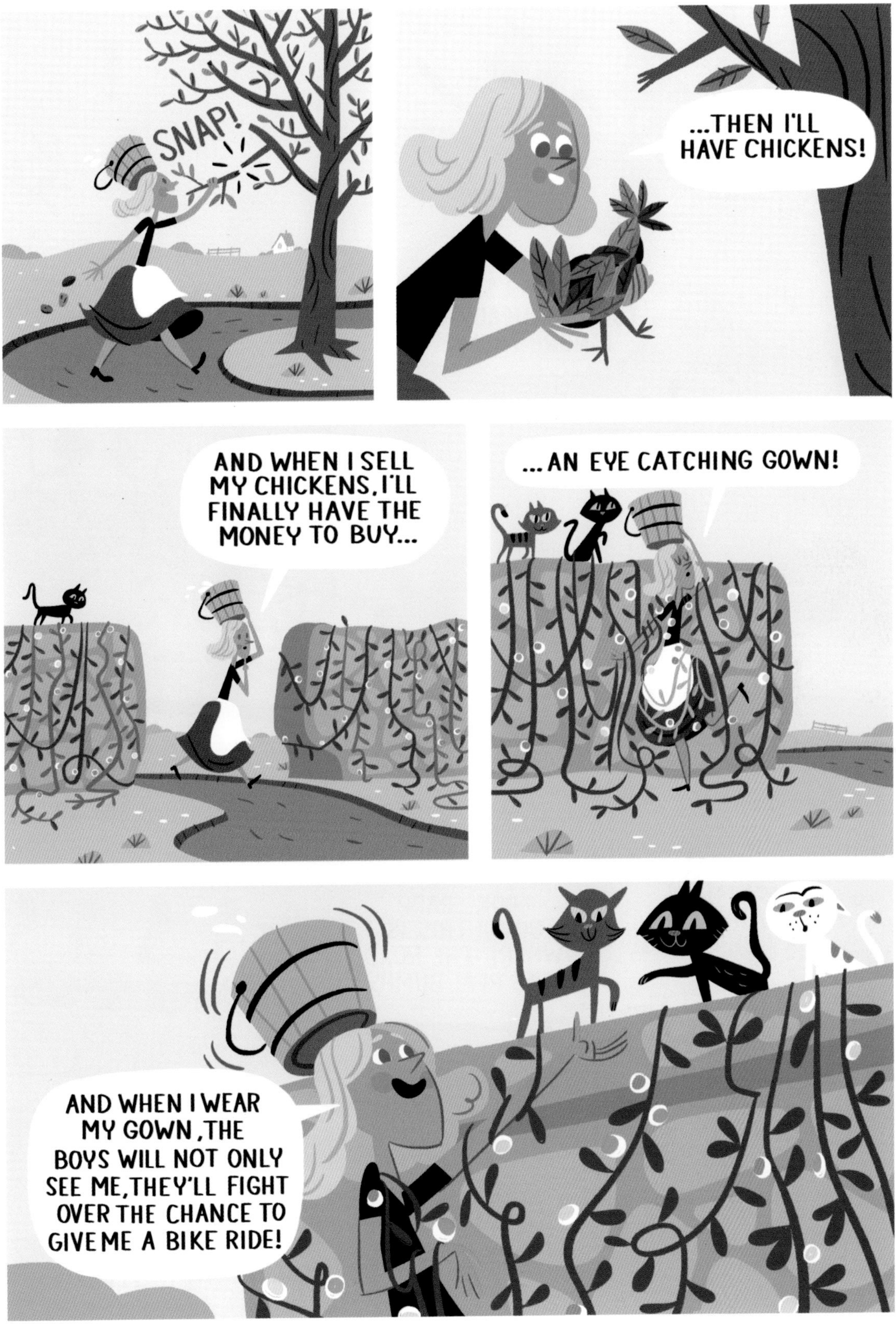
SNAP!
...THEN I'LL HAVE CHICKENS!
AND WHEN I SELL MY CHICKENS, I'LL FINALLY HAVE THE MONEY TO BUY...
...AN EYE CATCHING GOWN!
AND WHEN I WEAR MY GOWN, THE BOYS WILL NOT ONLY SEE ME, THEY'LL FIGHT OVER THE CHANCE TO GIVE ME A BIKE RIDE!

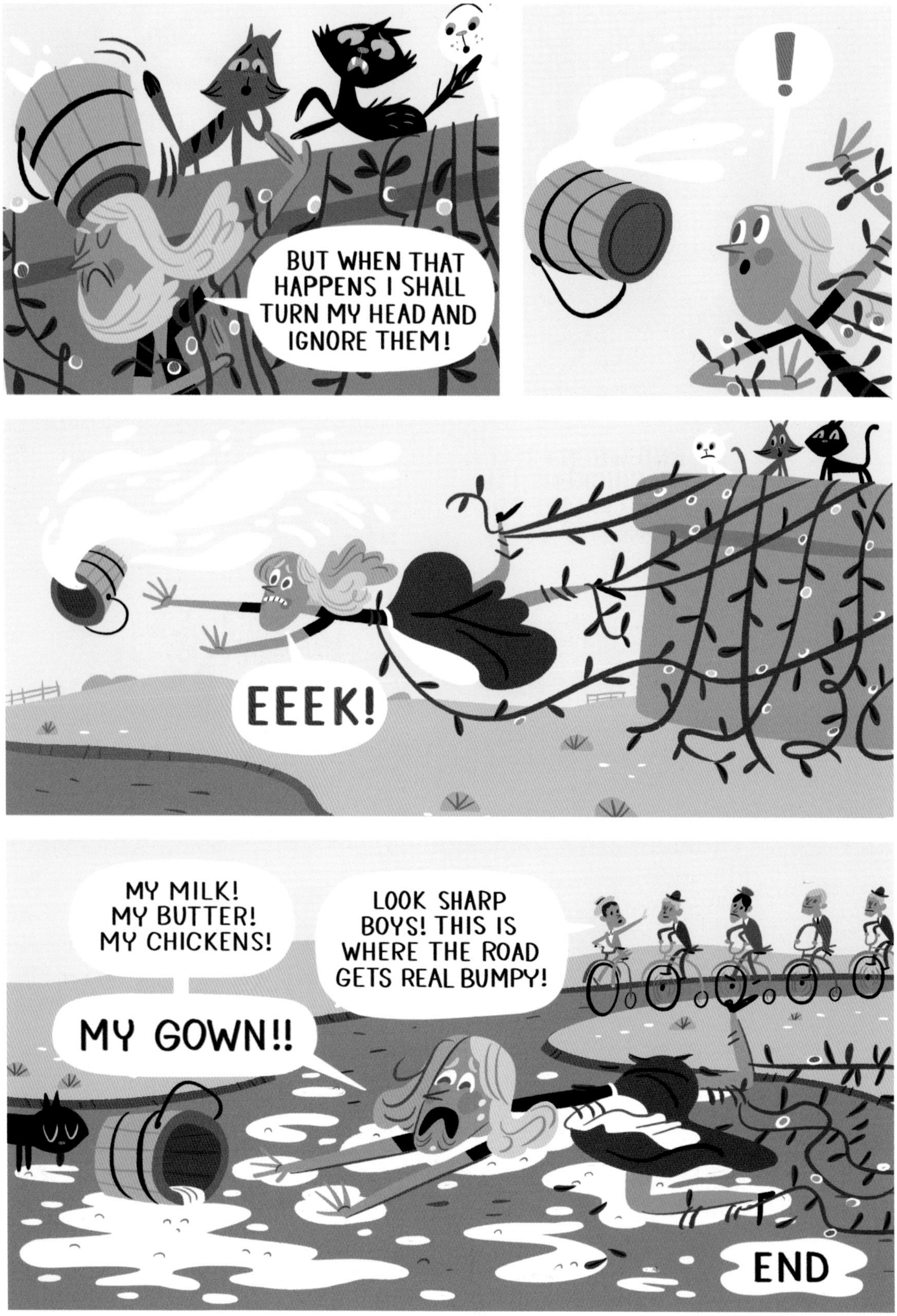

BUT WHEN THAT HAPPENS I SHALL TURN MY HEAD AND IGNORE THEM!
!
EEEK!
MY MILK! MY BUTTER! MY CHICKENS!
MY GOWN!!
LOOK SHARP BOYS! THIS IS WHERE THE ROAD GETS REAL BUMPY!
END

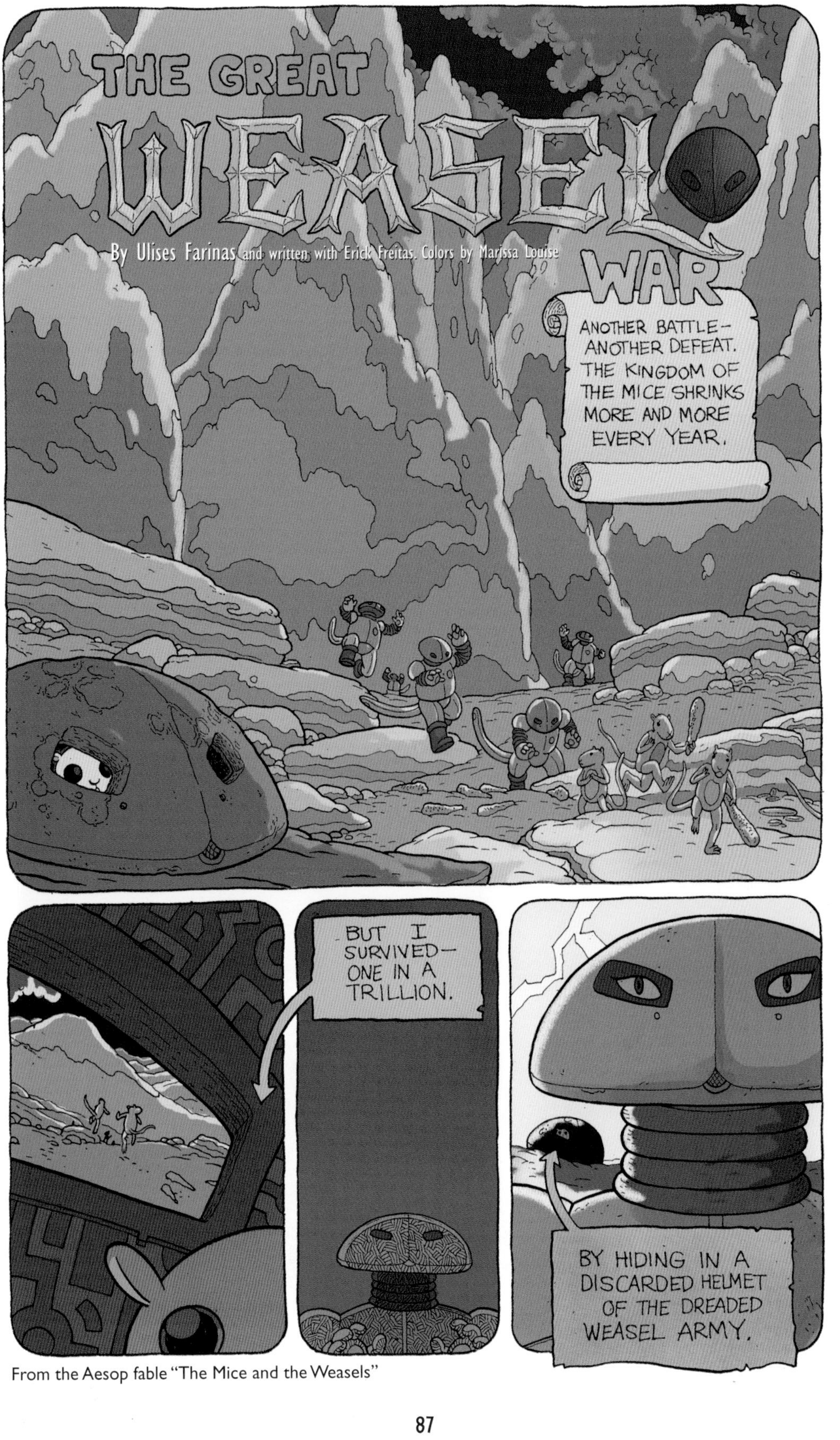
THE GREAT
WEASEL
WAR
By Ulises Farinas and written with Erick Freitas. Colors by Marissa Louise
ANOTHER BATTLE- ANOTHER DEFEAT. THE KINGDOM OF THE MICE SHRINKS MORE AND MORE EVERY YEAR.
BUT I SURVIVED- ONE IN A TRILLION.
BY HIDING IN A DISCARDED HELMET OF THE DREADED WEASEL ARMY.
From the Aesop fable "The Mice and the Weasels"

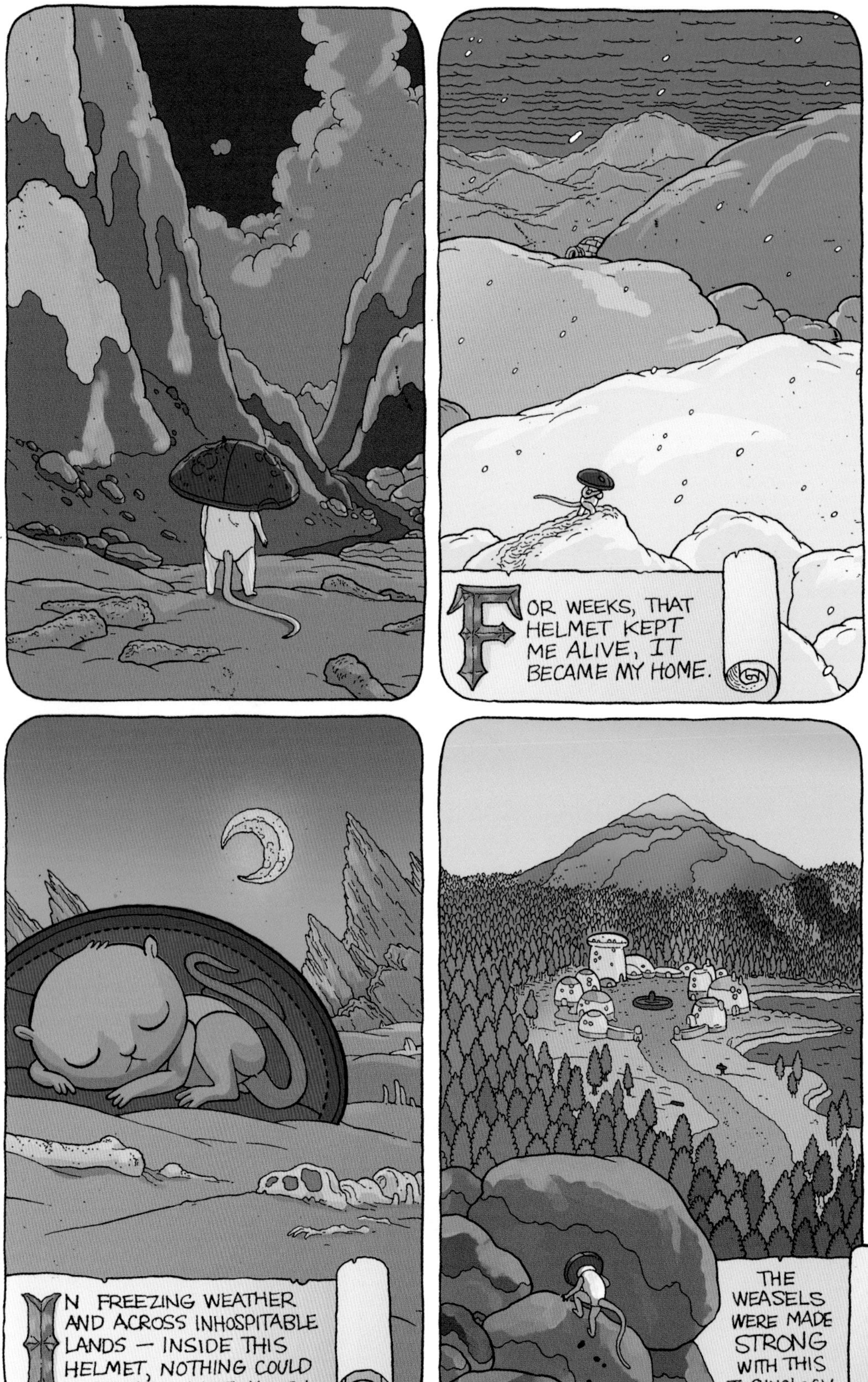
FOR WEEKS, THAT HELMET KEPT ME ALIVE, IT BECAME MY HOME.
IN FREEZING WEATHER AND ACROSS INHOSPITABLE LANDS — INSIDE THIS HELMET, NOTHING COULD HURT ME, NOTHING!
THE WEASELS WERE MADE STRONG WITH THIS TECHNOLOGY.

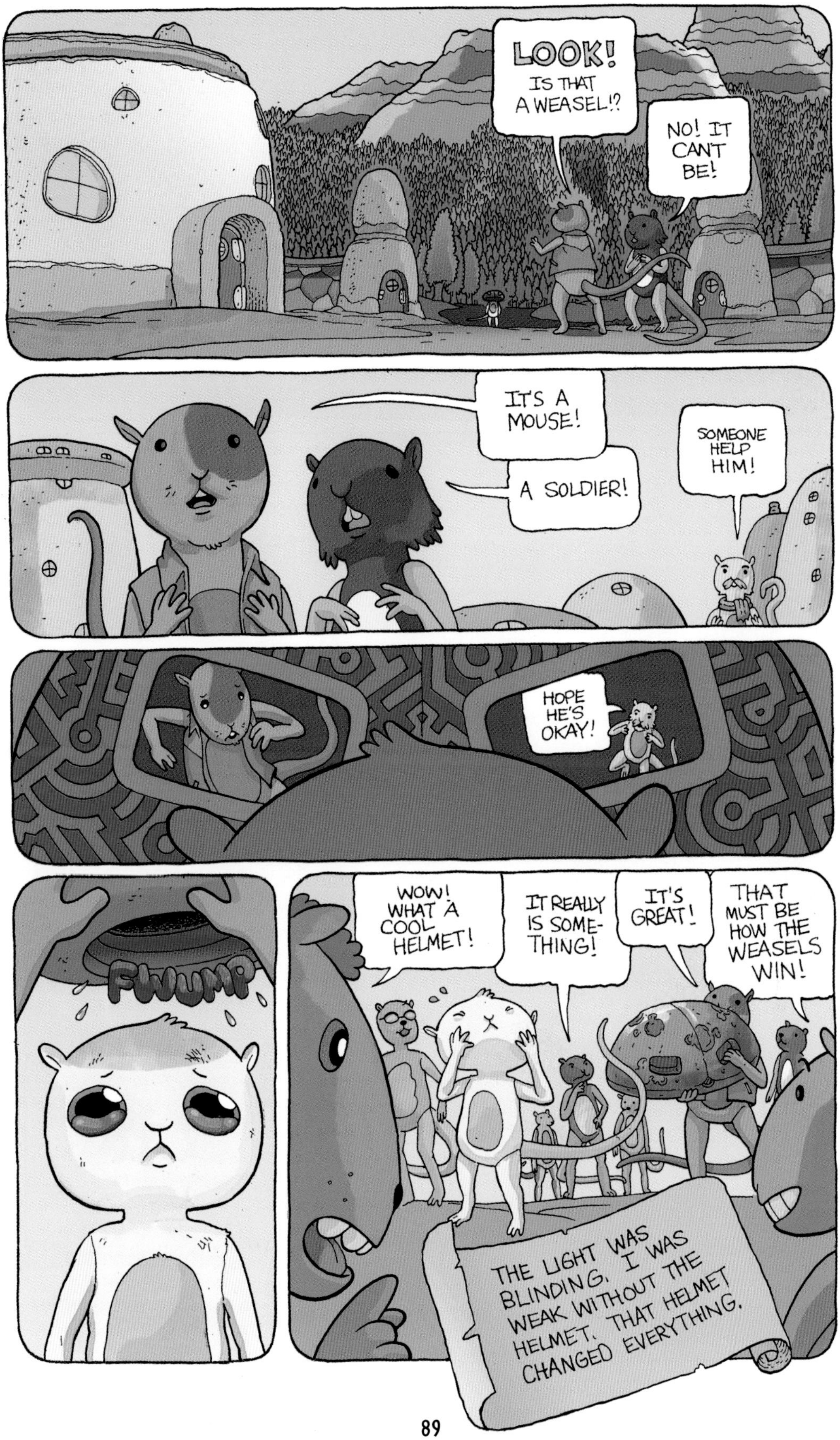
LOOK! IS THAT A WEASEL!?
NO! IT CAN'T BE!
IT'S A MOUSE!
A SOLDIER!
SOMEONE HELP HIM!
HOPE HE'S OKAY!
FWUMP
WOW! WHAT A COOL HELMET!
IT REALLY IS SOME-THING!
IT'S GREAT!
THAT MUST BE HOW THE WEASELS WIN!
THE LIGHT WAS BLINDING. I WAS WEAK WITHOUT THE HELMET. THAT HELMET CHANGED EVERYTHING.

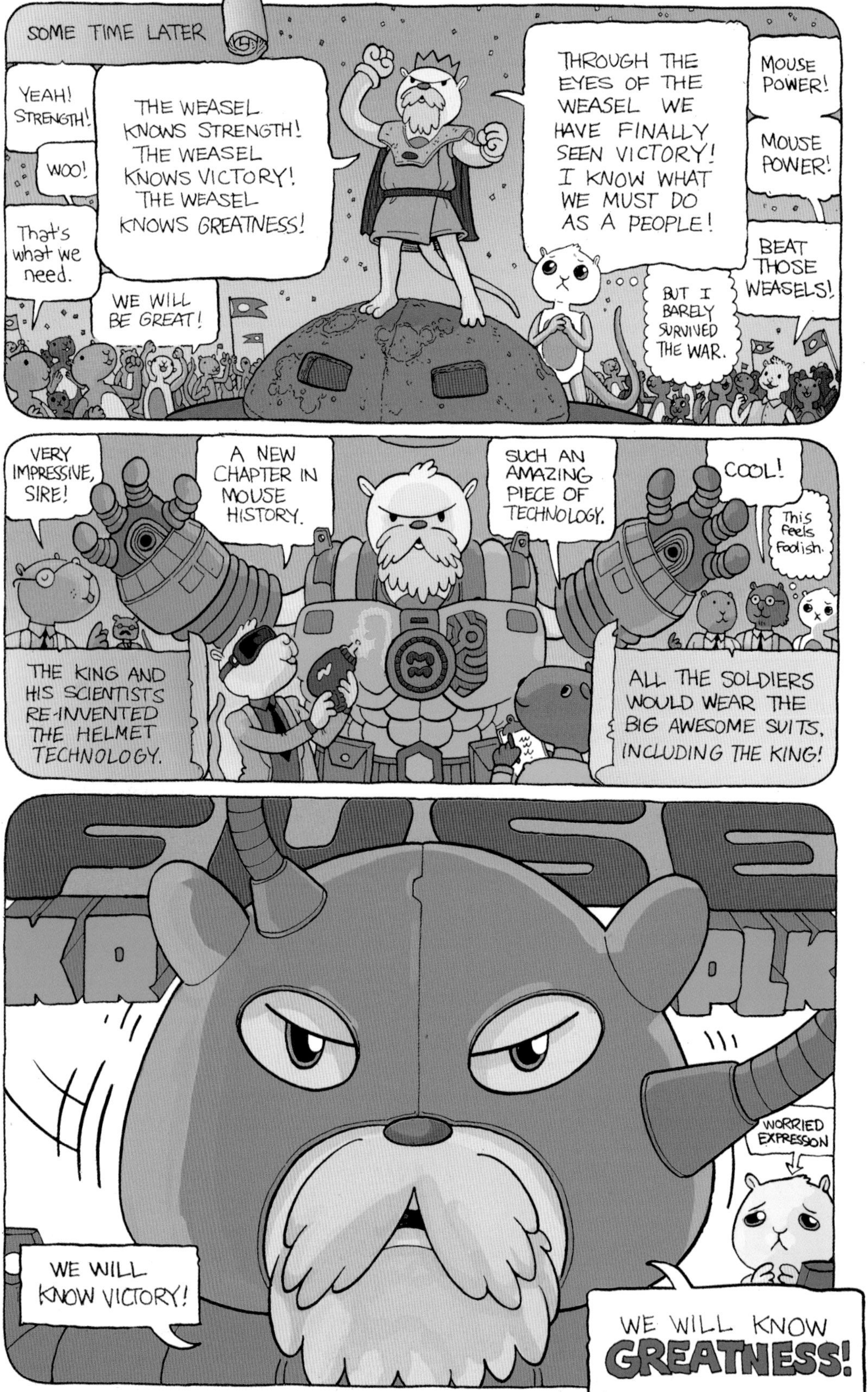
SOME TIME LATER
YEAH! STRENGTH!
WOO!
That's what we need.
THE WEASEL KNOWS STRENGTH! THE WEASEL KNOWS VICTORY! THE WEASEL KNOWS GREATNESS!
WE WILL BE GREAT!
THROUGH THE EYES OF THE WEASEL WE HAVE FINALLY SEEN VICTORY! I KNOW WHAT WE MUST DO AS A PEOPLE!
BUT I BARELY SURVIVED THE WAR.
MOUSE POWER!
MOUSE POWER!
BEAT THOSE WEASELS!
VERY IMPRESSIVE, SIRE!
A NEW CHAPTER IN MOUSE HISTORY.
SUCH AN AMAZING PIECE OF TECHNOLOGY.
COOL!
This feels foolish.
THE KING AND HIS SCIENTISTS RE-INVENTED THE HELMET TECHNOLOGY.
ALL THE SOLDIERS WOULD WEAR THE BIG AWESOME SUITS, INCLUDING THE KING!
WORRIED EXPRESSION
WE WILL KNOW VICTORY!
WE WILL KNOW **GREATNESS!**

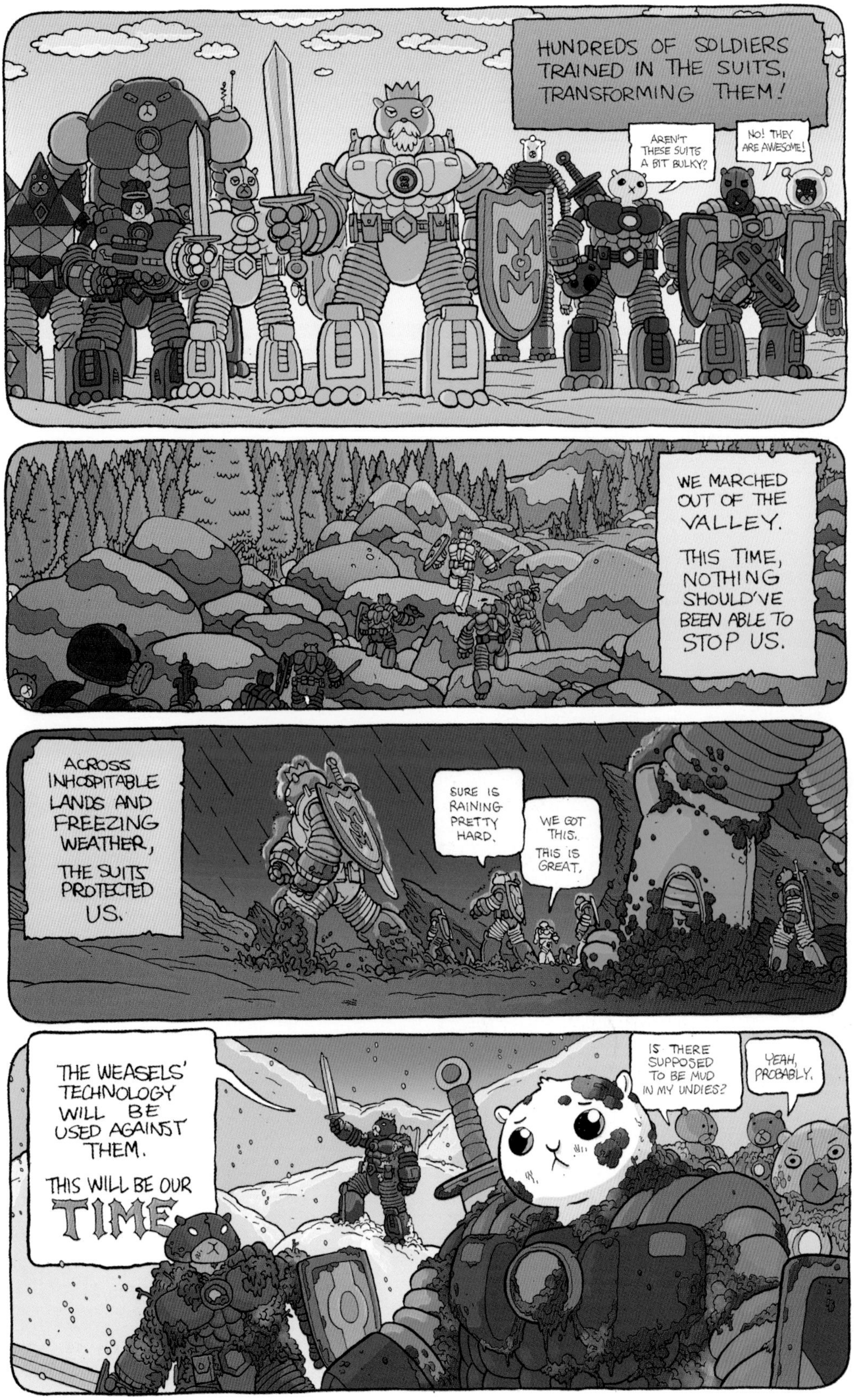
HUNDREDS OF SOLDIERS TRAINED IN THE SUITS, TRANSFORMING THEM!
AREN'T THESE SUITS A BIT BULKY?
NO! THEY ARE AWESOME!
WE MARCHED OUT OF THE VALLEY.
THIS TIME, NOTHING SHOULD'VE BEEN ABLE TO STOP US.
ACROSS INHOSPITABLE LANDS AND FREEZING WEATHER,
THE SUITS PROTECTED US.
SURE IS RAINING PRETTY HARD.
WE GOT THIS.
THIS IS GREAT.
THE WEASELS' TECHNOLOGY WILL BE USED AGAINST THEM.
THIS WILL BE OUR TIME
IS THERE SUPPOSED TO BE MUD IN MY UNDIES?
YEAH, PROBABLY.

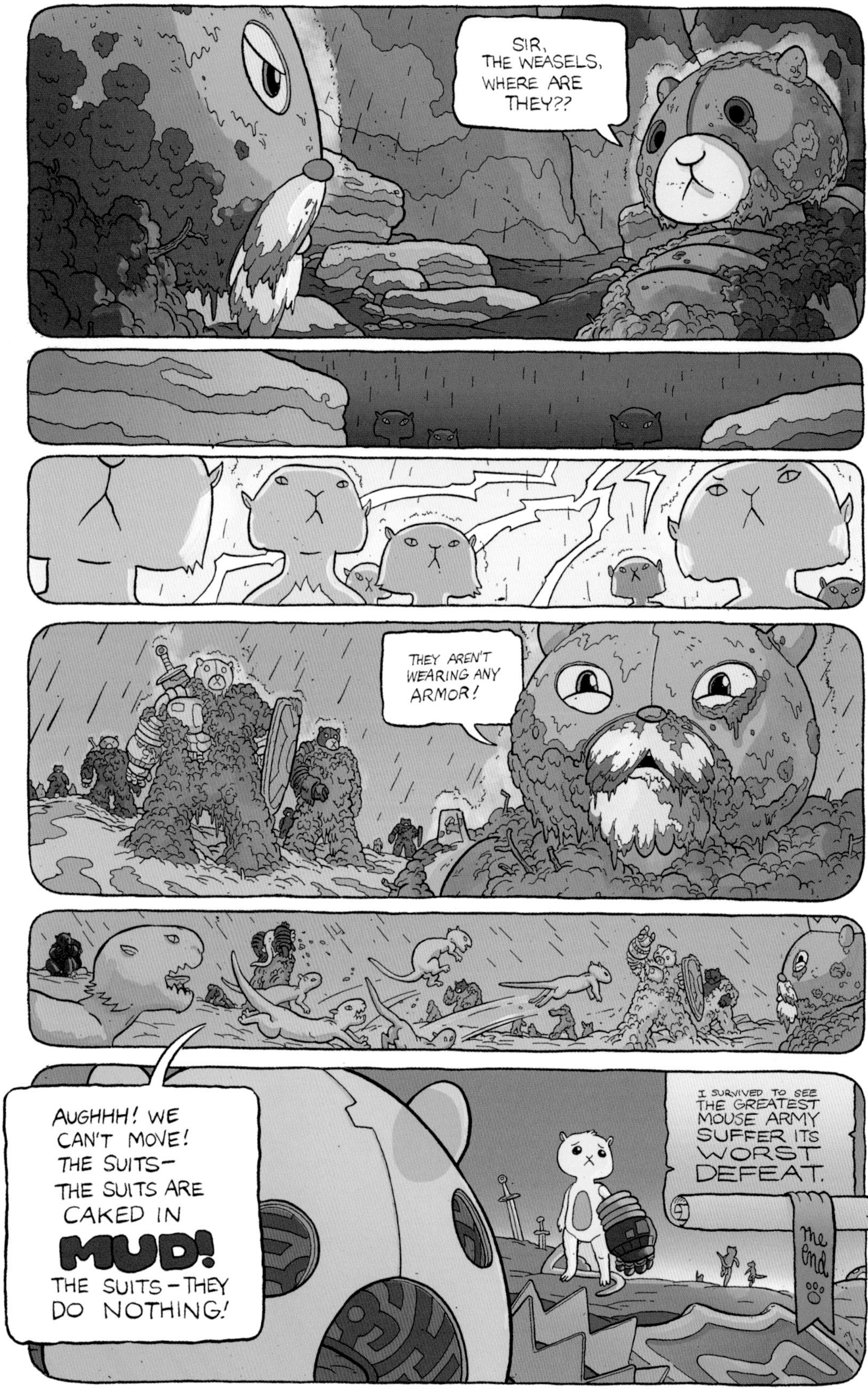
SIR, THE WEASELS, WHERE ARE THEY??
THEY AREN'T WEARING ANY ARMOR!
AUGHHH! WE CAN'T MOVE! THE SUITS— THE SUITS ARE CAKED IN MUD! THE SUITS—THEY DO NOTHING!
I SURVIVED TO SEE THE GREATEST MOUSE ARMY SUFFER ITS WORST DEFEAT.
the end

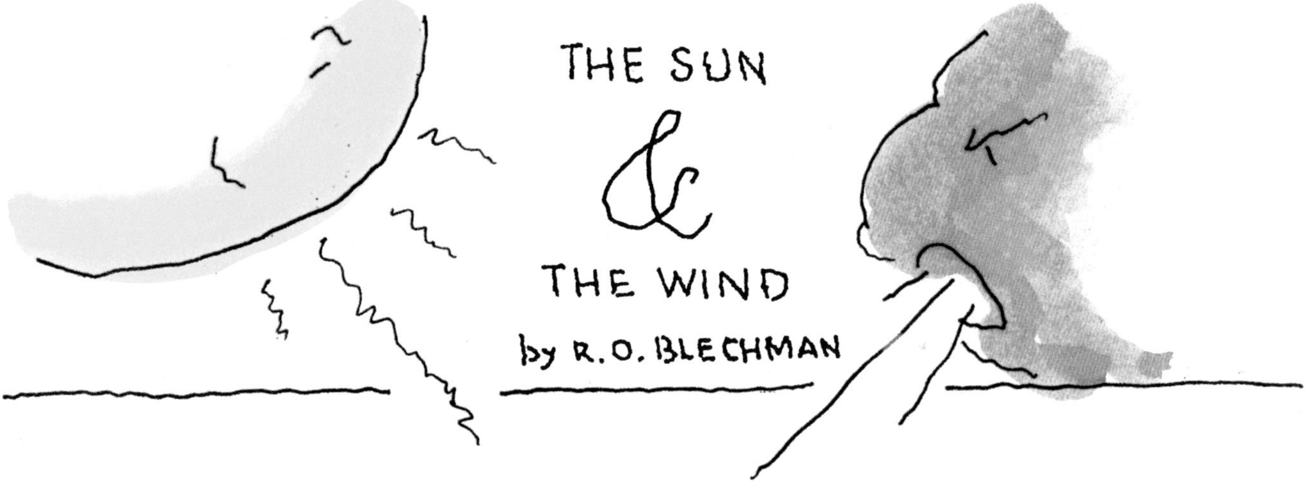
THE SUN
&
THE WIND
by R.O. BLECHMAN

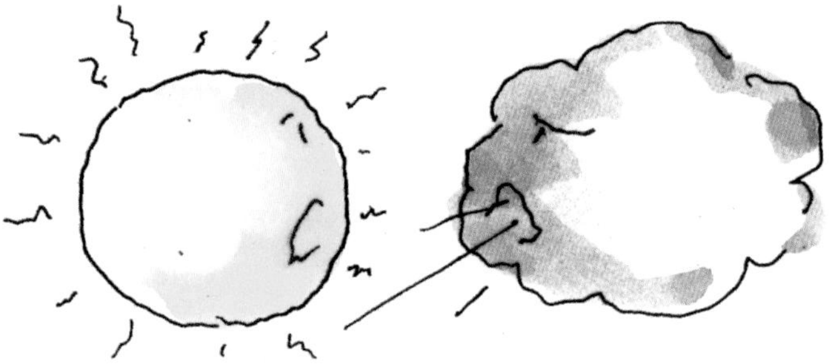

The sun and the wind once got into an argument over who was the stronger. (A silly argument, I know, but don't we often get into silly arguments?)

The sun said:

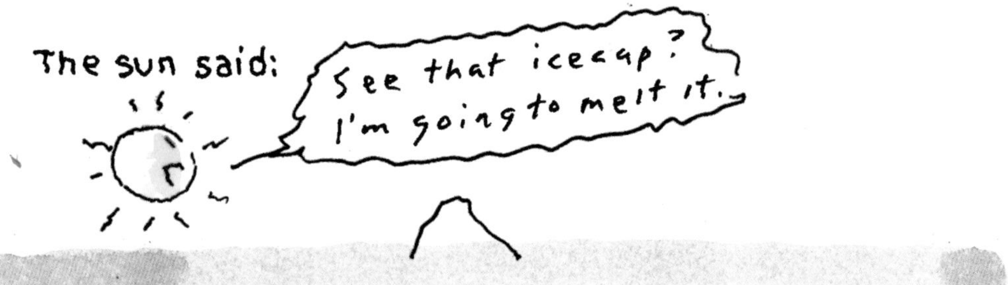
See that icecap? I'm going to melt it.

. . . and he melted it.

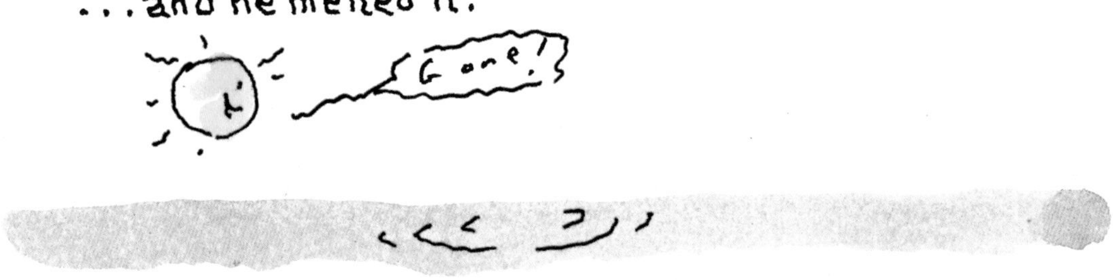
Gone!

From Aesop

Then the wind said:

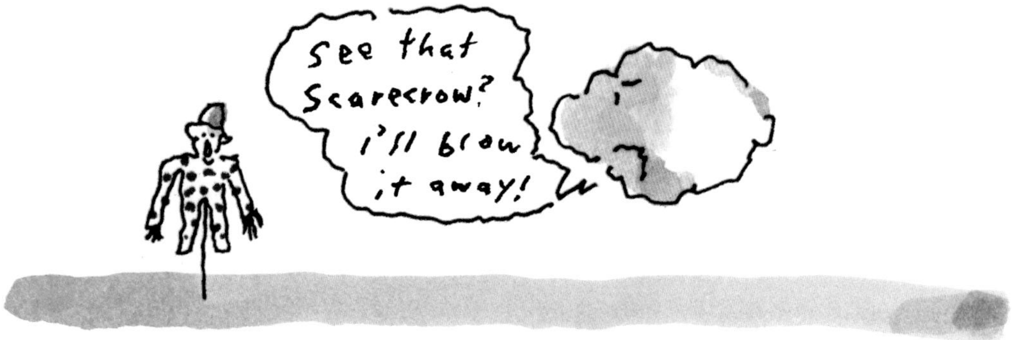
See that Scarecrow? I'll blow it away!

. . . and he blew it away.

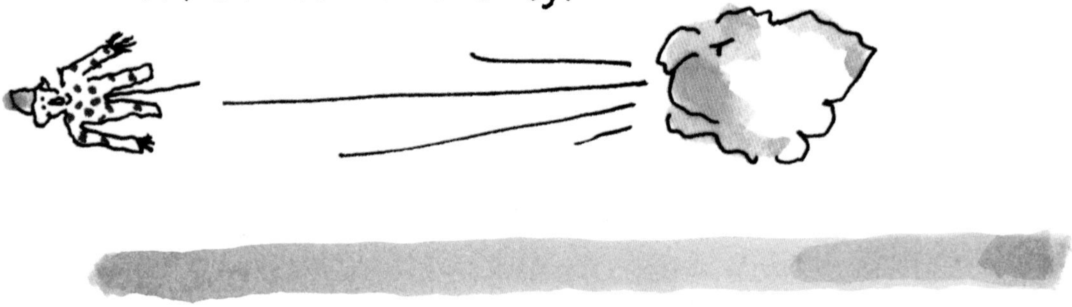

But neither of them convinced the other who was the stronger.

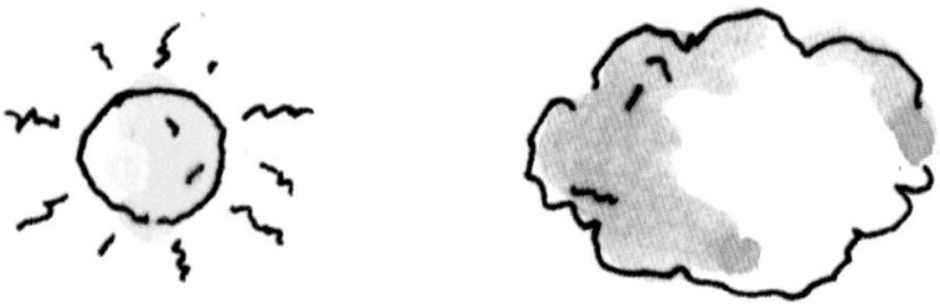

Then a traveler happened to pass by.

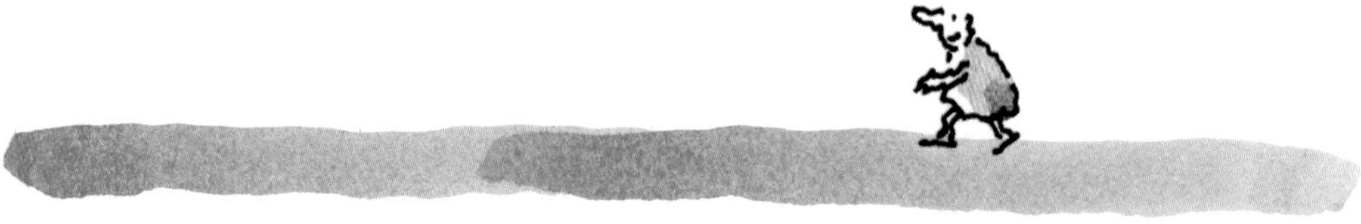

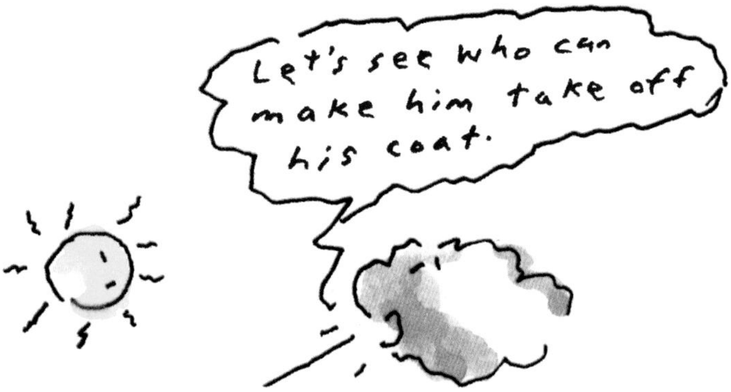
Let's see who can make him take off his coat.

So the wind blew . . .

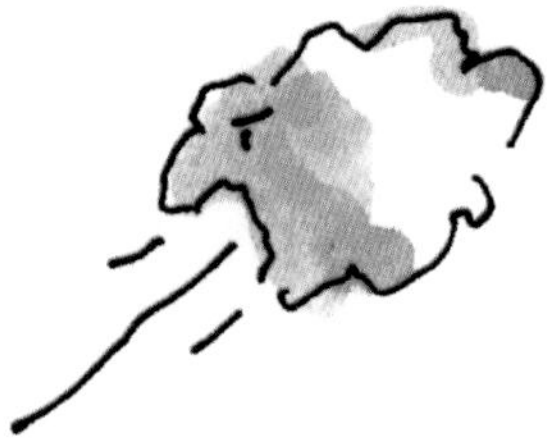

. . . and blew . . .

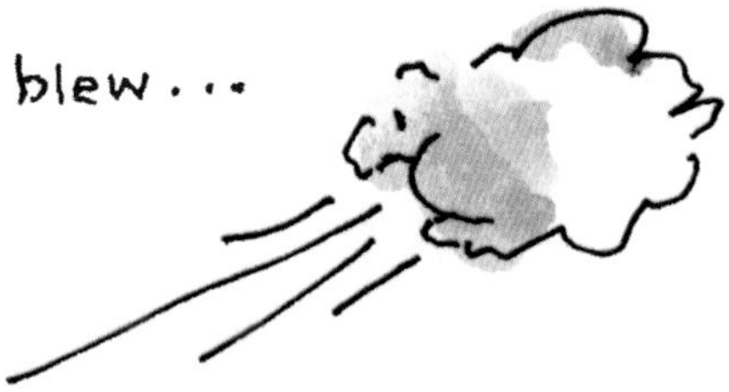

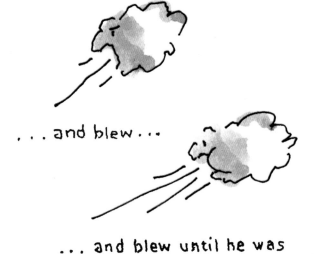

. . . and blew until he was red in the face, . . .

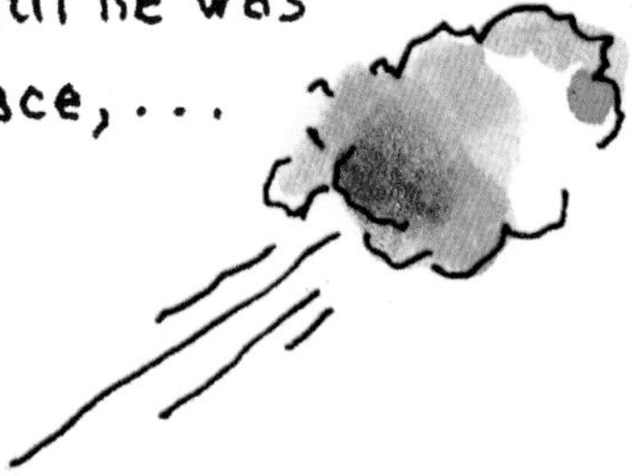

. . . but the man just kept pulling his coat tighter and tighter around himself.

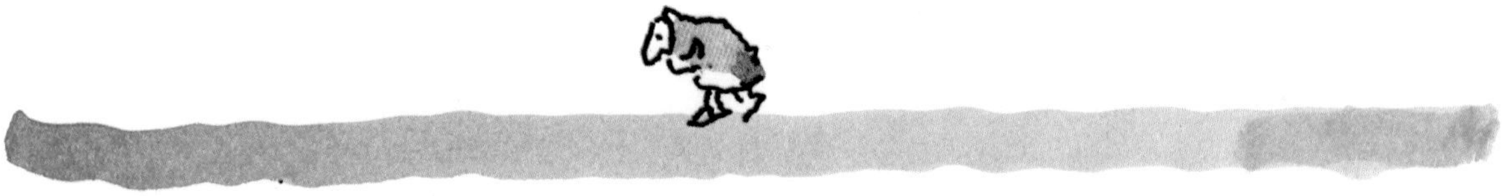

Then the sun shone gently on the man , . .

. . . and kept shining on him . . .

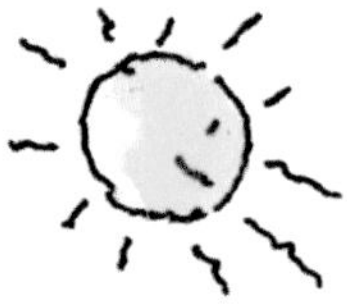

. . . as the man, feeling warmer and warmer and warmer , . . .

. . . took off his coat.

MORAL: Gentle persuasion is better than force

(sometimes).

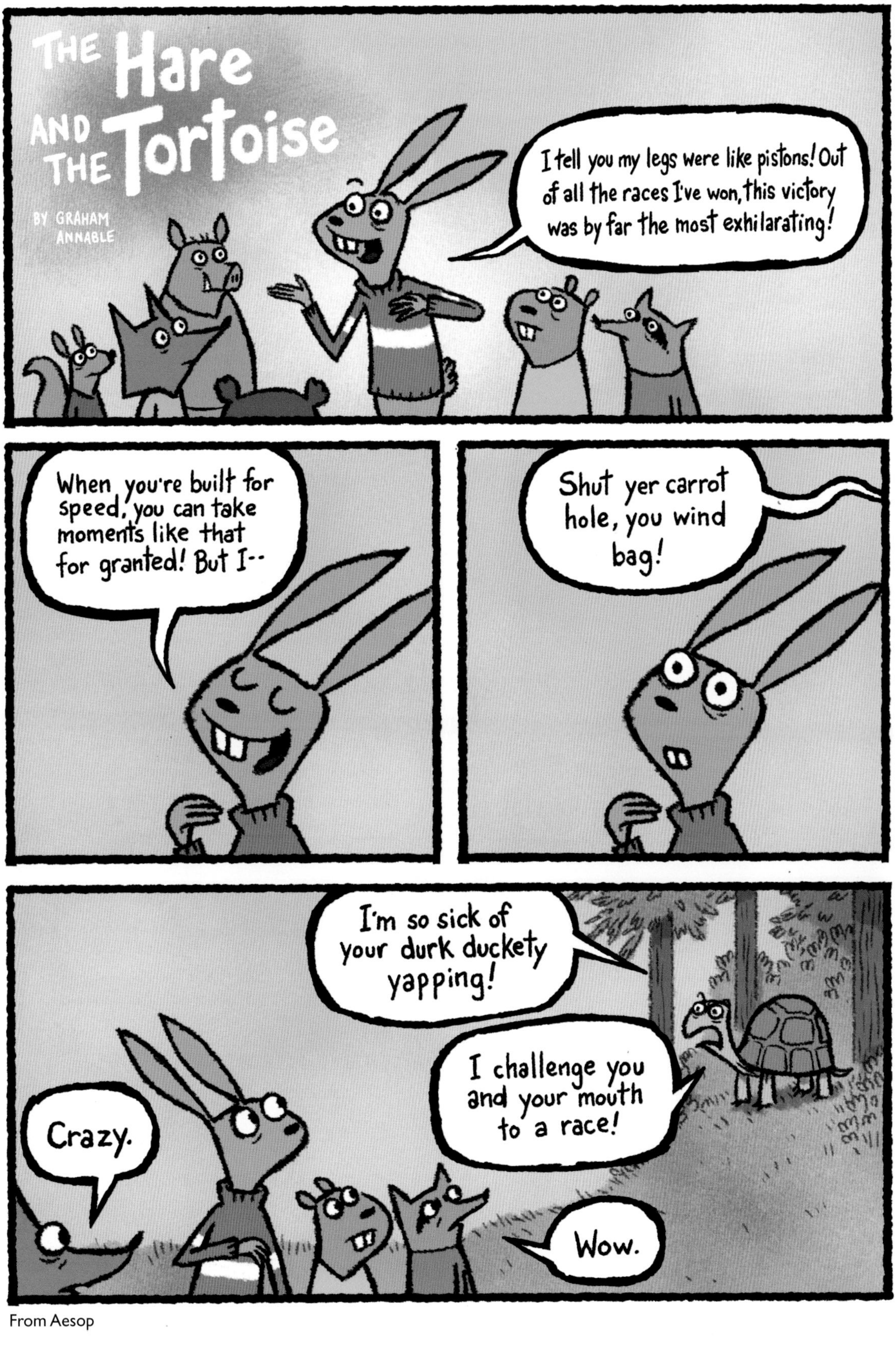
THE Hare AND THE Tortoise
BY GRAHAM ANNABLE
I tell you my legs were like pistons! Out of all the races I've won, this victory was by far the most exhilarating!
When you're built for speed, you can take moments like that for granted! But I--
Shut yer carrot hole, you wind bag!
I'm so sick of your durk duckety yapping!
I challenge you and your mouth to a race!
Crazy.
Wow.

From Aesop

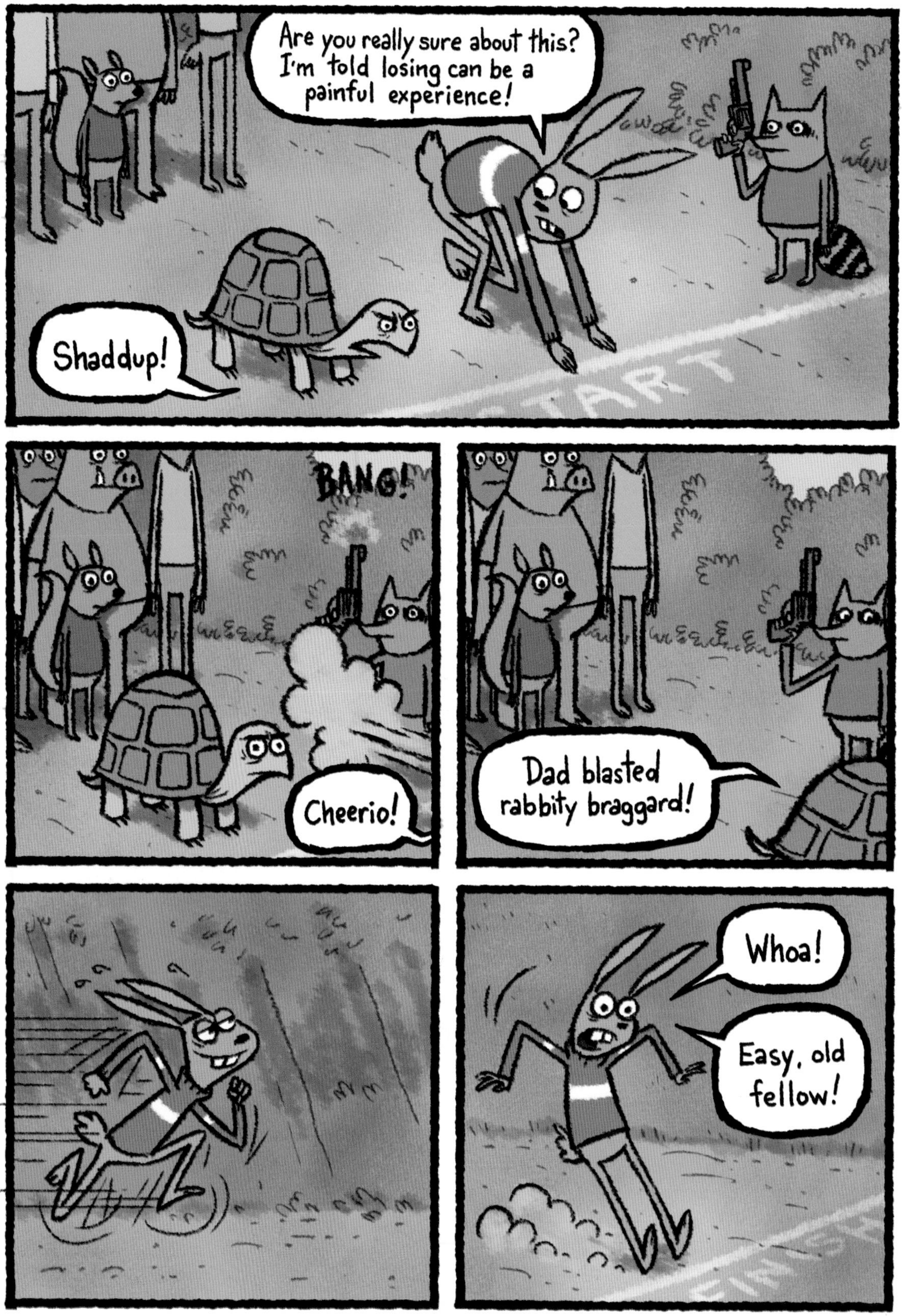
Are you really sure about this? I'm told losing can be a painful experience!
Shaddup!
BANG!
Cheerio!
Dad blasted rabbity braggard!
Whoa!
Easy, old fellow!
START
FINISH

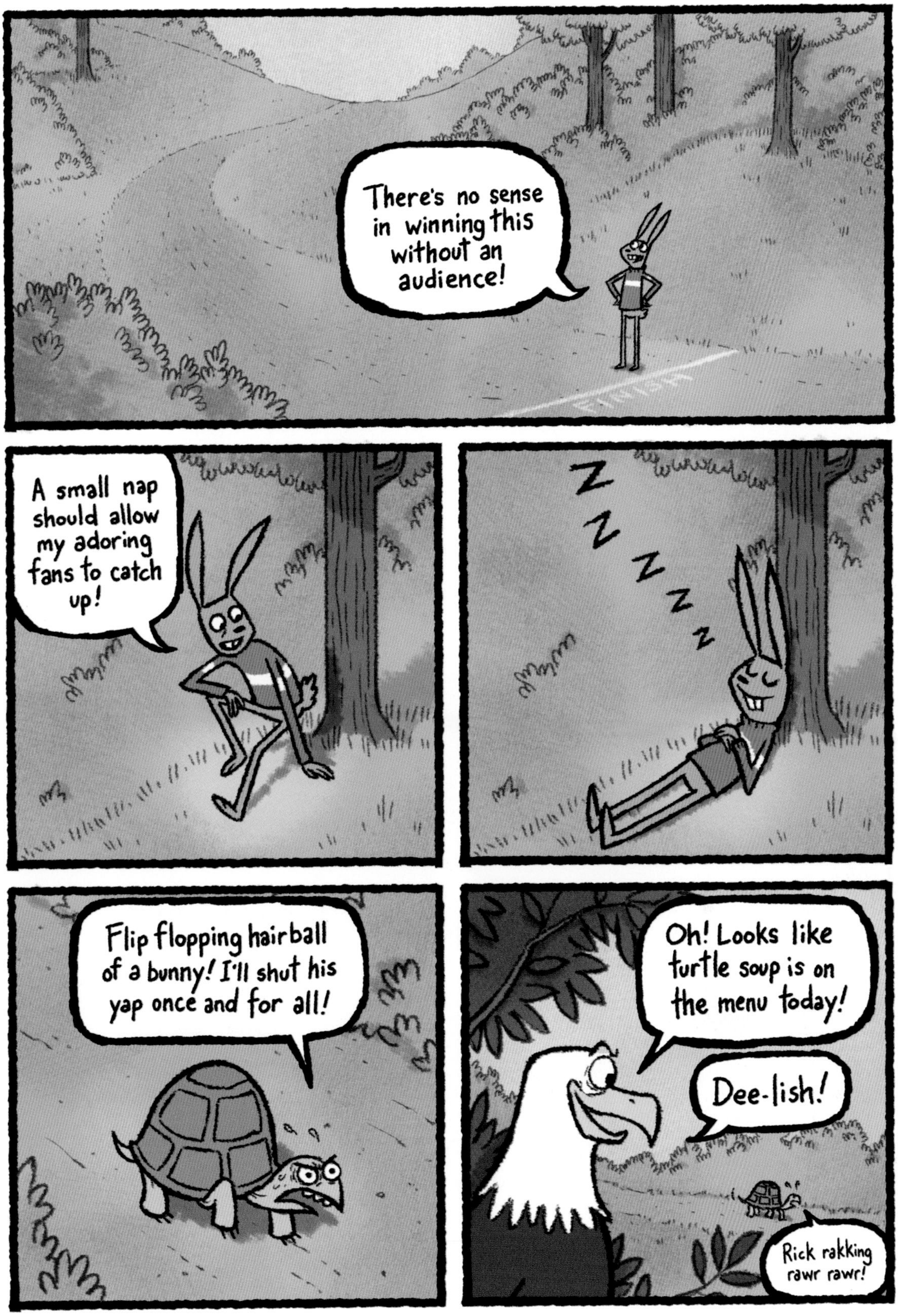
There's no sense in winning this without an audience!
A small nap should allow my adoring fans to catch up!
Z Z Z Z Z Z
Flip flopping hairball of a bunny! I'll shut his yap once and for all!
Oh! Looks like turtle soup is on the menu today!
Dee-lish!
Rick rakking rawr rawr!

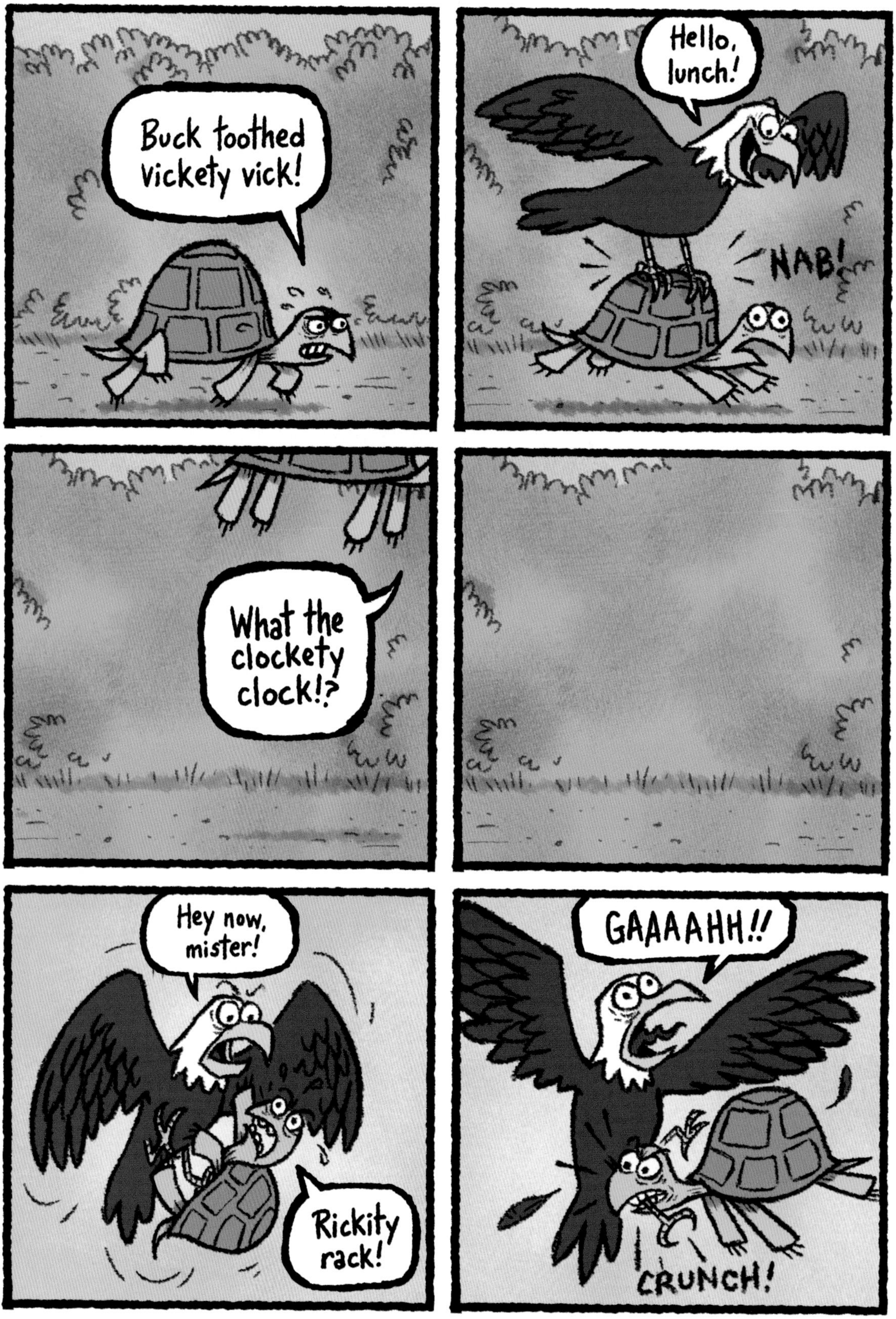
Buck toothed vickety vick!
Hello, lunch!
NAB!
What the clockety clock!?
Hey now, mister!
Rickity rack!
GAAAAHH!!
CRUNCH!

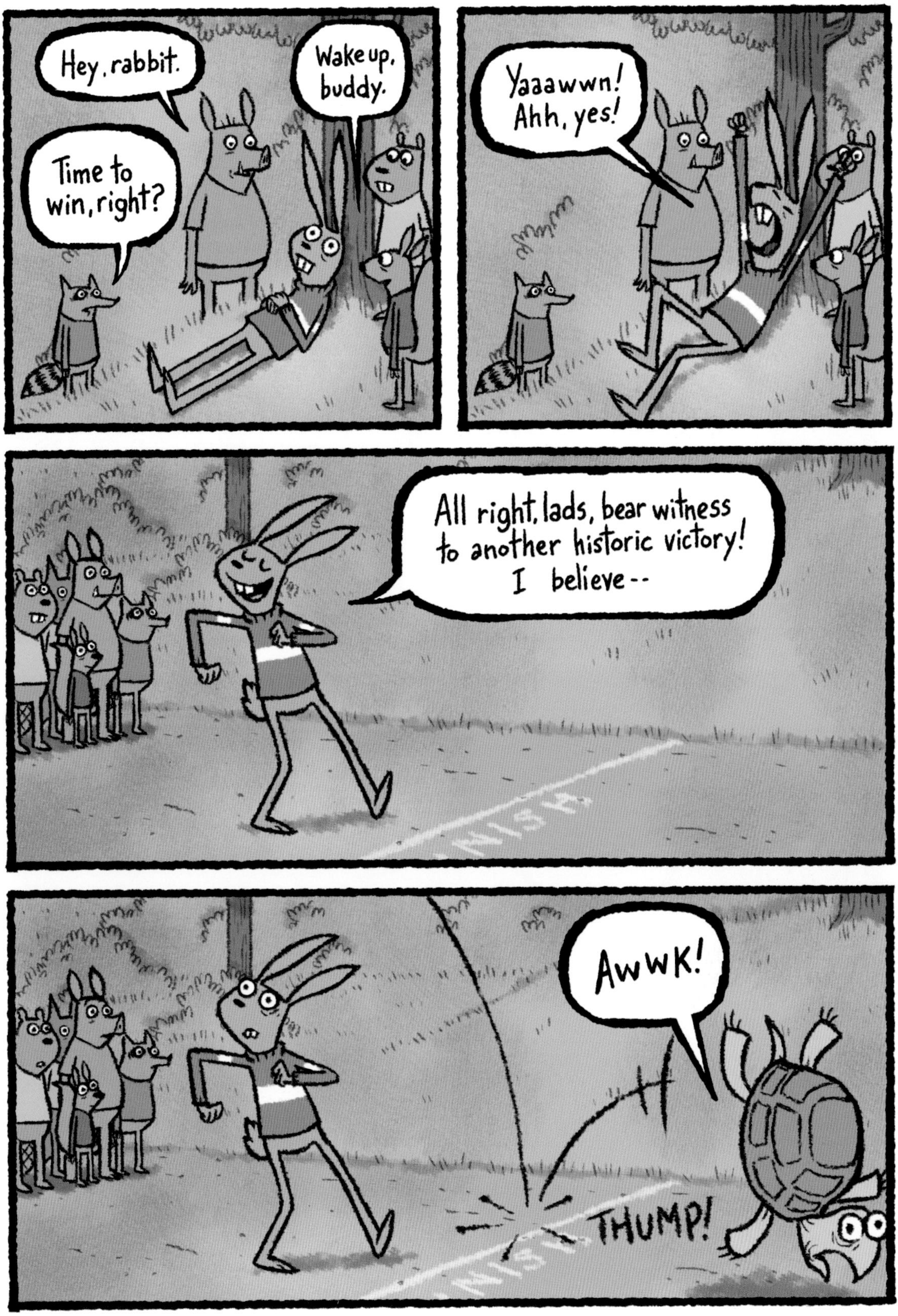
Hey, rabbit.
Time to win, right?
Wake up, buddy.
Yaaawwn! Ahh, yes!
All right, lads, bear witness to another historic victory! I believe--
AWWK!
THUMP!

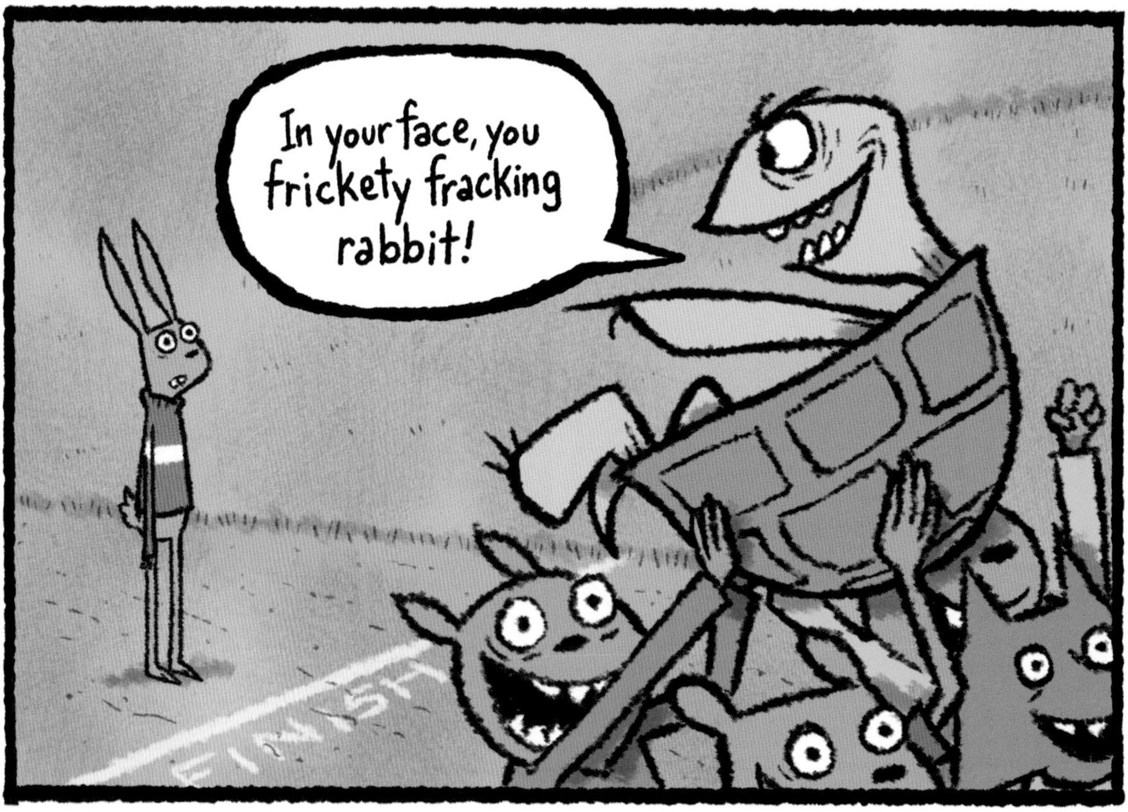
In your face, you frickety fracking rabbit!
FINISH

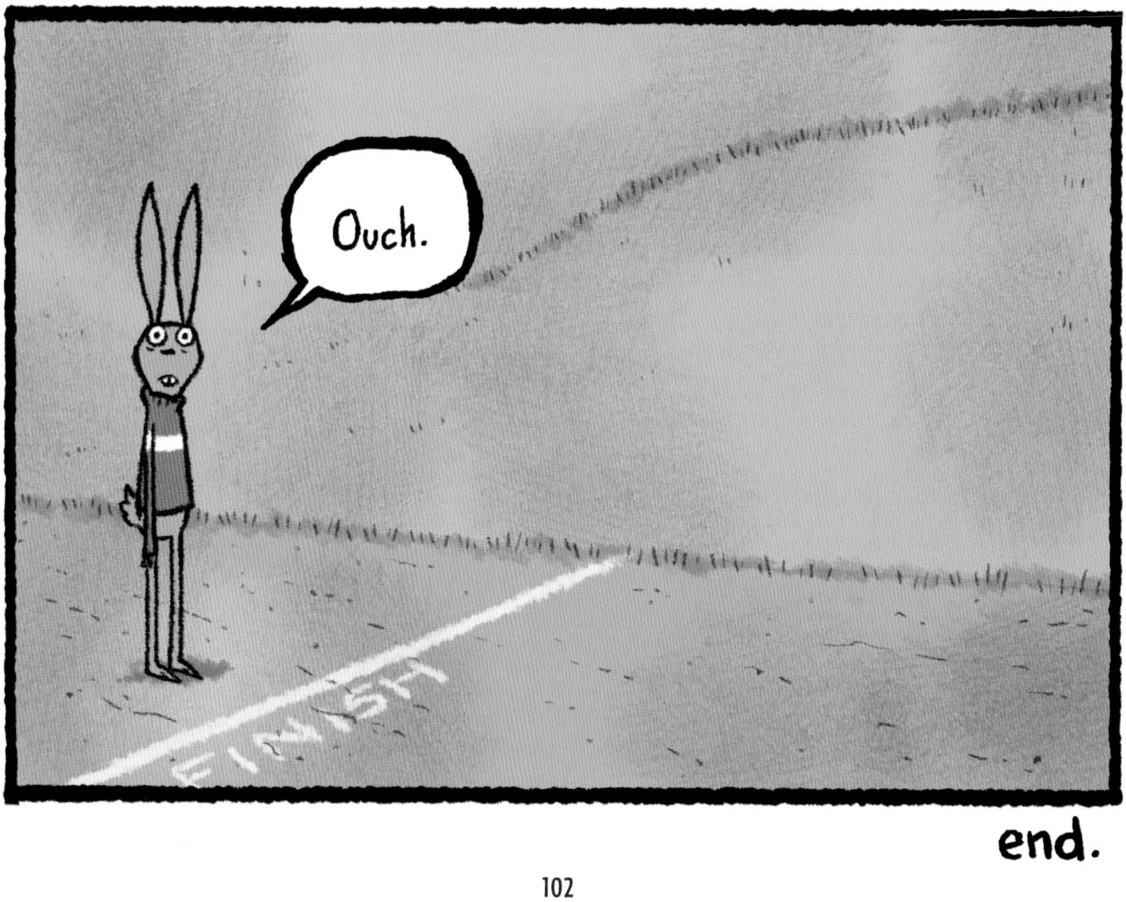
Ouch.
FINISH

end.

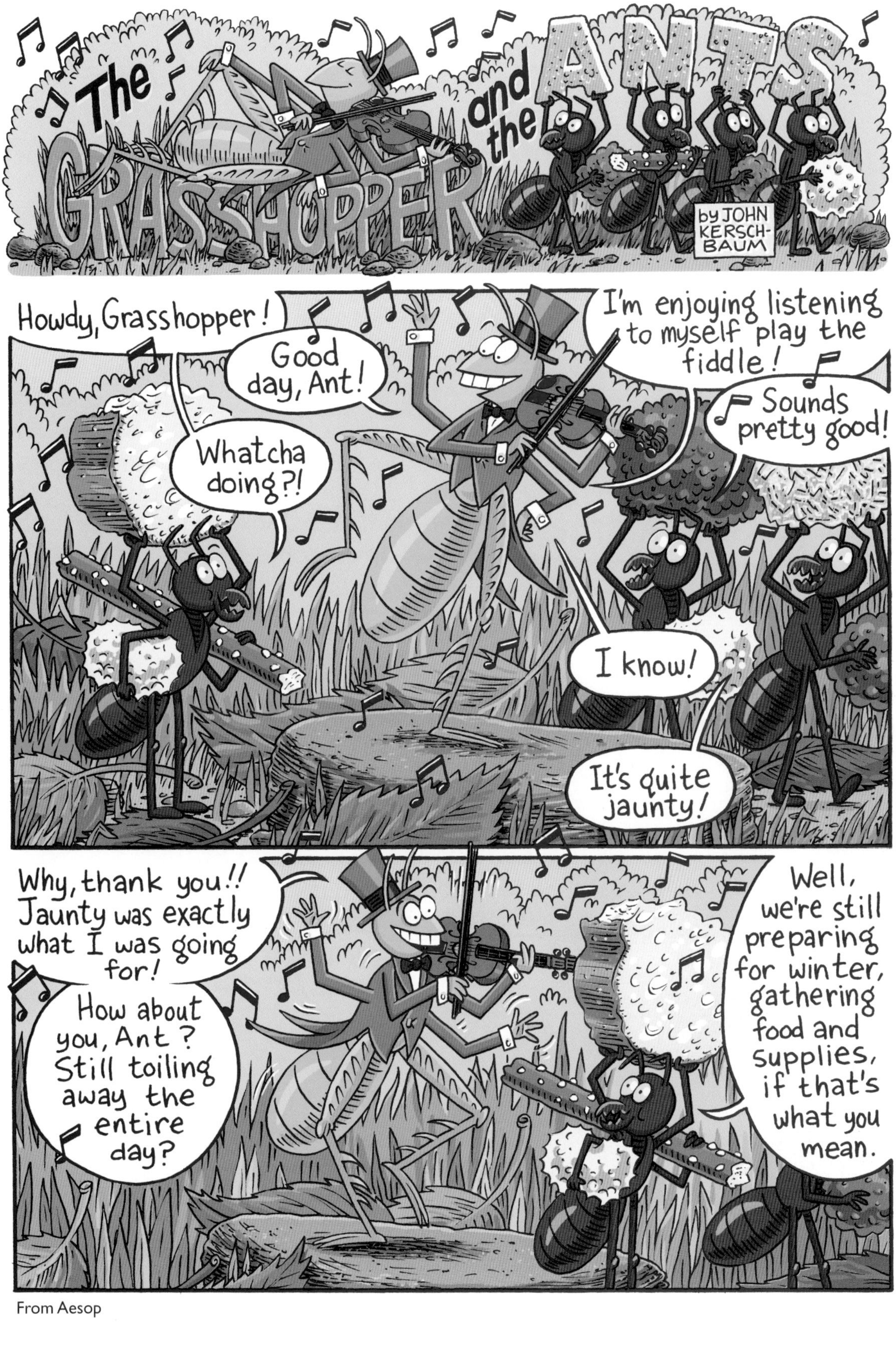
The GRASSHOPPER and the ANTS
by JOHN KERSCHBAUM
Howdy, Grasshopper!
Good day, Ant!
Whatcha doing?!
I'm enjoying listening to myself play the fiddle!
Sounds pretty good!
I know!
It's quite jaunty!
Why, thank you!! Jaunty was exactly what I was going for!
How about you, Ant? Still toiling away the entire day?
Well, we're still preparing for winter, gathering food and supplies, if that's what you mean.

From Aesop

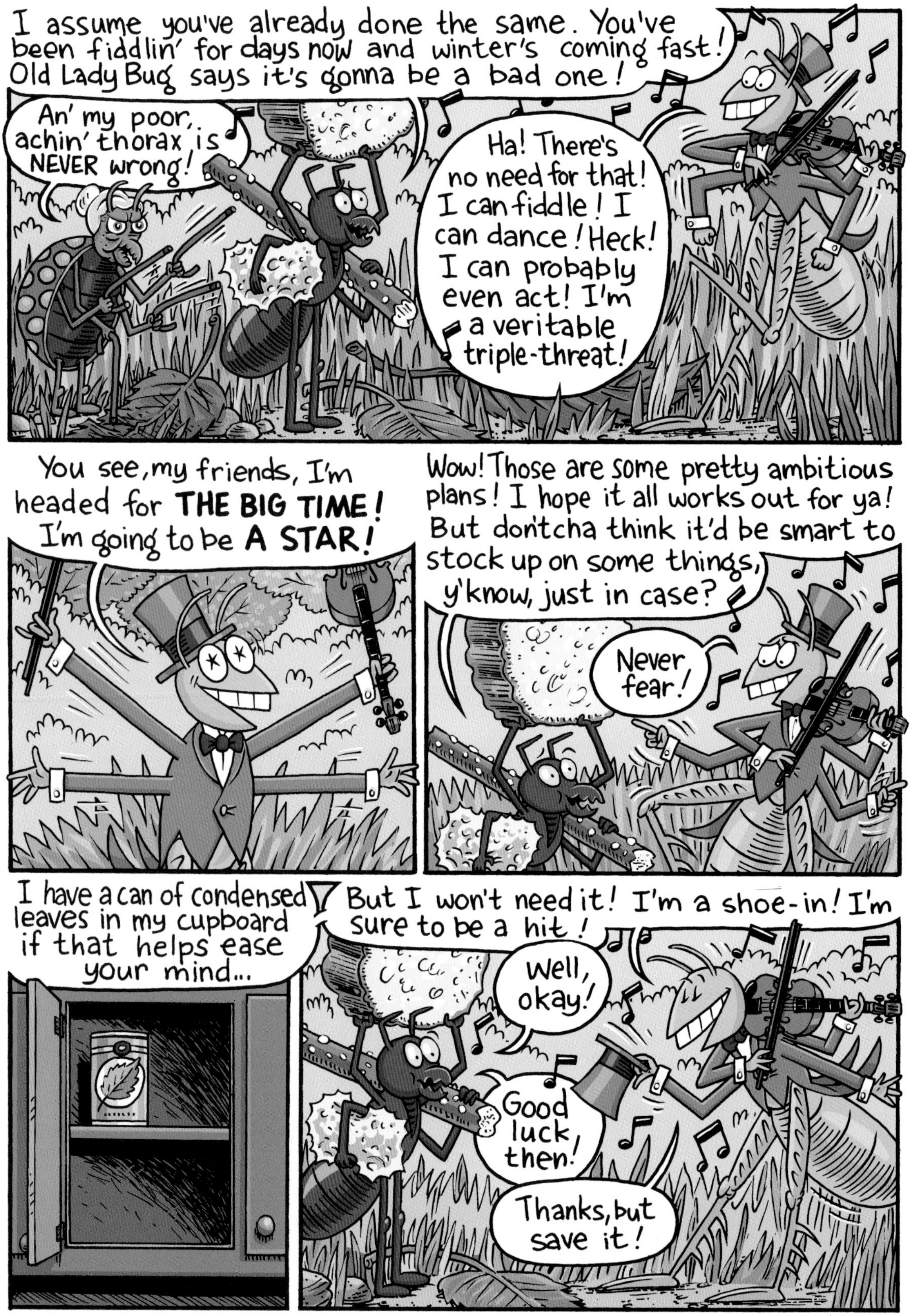

I assume you've already done the same. You've been fiddlin' for days now and winter's coming fast! Old Lady Bug says it's gonna be a bad one!
An' my poor, achin' thorax is NEVER wrong!
Ha! There's no need for that! I can fiddle! I can dance! Heck! I can probably even act! I'm a veritable triple-threat!
You see, my friends, I'm headed for THE BIG TIME! I'm going to be A STAR!
Wow! Those are some pretty ambitious plans! I hope it all works out for ya! But don'tcha think it'd be smart to stock up on some things, y'know, just in case?
Never fear!
I have a can of condensed leaves in my cupboard if that helps ease your mind...
But I won't need it! I'm a shoe-in! I'm sure to be a hit!
Well, okay!
Good luck, then!
Thanks, but save it!

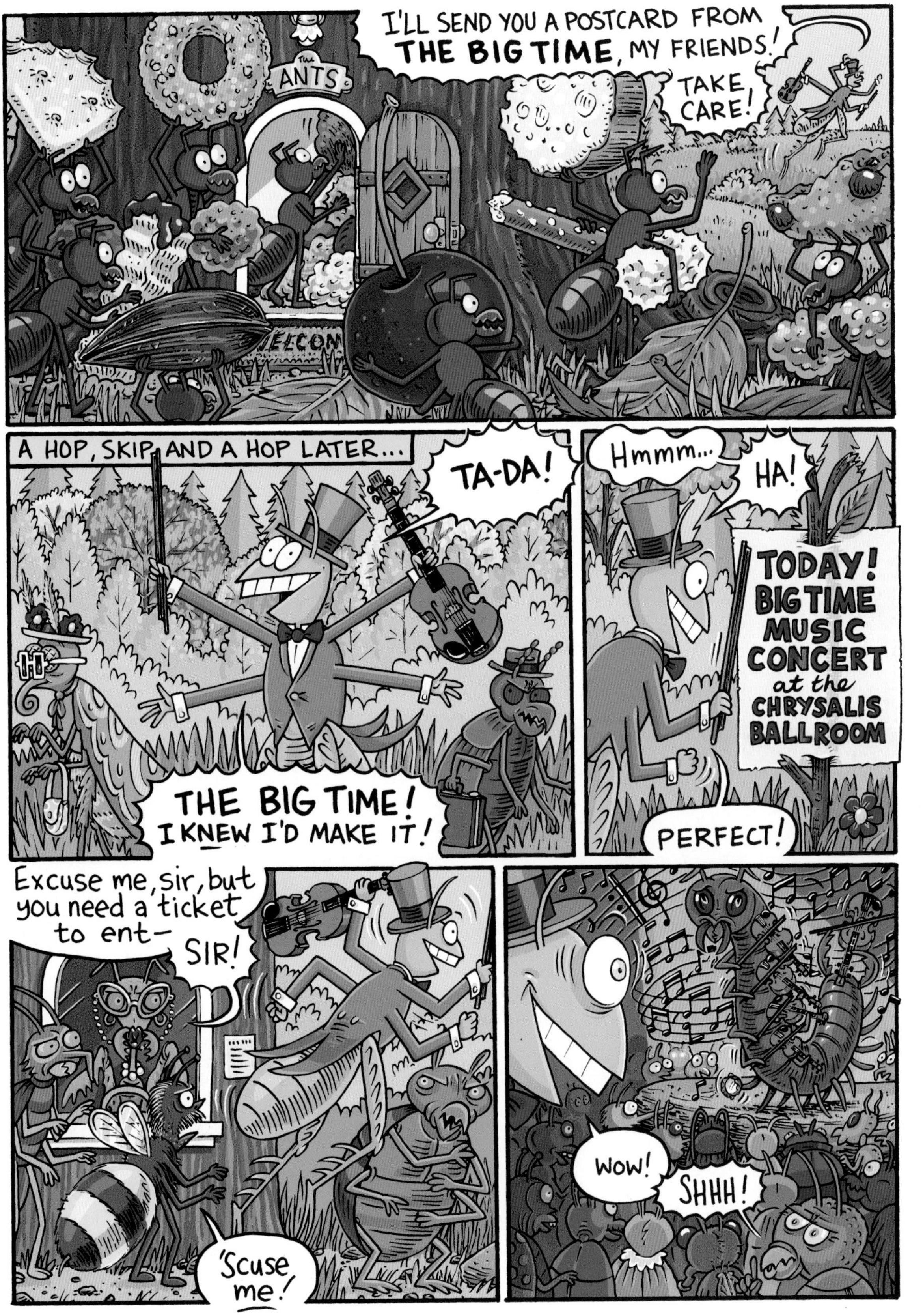
THE ANTS
I'LL SEND YOU A POSTCARD FROM THE BIG TIME, MY FRIENDS!
TAKE CARE!
WELCOM
A HOP, SKIP, AND A HOP LATER...
TA-DA!
THE BIG TIME! I KNEW I'D MAKE IT!
Hmmm...
HA!
TODAY! BIG TIME MUSIC CONCERT at the CHRYSALIS BALLROOM
PERFECT!
Excuse me, sir, but you need a ticket to ent—
SIR!
'Scuse me!
WOW!
SHHH!

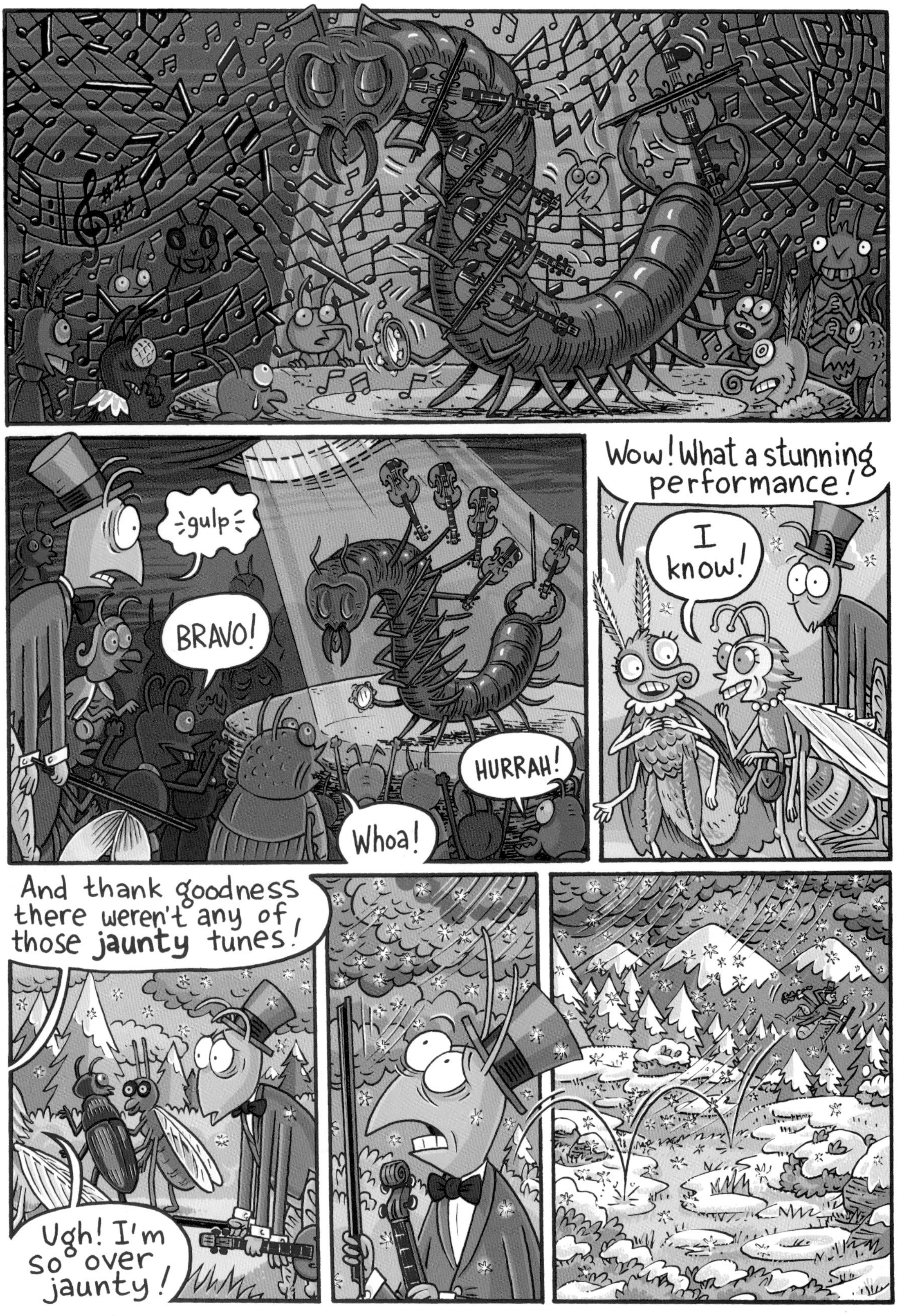

gulp
BRAVO!
HURRAH!
Whoa!
Wow! What a stunning performance!
I know!
And thank goodness there weren't any of those **jaunty** tunes!
Ugh! I'm so over jaunty!

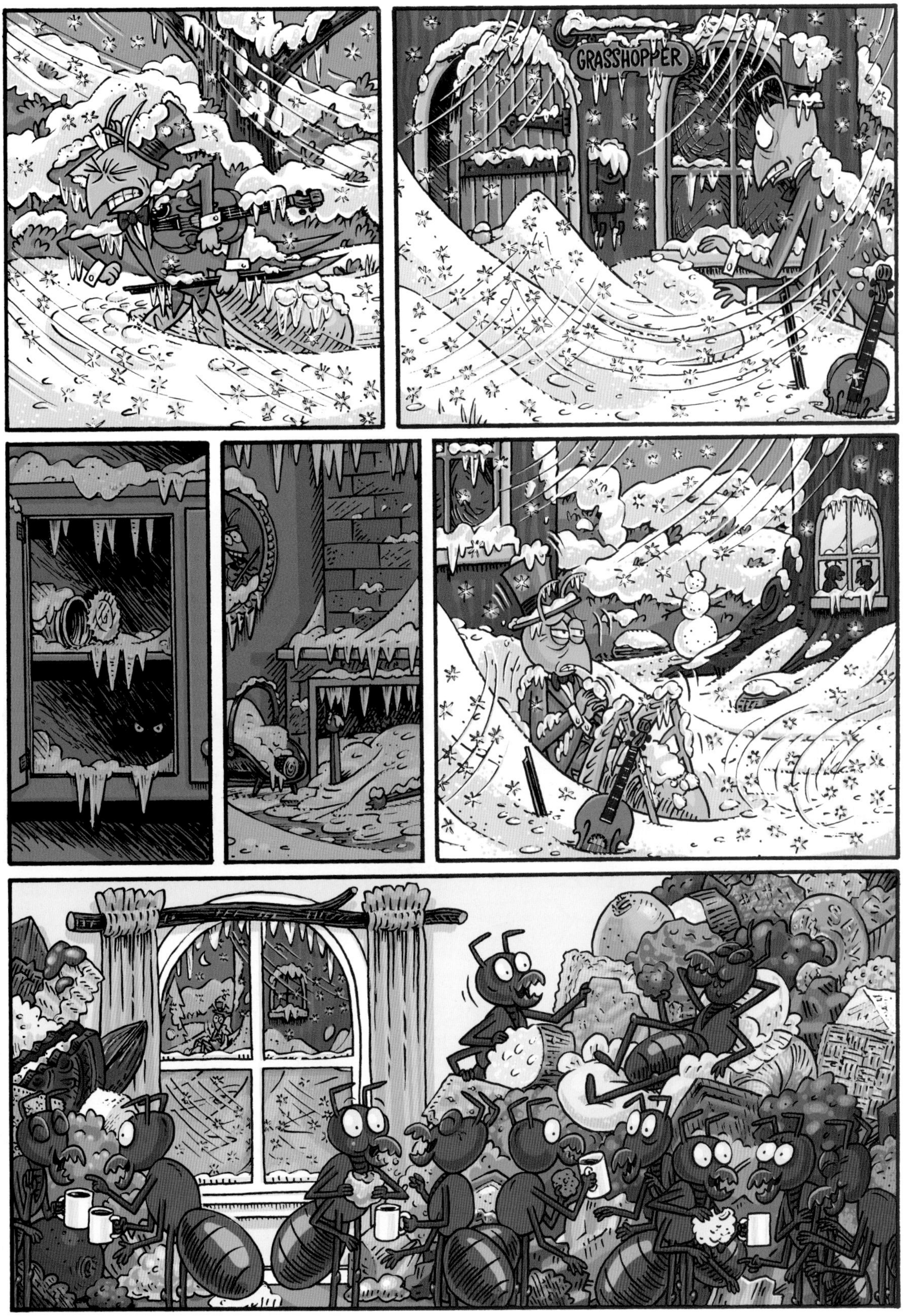
GRASSHOPPER

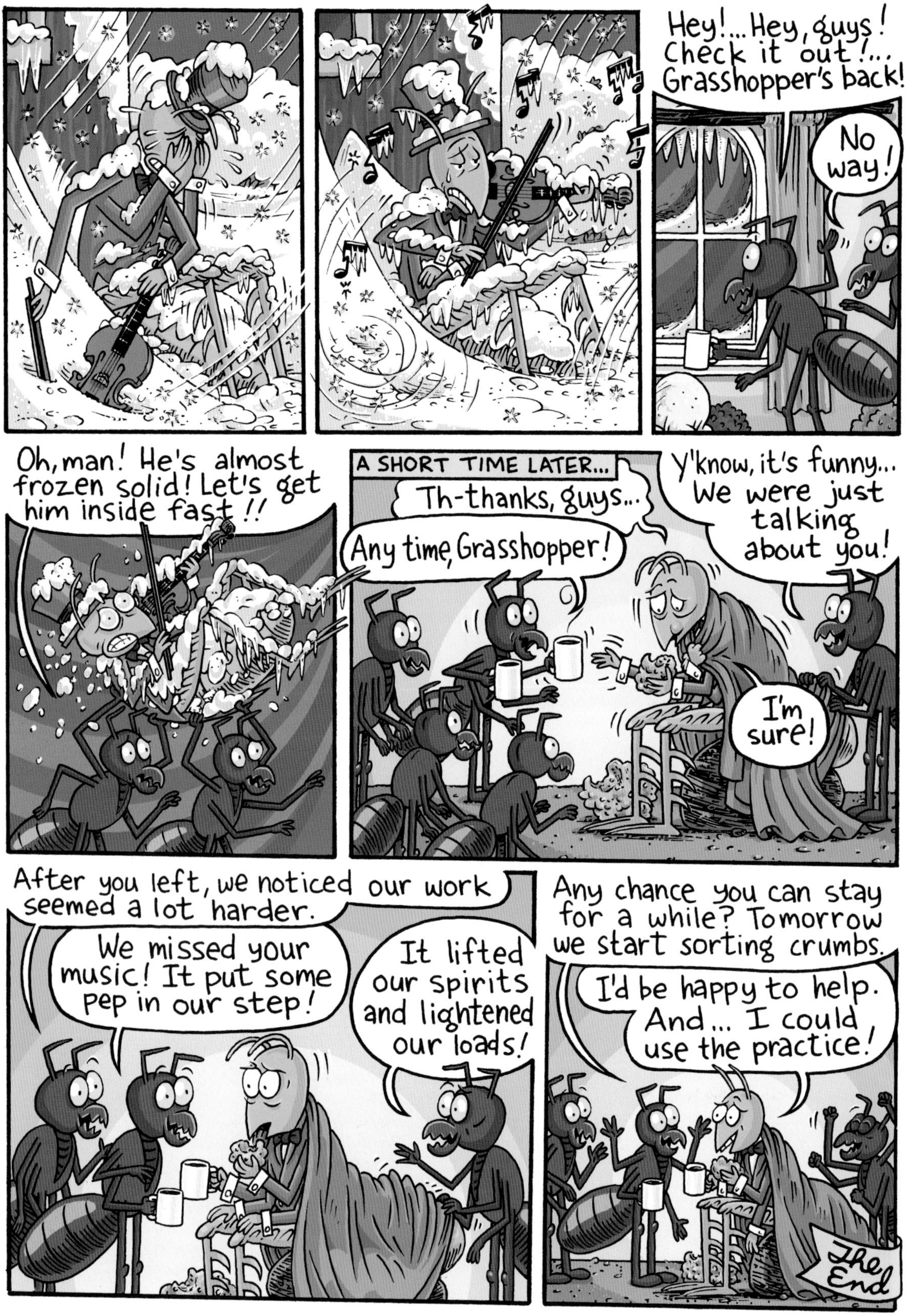
Hey!... Hey, guys! Check it out!... Grasshopper's back!
No way!
Oh, man! He's almost frozen solid! Let's get him inside fast!!
A SHORT TIME LATER...
Th-thanks, guys...
Any time, Grasshopper!
Y'know, it's funny... We were just talking about you!
I'm sure!
After you left, we noticed our work seemed a lot harder.
We missed your music! It put some pep in our step!
It lifted our spirits and lightened our loads!
Any chance you can stay for a while? Tomorrow we start sorting crumbs.
I'd be happy to help. And... I could use the practice!
The End

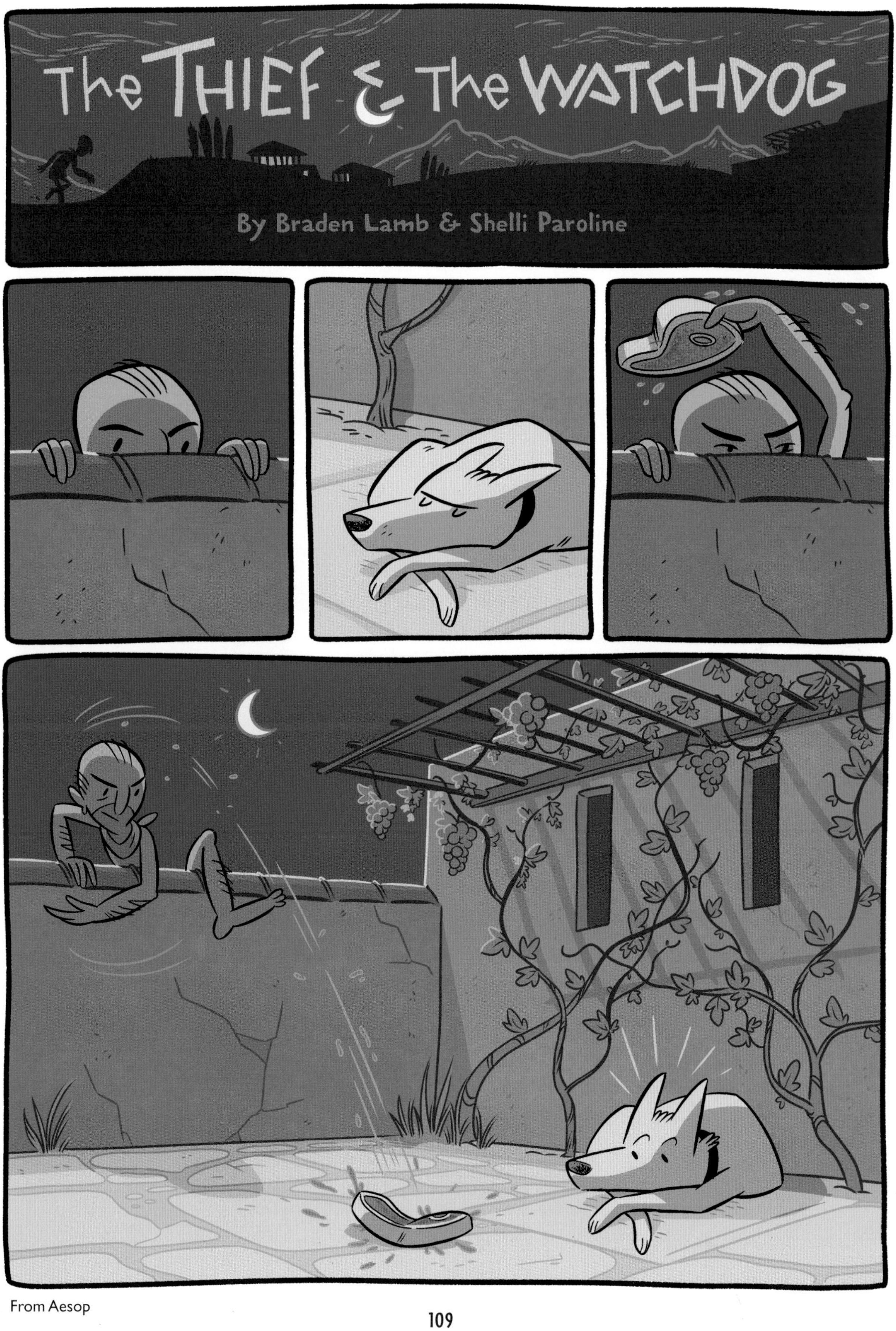
The THIEF & The WATCHDOG
By Braden Lamb & Shelli Paroline

From Aesop

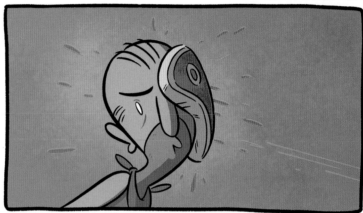

No, this will not do, for several reasons.

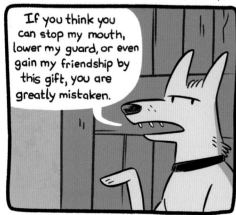

If you think you can stop my mouth, lower my guard, or even gain my friendship by this gift, you are greatly mistaken.

Your sudden kindness will only make me more watchful, in case you have some secret plans that would benefit you and injure my master.

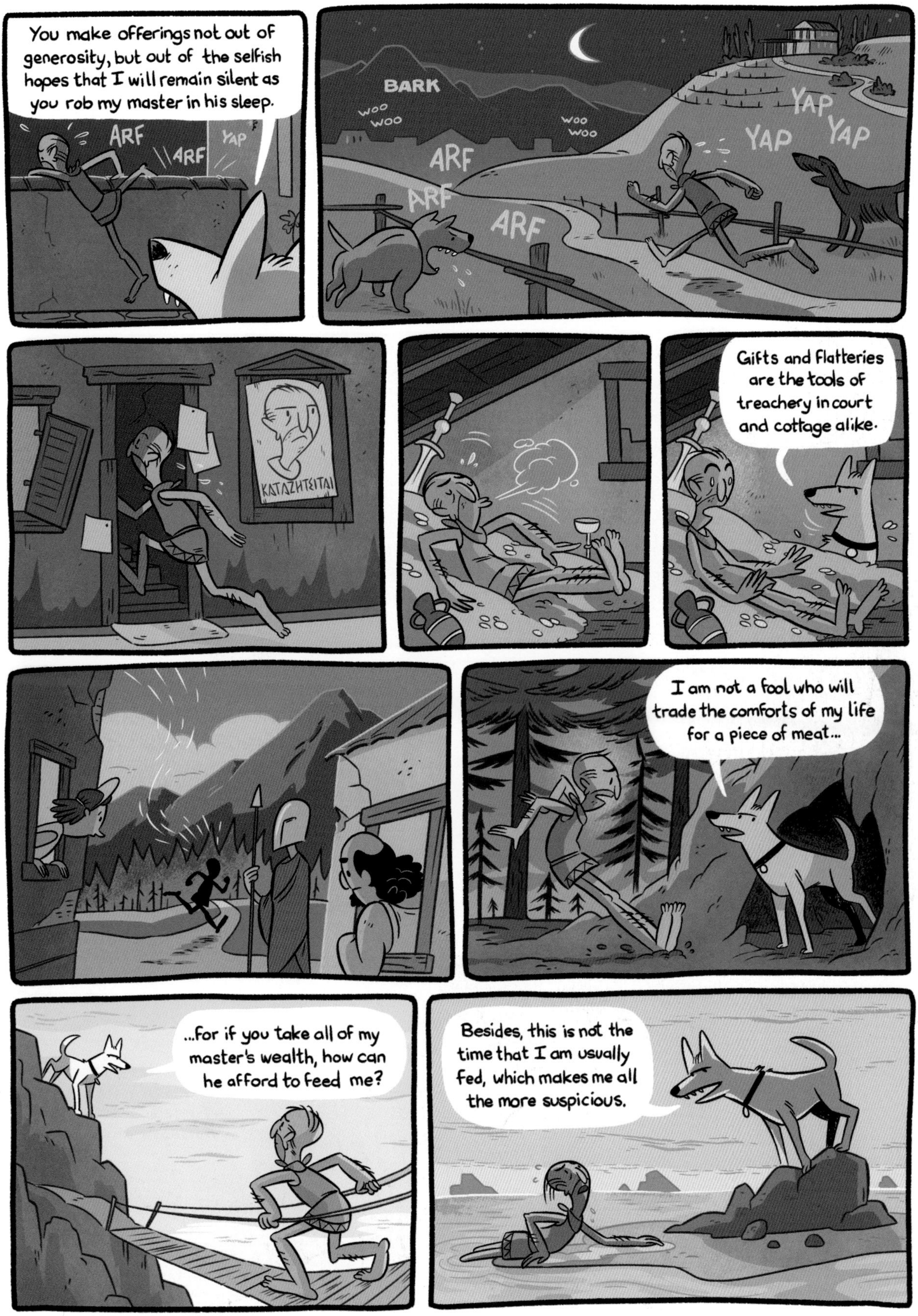

You make offerings not out of generosity, but out of the selfish hopes that I will remain silent as you rob my master in his sleep.
ARF
ARF
YAP
BARK
WOO WOO
WOO WOO
ARF
ARF
ARF
YAP
YAP
YAP
ΚΑΤΑΖΗΤΕΙΤΑΙ
Gifts and flatteries are the tools of treachery in court and cottage alike.
I am not a fool who will trade the comforts of my life for a piece of meat...
...for if you take all of my master's wealth, how can he afford to feed me?
Besides, this is not the time that I am usually fed, which makes me all the more suspicious.

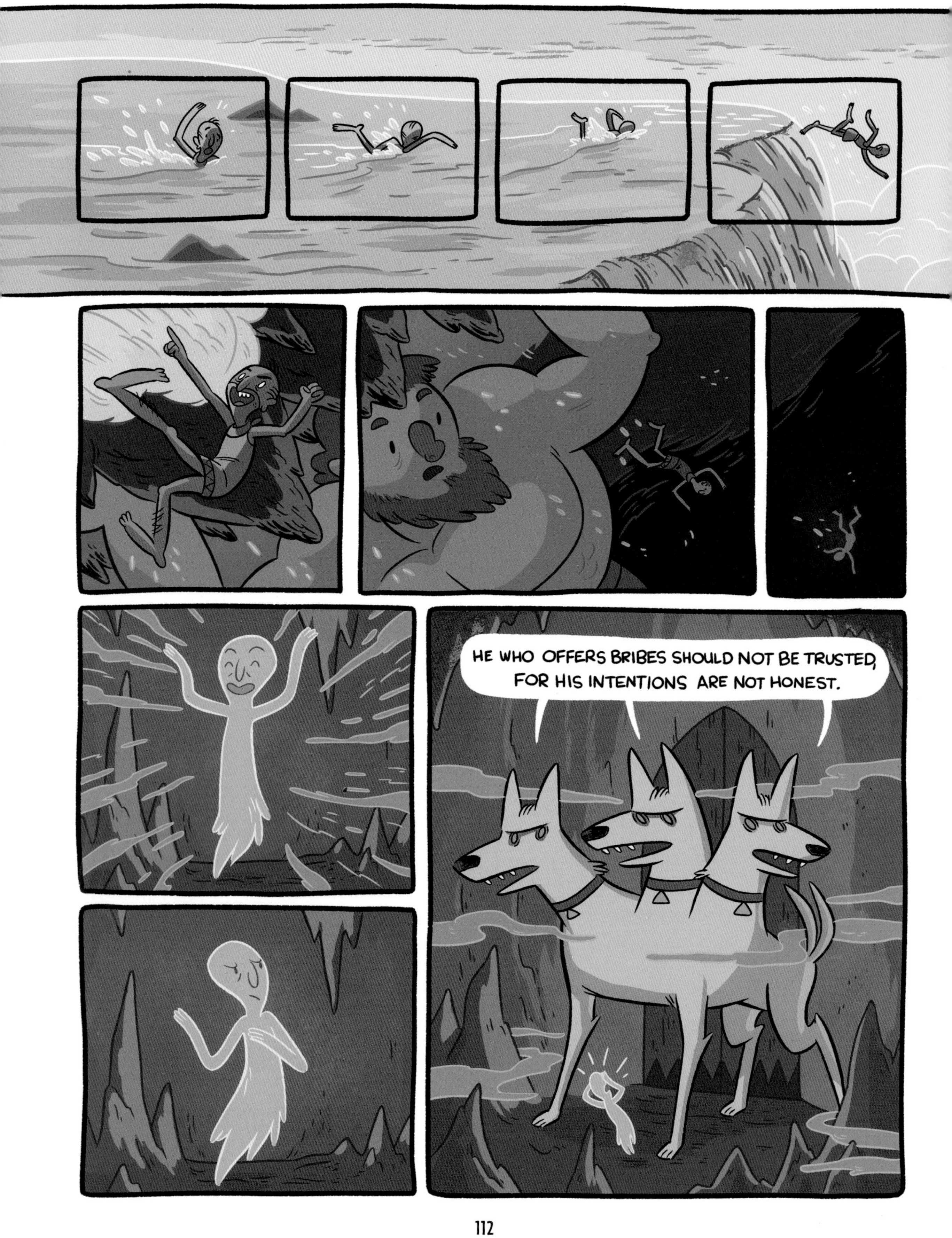
HE WHO OFFERS BRIBES SHOULD NOT BE TRUSTED, FOR HIS INTENTIONS ARE NOT HONEST.

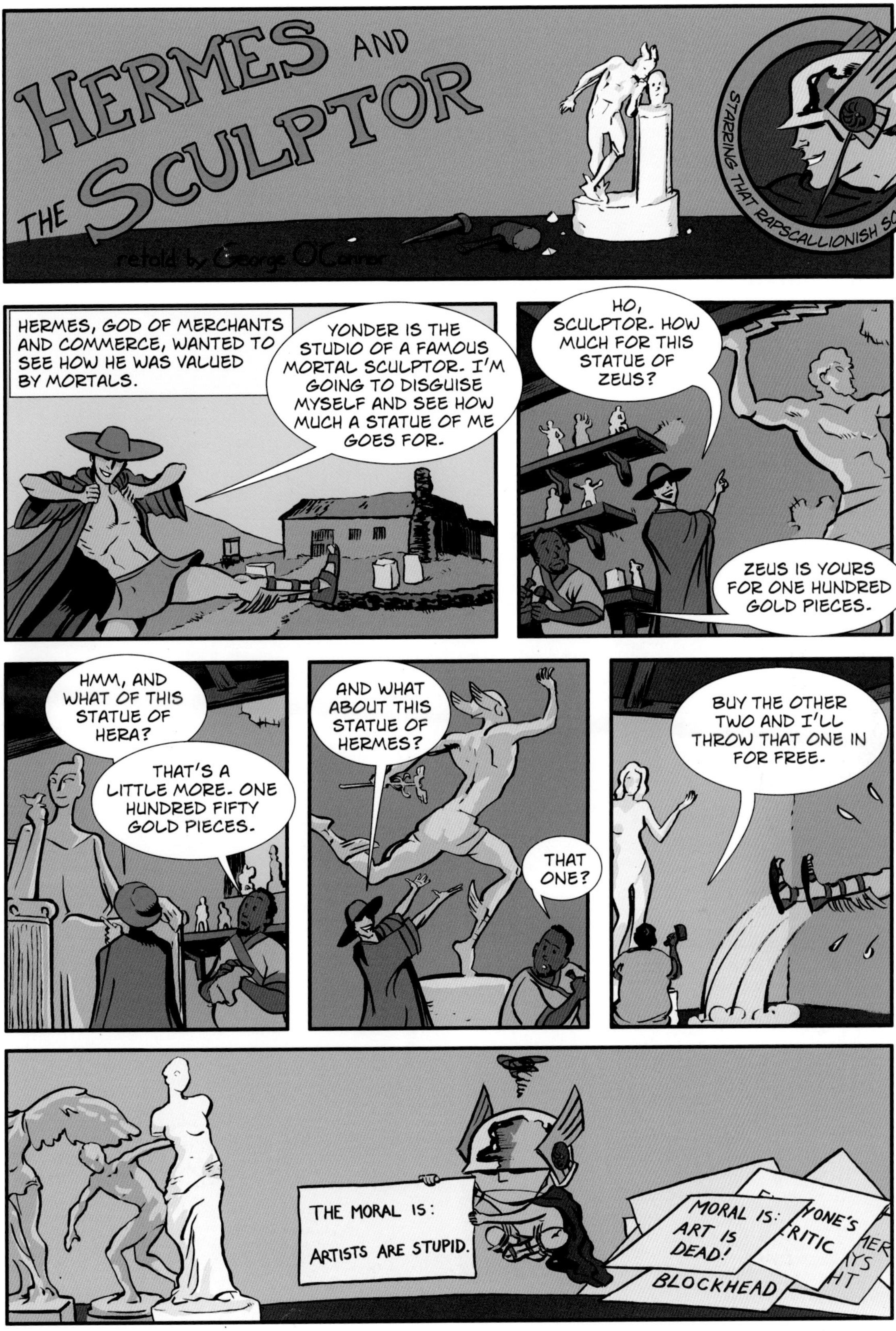
HERMES AND THE SCULPTOR
retold by George O'Connor
STARRING THAT RAPSCALLIONISH SCALAWAG, HERMES
HERMES, GOD OF MERCHANTS AND COMMERCE, WANTED TO SEE HOW HE WAS VALUED BY MORTALS.
YONDER IS THE STUDIO OF A FAMOUS MORTAL SCULPTOR. I'M GOING TO DISGUISE MYSELF AND SEE HOW MUCH A STATUE OF ME GOES FOR.
HO, SCULPTOR. HOW MUCH FOR THIS STATUE OF ZEUS?
ZEUS IS YOURS FOR ONE HUNDRED GOLD PIECES.
HMM, AND WHAT OF THIS STATUE OF HERA?
THAT'S A LITTLE MORE. ONE HUNDRED FIFTY GOLD PIECES.
AND WHAT ABOUT THIS STATUE OF HERMES?
THAT ONE?
BUY THE OTHER TWO AND I'LL THROW THAT ONE IN FOR FREE.
THE MORAL IS:
ARTISTS ARE STUPID.
MORAL IS: ART IS DEAD!
BLOCKHEAD

From Aesop

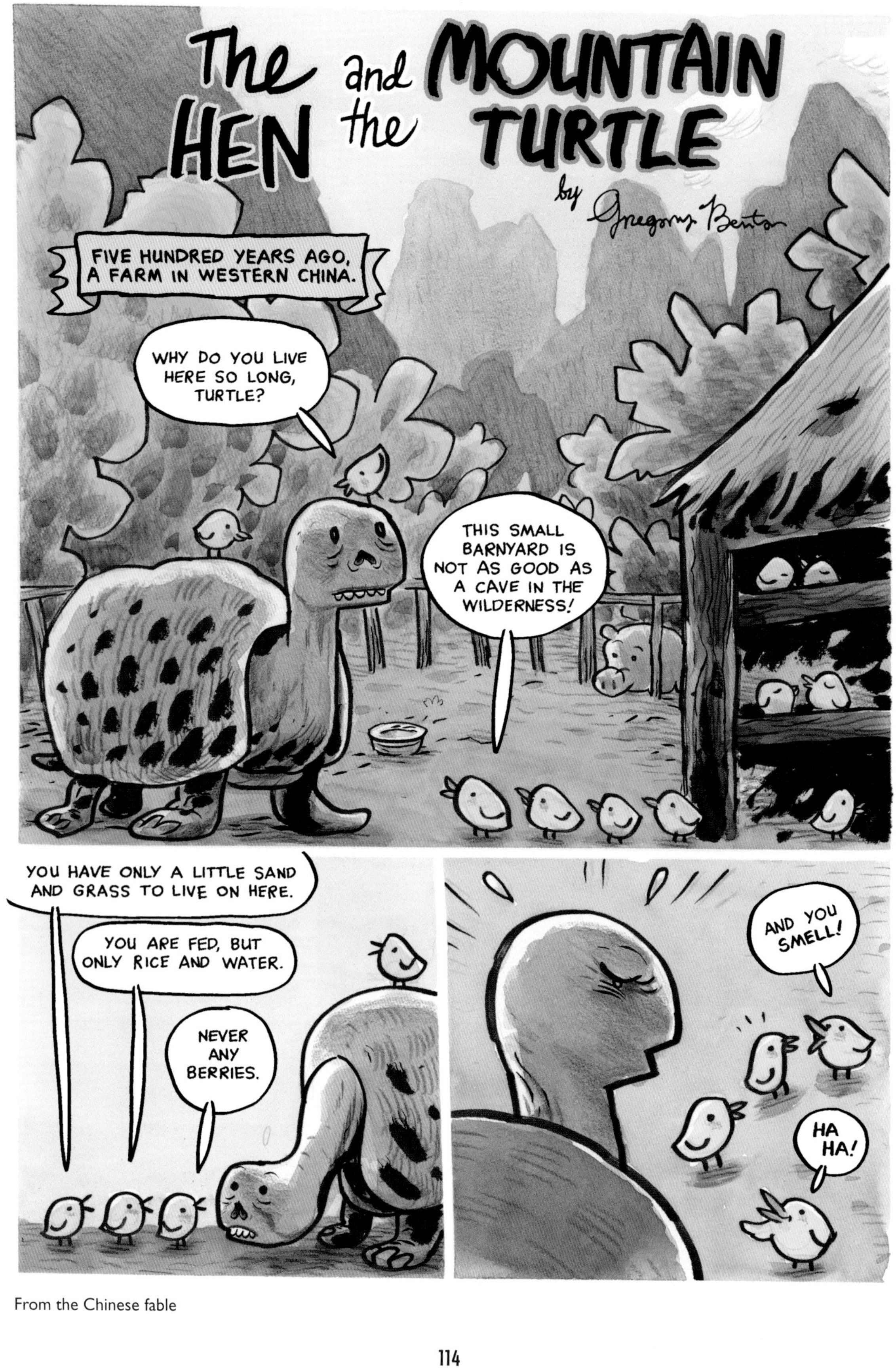
The Hen and the Mountain Turtle
by Gregory Benton
FIVE HUNDRED YEARS AGO, A FARM IN WESTERN CHINA.
WHY DO YOU LIVE HERE SO LONG, TURTLE?
THIS SMALL BARNYARD IS NOT AS GOOD AS A CAVE IN THE WILDERNESS!
YOU HAVE ONLY A LITTLE SAND AND GRASS TO LIVE ON HERE.
YOU ARE FED, BUT ONLY RICE AND WATER.
NEVER ANY BERRIES.
AND YOU SMELL!
HA HA!

From the Chinese fable

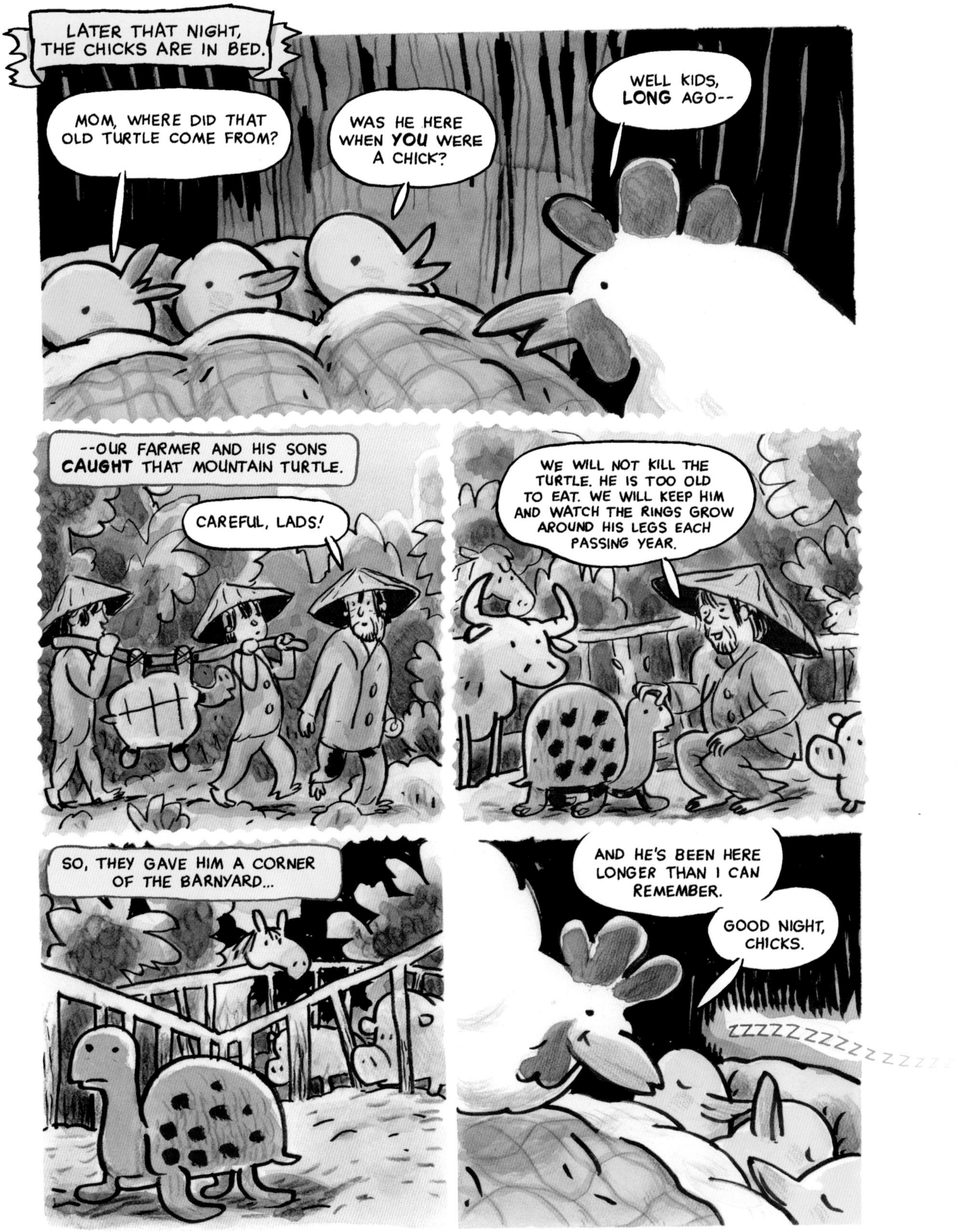
LATER THAT NIGHT, THE CHICKS ARE IN BED.
MOM, WHERE DID THAT OLD TURTLE COME FROM?
WAS HE HERE WHEN YOU WERE A CHICK?
WELL KIDS, LONG AGO--
--OUR FARMER AND HIS SONS CAUGHT THAT MOUNTAIN TURTLE.
CAREFUL, LADS!
WE WILL NOT KILL THE TURTLE. HE IS TOO OLD TO EAT. WE WILL KEEP HIM AND WATCH THE RINGS GROW AROUND HIS LEGS EACH PASSING YEAR.
SO, THEY GAVE HIM A CORNER OF THE BARNYARD...
AND HE'S BEEN HERE LONGER THAN I CAN REMEMBER.
GOOD NIGHT, CHICKS.
ZZZZZZZZZZZZZZZZZ

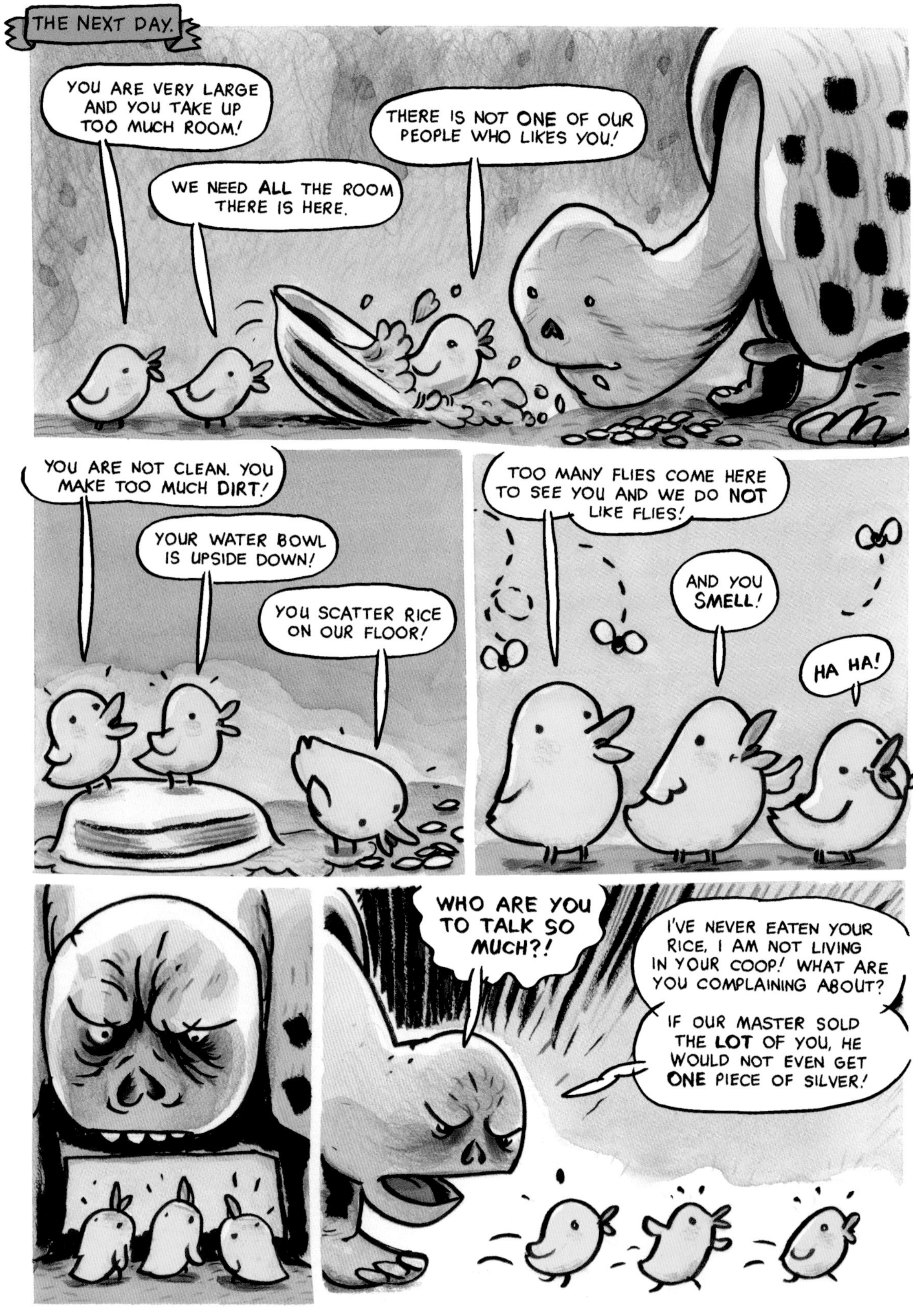
THE NEXT DAY.
YOU ARE VERY LARGE AND YOU TAKE UP TOO MUCH ROOM!
WE NEED ALL THE ROOM THERE IS HERE.
THERE IS NOT ONE OF OUR PEOPLE WHO LIKES YOU!
YOU ARE NOT CLEAN. YOU MAKE TOO MUCH DIRT!
YOUR WATER BOWL IS UPSIDE DOWN!
YOU SCATTER RICE ON OUR FLOOR!
TOO MANY FLIES COME HERE TO SEE YOU AND WE DO NOT LIKE FLIES!
AND YOU SMELL!
HA HA!
WHO ARE YOU TO TALK SO MUCH?!
I'VE NEVER EATEN YOUR RICE, I AM NOT LIVING IN YOUR COOP! WHAT ARE YOU COMPLAINING ABOUT?
IF OUR MASTER SOLD THE LOT OF YOU, HE WOULD NOT EVEN GET ONE PIECE OF SILVER!

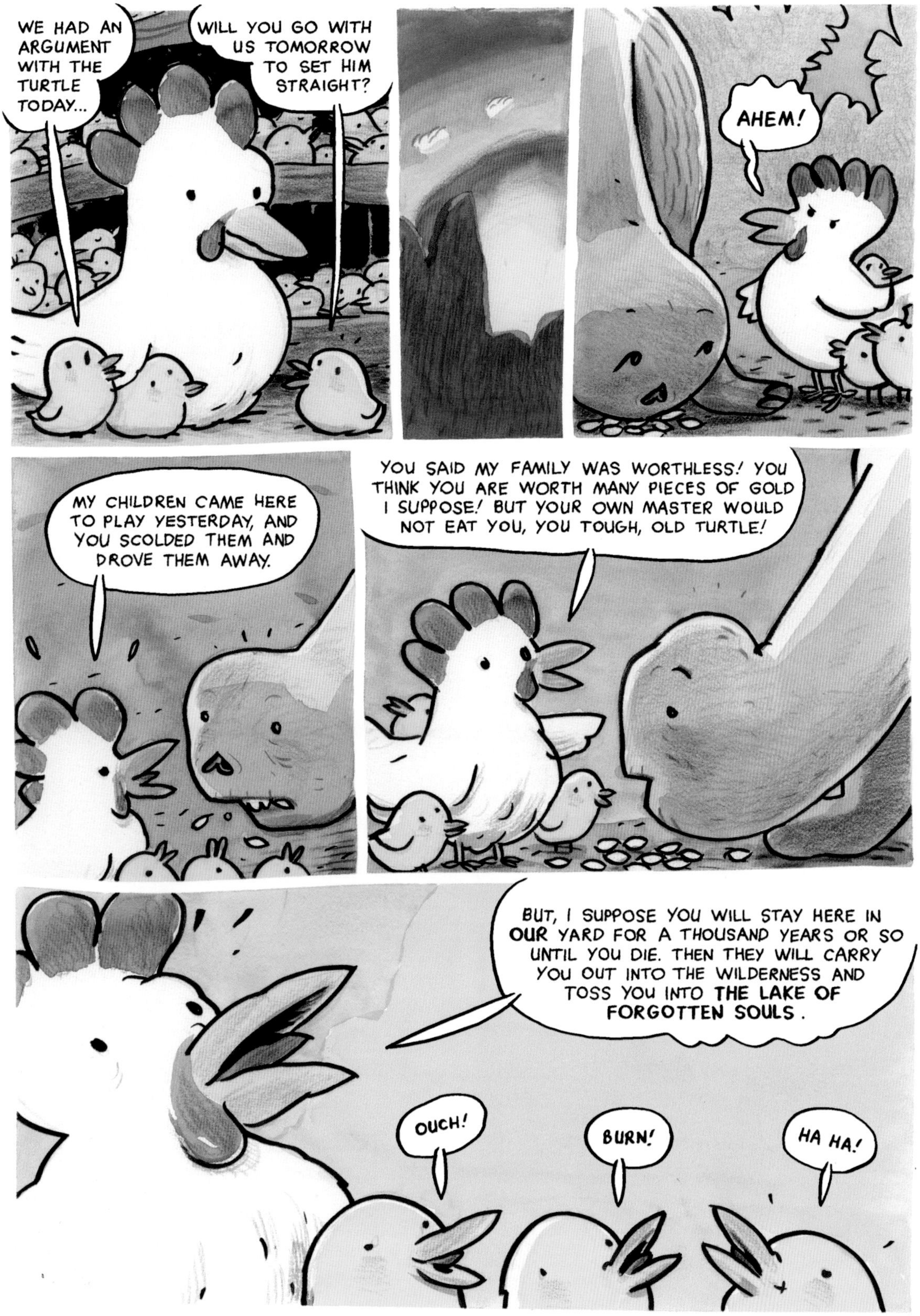
WE HAD AN ARGUMENT WITH THE TURTLE TODAY...
WILL YOU GO WITH US TOMORROW TO SET HIM STRAIGHT?
AHEM!
MY CHILDREN CAME HERE TO PLAY YESTERDAY, AND YOU SCOLDED THEM AND DROVE THEM AWAY.
YOU SAID MY FAMILY WAS WORTHLESS! YOU THINK YOU ARE WORTH MANY PIECES OF GOLD I SUPPOSE! BUT YOUR OWN MASTER WOULD NOT EAT YOU, YOU TOUGH, OLD TURTLE!
BUT, I SUPPOSE YOU WILL STAY HERE IN **OUR** YARD FOR A THOUSAND YEARS OR SO UNTIL YOU DIE. THEN THEY WILL CARRY YOU OUT INTO THE WILDERNESS AND TOSS YOU INTO **THE LAKE OF FORGOTTEN SOULS**.
OUCH!
BURN!
HA HA!

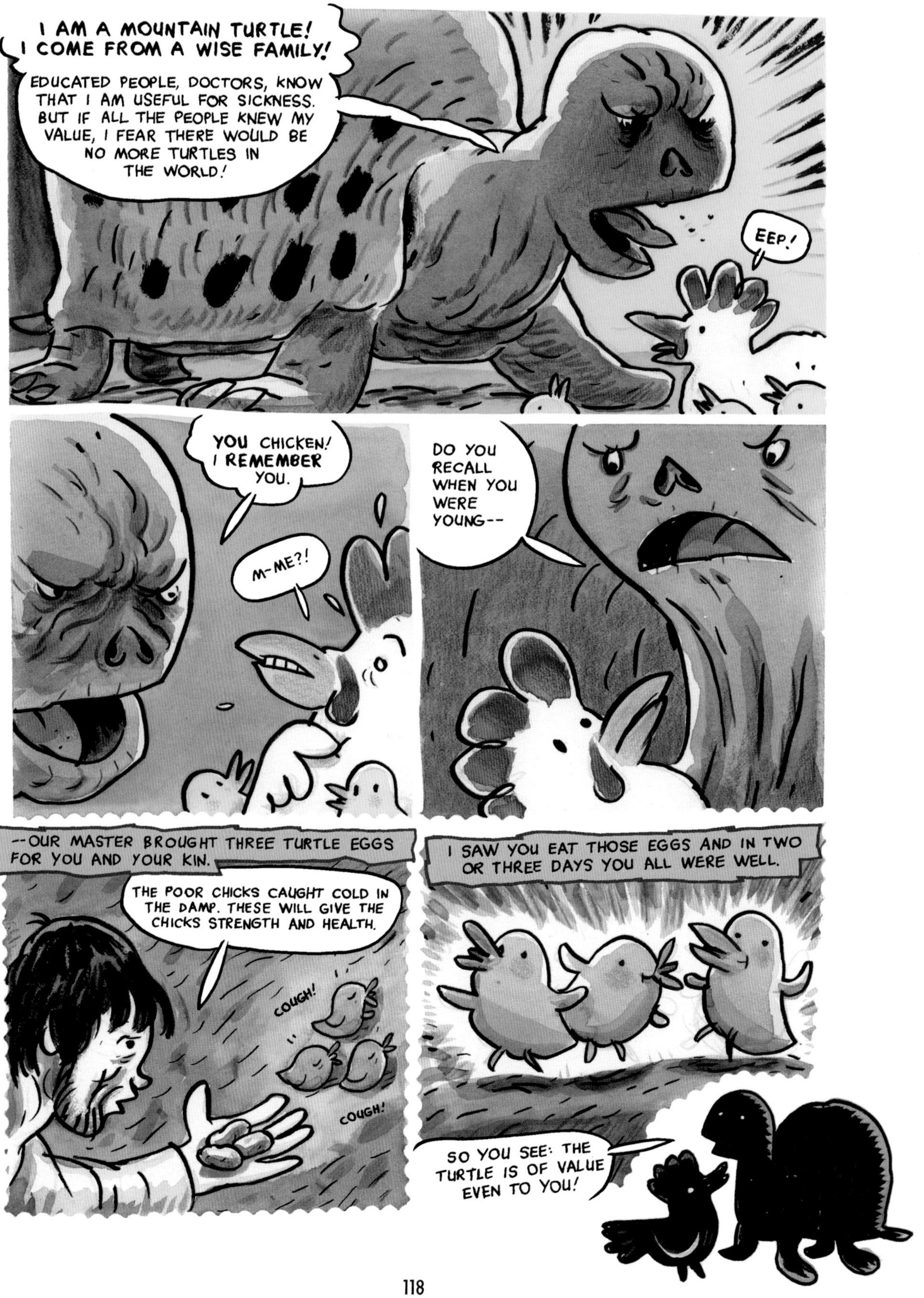
I AM A MOUNTAIN TURTLE! I COME FROM A WISE FAMILY!
EDUCATED PEOPLE, DOCTORS, KNOW THAT I AM USEFUL FOR SICKNESS. BUT IF ALL THE PEOPLE KNEW MY VALUE, I FEAR THERE WOULD BE NO MORE TURTLES IN THE WORLD!
EEP!
YOU CHICKEN! I REMEMBER YOU.
M-ME?!
DO YOU RECALL WHEN YOU WERE YOUNG--
--OUR MASTER BROUGHT THREE TURTLE EGGS FOR YOU AND YOUR KIN.
THE POOR CHICKS CAUGHT COLD IN THE DAMP. THESE WILL GIVE THE CHICKS STRENGTH AND HEALTH.
COUGH!
COUGH!
I SAW YOU EAT THOSE EGGS AND IN TWO OR THREE DAYS YOU ALL WERE WELL.
SO YOU SEE: THE TURTLE IS OF VALUE EVEN TO YOU!

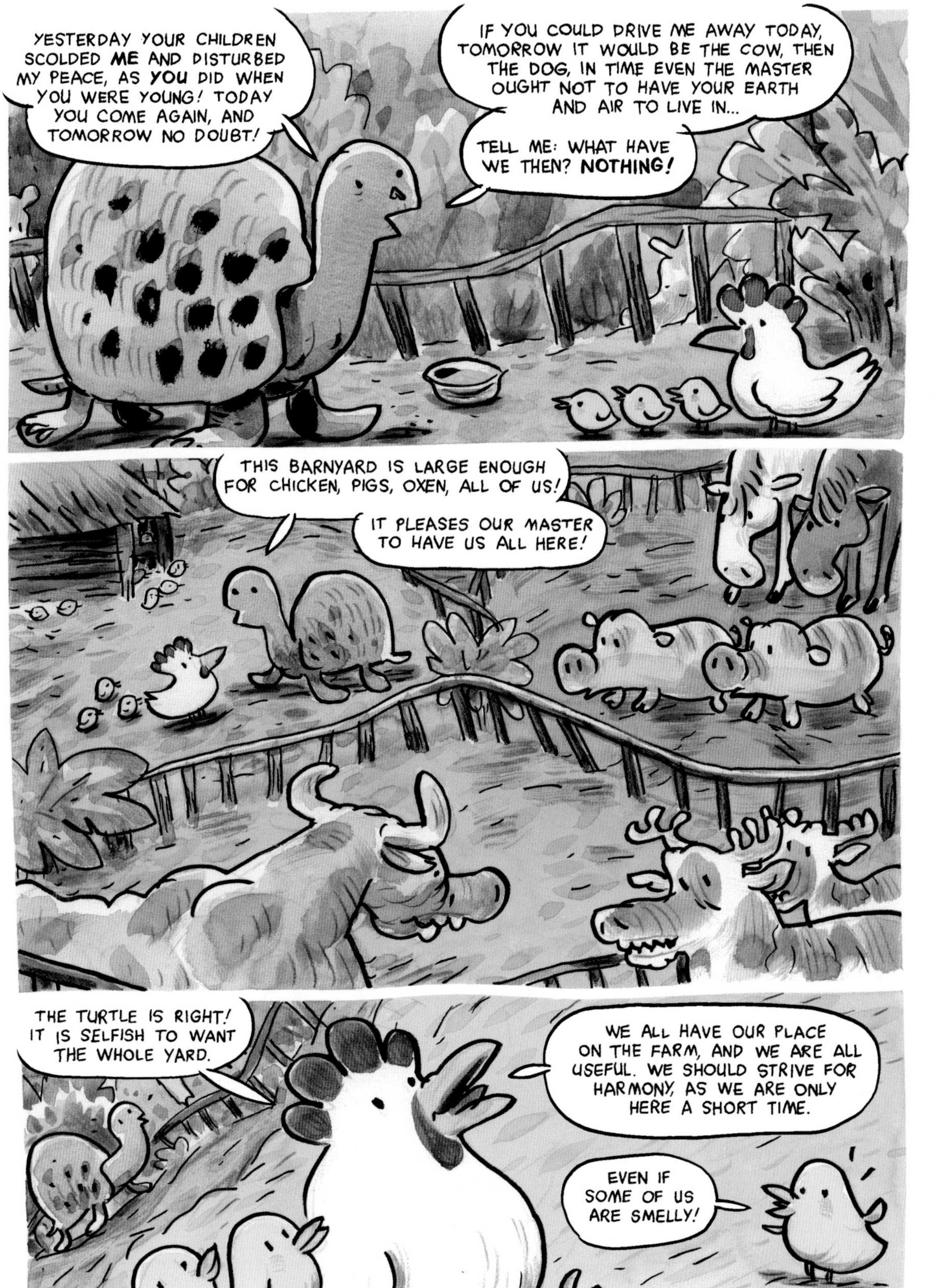
YESTERDAY YOUR CHILDREN SCOLDED **ME** AND DISTURBED MY PEACE, AS **YOU** DID WHEN YOU WERE YOUNG! TODAY YOU COME AGAIN, AND TOMORROW NO DOUBT!
IF YOU COULD DRIVE ME AWAY TODAY, TOMORROW IT WOULD BE THE COW, THEN THE DOG, IN TIME EVEN THE MASTER OUGHT NOT TO HAVE YOUR EARTH AND AIR TO LIVE IN...
TELL ME: WHAT HAVE WE THEN? **NOTHING!**
THIS BARNYARD IS LARGE ENOUGH FOR CHICKEN, PIGS, OXEN, ALL OF US!
IT PLEASES OUR MASTER TO HAVE US ALL HERE!
THE TURTLE IS RIGHT! IT IS SELFISH TO WANT THE WHOLE YARD.
WE ALL HAVE OUR PLACE ON THE FARM, AND WE ARE ALL USEFUL. WE SHOULD STRIVE FOR HARMONY, AS WE ARE ONLY HERE A SHORT TIME.
EVEN IF SOME OF US ARE SMELLY!
END

DEMADES AND HIS FABLE

ADAPTED BY ROGER LANGRIDGE

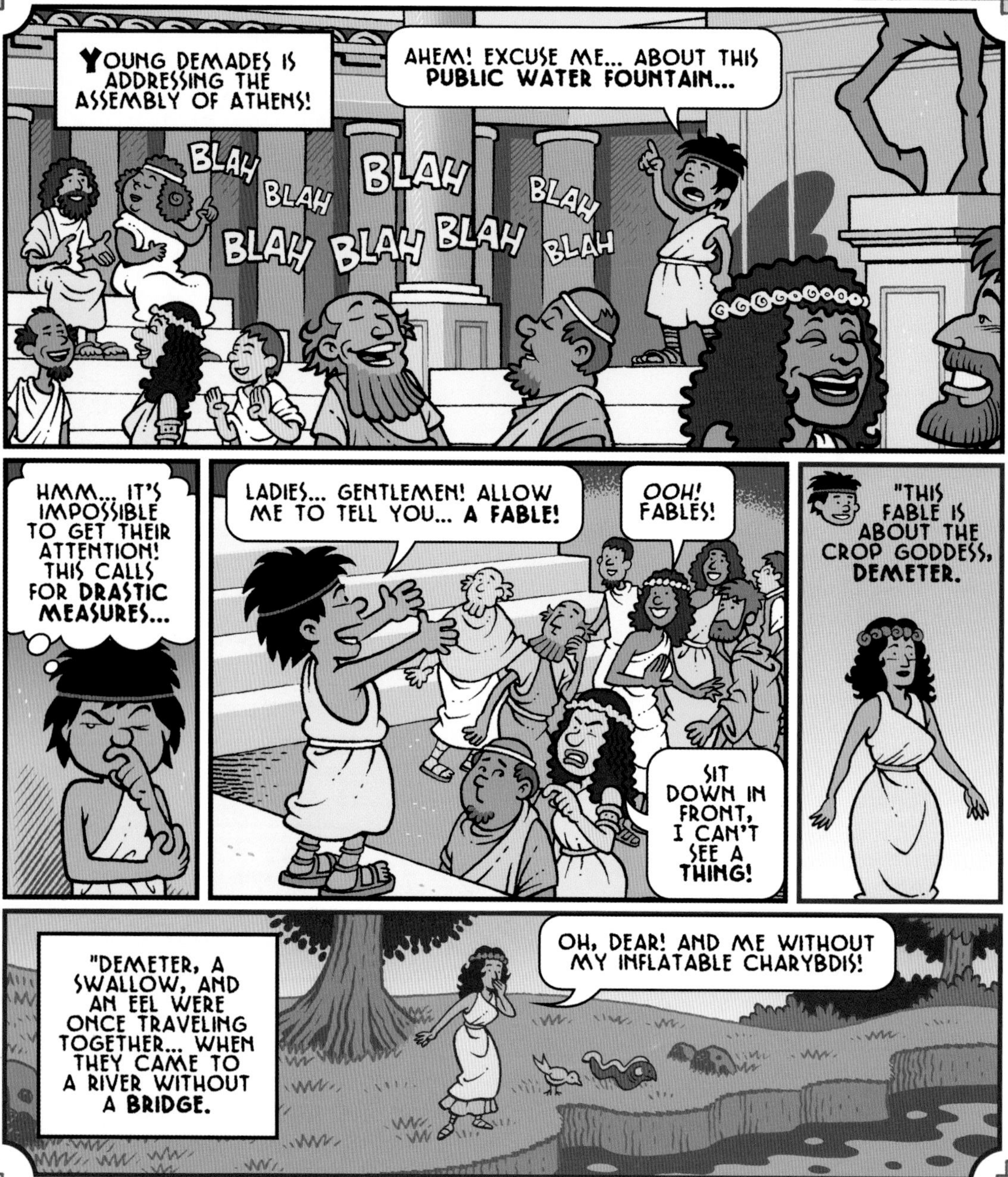
YOUNG DEMADES IS ADDRESSING THE ASSEMBLY OF ATHENS!
AHEM! EXCUSE ME... ABOUT THIS PUBLIC WATER FOUNTAIN...
BLAH BLAH BLAH BLAH BLAH BLAH BLAH BLAH
HMM... IT'S IMPOSSIBLE TO GET THEIR ATTENTION! THIS CALLS FOR DRASTIC MEASURES...
LADIES... GENTLEMEN! ALLOW ME TO TELL YOU... A FABLE!
OOH! FABLES!
SIT DOWN IN FRONT, I CAN'T SEE A THING!
"THIS FABLE IS ABOUT THE CROP GODDESS, DEMETER.
"DEMETER, A SWALLOW, AND AN EEL WERE ONCE TRAVELING TOGETHER... WHEN THEY CAME TO A RIVER WITHOUT A BRIDGE.
OH, DEAR! AND ME WITHOUT MY INFLATABLE CHARYBDIS!

From Aesop

WHY, THIS WILL BE NO TROUBLE AT ALL! I'LL JUST **FLY OVER** THE RIVER!

AND I'LL SWIM **ACROSS** IT! I COULD USE A BATH ANYWAY...

WELL, **THAT** WAS STRAIGHTFORWARD ENOUGH.

PIECE OF Π!

YOU KNOW, I'M **SURE** I'VE FORGOTTEN SOMETHING...

SANDWICHES?

...AND THAT'S THE STORY!

BUT... BUT WHAT ABOUT DEMETER?

YEAH! TELL US ABOUT DEMETER!

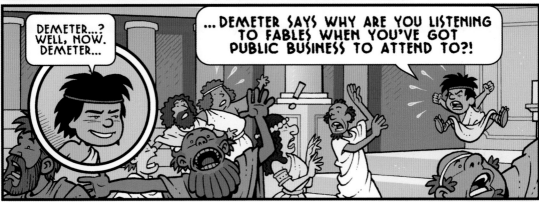

DEMETER...? WELL, NOW. DEMETER...

...DEMETER SAYS WHY ARE YOU LISTENING TO FABLES WHEN YOU'VE GOT PUBLIC BUSINESS TO ATTEND TO?!

EDITOR'S NOTE

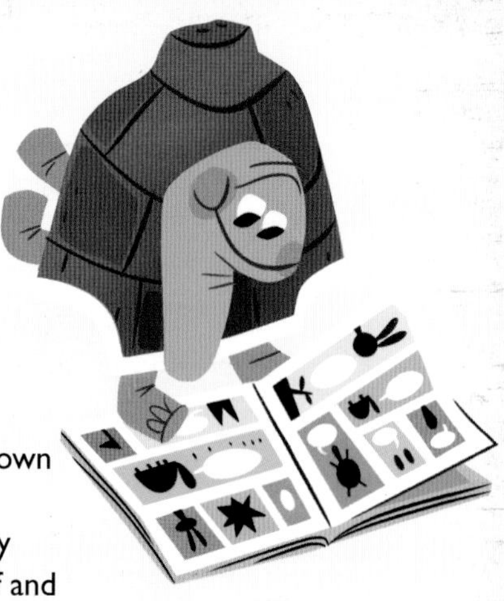

A FABLE IS A STORY with a lesson, usually–not always–starring animals. The lesson can be stated or it can be something to figure out. But they are, in essence, bossy stories with a message for you.

Fables come from all over. Aesop's fables and the Indian Panchatantra (a widely known body of fables throughout Asia and the Middle East) are in all likelihood assembled from many authors and sources, but they go back so far we don't really know. Many fables do have a known author, though, like the works of Russian satirist Ivan Krilof and American author Ambrose Bierce. But every culture has fables, many of them in the guise of folktales that get bossy.

For this collection, we wanted mostly Aesop fables, but we included a sampling of other traditions. Some star talking animals, others feature Greek gods, demons, people, and forces of nature. Cartoonists were allowed to embellish the stories (as they like to do) but we asked that a lesson still be in there.

–Chris Duffy

FURTHER READING:

Aesop's Fables (Oxford World's Classics), translated by Laura Gibbs, Oxford University Press, 2008.

The Panchatantra, Visnu Sarma, translated by Chandra Rajan, Penguin Classics, 2007.

The Talking Beasts: A Book of Fable Wisdom, edited by Kate Douglas Wiggin and Nora Archibald Smith. Project Gutenberg, 2004. www.gutenberg.org/ebooks/13815

gutenberg.org | archive.org | Both these sites have many public domain collections of fables.

pitt.edu/~dash/folktexts.html | Folklore and Mythology Electronic Texts is a remarkable compilation of world folklore, fables, and fairy tales compiled by D. L. Ashliman.

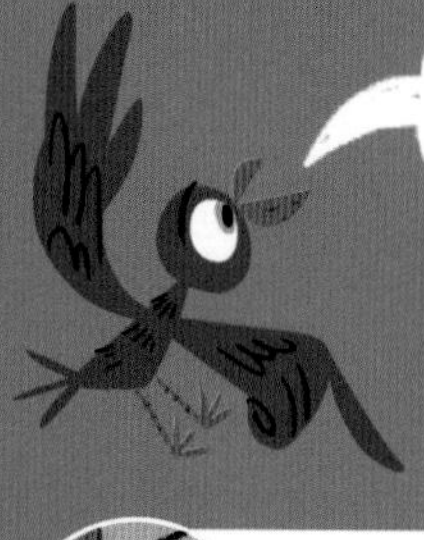

CONTRIBUTORS

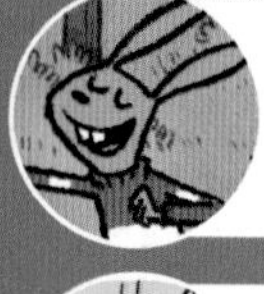

GRAHAM ANNABLE ("The Hare and the Tortoise") is a Canadian cartoonist living in Portland, Oregon. Between directing for feature films and creating the *Grickle* cartoons and comics, he finds time to illustrate a fable every now and again.

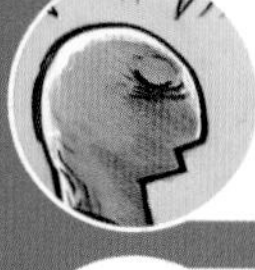

GREGORY BENTON ("The Hen and the Mountain Turtle") was bitten by a snapping turtle as a young boy. He has made many comics trying to reconcile that confusing early life event. This fable has helped Gregory to understand the turtle's point of view, and he is now able to get a good night's sleep.

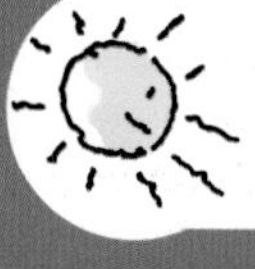

R. O. BLECHMAN ("The Sun and the Wind") is an illustrator and animated filmmaker. Among his many awards are his 1983 Emmy for animation, his 1999 induction into the Art Directors Hall of Fame, and a 2003 retrospective of his animated films at the Museum of Modern Art.

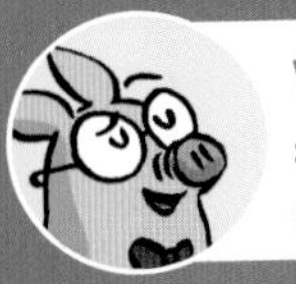

VERA BROSGOL ("The Hare and the Pig") lives in Portland, Oregon, where she draws storyboards for animated films, including *Coraline*, *Paranorman,* and *The Boxtrolls*. She also makes comics, such as short stories for the *Flight* anthologies and the Eisner Award–winning graphic novel *Anya's Ghost*.

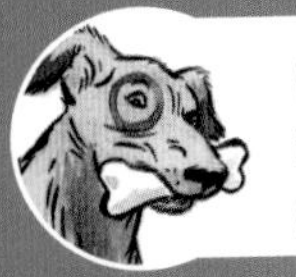

GRAHAM CHAFFEE ("The Dog and His Reflection") is a tattooist in Los Angeles. His other publications include *The Big Wheels, The Most Important Thing*, and *Good Dog*. He is currently working on a new graphic novel about cuckoldry and revenge, titled *To Have and to Hold*.

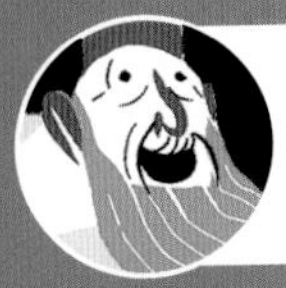

ELEANOR DAVIS ("The Old Man and Death") is a cartoonist and illustrator. She lives in Athens, Georgia, with her husband, Drew Weing, and three cats. doing-fine.com

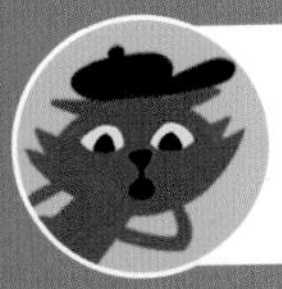

CHRIS DUFFY (editor) was comics editor of *Nickelodeon Magazine*, wrote a large chunk of *Bizarro Comics* for DC Comics, and has edited *Nursery Rhyme Comics, Fairy Tale Comics,* and *Above the Dreamless Dead* for First Second. He edits *SpongeBob Comics* for United Plankton Pictures.

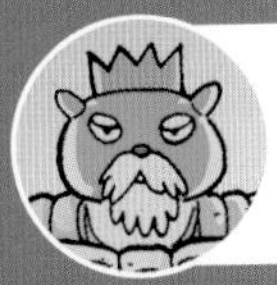

ULISES FARINAS ("The Great Weasel War") is a Portland, Oregon, based writer/artist. He has recently finished drawing *Judge Dredd: Mega City 2* and writes the titles *Amazing Forest* and *GAMMA*.

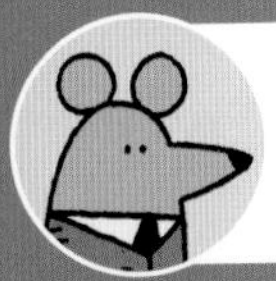

TOM GAULD ("The Town Mouse and the Country Mouse") lives and works in London, England. His cartoons and illustrations appear regularly in the *New York Times,* the *Guardian*, and *New Scientist*. He has published a number of comic books, including *Goliath* and *You're All Just Jealous of My Jetpack*.

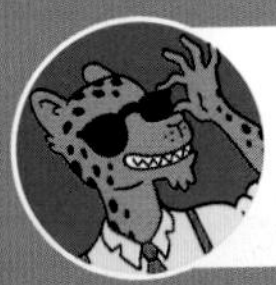

SOPHIE GOLDSTEIN ("Leopard Drums Up Dinner") grew up in Los Angeles but has lived in locations as various as New York City, Prague, South Korea, Vermont, and most recently Pittsburgh, Pennsylvania. Her work was featured in *Best American Comics 2013* and she won an Ignatz Award. redinkradio.com

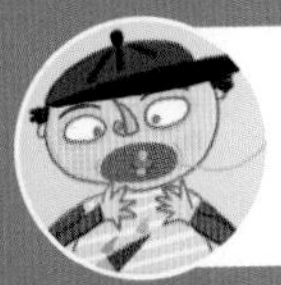

CHARISE HARPER ("The Belly and the Body Members") has written over fifty books for children. Before writing children's books, she penned a weekly comic strip. If she were paid money for every doodle she's made, she'd be a millionaire, but instead she's creatively happy.

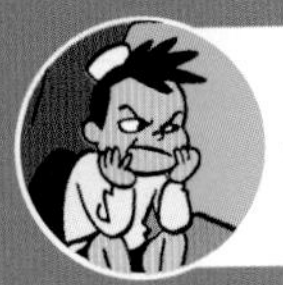

JAIME HERNANDEZ ("The Boy Who Cried Wolf") is on his fourth decade of drawing *Love and Rockets* and other comics. He can't think of a better job.

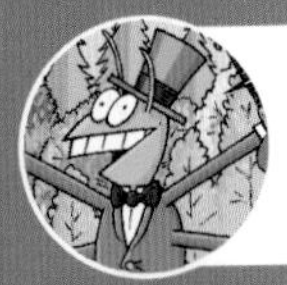

JOHN KERSCHBAUM ("The Grasshopper and the Ants") lives with his beautiful wife and daughter in Queens, New York, where he continues to practice the art of amusing cartoonery. www.johnkerschbaum.com

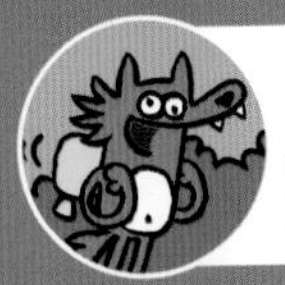

Eisner Award–winning cartoonist **JAMES KOCHALKA** ("The Fox and the Grapes") has drawn many graphic novels for kids including the Johnny Boo series, the Dragon Puncher series, and the Glorkian Warrior series. In 2011 he was named the first Cartoonist Laureate of Vermont.

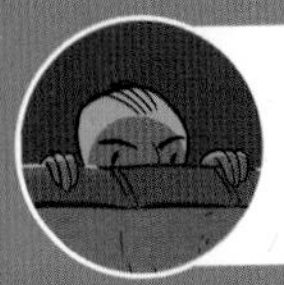

BRADEN LAMB ("The Thief and the Watchdog") grew up in Seattle, studied film in upstate New York, learned about vikings in Scandinavia, and now draws and colors comics in the Boston area. Recent books include the Eisner Award–winning *Adventure Time* comics and *The Midas Flesh*. bradenlamb.com

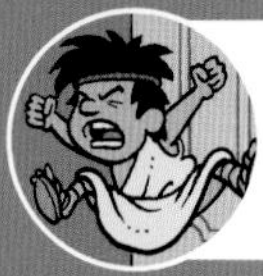

ROGER LANGRIDGE ("Demades and His Fable") is best known for his work on *The Muppet Show Comic Book* and for his Eisner Award–winning series *Snarked!* His most recent work is an adaptation of an unproduced Jim Henson TV special, *The Musical Monsters of Turkey Hollow.*

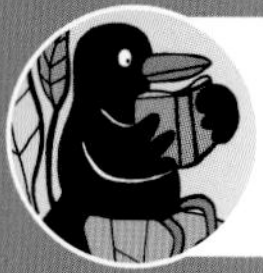

SIMONE LIA ("The Crow and the Pitcher") is a British comic artist. She is the author of *Fluffy* and *Please God, Find Me a Husband!* (Jonathan Cape). Her comic stories have been published in the *Guardian,* the *Independent,* The *Observer* and shown at the Tate Britain.

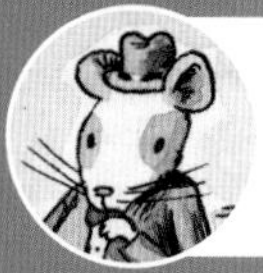

Ricardo **(LINIERS)** Siri ("The Mouse Council") lives in Buenos Aires with his wife and three daughters. Since 2002 he has drawn the comic strip *Macanudo* for *La Nacion,* an Argentine newspaper. He has published more than twenty books, including *The Big Wet Balloon* and *Macanudo #1* in the United States.

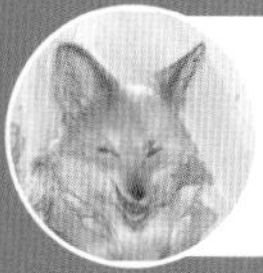

JENNIFER L. MEYER ("Fox and Crow") is an illustrator, comic artist, lover of animation, and eater of cupcakes. Her illustrated books include *Star Wars Adventures: Chewbacca* and *Jim Henson Storyteller: Puss in Boots*. She won a Bronze Award for comics from the Society of Illustrators West.

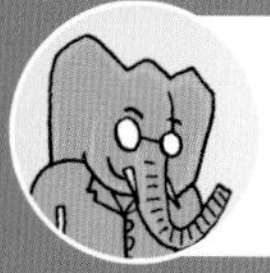

CORINNE MUCHA ("The Elephant in Favor") is a Chicago-based cartoonist, illustrator, and teaching artist. She is the author of three graphic novels, including *Get Over It!* published by Secret Acres. maidenhousefly.com.

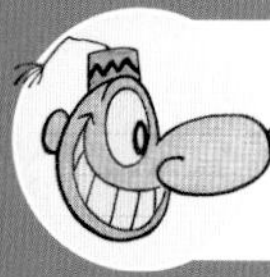

MARK NEWGARDEN ("Man and Wart") has been drawing abnormal proboscises since before you were born. He is currently living wart-free in Brooklyn, New York.

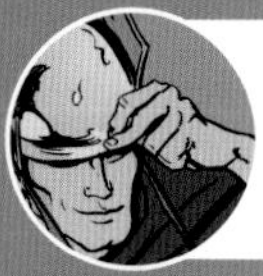

GEORGE O'CONNOR ("Hermes and the Man Who Was Bitten by an Ant," "Hermes and the Woodsman," "The Frogs Who Desired a King," and "Hermes and the Sculptor") is the bestselling author and illustrator of Olympians, a graphic novel series that retells Greek mythology, one god at a time. Hermes is his favorite obviously.

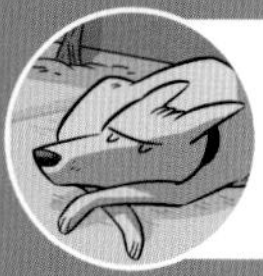

SHELLI PAROLINE ("The Thief and the Watchdog") escaped early on into the world of comics, cartoons, and science fiction. She has now returned to the Boston area as an unassuming cartoonist. Her credits include the Eisner Award–winning *Adventure Time* comics and *The Midas Flesh.* shelliparoline.com

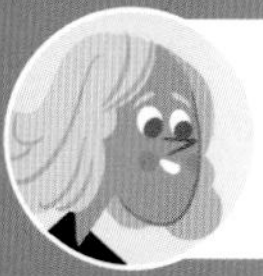

ISRAEL SANCHEZ ("The Milkmaid and Her Pail") lives in La Habra, California. His comics have appeared in the *Flight* anthology and *SpongeBob Comics*. Most of what he knows about life he has learned from stories about talking animals.

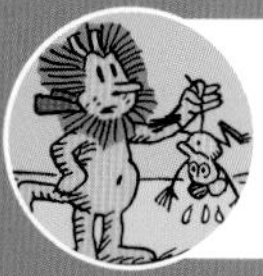

R. SIKORYAK ("Lion + Mouse") is the author of *Masterpiece Comics* (Drawn & Quarterly) and has contributed to the *New York Times, The Graphic Canon, Little Lit, SpongeBob Comics,* and many other publications. This comic is a tribute to cartoonist George Herriman and *Krazy Kat.*

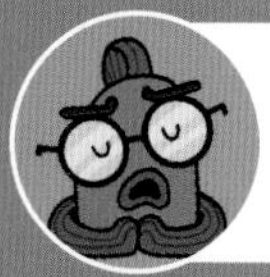

When **MARIS WICKS** ("The Dolphins, the Whales, and the Sprat") is not drawing whales with human arms, she is either making comics for First Second, *SpongeBob Comics*, Boom! Studios, Marvel Comics, and DC Comics, or teaching people about ocean critters at the New England Aquarium.

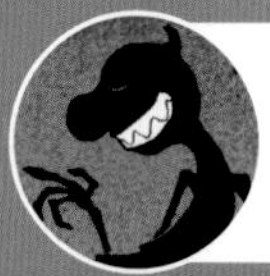

KENY WIDJAJA ("The Demon, the Thief, and the Hermit") is an Indonesian illustrator, designer, and cartoonist. He graduated from the Center for Cartoon Studies in Vermont and is currently living and working in Jakarta, drawing comics when he can.